From Ashes

By Molly McAdams

Taking Chances
From Ashes

From Ashes

Molly McAdams

WILLIAM MORROW

An Imprint of HarperCollins*Publishers*

HarperCollins books may be purchased for educational, business, or sales promotional use. For information please write: Special Markets Department, Harper-Collins Publishers, 10 East 53rd Street, New York, NY 10022.

FIRST EDITION

Designed by Diahann Sturge

Library of Congress Cataloging-in-Publication Data has been applied for.

ISBN 978-0-06-226772-6

13 14 15 16 17   OV/RRD   10 9 8 7 6 5 4 3 2

From Ashes

1

Cassidy

"DO YOU EVEN KNOW ANYONE who's going to be there, Ty?"

"Just Gage. But this will be good, this way we'll be able to meet new people right away."

I grumbled to myself. I wasn't the best at making friends; they didn't understand my need to always be near Tyler, and when I'd show up with bruises or stitches, everyone automatically thought I was either hurting myself or Tyler and I were in an abusive relationship. Of course that wasn't their fault; we never responded to them, so the rumors continued to fly.

"Cassi, no one will have any idea about your past, the last of your bruises will be gone in a few weeks, and you're gone from there now. Besides, I hate that you don't have anyone else. Trust me, I understand it, but I hate it for you. You need more people in your life."

"I know." I instinctively wrapped my arms around myself,

covering where some of the bruises were. Thank God none were visible right now unless I stripped down to my skivvies, but I couldn't say the same for some of the scars. At least scars were normal on a person, and the worst of them were covered by my clothes, so I just looked like I was accident-prone.

"Hey." Tyler grabbed one of my hands, taking it away from my side. "It's over, it will never happen again. And I'm always here for you, whether you make new friends or not. I'm here. But at least try. This is your chance at starting a new life—isn't that what that favorite bird of yours is all about anyway?"

"The phoenix isn't a real bird, Ty."

"Whatever, it's your favorite. Isn't that what they symbolize? New beginnings?"

"Rebirth and renewal," I muttered.

"Yeah, same thing. They die only to come back and start a new life, right? This is us starting a new life, Cass." He shook his head slightly and his face went completely serious. "But don't spontaneously burst into flames and die. I love you too much and a fire wouldn't be good for the leather seats."

I huffed a laugh and shoved his shoulder with my free hand. "You're such a punk, Ty; way to kill the warm and fuzzy moment you had going there."

He laughed out loud. "In all seriousness"—he kissed my hand, then met and held my gaze for a few seconds before looking back at the road—"new life, Cassi, and it starts right now."

Tyler and I weren't romantically involved, but we had a relationship that even people we'd grown up with didn't understand.

We grew up just a house away from each other, in a country club neighborhood. Both our fathers were doctors; our moms were the kind that stayed home with the kids and spent afternoons at the club gossiping and drinking martinis. On my sixth birthday, my dad died from a heart attack—while he was at work of all places. Now that I'm older, I don't understand how no one was able to save him; he worked in the ER, for crying out loud, and no one was able to save him? But at the time, I just knew my hero was gone.

Dad worked long hours, but I was his princess, and when he was home, it was just the two of us. He'd brave tiaras and boas to have tea parties with me; he knew the names of all of my stuffed animals, talked to them like they would respond; and he would always be the one to tell me stories at night. My mom was amazing, but she knew we had a special relationship, so she always stayed in the door frame, watching and smiling. Whenever I would get hurt, if he was at work, Mom would make a big show of how she couldn't make it better, and I'd have to hang on for dear life until Dad got home. She must have called him, because he would run into the house like I was dying—even though it was almost always just a scratch—pick me up, and place a Band-Aid wherever I was hurt, and miraculously I was all better. Like I said, my dad was my hero. Every little girl needs a dad like that. But now, other than precious memories, all I have left of him is his love for the phoenix. Mom had let Dad have his way with a large outline of a phoenix painted directly above my bed for when I started kindergarten, a painting that's still there today, though Mom constantly threatened to paint over it. And although I tried to keep a ring he'd had all his adult life with a phoenix on it, my mom had found and hidden it not long after he died, and I hadn't seen it since.

My mom started drinking obsessively when he died. Her morning coffee always had rum in it, by ten in the morning she was making margaritas, she'd continue to go to the club for martinis, and by the time I was home from school, she was drinking scotch or vodka straight out of the bottle. She made time for her girlfriends but stopped waking me up for school, stopped making me food, forgot to pick me up from school—pretty much just forgot I even existed. After that first day of being forgotten at school, and the next day not showing up because she wouldn't leave her room, Tyler's mom, Stephanie, started taking me to and from school without a word. She knew my mom was grieving, just not the extent of it.

After a week with no clean clothes and a few rounds of trial and error, I began doing my own laundry, attempted to figure out my homework by myself, and would make peanut butter and jelly sandwiches for both of us, always leaving one outside her bedroom door. Almost a year after Dad's death, Jeff came into the picture. He was rich, ran some big company—his last name was everywhere in Mission Viejo, California—but up until that day I'd never seen or heard of him. One day Stephanie dropped me off and he was just moved in, my mom already married to him.

That night was the first time I'd ever been hit, and it was by my own mother. My sweet, gentle mother who couldn't kill a spider, let alone spank her own daughter when she misbehaved, hit me. I asked who Jeff was and why he was telling me to call him Dad, and my mom hit me across the back with the new scotch bottle she'd been attempting to open. It didn't break, but it left one nasty-looking bruise. From that point on, I never went a day without some kind of injury inflicted by one of them. Usually it was fists or palms, and I began welcoming those, because when they started throwing coffee mugs, drinking glasses, or lamps, or when my mom took off her heels and repeatedly hit me in the head with the tip of her stiletto . . . I didn't know if I would still be alive the next day. About a week after the first hit was when I first got beat with Jeff's socket wrench, and that was the first night I opened my window, popped off the screen, and made my way to Tyler's window. At seven years old, he helped me into his room, gave me some of his pajamas since my night-shirt was covered in blood, and held my hand as we fell asleep in his bed.

Over the last eleven years, Tyler has begged me to let him tell his parents what was going on, but I couldn't let that happen. If Tyler told them, they would call someone and I knew they would take me away from Tyler. My hero had died, and the mom I loved had disappeared down a bottle; no way was I let-ting someone take me from Ty too. The only way I had gotten him to agree was agreeing myself that if he ever found me un-conscious, all promises were off and he could tell whomever he wanted. But that was just keeping Tyler quiet; we never had fac-tored in the neighbors . . .

After the first three years of the abuse, I stopped sneaking out to Ty's house every night, only doing so on the nights when it was something other than body parts hitting me, but Tyler was always waiting, no matter what. He kept a first aid kit in his room, and would clean up and bandage anything he was able to. We butterfly-bandaged almost all the cuts, but three times he forced me to get stitches. We told his dad I tripped over some-thing while going for a run outside each time. I'm not naïve, I knew his dad didn't believe me—especially since I was not one for running, and the only time I was involved with sports was watching it on Ty's TV—but we were always careful to hide my bruises around him and he never tried to figure out where I actually got the cuts from. I'd sit at their kitchen table and let him sew me up, they'd let me out the front door when they were sure I was okay, and Tyler would be waiting by his open window as soon as I rounded the house. Every night he had something ready for me to sleep in, and every night he would hold my hand and curl his body around mine until we fell asleep.

So when Tyler kissed my forehead, cheek, or hand, it never meant anything romantic. He was just comforting me in the same way he had since we were kids.

"Cassi? Did I lose you?" Tyler waved his hand in front of my face.

"Sorry. Life, starting over. Friends, yeah, this, uh—will be—I need to . . . friends." I'm pretty sure there was English somewhere in that sentence.

Ty barked out a laugh and squeezed my knee, and after a few silent minutes he thankfully changed the subject. "So what do you think about the apartment?"

"It's great. Are you sure you want me to stay with you? I can get my own place, or even sleep on the couch . . ." My own place? That was such a far-fetched idea it was almost funny; I didn't even have a hundred dollars to my name.

"No way, I've shared my bed with you for eleven years, I'm not about to change that now."

"Ty, but what about when you get a girlfriend? Are you really going to want to explain why I live with you? Why we share a dresser, closet, and bed?"

Tyler looked at me for a second before turning his eyes back to the road. His brown eyes had darkened, and his lips were mashed in a tight line. "You're staying with me, Cassi."

I sighed but didn't say anything else. We'd had a version of this argument plenty of times. Every relationship he'd ever had ultimately ended because of me and the fact that we were always together. I hated that I ruined his relationships, and whenever he was dating someone I would even stop coming to his room and answering his calls so he could focus on his girlfriend instead. That never lasted long though; he'd climb through my window, pick me up out of bed, and take me back to his house. We never had to worry about my boyfriends, since I'd never had one. What with Tyler's possessiveness and all, no one even attempted to get close enough to me. Not that it bothered me; the only guy I'd ever had feelings for was too old for me and had only been in my life for a few short minutes. The moment I'd answered the door to see him standing there, my stomach had started fluttering and I felt this weird connection with him I'd never felt with anyone, and even after he was gone I'd dreamed about his cool intensity and mesmerizing blue eyes. Ty didn't know about him though, because what was the point? I'd just barely turned sixteen and he was a cop; I knew I'd never see him again, and I didn't. Besides, other than my real dad and Ty, I had a problem with letting guys get close, strange connection or not. When my already-disturbed world turned completely upside down the minute a new man came into our house . . . trust issues were bound to happen.

Tyler had decided to go to the University of Texas in Austin, where his cousin Gage, who was two years older than us, was currently studying. I'd heard a lot about Gage and his family from Ty over the years, since they were his only cousins, and I was genuinely happy he was going. Gage was like a brother to him and Tyler hadn't seen him in a few years, so their sharing an apartment would be good for Ty. I wasn't sure what I was going to do when Tyler left; the only thing I did know was that I was getting away from the house I grew up in. I just had to make it another month until I turned eighteen and then I was gone. But Tyler, being Tyler, made my future plans for me. He crawled through my window, told me to pack my bag, and just before he could haul me off to his Jeep, he told Mom and Jeff exactly what he thought of them. I didn't have time to worry about the consequences of his telling them off, because before I knew it we were on the freeway and headed for Texas. We made the trip in just over a day, and now, after being here long enough to unpack his Jeep and shower separately, we were headed to some lake for a party to meet up with Gage and his friends.

Gage's family wasn't from Austin; I didn't know where in Texas they lived, but apparently they had a ranch. After hearing that, I'd had to bite the inside of my cheek to keep from asking what Gage was like. I understood we were in Texas now, but already Austin had blown my expectations of dirt roads and tumbleweeds away with its downtown buildings and greenery everywhere. I just didn't know how I'd handle living with a tight-Wranglered, big-belt-buckled, Stetson-wearing cowboy like I'd seen in rodeos and movies. I'd probably burst out laughing every time I saw him.

When we came up to the lake and the group of people, I sucked in a deep breath in a futile attempt to calm my nerves. I wasn't a fan of new people.

Tyler grabbed my hand and gave it a tight squeeze. "New beginning, Cassi. And I'll be right here next to you."

"I know. I can do this." His Jeep stopped and I immediately took that back. *Nope. No, I can't do this.* I had to think quickly of where every bruise was, making sure my clothes were covering them all, even though I'd already gone through this at the apartment. I just didn't want anyone here to know what kind of life I'd had.

I jumped out of Tyler's Jeep, took one more deep breath, and mentally pumped myself up. *New life. I can do this.* I turned and rounded the front and hadn't even made it to Tyler's side when

I saw him. I don't know if I made a conscious choice to stop walking or if I was still making my way to Tyler and didn't realize it; all I could focus on or see was the guy standing about ten feet from me. He was tall, taller than Tyler's six-foot frame, and had on loose, dark tan cargo shorts and a white button-up shirt, completely unbuttoned, revealing a tan, toned chest and abs. His arms were covered in muscles, but he didn't look like someone who spent hours in the gym or taking steroids. The only way I can describe them is natural, and labor-made. His jet-black hair had that messy, just-got-out-of-bed look, and my hand twitched just thinking about running my fingers through it. I couldn't see what color eyes he had from here, but they were locked on me, his mouth slightly open. He had a bottle of water in his hand, and it was raised like he had been about to take a drink out of it before he saw me. I had no idea what was happening to me, but my entire body started tingling, and my palms were sweating just looking at him.

I'd seen plenty of attractive guys—Tyler looked like an Abercrombie and Fitch model, for crying out loud. But Mr. New couldn't even be described as something as degrading as *attractive*. He looked like a god. My breath was becoming rougher, and my blood started warming as I took an unconscious step toward him. Just then a tall, leggy blonde bounced over to his side and wrapped her arms around his waist, kissing his strong jaw. It felt like someone punched me in the stomach and I was instantly jealous of whoever this girl was. Shaking my head, I forced my eyes to look away. *What the hell, Cassidy? Calm down.*

"Cassi, you coming?"

I blinked and looked over at Tyler, who had his hand outstretched to me. "Uh, yeah." I glanced back at Mr. New and saw he still hadn't moved. The perky blonde was chatting his ear off, and he didn't even seem to be hearing her. I felt a blush creep up my cheeks from the way he was looking at me, like he'd just seen the sun for the first time, and continued over to Tyler.

Tyler pulled me to his side and whispered in my ear, "You okay?"

"Yeah, I'm fine," I reassured him, trying to slow my heart down for a completely different reason now.

He kissed my cheek and pulled away. "Okay, well let me introduce you to Gage."

Right. Gage. Tyler dropped my hand, only to put his on the small of my back as he led me over to Mr. New and the leggy blonde. *Oh no. No no no no no.*

"'Sup, man?" Tyler slapped him on the back and Mr. New slowly dragged his eyes from me to the guy who'd just hit him.

Gage's eyes went wide when he saw Ty. "Tyler, hey! I didn't realize y'all were here yet."

Oh. Good. God. That voice. Even with that small sentence I could hear the drawl in it. It was deep and gravelly, and easily the sexiest thing I'd ever heard.

"Yeah, we just got here. Cassi, this is my cousin Gage. Gage, this is Cassi."

Gage brought his hand out. "It's a pleasure, Cassi. I'm glad y'all are finally here."

My knees went weak and a jolt of electricity went through me when I shook his hand. From how he glanced down at our hands quickly, he'd felt it too. "It's nice to meet you too." Now that I was up close, I could see his bright green eyes, hidden behind thick black lashes and eyebrows. He was the definition of masculine. From his strong jaw and brow, high cheekbones, defined nose, and perfectly kissable lips, his looks screamed *man*. The only thing offsetting the masculinity were his boyish deep dimples, which had me hooked. Yep, *god* was the only word out there that fit him.

Our hands didn't separate fast enough for the tall blonde, so she thrust her hand forward. "I'm Brynn, Gage's girlfriend." Her eyes narrowed on the last word.

I shouldn't have, but I glanced at Gage again. His brows were pulled down in either confusion or annoyance when he looked at Brynn. *You have got to be kidding me,* I thought. I didn't care if it had been only two seconds since I first saw him, this couldn't be a normal reaction for two people just meeting to have with each other, and he had a freaking girlfriend. It hadn't even felt like this with the cop who came to my door that night, and I'd thought about him for almost two years!

I squared my shoulders and dropped Gage's hand, focusing on Brynn. "It's great to meet you, Brynn!" I hoped my smile looked genuine. I didn't need an enemy yet, especially if she was dating the guy I was going to be living with. But hell, I'm not gonna lie—I was already thinking of ways to get her out of the picture.

Tyler and Brynn shook hands, and she looked back at me, noticing that I was doing everything to keep from looking at her boyfriend. Tyler and Gage were catching up, and every time Gage would speak I had to force myself not to shut my eyes and lose myself in the way his voice caused chills to go through my whole body.

"So, Cassi, what do you say we go introduce you to the rest of the girls?" Brynn finally said sweetly.

Tyler looked elated; this was exactly what he wanted. "Sounds great," I said, and stepped away from the guys. It felt wrong to walk away, but I could feel Gage watching me as I did.

"You and Tyler, huh?" Brynn nudged my shoulder.

"What do you mean?"

"Y'all make such a cute couple." She wasn't complimenting, she was reaching.

"Thanks, but no. Tyler and I are best friends, nothing more."

"You sure about that? I saw the way he was looking at you, and he had his arm around you."

"We're just different like that. We've been best friends our entire lives."

"Right. Are you going to UT too?" she asked, sounding a little too curious.

"Uh, no. I'm not planning on going to school at all."

"So why are you here?" If it hadn't been for the curled-up lip, she would have just simply sounded interested.

"Honestly? I have no idea. Tyler packed my bag and threw me in his Jeep. Apparently Gage didn't care if I lived with them." I smirked and turned to begin the introductions with the girls who were now right next to us.

Gage

WHAT THE HELL *was* that? Nothing like that had ever happened to me. One look at Cassi and it felt like my world stopped. All I could think about was closing the distance between us. I don't know how to describe it, but I needed to go to her. Unfortunately, I was frozen in place, taking in the most beautiful girl I'd ever seen. Her long brown hair was windblown, and those wide honey-colored eyes made me want to get lost in them. She looked so sweet and fragile, I wanted to wrap my arms around her and protect her from seeing anything bad in the world, but something in her eyes told me she knew too well what the world was like and could take care of herself. Which is why it was so damn confusing that she clung to my cousin like he was a lifeline.

Tyler told me he was bringing his friend to live with us, and that she was a girl. I'd remembered hearing her name over the years, but whenever he spoke about her, it seemed like they were only friends, so why did he hold her hand and kiss her damn cheek? I couldn't even stop the growl that came from my throat when I saw it. Then freakin' Brynn. Girlfriend? Really? We'd gone on two god-awful dates last year and I told her before school let out that I didn't want any form of a relationship with her. I thought we'd been clear since she'd avoided me all afternoon until Cassi and Ty showed up.

When Cassi first spoke, I had to force myself to breathe. Her voice was soft and melodic. It fit her perfectly. She was petite and even with how short she was, those legs in those shorts could make any guy fall on his knees and beg. I couldn't stop thinking about how she'd feel in my arms, how she'd look in my truck or on my horse. And yeah, I'm not gonna lie, I'd already pictured her beneath me . . . but one look at her and there was no way not to.

After Brynn guided her away, it took a huge effort to stop watching her, but I didn't want to let on to Tyler that I was already completely taken with her.

"She's mine, Gage. Let's get that clear right now."

Okay, so maybe I'd been a little more obvious than I'd thought. "Thought you said y'all were friends."

"She's my best friend, but you'll see. She's mine."

I nodded and clapped his back, forcing my hand out of a fist. "I got you, man. Come on, let me get you a beer."

As the night wore on, I continued to get closer and closer to where she was. I felt like a creep, trying to be near her, but I couldn't stop it. I wanted to listen to her talk and laugh; I swear she sounded like an angel singing when she laughed. I almost groaned out loud—*Angel singing? What the hell is wrong with me?*

We were all sitting around the bonfire talking and drinking. I was just a few feet from Cassi when she got up to head over to Jackie. If it hadn't been for what happened immediately after, I would have punched Jake in the face for touching her. With one hand he grazed the front of her thigh, and with the other he grabbed her ass, causing her to stumble and fall right into me, her beer soaking my shirt.

Her big eyes got even wider and she sucked in a quick gasp. "Oh God, I'm so sorry!" The sun was setting and it was getting darker, but I could perfectly see her blush. I'm pretty sure Cassi blushing was my new favorite thing.

I laughed and grabbed her small shoulders to steady her, not caring one bit about my shirt. "You all right?"

Her eyes focused on my lips, her teeth lightly sinking into her bottom one. I wanted to replace her teeth with mine and without realizing it, I started to lean forward. She blinked quickly and glanced up, then looked at Jake on my right. "I'm fine. I'm really sorry about your shirt."

Aw hell, this isn't normal. She's said all of two sentences to me tonight and I was about to kiss her? "Don't worry about it," I murmured as she righted herself and continued toward Jackie, only to be quickly pulled away by Tyler as he spoke in her ear, his arms around her.

"Damn, when you said your cousin was bringing a chick, I wasn't expecting her to be so hot," Jake said.

"Jake, touch her again . . . see what fuckin' happens."

"Whoa, got it bad for your cousin's girl already, huh? You gonna try to get with that?"

I eyed Cassi in Ty's arms and shook my head as I brought my beer up to take another long drink. "Nope." *Yes, yes, I am.*

"Well, if you're not, I sure as hell am."

"Jake," I growled.

"All right, all right. Chill, Gage. I won't touch her and you heard her . . . she's fine." Jake leaned forward to grab another beer out of the ice chest and settled back into his chair, his eyes already off Cassi and onto Lanie.

After a quick glance to see Cassi and Tyler still quietly talking, I got up and walked back to where all the trucks were parked. I took my wet shirt off and hung it off the bed of my truck before grabbing a clean one out of the backseat. When I turned around, Tyler was walking up to me.

"I'm real glad you're here, bro," I said.

"Me too." He took a long drink out of his can before setting it down on the tailgate. "We couldn't get here fast enough. Cali was really starting to wear on me; I was ready for someplace new. And hey, I know I've said this, but I appreciate you letting us room with you. I know you could've had anyone share your apartment with you, and he probably wouldn't have brought a girl with him."

"Don't worry about it, you're family. To be honest, I was kinda surprised when you said you were coming to Austin to go to school with me. After you started refusing to come to the ranch with Aunt Steph and Uncle Jim the last few years, I just figured you didn't like us much anymore."

"Nah, it had nothing to do with you. I just hated leaving Cassi behind. Sorry I made you think that though."

I took a deep breath, reminding myself Cassi *had* followed

him to Texas. "Really? I don't get it, Ty, you said she was a friend. Then she follows you here, and now you're saying you wouldn't come visit because you didn't want to leave her? How come you never just told me how it really was with y'all?"

"It's complicated; we really were just friends. But she needed me; I couldn't just leave her. And I'm in love with her, man."

Holy hell. I felt like someone had just knocked the air outta me. How was I already so into this girl that it physically hurt to think of her being with Ty? With anyone, for that matter? Seriously. This was not. Fucking. Normal. "What do you mean she needed you?"

Tyler sighed and shook his head. "Like I said, it's complicated."

We both looked up when we heard girls squealing and splashing. Some of the guys were throwing them into the lake, and I couldn't stop myself from going to Jake when he picked Cassi up and threw her over his shoulder. My hands were already balled into fists for when he put her down. Her long hair was hiding her face as she pounded her little hands on his back.

"Put me down! I'm not wearing a suit!" She sounded so determined for a little thing that I almost smiled. Almost. "I'm serious, put me down!"

"Jake, I told you not to touch her. Put her down." I was standing right behind them then. Cassi grabbed the top of his jeans to push herself up and look at me, but Jake turned so he was now facing me. She was trying to kick him as well and his hands high up on her thighs had my hands fisting again.

"Come on, Gage." He sounded annoyed. "All the other girls went in."

"She doesn't want to—" Jake slid her down, causing her shirt to ride up high on her back. I choked on my next words, and at least two other people gasped behind me. *WHAT THE HELL?!*

Tyler grabbed Cassi and started pulling her away. He looked at her sympathetically, and when his eyes met mine they looked worried. Cassi's face was bright red again and her lips were smashed together tight as she let Tyler lead her to his Jeep.

Jake looked at me like I was insane; if it wasn't for the other guys having the same reaction, I woulda felt like it too. I turned and followed Tyler and Cassi to the Jeep, waiting until I was sure no one could hear us. "What the hell did I just see?"

Tyler helped her into the Jeep before going to the driver's side and opening up his own door. Cassi was looking straight ahead, her jaw still clenched.

"Ty, man, what was that?"

"Nothing. We'll see you whenever you get back to the apartment."

"That wasn't nothing!"

He sighed and stepped away from the door, leaning close so she couldn't hear him. "Look, we were trying to avoid something like this, but since you already saw, I'll explain it later. But this is exactly what I was getting her away from, so I'm going to take her back to the apartment now if you don't mind."

I didn't wait for anything else. I practically ran to my truck, grabbed my wet shirt as I put the tailgate up, hopped in, and drove back with them. A million things went through my mind on the way back to the apartment, and each one had me gripping the steering wheel hard. It was dark enough that I couldn't be sure what I'd seen, but it looked like bruises. Lots of them. I'd heard of people with some illnesses who are covered in them. I tried to think of what it could be and thought about her too-small frame. If her face didn't look so healthy, I would have been sure it was that. But the way Tyler talked about not wanting to leave her behind, I couldn't dismiss it either. I refused to think about the obvious; there was no way someone would hurt her. I'd hunt them down if they did.

Why was I so protective of her? I didn't know her from Eve, and we'd barely said anything to each other all night. I was hardly like this when it came to my sisters, and I loved them more than anything. I didn't know what it was about that girl, but she was already completely under my skin. And I wasn't sure if I liked that or not yet.

The drive took forever, and I let out a long sigh when I finally pulled into my spot. When they pulled up next to me, I jogged over to the passenger door and opened it. Cassi's face made me take a step back. There was absolutely no emotion there, and though she wouldn't meet my eyes, hers looked dead. I held my hand out to help her down, but Tyler pushed through me, glaring at me, and helped her out himself. He kept an arm around her as he led her to our place and took her right into his bedroom. I stood in the living room waiting for them to come out, but thirty minutes passed and the door still hadn't opened. With a heavy sigh, I turned and went to my bathroom to take a shower since I still smelled like the beer Cassi'd spilled on me. Thank God I hadn't gotten pulled over on the way home. When I got back to my room, Tyler was sitting on my bed.

"Sorry, Gage, she didn't want to talk to you when we got here."

"Is she sick, Ty?"

Tyler started. "What? No, she's not sick. Why would you— Oh. No. She's not."

Part of me was relieved, but now that I knew that wasn't it, I felt sick knowing what must've happened. "That why you never wanted to leave her?" I asked quietly.

"Yeah, that's why."

"Boyfriend?"

He shook his head.

"Parents?" I gritted my teeth hard when he nodded.

"Hold on a sec." Tyler walked quickly to the other side of the apartment, and I heard his door open and shut twice before he came back to my room, closing the door. "I wanted to make sure she was sleeping; she doesn't want you to know. But since you saw it, I have to tell you—I need to tell someone." He dropped his head into his hands and took a deep breath as his body started shuddering. "I haven't told anyone in eleven years. Do you know what it's been like, knowing what's happening and not being able to say anything?"

"Eleven years?!" I hissed, and made myself lean back against the wall so I wouldn't go after him. "This has been going on for eleven fucking years and you didn't tell anyone? What the hell is wrong with you?"

"She made me promise I wouldn't! She was terrified they would take her away."

"Did you not see that? Her entire back was black and blue!"

Tyler hung his head again. "That's not the worst it's ever been. She'd come over with concussions; a few times I made her agree to stitches. Swear to God, that girl is tougher than most men I know, because without any pain medication she'd let Dad sew her up right there in the kitchen. Then there were times she couldn't even get off the floor. When she was young, sometimes she'd lie there for hours before she could move; when we got older and got her a phone, she'd have to text me and I'd come get her."

I tried to swallow the throw-up that was rising in my throat. "It got that bad and you never said a word. What would you have done if they killed her one of those times, Ty?"

A sob came from where he sat hunched in on himself. "I hate myself for letting her go through that. But every time I tried to confront them, she'd flip out and make me leave, and when I would, that night or the next day would be one of those days where they'd beat her so hard she wouldn't be able to pick herself up."

"That isn't an excuse, you could have taken her away from them. Uncle Jim could have done something!"

"Look, Gage, you can't make me feel any worse than I already do! I'm the one who had to clean the blood off her, I'm the one who had to bandage her up even during the dozens of times when she should have gotten stitches. I had to buy a mini freezer for my room so I could have ice for when she came over!" He pulled his phone out of his pocket, tapped the screen a few times, and stifled another sob as he handed it over to me.

"What is this?" Whatever these fresh bruises were, they definitely weren't done by hands. The small rectangles looked familiar, but I couldn't place what I thought they were.

"Golf club. I didn't even know about this last time. She just told me about it on the way back here, and I took the pictures before I came in here. She said it happened yesterday morning before I came and packed her bags."

"Are there more pictures?"

He raised his head for a second to nod. "Ever since I got my first phone I've taken pictures every time she came over, and I always transfer them to my new phones so I'll have them. They're all backed up too. She wouldn't let me say anything, but I wanted to have photos in case . . ." His voice trailed off. There wasn't a need for him to finish that sentence anyway; I got the message.

Flipping through some of his pictures, I couldn't believe this was the same sweet Cassi I'd just met a few hours ago. Bruises of all shapes, sizes, and colors covered her body and it was killing me to look at them, but I couldn't stop. You could see all the ones that were fading slowly get covered up by new ones, and other pictures showed her back, arms, and face covered in blood. What killed me was that whenever her face was in the picture, she wore the same expression I'd just seen outside. No emotion, dead eyes, and absolutely no tears.

"What would they do to her?"

"You don't want to know."

Like hell I didn't. I was already planning on going to California with my twelve-gauge. "What. Would. They. Do?"

He was quiet for so long I didn't think he was going to answer. "When it first started, it was *usually* just hitting and kicking. The older she got, the more it turned into whatever they had in their hands or could grab quickly. Once that started, she only came over if it was other objects. She lived for the days when it was only hands."

"So what I saw tonight, you said it isn't the worst?"

"Not even close."

"What was?"

Tyler sighed and looked up at me, tears streaming down his face. "I don't know, there were a few that really stood out, but I couldn't name one that was the worst."

I just kept glaring at him; he needed a beatin' just for letting this go on for so long. She was seventeen or eighteen now, so she had been six or seven when this all started. And he'd known the entire time.

"A couple years ago, the cops showed up one night—"

"I thought you said she wouldn't let you call?"

"I didn't." He sighed and ran his hands through his hair a few times. "The old lady that lived in between us heard her screaming one night, called the cops."

I shoved off the wall and flung my arms out. "You had a perfect opportunity and you still didn't do anything? *They* didn't do anything?!"

"Gage, I didn't even know the cops were called until she texted me hours after they'd left!"

"What happened?" I demanded, and forced myself back against the wall.

"Cassi opened the door, her mom and stepdad right behind her. None of her bruises were visible then and they all denied the screaming, including Cass."

Seriously? What the fuck?

"When the cops left, her mom took off her high heels, used the pointy heel part to hit her head repeatedly. There was so much blood when I got there, Gage, and she couldn't lay her head even on a pillow for almost a week after that. Another time her stepdad threw a glass of alcohol at her, she ducked, and it shattered against a wall. Since she didn't get hit by it, he grabbed her by the throat, dragged her to where it was, and just kept slicing her forehead, arms, stomach, and back with one of the pieces. She wore a scarf every day 'til the finger marks were gone. That's why she wears her hair with those things, what are they called? Bangs. She got those scars when she was ten and the one on her head isn't very noticeable anymore, but she still tries to hide it. She tries to hide all of them, but some she can't unless she wants to wear jeans and long sleeves in the summer."

I stood there in shock, trying to make the connection between this girl he was telling me about and the girl I'd just met. Even with seeing the pictures it wasn't clicking for me; I couldn't imagine someone touching her, or her being so willing to let it continue. "You're a poor excuse for a man, Tyler." I opened my door and stood next to it, arms crossed over my chest.

He looked like he crumpled in on himself. "You think I don't know that?"

I couldn't say anything else to him. As soon as he was out of my room I slammed the door and fell on my bed. I wanted to make him stay in my room and go to her myself. Hold her and tell her I'd never let anyone else hurt her again. But for whatever reason she wanted him, and we didn't know each other so it would be even creepier than my trying to be close enough to hear her talk tonight.

My whole body shook as I thought about anyone laying a hand on her, let alone sharp objects. Sweet Cassi, she deserved parents and a man who cherished her. Not ones who beat her and a boy who sat back and let it happen. I swallowed back vomit for the third time since I found out what happened and forced myself to stay in my bed.

I closed my eyes and tried to steady my breathing, focusing on her face and honey-colored eyes instead of what I saw on her back and the images that Tyler's phone had seared into my brain. I thought about running my hands through that long, dark hair. Pressing my mouth to her neck, her cheeks, and finally those lips that were full and inviting. *Tyler doesn't deserve her. Not at all.* I thought about taking her in my arms and taking her to the ranch so I could keep her safe for the rest of her life. But she'd already been living a life she didn't choose, so I wouldn't choose for her either; I would wait for her to leave him and come to me.

2

Cassidy

WE HADN'T BEEN in Austin for more than six hours before someone saw the bruises. And not just anyone, Tyler's cousin, our new roommate, and the guy who wouldn't leave my every waking thought. I told Tyler not to tell him—let him make his own assumptions—but of course Tyler didn't listen and told him way more than he should have. I couldn't blame him though; I'd made him keep a secret no kid should have to. I know he thought I was sleeping, but even if I had been, Gage yelling at Tyler, or Tyler coming back into our room to hold me and tell me how sorry he was while he cried, would have woken me up. I'd learned long ago that if I cried, I got hit harder until I finally stopped, so I'd become a master at turning off my emotions. But I knew if I had opened my eyes to watch him cry, it definitely would have broken through that wall and I would have been crying right there with him. So I lay completely still, emotions turned off and eyes shut, while Tyler cried himself to sleep.

Once Tyler got in the shower the next morning, I slipped into the kitchen to start some coffee. We'd spent so many nights without sleeping over the years, we'd both started drinking it early on, and I was glad that now he didn't have to sneak an extra cup for me since his parents hadn't exactly known that I stayed the night all those years.

I shut the door quietly and turned to tiptoe across the hardwood floors when I saw Gage, and my heart instantly picked up its pace. He was dressed only in jersey shorts and shoes, his body still glistening with sweat. God, he looked amazing, and my breath caught at how perfect his body and face were. I'd barely caught a glimpse of him without his shirt on last night before Tyler had caught me staring, and now I couldn't make my eyes look away.

"Morning."

My eyes finally snapped up to meet his. In the light and this close, I could see the gold flecks scattered throughout the green of his eyes. They were the most beautiful eyes I'd ever seen. "Good morning, Gage."

"How, uh—how are you today?"

I sighed and walked over to the coffeepot. "I know he talked to you, I could hear you guys last night. I don't want you to be awkward around me now because of what you know."

"Cassi, those things should have never happened to you. He should have told someone."

I turned to find him right in front of me again. "I made him promise he wouldn't."

"Well he shouldn't have listened to you."

"You don't get it, Gage. You weren't there. I couldn't let him."

His eyes narrowed. "No, I wasn't there. But if I had been, something would have been done the first time it ever happened. Why didn't you say anything the night the cops showed?"

I shook my head; there was no point in trying to make him understand.

Gage put a hand on each side of my face and leaned closer. I swear I thought he was about to kiss me, like last night, and it didn't matter that I hardly knew him; I wanted him to. "You didn't deserve that, Cassi, you know that, right?"

"I do."

Before I could realize what he was doing, he brushed my swoop bangs back and traced his thumb over a scar from Jeff's glass. My body instantly stiffened and Gage's eyes turned dark as he looked at it. He slowly tore his gaze from the scar to my eyes and spoke softly. "Didn't deserve any of that."

I took a step back and turned to look at the almost-full pot of coffee.

He reached around me and brought down two mugs before pouring coffee in each one. "I'm sorry if you like cream," he drawled. "I don't have any here."

"That's fine." I breathed a quiet sigh of relief as I walked over to the fridge and grabbed the milk. "I'll go to the store later and get some."

When I was done pouring it in, he put the cap on for me and put it back in the fridge. Walking back over to me, he put a finger under my chin and tilted my head up so I was looking at him. "How often did it happen, Cassi?"

My breaths started coming quicker. What was it about him that made me want to fall into his arms and not ever leave? It took his repeating his question for me to come out of my daydream. I was up against the counter, so I couldn't step back, but I moved my head away from his hand and stared past his shoulder into the living room.

He guessed when he saw I wasn't going to answer. "Every day?"

I still didn't respond; if it was a weekend, it happened at least twice a day. But that was something even Tyler didn't know. My body started involuntarily shaking and I hated that I was showing any sign of weakness in front of him.

"Never again, Cassi," he whispered while he studied my face.

My eyes flew back to meet his and my throat tightened. He sounded like he was in pain just talking about it and I had no idea why. But I'd be lying if I said it didn't make me want his arms wrapped around me. I cleared my throat and forced myself to continue to meet his gaze. "Cassidy."

"What?"

"My name is Cassidy."

"Oh." He looked a little sheepish. "My apologies, I didn't realize."

"No. Um, Tyler doesn't like it. He calls me Cassi. I just wanted to tell you my real name." Really I just wanted to hear it in his gravelly voice.

He smiled softly as he studied me for a minute and took a sip of his black coffee. "I like Cassidy, it fits."

Oh damn . . . yep. I was right in wanting to hear him say that. My arms were covered in goose bumps and I even shivered. Yeah— his voice was *that* sexy.

When I didn't say anything he walked around to the table and held out a chair, waiting for me to sit in it. We sat in silence for a while before I finally looked up at him again.

"This might be rude, but can I ask you something?"

One side of his mouth lifted up in a smile. "I think I already cornered the market on rude questions this morning, so go ahead."

And cue the freaking dimples! I got so lost staring at them I forgot to ask my question and his smirk went to a full-blown Gage smile. At this rate I'd need to start wearing a sleeping mask and earplugs around him in order not to make myself look like an idiot. Though I'd look ridiculous either way. "Well, um, Tyler said you live on a ranch?"

"I do."

"I was kind of thinking you'd look more like a cowboy . . ."

Gage's laugh bounced back off the walls, and I felt my body relax just listening to it. "And how exactly were you expecting me to look?"

"You know, boots, hat, big belt buckle, super-tight bright blue jeans," I replied, a little embarrassed.

"Well I definitely have the boots, and the hats, but I don't think my sisters or Mama would ever let me dress like Dad."

"Oh."

"My dad even has the big mustache, looks like Sam Elliott."

It took me a second to figure out who that was, and then I laughed. "Seriously?"

"Swear, they could be twins."

"I'd love to see that. So where was your hat last night?"

He shrugged. "I leave all that at the ranch."

"What? Why?"

"I don't wear them as a fashion statement, and I definitely don't have any kind of work that would require them here in hippie town."

"Hippie town?" I deadpanned.

"Just wait until we go out anywhere. You'll see."

I nodded. "What kind of work? What kind of ranch do you have?"

"Cattle ranch, and whatever needs to be done that day. Taking care of the animals, moving the cattle to different parts of the ranch, fixing fences, branding . . ." He drifted off. "Just depends."

"How many cows do you have?"

"About sixteen."

Okay, I understand I don't know a thing about ranches, but I figured you'd need more than sixteen cows to make it a cattle ranch. "You have sixteen cows?"

He huffed a laugh and smiled wide at me. "Hundred. Sixteen hundred."

"Dear Lord, that's a lot of cows."

He shrugged. "We'll be getting more soon, we have the land."

"How many acres is the ranch?"

"Twenty."

"Hundred?"

"Thousand."

"Twenty thousand acres?!" My jaw dropped. Why on earth would anyone need or want that much land?

"Yes, ma'am." He spun his mug around on the table.

" 'Ma'am'? Really?"

One of his eyebrows raised. "What?"

"I'm not some grandma—I'm younger than you."

Gage rolled his eyes. "I didn't mean you're old, it's respectful." When he looked at my expression he shook his head and chuckled. "Yankees."

"Uh, get a clue, cowboy . . . I'm not from the North."

"You're not from the South either. Yankee." He smirked, and if I thought that was going to melt me, when he added a wink I knew I was done for.

"Are you going on about Yankees again, bro?" Tyler asked, walking into the kitchen.

Gage just shrugged and his green eyes met mine from under those dark brows again. "She didn't like that I called her 'ma'am.' "

"Get used to it, Cassi, we may be in the city, but it's different here."

I grumbled to myself and Gage laughed.

"So what are you guys talking about?" Tyler sat in the seat on my other side.

"Their huge ranch with too many cows," I answered.

"She's right about that, there are way too many cows there," Tyler said between sips of his coffee.

"You'd like it." Gage looked at me with an odd expression.

"Hell no, she wouldn't! Cassi doesn't like getting dirty, and she hates bugs. Your ranch would be the worst place for her."

Gage flicked a quick glare at his cousin, then looked back to me. "We have horses."

I gasped. "You do? I've never been on a horse!"

"Eight Arabians. I'll teach you to ride when you come to visit." He sat back in his chair and folded his arms, smirking at Tyler like he'd just won something.

Tyler and I both got quiet. My dad told me he was going to let me start taking riding lessons for my sixth birthday and buy me a horse for my seventh. Obviously those things never happened. Not that we didn't have the money, but my mom wouldn't even cook for me; no way she would let me do those things. It didn't help that even though I still loved horses, whenever I saw them I couldn't stop thinking about my dad.

"Did I say something wrong?" Gage looked confused but kept his eyes on Tyler.

"No," I said with a soft smile. "I'd like that."

After a few awkward minutes, Gage stood up and put his mug in the dishwasher before walking toward his room, "Well, I'm gonna take a shower. If there's anything y'all wanna do today, let me know."

Tyler scooted my chair closer to him. "You okay, Cassi? Is it because of your dad?"

"No, it's fine. I mean, I was thinking about him. But I just can't believe he's been gone for almost twelve years. I feel like I should be over it, I was so young when it happened, but I don't think I was ever allowed to grieve, and that's why it's still hard. I'm not looking forward to this birthday. I always thought when I got away from Mom and Jeff, I would finally enjoy my birthdays again, but I'm looking forward to it less than ever. I think we need to give me a new birthday, Ty." I huffed a light laugh. "No one wants a birthday on the anniversary of their father's death."

He pulled me onto his lap and held me loosely so he wouldn't hurt my back. "He was a great dad; you aren't supposed to get over him, Cassi, you'll always miss him. And no new birthdays, you're keeping the one you have and I'll make sure they get better and better every year."

I let him hold me for a few minutes before speaking again. "Thanks, Ty, I love you."

"Love you too, Cassi."

Gage

OH MY GOD, *her dad died on her birthday? What else has happened to this girl?* Okay, I'll admit I left the bathroom door cracked for a few minutes before shutting it and starting my shower. But the way they'd both got so quiet there at the end, I knew I'd said something I shouldn't have, and I figured Tyler would bring it up as soon as I was gone. I knew she'd be hooked as soon as I mentioned the horses, and she was; I just didn't know telling her

I'd teach her to ride would take them back down memory lane to her dad, who was obviously nothing like her mom or stepdad.

Sitting there talking to her before Tyler had come in was the best morning I think I'd ever had, and it didn't even last ten minutes. She smiled so much it made my heart swell each time, and God, that laugh. I was right; it sounded just like freakin' angels. I wanted to die every time she'd start to relax into the chair. Her eyes would go wide for a split second and she'd sit right back up like she'd forgotten about the bruises on her back for a minute. I didn't have to ask her to know she was in pain; there was no way she could have been comfortable with what I'd seen last night. But even with that, her smile never faltered, and that may have killed me even more. She should have been depressed or crying or something. What kind of person goes through that kind of life, as recent as two days ago, and still finds reasons to smile?

When I walked out of the bathroom, she was still curled up on Tyler's lap and I blew out a frustrated sigh. I needed to get over her soon, or living there with them was going to be a challenge.

"Hey, Gage?" Tyler called before I could shut my door.

"What?"

"You up to showing us around the city today?"

No. I want to show Cassidy the city, I want you to go the hell back to California. "Sure."

I shut the door behind me and had just finished getting my jeans on when Tyler walked in.

"You okay, man? We don't have to go out today, I was just asking. Or Cassi and I could go by ourselves. It's not a big deal either way, I just figured since you knew the area . . ."

I never asked Cassidy why Tyler didn't like her name. It was so perfect for her, and why would he even tell her he didn't like it? Seriously, how were we related? "No, it's fine, I just have a lot on my mind. I'll be ready in a minute, we can go whenever."

"All right, well I'm sure she wants to shower. So it'll probably be a while," he called as he walked back out of my room.

I grabbed a shirt and headed out to the living room. Tyler wasn't there, but Cassidy was sitting at the kitchen table, staring intently at her hands. "You okay, Cassidy?"

She jumped and looked up at me, her brows pulled together in confusion and hurt. She didn't say anything, just studied my face for a minute, before blowing out a deep sigh and standing up to walk toward their room.

"I'm sorry for reminding you about your dad. I didn't know." I still didn't know. What did horses have to do with her dad?

Cassidy stopped walking and looked over her shoulder at me for a second, then continued to the door.

I stood there staring at the door, feeling like an ass, even after Tyler walked out of the room and started hooking a gaming system to the TV. Did telling Cassidy I'd teach her to ride really hurt her so much that the girl who asked why I didn't dress like a cowboy just disappeared? Everything in me screamed to go to her and talk to her, but the shower started, so I turned back to the living room. I told Tyler I'd watch him play and flopped onto the couch. I tried not to picture Cassidy in the shower while I listened to the water running, but that was damn hard, so I focused as much of my attention as I could on Tyler shooting people and tried not to think about her and the hard-on I was trying to cover with a pillow.

When Cassidy came out less than an hour later, her hair was wild and slightly wavy, and she had less makeup on than last night too. She looked beautiful. Without all that dark stuff around her eyes and stuff on her face, her honey-colored eyes looked even brighter and you could see a splatter of very light freckles on her nose. Not saying she hadn't looked gorgeous last night, because she had. She took my breath away. But I preferred this almost completely natural look. She was wearing green Chucks, jeans with the bottoms rolled up to her calves, and a worn black Boston concert shirt. *Boston. This girl is perfect.*

"Ty, I'm ready."

She still had yet to look at me since she walked in the room, and though I wanted her to, I was enjoying being able to take her in. I noticed her bottom lip was a little too full for her top lip, and her nose couldn't have been more perfect if she'd chosen it herself. Her eyes flitted over to me quickly, then right back to Tyler; her cheeks got red and I couldn't help but grin. *There's no way she doesn't feel this too.* She started biting her bottom lip, and again I thought about what it would feel like to kiss those lips. I'd never wanted to kiss a girl this damn bad.

"Tyler!" She tapped his leg with her foot and he looked at her, then back at the screen.

"What's up?"

"I'm ready, are we going or not?"

"Yeah, just let me finish this match and we can go. Like eight minutes."

I had already sat up when she entered the room so she could sit on the couch with me, and she was eyeing it now, but instead turned and went into the bedroom. She stayed in there while Tyler played two more matches and didn't come out until he went to get her.

I took them all over Austin that afternoon, and while she was polite and would respond whenever I asked her a question, she wouldn't hold a conversation with me and made sure she was always by Tyler's side, farthest away from me. Maybe I was wrong about her feeling whatever this connection was, because she definitely didn't seem like she was having a hard time not touching me. It was all I could do not to grab her hand and keep her by my side.

When we were on the way back, she asked if we could stop by the grocery store, and we let her take over the shopping after her third eye-roll at our food choices.

"Don't worry," Tyler whispered as she compared packages of ground beef, "she's been cooking for herself since she was six; she's better than my mom."

I hadn't been worried, and now that added just one more thing I wished I could have protected her from. Because my dad and I worked from sunup to sundown most days, I was only ever in the kitchen to help with dishes. I thanked Mom and my sisters daily for making the food, but I couldn't imagine having to do it on my own when I was just a little kid. I'd have to thank them again.

Other than letting us carry the groceries in for her, she wouldn't let us help put them away and immediately started on cooking dinner for the three of us. I lay down on the couch just watching her move around the kitchen while Tyler played his game again. At one point it looked like she started dancing for a few seconds before she stopped herself, and God, if that wasn't the cutest thing I'd ever seen. When Ty was fully engrossed in the game, I got up and wandered into the kitchen, stepping right up behind her.

"Do you need help with anything?"

Her body tensed for a moment, and once it relaxed she turned her head up to look at me. "No, I'm fine. Thanks though."

"Could I help anyway?"

She continued to watch me with that same hurt and confused

look from that morning. "Yeah, sure. You can make the salad." She grabbed a few things out of the fridge and brought them over to me before grabbing a couple more items that she'd bought at the store out of a bowl on the counter. "Dice these, and—wait, do you even like avocados?"

"I'll eat anything, darlin'."

Her mouth tilted up at the corners and her cheeks got red; I smiled to myself and made a mental note to call her that more often. "Well, if you don't like them, I can just put them in my bowl."

I grabbed the avocado from her and looked at it, a little confused. "Like I said, I'll eat anything. But how do you cut this thing?"

She laughed lightly and took it from my hand, sliding the cucumber and tomato in front of me. "Dice these first, then I'll show you how to cut the avocado." She handed me a knife and turned back to the stove.

I was flat-out awful at dicing those vegetables, but being in the kitchen with her had me smiling the entire time, and whatever she was cooking smelled damn good. "I think I did it right."

"There's really no way to mess up dicing veggies for a salad." She turned and looked. "You did it just fine. Haven't you ever diced something before?" I shook my head and she grinned at me. "Really? Well you did great. Let me show you how to do these."

She grabbed both avocados and handed me one of them before picking up her own knife. I'm not gonna lie, I purposefully kept messing up getting the seed out so that she finally had to reach over and grab my hands to show me what to do. I heard her intake of breath as soon as our hands touched, and I had to look away so she wouldn't see how wide I was smiling.

Hell. Yeah.

She finished showing me how to cut up the avocado and had me grab bowls and plates while she finished up whatever was on the stove. Every time I looked at it, she'd turn me away and say I wasn't allowed to see her secrets. I didn't know what was going on all day, but she was now acting just like she had that morning. Every smile and every touch had me falling for her that much more.

I touched her arm so she'd look up at me and I almost forgot what I was gonna ask as soon as her eyes met mine. "Uh, did I upset you this morning? I swear I didn't mean to. I had no idea about your dad."

She looked down, then back at the stove. "I didn't expect you to know about him. And what were you thinking upset me?"

"When I told you I'd teach you how to ride."

Cassidy huffed and shook her head once. "No, Gage, that didn't upset me. I would really like to learn how to ride, if you ever want to show me."

Did she think I would offer if I didn't want to? And would it be bad if I asked what those two things had to do with each other? "Of course I will. I mean, I heard what Tyler said, but I do think you'd like the ranch. I can't wait to take you there." Ah, too much. Too much.

"Sounds great." She picked up a spoon, then set it right back down and put both her hands on the counter before looking back at me. Her mouth opened and her eyebrows pulled together, then she looked into the living room at Tyler and back at me. "Dinner is about ready," she said softly. "Would you mind putting the salad on the table?"

When I turned around with the bowls, I saw Tyler staring at us and held back a sigh. I was gonna get crap for this later.

Cassidy had made crispy chicken fettuccine Alfredo, and all I could say was damn. I had to agree with Tyler that it was better than Aunt Steph's, and it rivaled Mama's cooking.

I stood up to help when she started clearing the dishes, but Tyler stepped in front of me before I got far. "I'm serious, man, she's mine."

"I heard you the first time."

"You sure about that?"

I glanced back at Cassidy. "Yeah, I'm sure. But you're the one who brought her here; you can't expect me to never talk to her, or offer my help when she's making us food. If we're all gonna live together, you need to get over the fact that I'm gonna be friends with her."

He remained quiet and smiled, waiting for Cassidy to return to the kitchen. "I couldn't care less if you're friends with her. Just don't forget that I'm the one who's been there for her every day for the last eleven years. Not you. I still see how you're look-ing at her, I'm not fucking blind, Gage."

Cassidy

"I'M KIND OF TIRED, I'm going to bed. Thanks for showing us around today, Gage."

Tyler stood and walked over to me. "Want me to come with you?"

I shot a quick glance behind Ty to Gage, who was openly glaring at his cousin. "No, you guys need to catch up, I'll see you later."

"Sleep well, Cassidy," Gage said.

I smiled and waved like an idiot. "Night."

Tyler hugged me and Gage winked when I looked over Ty's shoulder at him. Seriously, this guy was so confusing! I walked to the bathroom I shared with Tyler to wash my face and brush my teeth before slipping into some pajamas and crawling into bed. I could hear the boys talking and Gage started laughing, warming my entire body. I sighed and flipped onto my side. I didn't understand him at all. First, he had a girlfriend, then he'd almost kissed me last night, and this morning I could have sworn he was flirting with me. Then he got upset when we wanted to go out this morning and Tyler told me that when he went to talk to him about it, Gage said he didn't want me living here, but tonight in the kitchen he kept finding a reason to touch me and wouldn't stop smiling at me. What the heck? I didn't know how to even act around him.

I must have fallen asleep, because I felt a little groggy when Tyler slipped into the bed later that night.

"Sorry, I didn't mean to wake you," he said softly.

"It's fine, I meant to wait up for you. I guess I was more tired than I realized."

He pulled me close to his body and wrapped his arms around me. "You've had a long last three days, you needed to sleep."

"True. Did you guys have fun talking?"

"Yeah, it's good to see him again. It's been a long time since we hung out."

"I'm sorry I'm ruining that; you really shouldn't have brought me, Ty."

He leaned back a little so he could see my face. "Cassi, I'll take you with me everywhere I go. And don't worry about Gage, he'll get over it eventually. I'm sure it's not you that he doesn't like, he just said it's going to mess up his relationship with Brynn having a girl live with him."

"I don't want to do that." *Yes, yes, I do.* I'd never experienced jealousy until I met Gage last night, and it was one ugly feeling. "When I turn eighteen, I'll get my own place, Ty."

"No, you won't. He'll get over it, and I want you with me, okay?"

I curled into his chest and nodded. "Love you."

Tyler leaned back again and tilted my face up to his. "I love you too, Cassi." His lips fell onto mine and I scrambled back, pushing against his chest as hard as I could.

"What the hell, Tyler?!" We slept in bed with each other, but we'd never actually kissed before.

"I'm sorry! I thought you wanted me to."

"What? Why would I want you to?" *Oh my God, seriously, what the hell just happened?!*

He sighed and relaxed his hold on me. "I don't—I don't know what got into me. I'm sorry, that was really stupid."

"Is that why you brought me to Texas with you?"

"No, it's not, I swear. You're my best friend, I would have never left you there. I'm sorry, like I said, that was really stupid."

I crawled off the bed and grabbed my pillow. "Maybe I should sleep on the couch tonight."

"No! Cassi, come on, don't do that. I'm sorry."

"It's fine, it hasn't just been a long three days for me. It's been even longer for you. I think we're both too tired and we aren't thinking clearly."

"Cass." He sighed and got out of the bed as well. "I'm sorry, I don't know what I was thinking doing that." He hugged me loosely and stepped back. "Please get back in bed."

"It's all right, I promise. I'm just going to sleep out there to-night—I think it would be best for us. I'll be back in here tomorrow, okay?"

"I'll go out there, you can stay in the bed."

I put my hand on his chest and pushed him onto the bed. "I'm way shorter than you; that couch was practically made for me. Good night, Ty, see you in the morning."

3

Gage

I COULDN'T SLEEP. I already hated thinking about what probably happened between Tyler and Cassidy, but having Tyler tell me he was about to go screw her made it that much worse. I'm sorry, not screw her, bang her. Like it was no big deal, just announced, "I'm gonna go bang my girl," and left without another word. A girl like Cassidy needs to be loved and worshipped, not *banged*. I knew he was just trying to get a rise out of me—I doubted he'd treat her with such little respect to her face—but I fell right into his trap, 'cause now there I was wearing a freakin' hole in my floor pacing back and forth. And what happened during dinner? I thought I'd been making progress in the kitchen, she'd started flirting with me again, bantering back and forth and smiling like I was the most interesting person she'd ever talked to. Then dinner started and she went right back to being polite and unin- terested. I swear I was getting whiplash with this girl.

After taking a calming breath, I headed out into the kitchen so I could grab some water. I tried not to, but my eyes betrayed me and flashed over to their door. I was itching to knock it down and drag her to my bed; I didn't want him touching her at all. Dear Lord, since when did I get this possessive over a girl? I was about to go caveman on Ty's ass and put my claim on her. Turning away from the door, I almost choked when I saw sweet Cassidy curled up asleep on the couch. After downing the rest of the water, I walked quietly into the living room and smiled at the sight of her. She had her arms and legs inside what must have been one of Tyler's shirts, and was curled into a tight ball in the corner of the couch.

Part of me was happy because I didn't think she'd come out here after having sex with Ty; the rest was annoyed that he'd done something to upset her enough that she felt like she needed to sleep out here. I called her name and touched her shoulder gently; when she didn't respond I picked her up and carried her to my room. She was a small girl anyway, but I'd lifted hay bales heavier than her, and I was feeling too many bones. I didn't even want to think about how her spine and shoulder blades had jutted out in those pictures. Whether she wasn't allowed to cook often or didn't have enough food in the house, she'd obviously missed too many meals. I'd have to make sure we always had enough food here; Cassidy needed to put on at least twenty more pounds just to look healthy.

Flipping back the comforter on my bed, I lowered her to the mattress and pulled the covers back over her. Her hair had fallen in her face, and I tucked it behind her ear so I could see her better. God, she was beautiful. I was aching to slide into the bed with her and hold her all night, but I'd probably be woken up by either her or Tyler punching me. Afraid she'd wake up and see me starin' at her, I walked to my dresser and changed into some workout shorts and headed out to the couch. I almost groaned out loud when I lay down and was surrounded in her scent trapped in the pillow. How did Ty fall asleep with her in his bed every night? I could barely relax just thinking about her in my bed, and we were separated by a few walls.

"GAGE." I FELT a hand on my arm. "Gage." This was a better dream than most; I swore I could smell her sweet scent in this one. "Gage, you gotta wake up!"

The pillow slipped out from under me and my head hit the hard arm of the couch. "What the fuck?" My eyes flew open and I saw Cassidy standing right in front of me, clutching her pillow to her chest. "Oh, Cass, I'm sorry."

She rolled her eyes and smiled. "For the last time, your cussing doesn't offend me."

Yeah, but once again, Mama would smack me upside the head for even saying that in front of a girl. I smiled back. "Mornin'."

"Ty's going to wake up soon, you need to get up. I swear, Gage, you have got to stop putting me in your bed. One of these times he's going to find out you do that and he'll be mad."

"I don't know what happens between y'all that you feel the need to sleep out here sometimes, but it's not right. He's the guy so he should be out here, not the other way around." Besides, I loved seeing her in my bed. This was the fifth time in the last month since they moved in that I'd found her on the couch at night. That didn't include the mornings I would be leaving for my run and find her then.

"Well, I don't come out here so you'll take my place. If you keep doing this I'll just start sleeping in the tub. Now, get up."

She was already stepping away from the couch and folding the blanket she had bought for her nights out here.

I took the blanket from her and put it in the closet before heading to my room to get ready for a run. When I took my phone off the charger I caught a glimpse of the date and practically jogged out to the kitchen. She was getting the coffee ready and had her back to me, so I wrapped my arms around her and leaned in close. "Happy birthday, Cassidy."

It wasn't weird for me to hug her anymore; every morning one of us got the coffee ready, and she came in for her "morning hug," as she called it. I thought it was adorable, and I lived for it. It was the one time Tyler didn't give me crap for being near her, mostly because he wasn't there to see it. But this morning she didn't hug me back, she just continued to get the coffeepot ready, even with my arms wrapped around her. I almost cursed out loud when I realized what else today was.

Spinning her around so she was facing me, I cupped her cheeks and bent down so I was closer to her eye level. "You gonna be okay today, darlin'?"

She nodded and gave me a sad smile, her arms lightly wrapping around my waist. "I'm fine, it's just hard. I wish he was here."

"I know you do." I heard Tyler moving around so I let her go and pressed start on the coffeepot. "So what do you have planned for today? Tattoos, buying cigarettes, voting?" I winked and nudged her shoulder.

"You're so dumb. No, to all of the above. I don't have many plans; I need to go to the bank though. Now that I'm eighteen, the bank accounts are in my name and I can use them."

"Bank accounts?"

"Yeah, before he died, my dad started a savings account and a college account in both our names. But I wasn't allowed to touch them until I turned eighteen. I wish I already had some of my own money, but when I turned sixteen and said I was going to get a job, Mom . . . well . . . let's just say I wasn't allowed."

I ground my teeth and forced my hands not to ball into fists. "You need a ride? I mean, you can wait for Ty if you want, but I don't have any classes today, so I'll take you if you want to get it done early."

"That'd be great, thanks, Gage." She set about pouring the coffee into two mugs for us, and a travel mug for Tyler.

Just as she finished, Tyler walked out and grabbed her hand, taking her to their room. I was glad they weren't in there for more than two minutes; not much they could have done in that time.

"What's up, man?" Tyler shouldered past me as he grabbed his cup. "Take care of my woman this morning for me, okay?"

I knew Cassidy must not have come back in with him if he was being all possessive. "Sure thing. Gonna go for a run, then I'll take her to the bank to get all that stuff taken care of." I looked around at the hall, then back at him. "We still taking her out tonight?"

"Yep, you call everyone?"

"Yeah, most of them are coming. Jackie, Dana, and Lanie for sure; Adam, Ethan, Grant, and some of the other guys will be there."

"Sounds good, I'll see you later this afternoon."

"Later."

I sat at the table and started drinking my coffee, waiting for Cassidy to come join me like she did every morning, but she ran into the kitchen, gave me a small smile, and ran back to the room with her mug in her hand. Couple minutes later I heard the shower turn on so I put my mug in the sink and left to run.

When I got back she was sitting on the kitchen counter holding a bottled water for me. I gave her knee a light squeeze and downed the bottle. I kept catching her staring at me and tried not to smile. At this point, I honestly had no idea what was going on between her and Tyler. If they were actually dating, they were one odd couple. She always wanted to be near him, but he never talked about their being a couple unless she wasn't around. And even then, it seemed like he was just trying to remind me that she wasn't available. Most days we slipped into comfortable banter, and our mornings alone usually resulted in subtle flirting, but there were still the days when she'd look at me like I'd hurt her and shut off. Today wasn't either of those days. She was quiet and looked crushed, but I knew it had nothing to do with me.

After my shower, I walked back into the kitchen to find her in the same spot and jumped up onto the counter next to her. I sat there silently until she leaned into me, resting her head on my shoulder. We sat there for a few minutes without speaking, and my arm kept twitching. I wanted to put it around her so bad, but I didn't know if it would bother her, so I kept it at my side. When she sighed and sat straight up, I figured it was better that I hadn't.

"You ready?"

She nodded and slid off the counter, looking at me expectantly.

"I promise we'll make this a good day for you, okay?"

"I know."

She remained silent until we were at the bank and the banking officer called her into his office. Cassidy grabbed my arm and pulled me in there with her; her whole body was shaking.

I'd never done it before, but when we sat down I intertwined my fingers with hers and smiled in relief when she clutched my hand tighter, rather than removing it.

"Hmm . . . you said Cassidy Jameson?"

"That's correct."

"It looks like the primary account holder withdrew all the money last week."

Cassidy blanched and instantly stopped shaking. "Th-that's not possible. My dad was the primary on the accounts. He died twelve years ago."

The banker looked at her with a scrunched brow, then began typing something into his computer. "Is your mother Karen Jameson Kross?"

"Yes."

"She must have become the primary when he died." He typed a few more things. "Yes, yes, she did. It shows here everything was transferred to her name, and she withdrew the money out of both accounts last Thursday."

"Can you please tell me how much she took?" Cassidy asked through clenched teeth.

"Sure, just one second." He went back to clicking and typing for another minute.

I kept my eyes on Cassidy; she looked like she was going to pass out at any moment. I couldn't believe this was happening.

The banker printed out a piece of paper and slid it across the desk to us; he'd circled the total of the two accounts, just under one hundred grand.

All the air left Cassidy as if someone had punched her, and I kept my grip tight on her hand. "I'm sorry, sir," I started, "but there's been a mistake. That woman wasn't supposed to be able to touch that money."

"She's your mother, right, Miss Jameson?"

Cassidy didn't move; her eyes were huge and she was staring at the floor. "*Mother* is a very loose term for her," I answered.

"Was she still the legal guardian?" The banker started to sweat and was reaching for his phone.

Cassidy jumped out of the seat. "Just let her have it," she blurted out, and turned for the door.

I ran after her, catching her just before she hit the doors of the lobby. "Cass, look at me."

She turned around and my heart sank when I saw her emotionless mask back on.

"Talk to me."

"There's nothing to say. She took it, that's the end of it."

"What can I do?"

"Nothing." She shrugged out of my grasp and continued out to my truck. "I'm just going to get a job and get over it."

I bit my tongue and held the door open for her before going to the driver's side and sliding in. "Cassidy, you can talk to me. I know this upsets you, don't act like it doesn't."

"What do you want me to say, Gage?!" she snapped as she struggled to get her seat belt buckled. I reached over and took it out of her hands, buckling it for her. She sat back with a huff and mashed her lips into a line.

After cranking the car and turning on the AC, I left the car in park and just watched her, hoping she'd finally let me in. We could talk for hours, but as soon as it got personal like this, she shut off and would run to Tyler. Every. Time. Her phone chimed and while she searched through her purse it chimed again. She read it, her jaw dropped, and she shakily started tapping on the screen, holding it to her ear. I saw her eyes fill with tears.

"Ty," she choked out, "Ty, please call me back." A line of tears fell down her left cheek as she ended the call. I'd never even seen her tear up before this.

"Cassidy." The need to hold her was too much; I took off her seat belt and pulled her over to me. "Please talk to me, who texted you?"

Her shoulders shook as she clung to my arm, but she didn't respond. Her phone was resting on her leg and I picked it up. Giving her the time to stop me, I opened up her texts and had to read them twice to make sure I was reading them correctly.

> MOM
>
> *Just got a call saying you tried to withdraw money from the accounts. You really think you did anything to deserve that money? I had to put up with you for 18 years, someone needed to pay me for that.*

> MOM
>
> *OH! Almost forgot . . . Happy you-killed-your-father day.*

I cursed and squeezed her tighter to me. "Cassidy, I'm so sorry. You don't deserve that." I cupped her face and stared deep into her whiskey-colored eyes; my heart broke seeing this beautiful girl cry. "You're amazing and perfect, and your mom is a worthless human being."

"I just don't understand why she hates me." She sobbed and put her face on my chest. "I understand some of the drinking, but not Jeff, not her leaving me to completely fend for myself, not the—not the—" She choked on another sob and tried to pull away but I held her there.

There was nothing else I could say in that moment. If there

were words that could have comforted her, I would have said every single one of them. But she didn't need words, she just needed someone there. I leaned back against the driver's-side door and pulled her onto me so she was leaning into my chest. Wrapping my arms around her, I tried to let her feel everything I wasn't allowed to tell her. That she was unlike any other girl in the world, that she was wanted and cherished, that I loved her with everything in me. No reason trying to tell myself that wasn't what this was anymore; there was no doubt in my mind I was in love with Cassidy. She consumed me in a way I never thought imaginable, and hell if I didn't love that too.

Her phone rang and she sat up suddenly. "Ty?" There was a short pause. "I need you. Can you go home?"

And there went my heart.

"I'll meet you there, I love you too." She wiped under her eyes and I watched as her face went into that carefully composed mask of indifference.

I held in a painful sigh as I put my truck in reverse and started home. Nothing like hearing the girl of your dreams tell someone else she needs and loves him.

The drive home was silent and uncomfortable. I wanted to touch her, hold her hand, anything. But I knew that wouldn't help, since I wasn't the person who had always helped her through her hard times. When we pulled into the lot and she saw Tyler's Jeep, she jumped out of the truck before I even put it in park and ran for our apartment. I jogged after her, and immediately wished I hadn't. Ty swung the door open and she jumped into his arms, wrapping her arms around his neck and burying her face in his chest. He spoke softly to her as he walked them back to their room, and though I wanted to be anywhere but near the two of them, I couldn't make myself leave. Didn't matter if she didn't need me; I needed to know she was okay, so I sat down on the couch and waited for them to come back out.

They didn't come out until it was time to leave for her dinner. I stood up when the door opened and my jaw dropped when Cassidy came practically bouncing out of the room, a big smile on her face. Had I just imagined that morning? Or did they just have that good of a time—never mind, I didn't want to think about that.

"Ty said we're going out, are you ready?" She beamed her bright smile at me.

"Uh, yeah. I guess."

"Oh. Well, you don't have to go if you don't want to. I understand."

Understand what? "No, I'll go."

"Really?" She seemed genuinely surprised; her eyes lit up and her smile changed. It softened but was even more beautiful. Then suddenly it fell and she whispered softly, "I know you're worried about it, Gage, but I will get a job so you and Ty aren't paying for me anymore. I'm sorry you had to be there for that today."

What. The. Hell. Just—what?! Before I could ask where she would even get an idea as dumb as that, Tyler stepped into the living room.

"Ready, birthday girl?"

Cassidy just rolled her eyes and laughed as we all left the apartment. I'm sure Tyler was getting pissed by the end of dinner, but I couldn't seem to do anything other than stare at her the entire night. The last thing she wanted was for her birthday to roll around, and then after this morning I was prepared to cancel on everyone tonight. But there she sat, bubbly and adorable as ever. Not one of those people would have imagined anything bad had happened to her, or that today was harder for her than she could describe. I knew how rare it was for her to break down like she had that morning, but this was blowing my mind. She was ridiculously happy; her cheeks had to be hurting from how much she was laughing and smiling. And even when Lanie got teary eyed telling Cassidy that her boyfriend broke up with her, Cassidy was sad for her, and helped her plot a girls' night to help her get over the dick. This was her day, and a hard day, but not one ounce of Cassidy was thinking about herself. Though I still wished I could take her away and give her the opportunity to actually grieve and be upset over things that had happened, it was times like this that made me fall in love with her more.

4

Cassidy

FLOPPING ONTO THE COUCH, I sighed heavily and was grateful the guys would be gone most of the day so I could rest. Trying to avoid Gage's knowing I was sleeping on the couch, and getting away from Tyler's hard-on—which just *had* to continue to remind me that it was there—made for a night of practically no sleep. We'd gotten into a very comfortable routine over the last couple months, and most days it worked perfectly. Just not that day.

WAKING UP EARLY, I slipped out the door and went for a walk. After Tyler had helped me calm down yesterday from the shock of my mom taking all the money my dad had left me, I'd put on a brave face like I always do and went to enjoy my birthday dinner. I had felt so weak breaking down in front of Gage like that; it wasn't like me at all. No one other than Tyler was around for my hard times, and though Gage now knew that I'd had a different home life, he would never understand everything I went through. Not like Tyler did. But like I said before, I learned a long time ago that crying only got you hit harder and longer; I couldn't remember actually letting tears out since before I was a teenager. Then yesterday in Gage's truck, I couldn't hold it back anymore.

I don't know if it was because I felt like he was getting a glimpse of how heartless my mom could be, or if her cruel texts had finally pushed me over the edge. Whatever the reason, I'd cried, and he held me in his arms, comforting me. If Ty hadn't called me back, I would have stayed in Gage's arms all day. I hadn't felt so whole since Dad died, and I never wanted the feeling to end. But it did, and last night Gage went back to not speaking to me again.

I asked probably too frequently, and Ty was now saying that Gage was beginning to tolerate me, but sometimes it still felt like more than that. Or maybe it was just my wanting him so much that made me stupidly think he might want me too. Maybe I imagined how he always seemed to shift closer to me, or how in the mornings before Ty woke up, he was happier than ever. Maybe he only curled up onto the sofa to talk to me for hours because he felt obligated since I lived with and cooked for him. At first I thought his distance was because he had a girlfriend, but that option flew out the window a couple weeks after we moved in. I knew now that he wasn't actually dating Brynn; I'd overheard him telling Ty about their disastrous dates at the end of last year. And I'm not going to lie, I grinned like an idiot for the next few hours knowing he was available. But then he wasn't there for our morning hug and coffee and didn't speak to me for three whole days after I overheard that conversation.

This whole flirting, then avoiding me thing was wearing on me, and you can't imagine how often I wished I didn't feel the electricity between us; it would have made my life so much easier. I knew when he was in the same room with me now; the hairs on the back of my neck would stand up before I could even hear him, and it drove me nuts. It also didn't help that he was by far the sexiest guy I'd ever seen, or that when we would talk . . . he was incredibly sweet. That whole Southern-charm nonsense? Dear. Lord. So hot. It wasn't like he tried to be a gentleman; it just came naturally for him. It made me laugh when he let a cuss word slip and he'd realize I was around; his eyes would go big and I swear sometimes he flinched. The fact that he was always worried his "mama" was gonna come smack him for it cracked me up, and this may sound weird, but when he'd call me "darlin'," my heart would melt. Any other guy and I'd probably have laughed at him, but it just rolled off Gage's tongue like a caress, and I loved it.

I loved everything about him.

I loved him.

I just didn't know what I was going to do about him. At least when Tyler and I would have our talks, his reminders of how much of a nuisance I was for Gage usually kept my head on straight when I was around Gage for the next day or so. But after that I'd start letting myself get too comfortable around him, and then things like yesterday happened.

Looking up, I saw Starbucks was only a block away and decided to sit in there for a while, trying to figure out what I was going to do now that my backup had fallen through. Opening up my wallet, I saw I had a whole ten dollars to my name. Awesome. I knew Tyler would give me anything I wanted or needed, but I'd already been living off his parents and Gage for the past month, and I didn't want to continue. Glancing at my wallet again, I decided. Ten dollars or not, I needed an indulgence.

I walked up to the counter and waited while the barista switched out the coffee. Just as she was turning around to me, a person I guessed was the manager walked up in a huff.

"I don't believe this. Victoria *and* Cody just quit! I've been calling them like crazy all morning, and they finally answered and said they wouldn't be back." She slapped the cordless phone onto the counter, picking it back up quickly to make sure she hadn't broken anything.

"Are you serious?" the barista asked, her face blanching.

"That's half my morning crew. No one else can work mornings here! Everyone has too many early classes."

"Excuse me?"

They both jumped like they'd forgotten I was standing there. The manager's face instantly went into a bright smile. "Welcome! What can we get for you?"

"Well, how about an application?"

"I'm sorry, honey, but I just can't afford to hire any more students. I need full-time employees."

"I guess it's a good thing I have absolutely nothing to do all day, every day," I said with a smile so she didn't think I was being rude.

"I need someone to open Monday through Saturday," she said, challenging me, "six hours on the weekdays, four hours on Saturday."

"Perfect! I'm a morning person," I lied.

The manager gave me a once-over, her eyebrow quirked. "Have you ever worked for Starbucks or another coffee shop before?"

"No, ma'am."

"Have you ever had a job before?"

"No, but I'm dedicated and pour myself into everything I do."
Pun *so* not intended.

"If I considered this, when would you be able to start training?"

"Right now."

Her smile widened again and she nodded her head toward the
back door she'd just come through. "Let's go talk."

WE ENDED UP TALKING and had a formal interview in the back
room for almost an hour, and after telling me the uniform I
would need to go buy, she told me to come back in five hours
for my first day of training. After the week of training and two
classes, I started opening six days a week, just like she said.

The boys were thrilled that I was doing something, but Tyler
started grumbling soon after I started about never waking up
next to me anymore. I'd rolled my eyes at him. I hadn't been
aware that waking up next to each other had become a favorite
part of his day. Especially since he fell right back to sleep, and I
would go to the kitchen to hang out with Gage. But Tyler was
my best friend; if he wanted to grumble about something like
that, then I would let him. As for Gage, we didn't get to drink
coffee together but I still got my morning hug from him. Only
now it was as I was jumping out of his truck when he dropped
me off in the mornings.

I had protested at first, but he usually woke up anywhere from
quarter 'til to five, so waking up the extra thirty minutes early
wasn't a big deal, according to him. Honestly, I think he and Ty
were just terrified thinking of my walking the mile and a half
to work in the dark, because they let me walk home every day.
Not like they had a choice; they'd both be in class unless it was
Saturday.

So that's how we were now: Gage would drop me off in the morning, I would come home and fall asleep for a few hours while they were in classes, and then I'd make dinner for when they got home. At first, it was just the three of us, but then all their other friends started finding out that I actually cooked, and now three days a week, I cook for six ridiculously obnoxious college guys while they all take turns playing Xbox. Thank God tonight wasn't one of those nights, because I hadn't slept at all the night before, which meant I slept straight through their classes and then some.

"Wake up, darlin'." My eyes flew open when Gage's deep voice drawled in my ear.

"You're home?" I croaked, my voice raspy from how long I'd slept.

"We've been home for a while, but Tyler had to go to some study group. Said he would be gone 'til eleven."

I glanced at the clock and gasped when I saw I'd slept for six hours. "Crap, I'm so sorry. Let me make dinner."

"No way, you do too much for us. Besides, I was kinda hoping you'd let me take you out tonight."

"Out?"

"Yeah, I wanna go driving."

My face fell. "Oh. Okay."

He chuckled and pulled me off the couch. "Go change, we'll grab some food on the way."

"Where are we driving to?"

"Not sure, we'll see when we get there."

I gave him a confused look but rushed into the bathroom to rinse off my body since I still smelled like coffee. Even though it was the middle of November, it was still pretty warm, but I'd already learned far too well that could change quickly. So I pulled on some jeans, rolling up the bottoms, and a light long-sleeved deep-V-neck shirt before grabbing my jacket and running back to the living room.

"Ready!" Gage's smile stopped me in my tracks. Dear Lord, he was so handsome. And there were those dang dimples again. Those things alone could reduce me to a puddle on the floor.

"If you want, we can go eat somewhere, or we can just grab some burgers."

"And you aren't going to tell me where we're going?"

He put a hand on the small of my back as he led me out of the apartment. "I don't even know where we're going, Cass. Really. I just wanted to go for a drive with you."

"Fine, don't tell me. Burgers are fine."

Gage chuckled and shook his head as he shut my door.

Okay, so he was being serious. He really did just want to go for a drive. We'd drive, and if we came to a T in the road, he told me to choose which way to go, and every now and then we'd take a random road just because it was the first one we'd come across in a while. After a little over an hour and a half, it was already dark outside and he pulled over into a small field.

"Uh, is this the part where you kill me and leave me in the woods?"

"Now, why would I do that? Who would keep me fed?"

I smacked his arm and he pretended it actually hurt. "Rude."

"You in a hurry to get home?"

"Doesn't matter." Lie. I didn't want this night to end. We'd kept the windows down and sang to the radio. I'd propped my feet up on the dash, and Gage had his arm resting behind me on top of the seat. In between songs we'd tease each other, and I don't think either of us had stopped smiling since we'd gotten in the truck. Tonight was simple and perfect. "Up to you."

"Well then." He put his truck into park, turned it off, and got out.

"Where are you going?" I asked as he rounded the front, coming to me. He opened up my door and stepped back, waiting for me to join him. When I did, he reached in the back and pulled out a blanket.

"Why don't you join me?" He climbed into the bed of his truck, reaching down to give me a hand as well. After we were sitting down, our backs up against the cab, he wrapped the blanket around us and I snuggled closer to his side.

I was wrong. *Now* it was a perfect night. "I like this. It's so quiet and peaceful."

He grunted an agreement and held me tighter. "Makes me miss the ranch."

"When are you going back?"

"Christmas probably. You gonna come with me?"

"I don't know, I haven't even thought about the holidays. I'll probably have to work. I do want to go though; you *did* promise to teach me how to ride."

"I'll teach you a lot of things there. How to ride, how we take care of the place, how to shoot."

"Shoot?" I leaned away and looked at his face, my eyes wide. "Guns? Like, real guns?"

"Uh, yeah. Do you not want to?"

I was shaking just thinking about it. "Are you insane?"

"You shouldn't be scared of them. Guns should be respected, not feared."

"Gage! They kill people!"

His expression deadpan, he said, "Cars kill people too, Cass." He sighed and pulled me to his side again. "They do, but it's the people who do the killing. Anything you come in contact with on a regular basis can kill someone." His voice got soft and he started making lazy circles on my arm.

"But that's just it—things I come in contact with on a regular basis, which makes them normal. I've only seen a gun on TV, so they're definitely not normal to me."

"Cassidy, I have two in my room."

"*What?!* Why? Why would you need them in your room?"

Gage laughed lightly. "To protect you, darlin'. You should see in our house on the ranch. We have so many we don't know what to do with them all."

"Gage, that's weird. Why do you have them?"

"It's not weird. This is Texas, I assure you it's common. Out on the ranch, they come in handy with things that wander onto the property that shouldn't be there. But here, they're just to protect us if someone breaks in." He chuckled and rubbed my arm. "Why are you shaking?"

"I rank guns right up there with spiders."

Gage laughed louder. "Well, I'll help you with the guns. But I can't help you with your fear of the last one, except to come runnin' when you scream because there's a spider on the wall." He raised an eyebrow at me.

"That evil bastard jumped at me!"

"Cass, it was microscopic."

"Doesn't matter. They're nasty and have too many legs."

"Perfect . . . guns don't have legs."

"It's not like that automatically drops the scary factor and makes them okay all of a sudden! God, I can't believe you have them in your room." I whispered the last part to myself.

"You've been there for over three months now, and you had no idea. It'll be fine."

"But now I know they're there," I reasoned. "Way different."

"I promise they won't hurt you."

"Can we talk about something else? I'm still freaking out and they're not even near us."

He stiffened.

"Gage?"

"So how's work going?"

"Gage!"

Tilting my head back so he could look in my eyes, he spoke softly and watched closely for my reaction. "My shotgun is in the backseat."

My breath caught. How many times had I been in his truck, and I'd never noticed this? "Nope." I shook my head and forced myself to relax into him. "No, I'm pretty sure that's incorrect. There isn't a shotgun in your truck."

He laughed. "Yes, ma'am. Whatever you say."

"So work is going great."

He laughed even louder. "I'm glad. Though now we have so much coffee in the apartment, I don't think we'll ever go through it all."

"Probably not. I'll send some with you to the ranch."

"They'd like that." He was quiet for a moment. "They'd like you too. I hope you come with me sometime."

"I will," I promised.

We slid down so we were now lying in the truck, looking up at the stars. He kept an arm around me, and I stayed curled into his side, my head resting on his shoulder. Our morning hugs were the most we ever touched now, so I closed my eyes and enjoyed every bit of this, knowing it wouldn't last forever. I listened to his heartbeat, breathed in his clean, masculine scent, and memorized the way my body felt pressed up against his. His heartbeat picked up when I lightly ran my fingers across his chest and I smiled to myself.

His chest rumbled as he said, "What do you want to do for the rest of your life, Cassidy?"

Stay here with you. "What do you mean?"

"Well, I know you don't want to go to school. Just wondered what you wanted to do. If you had a certain career in mind." Gage's deep voice got even huskier as he continued. "If you actually wanted to do something with your photography, or get married and have kids, if there's somewhere you want to move to . . ." He trailed off.

No kids. I refuse to have children. "I don't really know. I've never thought about it."

"Seriously? You've never thought about your future and where you'd like to be? What you'd like to be?"

"Not once." The most I'd ever thought about the future was in terms of weeks.

"I thought girls start planning their weddings when they're little, and have crazy dreams like being an actress or a singer."

I shrugged. When I was little, I wanted to grow up to be a princess. But my dad treated me like one, so I'd already thought I was one. The day he died, all dreams of the future stopped, and I hadn't had one since. "What about you?"

"I want to finish college and move back to the ranch so I can take it over for my dad. Other than a family, that's all I've ever wanted."

"That sounds perfect for you." I was already jealous of his future wife.

"You've really never thought about it? Never aspired to be a doctor, or a scientist, or a coffee shop girl?"

I laughed and rolled my eyes even though he couldn't see. "Nope."

"Everyone thinks about their future, but if you don't want to tell me, that's fine, I get it," he joked, and squeezed me tighter. When I didn't say anything for a few minutes, he whispered, "Are you with me, or did you fall asleep?"

"Gage, can I tell you something I've never told anyone?" I asked softly.

"Of course you can."

"I wasn't lying to you, I really haven't ever thought about what I wanted to do with my life. I, uh . . ." Clearing my throat, I tried again. "I never thought I'd live long enough to be able to move out of that house, so it seemed pointless to think about the future."

"Cass," he breathed, "I'm so—"

"No, I didn't tell you that so you'd feel sorry for me. I just didn't want you to think I was keeping something from you. I want you to know who I really am, Gage."

He didn't talk for a moment. "Thank you for trusting me with that." He rolled me onto my back, his left arm still under me, and propped himself on his elbow. Brushing back loose strands of hair, he ran his fingers down my jaw; my eyes shut and I tilted my head back when he continued the line down my neck. "You're away from them; you'll never have to see them again. You have your whole life ahead of you, darlin'." His voice dropped another octave and my eyes shot back open when I felt his breath on my lips. "It's okay to dream about the future."

My heart started racing as he slowly lowered his body to mine. Heat zinged through my entire body when his chest pressed against me, his lips still hovering less than an inch from my own. Our eyes searched each other, and his green eyes darkened as he leaned in closer to brush his lips across my forehead and both cheeks. Pulling back slightly, he waited, giving me the opportunity to stop him. I ran a hand through his messy black hair and curled it around the back of his neck, giving the slightest pressure so he'd know I wanted this too. A soft smile broke across his face and he leaned toward me again. Just before his lips could meet mine, my cell phone blared Tyler's ringtone.

We both started and stared at each other for a long moment before I reached into my pocket and grabbed my phone. "Hey, Tyler."

"Hey! God, I can't wait to see you, you won't believe what a shitty day it's been. I'm about to leave but I'm starving. Do you want me to pick up some food?"

Gage was still hovering less than an inch above my face, his eyes locked on mine.

"Uh, no. We already ate. We went for a drive though, so you might make it home before we do."

"Oh. Yeah, okay."

I sighed and shut my eyes. I hated not being there for Tyler, even if it was just when he got home from a long day at school. He'd been there for me almost every night for eleven years; I owed it to him to be waiting for him when he got back. "We're on our way, promise. See you soon."

"All right, love you, Cassi."

"Love you too, Ty."

Gage was off me and out of the bed of the truck before I could even end the call. I knew I'd ruined the moment the second I'd grabbed for the phone, but there was no way I could ignore a call from Ty. Surely he knew that.

"We better get going." He acted like nothing had just happened. "It's already really late, and you have to work in the morning."

I wanted to groan into my hands. I couldn't believe I'd just stopped that kiss from happening. And there was no way I could salvage the situation now. Gage didn't say anything the entire way back; his right hand was on the steering wheel, making his body lean away from me. I knew this was my fault, so I stayed pressed against the passenger-side door and didn't push him to talk to me either. Tyler tried to take me into the bedroom as soon as we got home, but Gage stopped us.

"Tyler, can I talk to you for a minute first?"

"Sure, man." He hugged me quickly and told me he'd meet me in our room after.

I waited anxiously on the edge of the bed for when he'd come back, my knees bouncing up and down. Thankfully he wasn't in there long and not five minutes later he was walking into our room, shutting and locking the door behind him.

"Cassi, you need to leave Gage alone for a while."

I froze. "What? Why?"

He looked at the door, then back to me, speaking softly. "Look, I don't know what happened between you two tonight. But he's pissed, said you needed to understand that you're like a sister to him and nothing more."

I let my face fall into my expressionless mask, but inside I felt like I'd been punched and was trying to catch my breath. I didn't understand—Gage had been about to kiss me. *He'd* been the one pressing his body to mine, brushing featherlight kisses on my face. Why would he do that if he didn't actually like me? My stomach churned at the thought of him seeing me as his sister. But this was probably for the best. I had been getting in too deep with him, and I needed to guard myself. My father and Tyler—the only men I would ever need in my life. I didn't have room in my eternally shattered heart for anyone else . . . including Gage

Carson. My chest tightened and I had to blink my eyes rapidly as that lie almost forced me to tears again. When I had a handle on my emotions, I looked up at Ty and gave him a weak smile.

"I understand." I stood up and went to the bathroom to quickly get ready for bed before slipping under the covers with Tyler. He curled his body around mine and I was once again so thankful for him. My rock. He always made everything better by holding me, even heartache.

THE NEXT MORNING I got dressed for my opening shift and headed out to the kitchen. Ty was letting me borrow his Jeep today, so I wouldn't have to further impose on Gage. Apparently he'd also been complaining about having to "be my chauffeur." It's not like I asked him to drive me, he just never gave me a choice. I rounded the corner and smacked right into his brick wall of a chest.

Gage laughed softly and wrapped his arms around me. "Morning, darlin'."

Placing both hands on his chest, I pushed him off me and stepped around him to grab a granola bar. I knew I was being rude, but I'd spent the majority of the night trying not to cry at the thought of the man I loved seeing me as his sister, so I was extremely grouchy this morning. Walking back around him, I continued for the front door and didn't stop 'til he caught my arm and turned me back to him.

His eyebrows were scrunched together in confusion. "Are you gonna at least wait for me to get my keys?"

"I'm driving myself." I dangled Tyler's keys between us. "Have a good day."

"Wait, Cassidy, wh—"

"What, Gage?" I hissed. "What do you want?"

He dropped my arm and took a step back. "I th—talked to Tyler last night, I thought you'd be . . ." He trailed off as my eyes narrowed at him.

"You thought what, Gage? Thought I'd be happy? Or I'd be okay with that?" I laughed humorlessly and took a few more steps toward the cars before turning back to him. "Do you have any idea how frustrating you are?"

"Cass." He took a few tentative steps toward me, reaching his hand to me.

"Don't! Don't touch me. I'm sure in a few weeks, I'll look back and realize how stupid I'm being right now. And maybe by then I'll be okay with what you want, but right now I don't want to talk to you, I don't want you to touch me, and I don't want to see you." Hell, I already knew that I was overreacting. But I could have sworn he felt something for me too, something more than a sibling bond. And he'd let me believe that, he'd even encouraged it, just to have Tyler tell me to back off. No freaking wonder Brynn had thought they were a couple. He probably went around doing these kinds of things to every girl.

His green eyes hardened and he looked crushed. Though that threw me off balance for a moment, I didn't have time to care about how he felt right now. He was the one playing with my emotions. He was the one breaking *my* heart.

Gage

AFTER CASSIDY DROVE AWAY, I forced myself to breathe and go back into the apartment. I felt like she'd just ripped my heart out. This girl I'd fallen in love with the moment I saw her, this girl I would do anything for . . . didn't want me.

"Hey, you okay, Gage?" Tyler asked from the kitchen table.

I sat down numbly, just staring at the table.

"Oh—I guess it didn't go well this morning?"

When Cassidy and I had gotten home last night, I'd pulled Tyler into my room so I could tell him exactly what I felt for her. He'd told me that no matter how much he loved her, he knew how we both felt for each other and wouldn't stand in our way anymore. I'd been blown away and could barely wait to see her this morning. I was going to finish what I'd started so many times, including last night. I was going to pull her body to mine and kiss her 'til she couldn't stay standing anymore. Even sleeping had been difficult; I was too distracted thinking about where this could take Cassidy and me.

"She was pissed. Like beyond pissed. Told me she didn't even want to see me. I don't understand. After last night, I thought—well . . . it doesn't matter what I thought."

Tyler rinsed his mug out and clapped me on the back as he walked toward his room. "That's a bummer, man, I really thought she liked you too."

5

Gage

I WAS MISERABLE. It had been eight months since Cassidy had crushed my heart that morning before she went to work. Eight months of trying to ignore the pull I still felt, now more than ever. Eight months of being her friend and nothing more. The first six months of which I had to watch her run to Tyler every damn time something happened. Now for the last two months I'd barely had what you could even consider a conversation with her. Two months of no morning hugs and conversations, and one month until I moved back in with the happy couple.

It was the end of July and I'd moved back to the ranch like I do every summer. It had killed me to know I was going to be without Cassidy for three months, but not as bad as watching her go into his bed every night, and watching her walk out of their room every morning in his shirt. After that morning, it had taken almost a week for us to even say hello to each other. Apparently my wanting to be with her was so awful she couldn't stand to look at me that entire time too. Tyler was kind enough to wait two weeks before talking about their relationship again. Asshole. I loved the guy, I'd do anything for him, but I knew he didn't feel for her what I did. And if she would have chosen to be with me, I wouldn't have rubbed it in his face every chance I got. Loving him like a brother and hating him for being with the girl who held my heart was a hell of an emotional trip.

"Are you hearing a damn word I'm saying, son?"

I stopped fixing the post and looked up at my dad. "Sorry—no, can you repeat that?"

He sighed heavily. "Take a break, Gage. Let's talk."

Dropping the post and tools, I followed him over to a tree and leaned up against the base.

"Your mother and I are worried about you."

I looked at him, confused, but kept my mouth shut. You didn't interrupt my parents.

"Over the winter break, we just figured you were sick or something, but these last two months have been beyond ridiculous. You don't talk to us, you don't talk to your sisters, you look like a damn zombie. All you do is work, eat, and sleep. Are you on drugs?"

"What?! Dad, are you being serious right now?"

"Well shit, Gage, what are we supposed to think? This isn't who you are at all. If you aren't on drugs, then tell me what's goin' on. That, or leave. You're being completely disrespectful to your family; this isn't how we raised you."

I sank down to the ground and let my head fall into my hands. "Sorry. Honestly, I thought I was hiding this a lot better. Guess I was wrong."

"Hiding what?"

"Dad?" I took a deep breath in and out. "When you met Mom, did you know right away you were going to marry her?"

That shocked him; he hadn't been expecting that turn in the conversation. "Does this have to do with your attitude?"

I nodded.

"No, I reckon I didn't. She was my best friend for a long time. We all viewed her like one of the guys. One night when we were seventeen, there was a dance at the Miller ranch, and I remember seeing her. Like I was actually seeing her for the first time. She'd done her hair and put on some makeup, and was wearing a dress. I didn't realize it was your mama until I got the nerve to ask her to dance with me. But of course by then all the other guys had noticed her too. You shoulda seen us all fightin' over her, trying our damnedest to get your grandpa to let us court her."

I laughed. I could only imagine Dad being all awkward trying to get the courage to go up to Grandpa. That was one terrifying man.

"Took four months for her to finally agree to a date with me. I still didn't know I was in love with her, not for a few more months after that. I just woke up one day and realized I couldn't live without her. Gave her a promise ring that night, an engagement ring a year later, and we were married six months after that." He looked at me for a minute. "I'd ask if you're in love, Gage, but love makes you alive. You look dead."

"Yeah, about that." I huffed and ran a hand through my hair, grabbing a good chunk in my fist. "I was kinda hoping your answer would be different. I know what's happening between us isn't normal. Well, not between us, I guess . . . she doesn't feel the same way for me."

"Ah. I see. So why don't you tell me what's happening for you."

I looked at my dad for a minute, and I suddenly couldn't hold it back anymore. I'd told Tyler I loved her, but I hadn't talked to anyone about the depth of my feelings. "It's like I'm being pulled to her. Like something in her calls to me. I know that sounds dumb, but that's the only way to describe it. The first night I met her, I felt her before I even saw her. It's like I *had* to look up at her, and when I did . . . I swear to God the world stopped moving. When she shook my hand, it felt like—not a spark, but like a jolt of electricity went through me. All I can think about is her, and I could have sworn she felt it too. But when she found out my feelings, she got pissed. Wouldn't talk to me for a week. I've tried, Dad, you have no idea how damn hard I've tried to get over her. But I know I'm supposed to be with her, I know I'm going to marry her. I knew it the moment she hopped out of Ty's Jeep."

"Ty Bradley? Your cousin Tyler?"

"Yep."

"So you met her through him?"

I laughed hard. "You could say that."

"You're gonna have to help your old man out here, I don't get what I'm missing. You having problems with him?"

"Do you remember me telling you Ty was bringing his friend Cassi from California to live with us?"

"Yeah . . ." He drew out the word.

"Well Tyler's *girlfriend,* Cassi, my new roommate, is the same girl who consumes my every thought."

"Shit."

"Yep." I let my head fall back against the tree and rubbed my chest where the ache that never went away intensified from just thinking about her. "God, Dad, am I crazy? This isn't normal, right? This can't be healthy. She doesn't even want me."

"And you're sure about that?"

"Yeah. She made herself pretty clear. What makes it harder is that even though she's his girlfriend, and she doesn't want me, I can't stop being near her. I hate just being her friend, but I would rather be her friend than not have her at all. I thought this summer would be good for me, to get her out of my head; instead I just feel like I'm dying the longer I'm away from her."

Dad was quiet again for a moment. "Well, I haven't ever experienced this, uh—pull you're talking about. But I don't think you're crazy. The only advice I have for you is don't give up. If you're sure you want her, then you gotta fight for her."

"But she's with Tyler. If it was anyone else I wouldn't have a problem with it. But Ty?"

"That does make your situation a little difficult. Have you talked to Tyler about her?"

"Oh yeah, at first he was pissed that I wouldn't stop looking at her, then one night he finally said he'd step back and let us be together. That next morning was when she yelled at me, told me she didn't want to see me. And it's hard, because even though I'm positive she's not in love with Tyler, and honestly I don't think they're even actually *together*, she can't leave him. Same way he can't leave her."

"I'm just going to assume you're about to explain that. 'Cause that little statement is confusing as hell."

"Well, since you'll probably never meet her, I guess it's safe to tell you about her childhood. Her dad died when she was real young, on her birthday actually. It really screwed her mom up; she turned into an alcoholic and married some guy. From the day he died, Cassidy had to raise herself; her mom stopped feeding her, washing her clothes, even talking to her. And she was only six. Then after her stepdad moved in, they started beating her. Up until the day Tyler packed her shit up and moved her to Texas."

"You got some beatings yourself, son."

"No, Dad, not like getting spanked by Mom when I was little. They didn't just take off their belts and hit her with that or a wooden spoon when she was in trouble. They could've killed her. Tyler told me about some of the times, and I saw pictures from after a few of the tamer times and it's enough to make you sick. Uncle Jim would have to stitch her up sometimes, others she'd be so messed up she wouldn't be able to walk. Her bruises when she moved in were like nothing I've ever seen. Her entire back and sides were black, blue, green, and yellow. They're obviously all gone now though, but Ty said she's really careful about what she wears around people because of the scars she has from some of the bad beatings."

"How people can do that to their own kid is beyond me. People like that need to be arrested, or shot. I'm sure we can find some ditches." He smiled under his massive mustache.

"I swear I wanted to drive there and have a conversation with them and my shotgun. It about killed me; she's the sweetest person you've ever met. And she wouldn't let Tyler turn them in. Her mom's a heartless bitch, and yet Cassidy still would never do anything against her."

Dad just shook his head and relaxed against the tree. "Don't give up on her, Gage. You don't feel this way for no reason. What do you say we finish this post and call it a day? You need to explain to your mama what's been going on. She might have better advice than your old man. And you better apologize to her. She's been making herself sick with worry."

I nodded. "Sorry for putting y'all through this. I honestly didn't realize I was letting it show so much."

"You're forgiven. Come on, I'm hungry and your mama and sisters are makin' chili and corn bread."

I missed Cassidy's cooking. I missed trying to help her cook, even though I messed everything up more times than not. I missed her laugh and smile, and the way she felt in my arms every morning. I just missed her. God, I felt like such a fuckin' girl.

We fixed the broken parts of the fence and were on our way back to the house within ten minutes. We rode slowly back, and I told Dad more about Cassidy and our lives together with Tyler. Not even halfway back to the house, my sister Amanda texted me to say Ty, his parents, and a girl were at the main house and for us to come back. I didn't need to ask who the girl was; there wasn't anyone else they'd bring.

"Gage, what's wrong?"

I realized I'd stopped my horse Bear and was just staring in the direction of the house. Looking up at him, I could only say one word. "Cassidy." If Bear sprinted, we'd be back in about fifteen minutes, and even that seemed too long. "*Hya!*"

"Gage!"

I couldn't look back at my dad. I heard his horse in a dead sprint behind us, and I knew he'd be pissed at me for taking off like that, but she was here. When we reached the house, I saw Tyler's Jeep out front and stood there for almost an entire minute trying to decide between taking care of Bear and going to her.

"She'll still be in there in five minutes. After what you just put Bear through, you may want to attend to him first."

I grunted in acknowledgment and jumped off my horse to walk him toward the stables. After he had everything off him, we sprayed him and my dad's horse down with a hose and let them out into the field. Dad put his hand on my shoulder to stop me, and I tried not to let him see how frustrated I was that he was continuing to keep me from Cassidy.

"Now, I have no doubt there's a reason she was put in your life, and I know I told you to fight for her. But fight smart, son. Tyler's like a brother to you; you don't want to ruin that because of her. And another thing: you running in there lookin' like you do will probably scare her shitless."

I looked down at my shirt. I'd been sweating all day from work and I'd thrown my shirt back on right before we started back here, but it wasn't like I was covered in bits of cow pies.

"I wasn't exaggerating when I said you looked like a zombie, Gage. With how dead you look, you may want to go easy on seeing her again. Take a deep breath, and walk in like a normal human being."

That was damn hard. My hands were balled into fists so I wouldn't reach out for her, and I couldn't even see her yet. I opened the door and walked through the living room, toward the voices in the kitchen. Cassidy laughed and it speared me to the floor. I took what felt like my first breath in two months and actually smiled. I glanced over at Dad and he patted my shoulder.

"Well, let's go meet my future daughter-in-law."

I punched his arm and took the last few steps before rounding the corner into the kitchen. And there she was. As perfect and beautiful as ever. "Cassidy," I breathed.

She launched herself at me and wrapped her arms around my neck, whispering into my ear. "I missed you so much, Gage."

"I missed you too, darlin'." God, she had no idea how much I'd missed her. I held her tight and memorized the feel of her. Trying not to be obvious, I breathed her in and relaxed even more. She was here. Really here. Squeezing her tighter, I was glad to feel even less of her ribs and shoulder blades. She'd been slowly putting on some more weight, and while she had at least another ten pounds to go, she was looking healthier and more beautiful all the time.

Tyler cleared his throat, and I reluctantly let her go. I tried not to let it show how much it hurt when she went right back to his side. Aunt Stephanie and Uncle Jim stepped up to give me hugs, and I caught Mom looking at me with wide, curious eyes. I cast a glance at Dad and saw him giving the same look at Cassidy. I knew exactly what he was thinking, because it was the same as me. How does she act like that toward me and not feel a damn thing for me?

"Gage?"

"Yeah, Mama?" I still couldn't take my eyes off Cassidy.

"Why don't you go get cleaned up. You've been working all day."

"All right."

After a minute of me not moving, she spoke up again. "That was code for 'you smell and look all kinds of tore up,' son. Go take a shower."

Not that I take long showers anyway, but I don't think I've ever taken a faster shower than I did just then. I wanted to get back to Cassidy, had to get back to her. I was stupid for thinking I could ever get over her; if anything, this time apart had shown me how impossible that would be. I ran into the bedroom and skidded to a stop, clutching the towel around my hips.

"Whoa, Ma, seriously?"

"Now, tell me why you thought you couldn't tell me what was going on, Gage."

I sighed and grabbed a shirt, focusing on buttoning all the buttons before speaking. "I'm real sorry, ma'am. Until Dad made me talk about it today, I hadn't realized I was acting any different toward y'all."

"We have been worried sick."

"I know, Mama."

"Now, your father already told me everything you told him, so I won't keep you much longer. But you know you can always talk to us." She stood up and walked toward my door, pausing just before she shut it. "She is dang cute, Gage."

I smiled widely at her. "I know she is."

With a quick wink, she shut the door behind her, and I went back to frantically trying to get ready. I tried not to charge down the stairs, but it didn't matter. She wasn't in the house. I heard Tyler say her name and walked out the front door and about choked on a laugh when I saw her. She was staring wide eyed at my dad, who was showing Uncle Jim and Tyler his new hunting rifle. She shot a quick glance in my direction, then went right back to the rifle.

"It won't bite you, Cass." I smirked as I reached her side.

"It might, you don't know that."

"We can go shooting right now and I'll show you they're fine."

Her eyes got even wider and she slowly shook her head back and forth. She still couldn't take her eyes off the rifle and I ground my teeth when she took an involuntary step toward Tyler.

"Let's start with something a little easier then." I lightly touched her arm and turned her the opposite way. "It's been a while since I promised you . . ." I trailed off and smiled when I heard her intake of breath.

I led her into the stables and over to my mare Star. She was dark chestnut brown with a white lopsided star on her forehead, and she was extremely calm. She would be perfect for Cassidy. I opened up her door and walked in, bringing Cassidy with me.

Tyler stayed up against the door and didn't say much as I let the girls meet.

I rubbed Star's long nose as she butted my chest. "Star, this is Cassidy; Cass, this is Star." Grabbing Cassidy's hand, I brought her closer to the horse and she slowly reached out a hand to Star's neck.

"Hey, Star," she said softly. "Is she yours?" she asked as she brought her other hand up to Star's jaw.

I nodded. "I think she'd be best for you to ride. She's a calm girl."

"She's beautiful," she breathed.

"That she is. Would you like to ride her today?"

"Can I?" Her smile was so beautiful, I'd let her do whatever she wanted.

"Let me get her ready." I looked back at Ty. "You wanna ride Beau?"

"Sure, I'll get him out." Tyler looked at Cassidy, gave me a warning glare, and went over to where Amanda's horse was.

When he was gone I grabbed Cass and hugged her tight to my body. God, I missed this. "I'm glad you're here."

She sighed and pressed her head into my chest. "It's been lonely without you, Gage. I'm ready for you to come home."

If only home wasn't where y'all share a bed, I wouldn't have been able to leave. I sighed and squeezed her tight before putting the saddle on Star and helping Cassidy up.

"CASSIDY." I WHISPERED so I wouldn't wake up Amanda from where she was on the other side of the room.

Cassidy moaned lightly and rolled onto her side, facing me.

"Cass." After nudging her shoulder with no results, I stretched out on the small sofa bed beside her and brushed her dark hair from her face. God, I loved watching her sleep. I memorized her relaxed expression before pressing my lips softly to her cheek.

She curled into a tighter ball and sighed my name.

My heart stopped when I realized she was still asleep. She was dreaming about me. I wrapped an arm around her waist and pulled her closer. "Wake up, darlin'," I said as I trailed her jaw with my fingertips.

Cassidy's eyes slowly fluttered open and widened when she saw me right in front of her. "What are you doing?" I'd expected her to freak out, but her voice, still husky from sleep, sounded almost dreamlike.

"I have to start working, but I wanted my morning hug first."

She smiled and wiggled her way deeper into my arms, wrapping one arm around my waist and placing the other on my chest, fingers splayed out. "Good morning, Gage." She yawned and buried her face deeper into my shirt.

"Morning." I held her to me and tried to savor every second of her warm body against mine, her long hair wild from her lying on it, her sweet scent engulfing me.

"What are you doing today?"

"Gotta feed everyone first, then we have to fix more of the fences. We stopped early yesterday and they need to be done before we can move the cattle into that area. Other than that, whatever pops up."

She nodded against me. "Do you need me to do anything?"

I didn't need a thing from her, but I wanted everything. I wanted her to leave Tyler, to love me, to want to live here with me for the rest of our lives. I wanted so damn much. "Just go back to sleep, then enjoy the rest of the day with the girls. I'll be back tonight."

"I'll be here waiting for you."

Closing my eyes, I took a deep breath in and held it. If only she knew what she did to me. I could see us, just like this. Whispering in the dark room before I started work each morning, her telling me she'd be waiting for me when I got back. God, I wanted to kiss her and stay in that bed all day, but just then I heard the front door open and shut and knew I had to get going. With one last squeeze, I reluctantly unwrapped us from each other and left the room.

Cassidy

"THOSE BOYS ARE TREATING YOU all right, aren't they, Cassidy?" Stephanie asked as she pulled up a chair at the breakfast bar where Gage's youngest sister, Emily, was coloring. "It was hard enough losing Tyler, and then you had to go with him. I feel like all my babies are gone and I just need to make sure you're all taking care of each other."

"They're great. I work early in the mornings, and Gage takes me; when I get home they're at school and by the time they're back I have dinner made for them. Everything's been great so far."

"Good, sweetie," she said, and I couldn't believe how much she and Gage's mom, Tessa, looked alike, and how Tessa looked nothing like her kids.

"You tell me if my boy's actin' up, all right, sweet girl? I don't care if that boy is grown, I'll still smack him upside the head." Tessa gave me a look and I didn't need to have seen Gage's flinching to know she would.

I laughed. "You don't have to worry about that, Gage is . . . Gage has been . . . he's great."

Tessa and Stephanie shared a look and Stephanie raised her eyebrows as she took a long drink of iced tea.

"All right, I'm sorry, but I have to ask. Are you dating Ty or not?" Amanda, Gage's oldest sister, put the stack of plates away and leaned back against the counter so she was facing me.

I paused, opening up the package of yellow cake mix, and looked at her, confused. "Uh, definitely not. Why?"

"Well . . ." She looked at her mom and other sister, Nikki, before continuing. "We've all heard about you since as far back as I can remember . . . and it just kinda looks like y'all are together."

Stephanie started laughing and I could only imagine the look of horror on my face. "No. Tyler's my best friend—really he was my only friend until we moved to Texas. We're just really close like that; he's like my family."

"So is there anyone you *are* dating?" Amanda asked, and I noticed even Tessa had stopped what she was doing and looked up at me.

"No." I drew out the word, uncertain as to why they were all looking at me like that.

"Interested in?" Tessa asked, seeming a little too concerned in what my answer was going to be.

"Um, well . . ." My cheeks flared and I had to bite down on my lips to stop my ridiculous smile. "I—"

Just then the front door opened and shut, and Gage's and Tyler's voices drifted in toward us. My eyes went wide and I swear I somehow blushed harder. Tessa took one look at me and smiled to herself before turning back around to the food she was preparing. When I looked over at Amanda, she was studying me intently. She shot a quick look at her brother and cousin when they came in and the same smile I'd just seen on her mom spread across her cheeks.

"You girls wanna go to a bonfire?" Gage drawled, and winked at me; I swear I somehow blushed harder.

"*I do!*" Nikki yelled, and ran up to the guys. Gage and Tessa started disagreeing immediately.

"Absolutely not!"

"No way, Nik."

"You said *girls,* Gage! I am a girl, you know!"

He kissed the top of her head and ruffled her hair. "When you're older, kid. Amanda and Cassidy," he clarified, and smirked when Nikki huffed, "do y'all wanna go?"

I stole a quick glance at Tyler and gave him a smile when I saw he was staring at me intently. "Sounds . . . fun?" When he nodded I looked back to Gage and nodded once. "Yeah, sure."

Amanda agreed and Gage grabbed two bottles of water out of the fridge, tossing one at Tyler. "All right, we'll leave after dinner."

"Gage!" Amanda looked quickly at the clock, then back at him. "Dinner's in like—three and a half hours!"

"And?"

"That gives us *no* time! We need to go into town!"

"Why?"

She just shook her head and grabbed my hand before towing me toward the front door. "We'll be back before dinner!" she called as we went out the door. "Do you have boots?"

"Uh, what?"

"Boots, do you have any?"

"No . . ."

She hopped into her car and I followed. "Figured as much. You can't go to a bonfire out in the country without 'em."

"Oh, if that's why we're going into town, we don't need to. I can just go in my flip-flops or Converse."

"Yankee," she mumbled, and I snorted.

"I FEEL LIKE I look like a cliché."

Amanda laughed and checked herself out in the mirror. "And why is that?"

"You put me in a plaid button-up and cowboy boots."

"Yeah? And you look hot! At least I didn't give you a torn denim miniskirt to match it with, because I have one. I can even get you a cowboy hat!" I looked at her, mortified, and she laughed. "Exactly. Now, *that* would be cliché; what you are wearing is perfect."

I fluffed my hair, which Amanda had curled before dinner; checked my makeup one last time; and stepped back to take in the entire thing. I did like my boots and shirt, which was an electric-blue, black, and gray combination and worked well with the dark skinny jeans I had on, but seriously. Walking cliché.

"All the guys there will love it, trust me."

"I don't exactly care about the guys we'll meet there," I mumbled, and followed her out of the room toward the stairs.

"Gage will love it." She shrugged and feigned indifference before turning to wink at me.

"He doesn't, I mean, I haven't—"

"You haven't told him? Yeah, I figured. You should change that."

"Change what?" Tyler asked, and I jumped, causing me to miss the next step and start sliding down. Ty caught me around my waist and smirked. "Always wanted to sweep you off your feet."

I laughed and pushed on his shoulder until he let go. "You're so dumb, Ty."

"You girls rea—" Gage cut himself off quickly; his green eyes widened and he just stared at me until Tyler cleared his throat. "Uh, y'all ready?"

We followed when Tyler started pushing him toward the door, and Amanda leaned in close. "Told ya, time to change that."

If only she knew just how bad I wished I could.

"WE'RE GONNA GO get more beers, y'all want some?" Gage asked. Amanda and I both shook our heads and went back to talking about this guy she was seeing off and on at A&M.

Other than the fact that we were out in the country instead of on the beach, and all the girls were dressed scarily similar to me and Amanda, this felt like one of the many bonfires I'd gone to with Ty whenever he'd tried to get me more socialized during high school. And like then, this really wasn't my scene. Even with moving to Austin, I still wasn't a huge fan of new people. I couldn't stand the looks some of the girls were giving Gage, and already we'd had an issue with one of the guys, Max.

We'd all been standing near the fire, and I must've gotten so caught up in thoughts of my dad and the phoenix while looking at it that I hadn't noticed Max watching me, or when he came up to my side to push me toward the fire, only to quickly wrap his arms around me and slam my body back to his chest. He'd thought it was hilarious until Gage pulled me away from him and proceeded to give him a verbal ass-kicking with Ty.

He'd avoided me the rest of the night, as had the rest of the guys there since Gage and Tyler had already made it known that they shouldn't mess with or come near me. But now that they had gone to get more drinks, Max was stumbling over toward me and Amanda, causing me to groan and Amanda to stop talking about her pseudo-boyfriend to glare at him.

"What do you say we head back to my truck? Have us a little alone time." His breath reeked of beer and his eyes were completely glazed over.

"Um, no thank you. And you should really consider giving someone your keys." I turned to look at Amanda when she snorted and I shook my head. Seriously? Who did this guy think he was? After the stunt he'd pulled earlier he really thought I'd go anywhere or do anything with him?

"I didn't say we'd be driving."

"Like I said, no—"

He grabbed my hips and turned me so I was facing him and pressed my body close to his. "I bet I have you screaming my name in no time."

"Ew. Max, leave her alone!" Amanda hissed, and I pulled away from him.

"I said no, you need to back off." I turned back to Amanda and grabbed for her hand, fully intending to go find Tyler and Gage, but Max gripped the top of my arm and roughly brought me back to him.

"And I said we're going to my truck." His hold on my left arm tightened and was past the point of being painful; that mixed with the alcohol on his breath had my body going rigid seconds before I started shaking uncontrollably.

"*Max!*" Amanda sounded appalled and began pulling me toward her. "What the hell is wrong with you?! Go sober up in your truck, *alone!*"

His hand had loosened slightly and I let Amanda pull me

away; just before I slipped out of his grasp, it tightened as much as my arm would allow and he yanked me toward him again. Only this time Amanda had a hold on me as well and that split second I was being pulled by both sent a sharp pain through my left shoulder. Amanda let go and I stumbled over myself, landing hard on my butt, causing the pain in my shoulder to intensify as Max yanked on the arm he still kept hold of.

Amanda gasped loudly, and though I tried to keep it in, a short cry of pain escaped my lips. I couldn't even try to get myself standing; my entire body was trembling too hard as I subconsciously waited for the blows to start. All I could seem to do was stare at my lap as flashes of different beatings quickly flipped through my mind. Suddenly, Max's hand was gone and Tyler was directly in front of me, pushing my chin up so I would look at him. His eyes were wide and he was speaking, but I couldn't hear him over the sounds of flesh hitting flesh, glass breaking, my screams, Jeff's grunts, and my mom's moans.

Tyler pulled me up and half carried, half walked me back to his Jeep. Sitting me on the passenger seat, he stood just inside the open door and between my legs, gently rubbing the throbbing ache on my arm, his other hand cupping the back of my neck and holding my forehead to his. Slowly, the nightmarish flashes disappeared and I could hear Tyler whispering softly.

". . . okay, I've got you. Never again, Cassi, they're gone, they can't touch you here. You're okay, I've got you. I'll always have you, Cass. They're gone—"

"Is she okay?!" Gage's voice broke through my immediate world of my rock, my Tyler, holding me.

"She'll be fine," Ty responded, and went back to whispering, "I've got you, you're going to be okay, sweetheart."

Next thing I knew, Gage was in the driver's seat of the Jeep and talking directly behind me. "Darlin', are you all right? Tell me what happened."

I couldn't bring myself to respond to him; I didn't want him seeing this. Didn't want him to know I was so messed up that from Max grabbing my arm, I'd begun having a full-on melt-down in front of everyone. Tyler gently squeezed the back of my neck as his whispering continued, over and over. I wrapped my arms around his waist and moved my head so it was resting against his chest. His lips pressed down on my head and his whispers slowed, changing slightly.

"That's it, sweetheart, you're okay. I'm here, I'm always here for you. I love you, Cass, you're all right, I got you."

"Ty—man, what happened?"

I felt Tyler's head shake as he continued whispering.

"Holy crap, Gage!" Amanda said loudly. "You knocked Max out cold. I think you busted his nose . . . again."

"Amanda," Tyler growled at the same time Gage hissed, "Shut up, Manda!"

My body started shaking harder, and I pulled myself closer to Tyler and farther from Gage. I didn't want to hear that, I didn't want to think about what had happened between him and Max. I focused on nothing but Tyler so those images wouldn't put themselves in my mind.

"I need to get her back to the house," Tyler said, still speaking softly. "Are we good to go?"

When the others agreed, he moved me so he could get onto the passenger seat as well and pulled me onto his lap. My head instantly dropped to the crook of his neck and I let his large arms, warm scent, and soft words continue to soothe me all the way back to the ranch.

Once we were back, Tyler gave me one of his shirts and gently pushed me into the bathroom. I took a quick shower; dressed in his shirt, which came down to my thighs; and made my way back to Amanda's room. Gage had been standing there with Tyler, but after one look at me, his expression turned worried and he didn't say a word as I walked past him and went to the sofa bed in the far corner of the bedroom. The guys left when Amanda came to get in her own bed, and once she was asleep Tyler was slipping under the comforter with me. My rock . . . my best friend. I didn't know what I would ever do without him. His arms went around me and I curled myself tighter into him, taking a deep breath in. Finally feeling safe in his arms, I closed my eyes as my shaking slowed to a stop and I drifted off to sleep.

6

Gage

I KEPT TOSSING and turning in bed. Cassidy was going back to Austin tomorrow, and I wouldn't see her for three weeks. This last week had been more torturous than living with them, and I was seriously considering not letting her go back with Ty. Despite the things that had happened in the last year, and what happened at the beginning of the week at the bonfire, I knew for sure she was in love with me too. Mama didn't have to tell me that she didn't look at Ty the way she looked at me; I'd known that from day one. But my entire family was now convinced she wanted me too, and I think that made watching her with Tyler harder than ever. Before, I kept telling myself I was only seeing what I wanted to; now I knew that wasn't it, and I needed to try to get in her head one more time. Besides, Mama and my sisters, especially Amanda, had taken a huge likin' to Cassidy, and I knew I wasn't the only one who wanted her in our family now.

Jumping out of bed, I threw on a pair of jeans and the first shirt my hands touched before quietly making my way to Amanda's room. After making sure my sister was completely out—since apparently she had been awake every morning when I woke Cassidy up for my hug and decided to fill Mama and my sisters in on that bit of information—I walked over to Cassidy's bed and didn't waste time. I brushed her hair away from her face and pressed my mouth to her neck and cheek before saying low in her ear, "Wake up, darlin'."

Her eyes shot open and she looked at me, confused, for a moment. "Gage? Is it already time for you to go to work?"

"Not even close."

"Oh." She yawned and tried to lean over to look at Amanda. "Then what are you doing?"

"You wanna go for a ride with me?"

She paused. "Right now?"

"If you want to go back to sleep we don't have to . . ." *God, this was a bad idea.*

"Who's going?"

"Just us."

Her eyes widened and a soft smile touched her lips. " 'Kay, let's go." She crawled out of bed and looked at me, then down at herself. "Uh . . . what should I wear?"

I looked at her little body in those short sleep shorts and that form-fitting sleeveless shirt; my body started burning and my pants got tighter just looking at her. "That."

Cassidy pulled her bottom lip into her mouth and even in the dark I could see her cheeks went red. "Guess I'm ready then."

Grabbing her hand, I led her through the dark house, snatching a blanket out of the closet on the way out, and had Bear saddled up and both of us on him in no time. I could have gotten Star ready for her, but I wanted this excuse to have my arms around her, her back against my chest.

I led Bear to a creek that ran through my favorite part of the ranch and tied his reins around a tree branch on top of the hill before spreading out the blanket and lying down with Cass. We talked for two hours about the ranch, the stars, the quiet other than the light wind and cicadas, and the fireflies, which were her favorites. Cassidy began yawning a lot and I started to wonder if I should take her back, but I wasn't ready to end this.

"I'm going to miss it here." She sighed softly. "It's so beautiful, all of it."

"You can come back as often as you'd like."

She smiled as she rolled on her side to look at me. "I'd wear out my welcome if I came here as much as I wanted to."

"Not possible, my family loves you." *I love you.*

"I'm going to miss them too; they're so amazing. I've never really been close with any other girls, even Jackie. I mean, she's a good friend and all, but it's just not how I feel with your mom and sisters. I wish I could've had family like that growing up."

God, there were so many things I wanted to say, but every single one of them was too much. I'd just scare her away. She yawned again and I sat up. "You're tired, I should get you back."

She grabbed my arm and pulled me back down, scooting up to lay her head on my chest. "Not yet. Going back means I have to leave you, and I don't want to."

My heart skipped a beat, then took off. "Cassidy." I placed my fingers under her chin and tilted her head back; her honey eyes were bright in the moonlight. I slid out from under her head and hovered over her, my lips within an inch of hers. "Please don't leave."

Brushing my mouth across hers, her breath caught and her eyes darkened before she wrapped her hands around my neck and crushed her mouth to mine. Our lips moved against each other, and a soft whimper escaped her throat when I caught her bottom lip between my teeth. Exactly the way I'd wanted to from the first night of meeting her. I pressed my body against hers and couldn't stop my groan when her tongue met mine and she ran her hands through my hair. Lowering my body to hers, I wanted to die when she hitched her knees onto my hips; placing both forearms on either side of her head to hold my weight, I ground my hips into hers and was rewarded with a sweet-as-sin moan. God, I wanted her, to feel her and hear her sigh my name, but I knew I needed to restrain myself from anything like that for now, which meant I needed to stop kissing her. I just didn't want to. I wanted to rip her shorts and shirt off and spend the rest of the night worshipping her body, I wanted to make her moan like that again and again . . . damn it, I *really* needed to stop. I forced our kisses to slow until our lips were barely brushing each other and tried not to think about slamming into her.

When I finally calmed down, I opened my eyes and saw her looking at me under heavy eyelids. "You're so beautiful, Cassidy," I whispered against her cheek before kissing it.

Her cheeks were still stained pink from our kiss and her lips tilted up in a soft smile I was beginning to realize she only ever gave me. My smile.

We stared at each other while her eyes slowly closed a little more and I knew I had two options: take her back to the main house and say good night, or keep her with me. "Come here." I pulled her into my arms and rolled onto my back so she was lying across my chest. Kissing the top of her head, I relaxed under her. "Get some sleep, darlin'."

She nodded against my chest and pressed her lips there twice before curling against me. "Good night, Gage."

Good night indeed.

Cassidy

I WOKE UP with my back curled into Gage's chest, my head resting on one of his arms, his other wrapped securely around my waist. *Last night wasn't a dream. Oh my God, Gage kissed me, and I slept in his arms.* I took a deep breath in and out and couldn't help the huge smile that broke across my face. Tyler had been wrong about everything; Gage did want me. His arm tightened around my waist before he intertwined my fingers with his and brought my hand back to his lips.

"Morning." His rich voice was even deeper from sleep.

"Good morning." I rolled over and blushed as I placed my lips to his neck. I wasn't sure how things were supposed to be this morning, but I couldn't stop myself. I held my breath for a few seconds until his wide smile and dimples came into view right before his lips pressed softly to mine. My whole body started tingling the instant his mouth was on me. Dear Lord, if I had known kissing Gage would feel like this, I would have tried to make it happen long ago.

He pulled away, but placed two more quick kisses on my lips before sitting up and pulling me with him. "Come on, I need to get back to the house." He must have seen the hurt in my eyes, because his went wide and he cupped my face. "I wouldn't go back unless I had to. My dad's probably already pissed that I wasn't there this morning. I'm not going to work today though; we'll get ready and I'll take you to another spot on the ranch that I want you to see. Just us. But I need to tell him I won't be around today." His eyes were bright and though he tried to contain his smile, his dimples gave him away.

I got up and helped him fold up the blanket. "I thought I'd seen the whole ranch."

"Not even close, you've only seen about half. Where I want to take you, though, it isn't too far from the house, but it's really secluded."

My stomach heated and I was suddenly extremely anxious to get to wherever he was talking about. Leaning into his side when he wrapped an arm around me, I smiled and let him lead me back to his horse. The ride back to the house was quiet, like last night, but it was nowhere near the same. He played with my hands, teased my neck with his lips, and made sure Bear took his sweet time going back. I was nervous when we came across Gage's dad, but he took one look at us, smiled wide, and told us to enjoy our day together.

"I need to take care of Bear. I'll meet you in the kitchen."

"Okay, I'm going to take a shower, but I'll try to hurry." I turned but he grabbed my hand and swung me back into his chest, kissing me deeply.

"See you soon."

My head felt light and my stomach fluttered as I quickly made my way up to Amanda's room to grab a change of clothes and rush through my shower. I couldn't wait to get back to him. For almost a year now he had consumed my every thought, and I believed I'd never be able to have him. It felt like it was too good to be true now that I did, or at least, I thought I did. I didn't know if this would change when I went back to Austin today, or when he came back in August. I shook my head to clear those thoughts. Gage wouldn't just drop me like that; even when I thought I was only his friend, he cared too much to treat me that way.

A startled yelp escaped from my chest when I bounced back into Amanda's room; she was gone and Ty was sitting on my bed. "Tyler! You scared the crap out of me!" I got a closer look and rushed over to him. "What's wrong, Ty?"

"Where were you this morning?"

I bit my lip and looked away. "I was with Gage."

"Cassi," he groaned, and flopped back onto the sofa bed, "why are you doing this? He's only going to hurt you."

"No, he won't."

"Do you not remember anything he's said about you since we moved in?"

How could I forget? He didn't want me living there, I needed to stop asking him to take me to work, I was like a sister to him, I was ruining his relationships with other girls by being in the apartment. "Maybe he changed his mind," I said softly.

Tyler shook his head and hugged me to his side. "If he hurts you, I'll kill him."

"He won't."

"Whatever you say, Cassi. I know I've stopped you from being in relationships before, but I won't anymore. If he's who you want, then you should be with him. But you're still my girl; you always will be."

"I love you, Ty. If it eases your mind, no one will ever replace you."

He smirked at me. "Duh."

I laughed and smacked his chest. "I feel bad for my future husband. He's going to have to share me with you."

"How about we just marry each other, save everyone the heartache?" he teased, and squeezed me closer.

"You're so dumb. All right, I gotta go do my hair really quick. He's taking me around the ranch today. I'll be back before we leave. Did your parents still want to leave tonight?" I dragged the last few words out.

"Probably earlier in the afternoon . . . am I missing something?"

I scrunched my face as I peeked at him from under my eye-lashes. "I don't want to leave; I want to stay here with Gage until he moves back. But I don't know if he'd be okay with that. I don't know if he'd want me here for the next few weeks."

Tyler's face fell, but he kissed my forehead and got off the bed. "Talk to him about it before you leave this morning; that way if you both decide you want to stay, my parents and I can leave earlier and you won't have to cut your day short."

"Hey." I reached for his hand and spoke softly. "Thanks, Ty."

"I love you. Be careful with this, Cassi."

I nodded and watched him walk out the door. Was he really that worried about me getting my heart broken? He looked so sad I almost told him I wouldn't stay on the ranch and would go back to Austin with them today. Almost.

Gage

MY HEART PICKED UP when I heard someone come down the stairs, but it went back to normal when I realized just how loud it was, right before Tyler rounded the corner. A huge shit-eating grin was on his face. "What's got you in such a good mood? You that happy to be leaving today?" My stomach clenched; I really didn't want Cassidy going back.

He raised an eyebrow at me and grabbed a mug. "If your girl woke you up by blowing you, you'd be happy too."

I choked on my coffee and had to wait a minute before I could speak again. "Excuse me?"

"What?"

"What did you just say?"

His brow furrowed and he looked at me, confused, then his

face relaxed and he smiled behind his mug. "Oh, about Cassi? I swear, the things that girl can do with her mouth."

I slammed my mug onto the table and the chair tipped over from how fast I stood up.

"Whoa, Gage, what's your deal? The cows will still be there if you're late."

Breathe. Just breathe. There was no way he was being serious; he was just trying to piss me off like always. He still had that cocky smirk and I wanted to punch him. *Breathe, Gage.* My hand fisted on top of the table and I turned to leave the house before I could act on it, but just before I hit the living room, I heard Cassidy coming down the stairs. I needed to ask her about their relationship myself; I was so damn tired going back and forth through Tyler. Turning on my heel, I headed back through the dining room, slowing down when I heard Tyler speak.

"Well, good morning, gorgeous!"

Cassidy laughed lightly. "You act like we didn't just say that a few minutes ago."

My stomach dropped when I heard that, right before I rounded the corner to see her fall into Tyler's arms. He squeezed her to him, kissing her cheek softly.

"Did you talk to him?" he asked when he pulled back to look at her face.

"Gage? No, not yet, but I will."

"Well, you need to do it soon."

She sighed and stepped away. "I know, I'm just nervous, I don't know how he'll react to this."

"Get out," I choked.

Cassidy jumped and turned to see me, her eyes wide. Tyler just raised an eyebrow at me.

"Gage?" She looked worried.

I can't believe I fell for her shit. "I said get the fuck out. Both of you."

"What?" She clutched her stomach, her eyes filled with tears.

Without another word, I stormed out of the main house and grabbed Bear, heading off toward the place I'd wanted to take Cass to. The house my dad and I had been slowly building since I was sixteen. Whenever I got married, this would be where we lived, and I'd never wanted to show it to anyone before meeting Cassidy.

Walking around it now, I thought about how perfect it would be for her. Over winter break and the first two months this summer we'd expanded the kitchen, and I knew Cassidy would have loved it. Hell, I'd expanded it *for* her. There was a large bathtub in the master bathroom as well, and I smiled remembering the conversation with her months ago about how she would kill to have a tub that she could relax in. The ones in our apartment weren't much in the way of relaxing, but this one was. I walked back out to what would be the living room and sank onto the wood floor, my head between my knees. Other than windows and the wraparound porch I still wanted to build, all the house needed was furniture, and it would be finished. But that would be up to Cassidy to pick all that out. No, not Cassidy. My wife. Whoever that might be, because obviously it wouldn't be her.

My heart ached and I kept replaying last night and that morning in my head. I'd been so sure last night before waking her up, and then after our time out by the creek, I knew I had been right. Cassidy and I belonged together. I thought about Tyler's statement and Cassidy's confirmation when she walked into the kitchen and I felt sick. Raking my hands through my hair, I fell back so I was lying on the floor and looked up at the ceiling through blurred eyes. God, what was happening to me? I couldn't remember the last time I cried. No . . . I did. It was when my grandma died when I was little. And now this girl, who apparently had no issues leading on one guy and messing around with another, was bringing it all out. I wanted to kick myself for falling for her. For spending an entire year miserable because I couldn't be with her, and for once again letting myself *think* I could.

The sun had begun setting when my dad walked into my house. "Figured I'd find you here."

"Here I am." I let one arm make a sweeping motion before bringing it back to rest on my chest.

"You want to tell me why I walked into a house full of my confused family and a seriously pissed off Bradley family?"

"Not really."

"What about why Cassidy seemed so odd? She wouldn't speak to anyone—hell, she looked about as messed up as you did before she got here."

"Are they gone?"

"Left a few hours ago."

"I can't move back in with them, Dad. I need to get my own place this year."

He sat down next to me and stared at the stone fireplace. "We're not leaving until you tell me what's going on. From what I saw this morning, I wouldn't have expected what I witnessed this afternoon." He looked down at me. "Or what I'm seeing right now."

"It doesn't matter," I said after a few silent minutes. "I thought she liked me. I was wrong. She's still completely hung up on Tyler."

"Sure didn't look like it this past week."

I groaned. "I know that, Dad. But trust me. They made it extremely clear this morning who she wanted to be with."

"How so?"

"I'd rather not repeat what I heard them saying."

"Maybe you didn't get the whole story."

"No, I'm pretty sure I heard the entire damn thing."

He stood up and stretched his back. "Well, I can't change your mind; no one can. But I just sat there listening to your sisters and mother trying to figure out what could have happened. And they all came to the conclusion that you hurt her. From the time they spent with her this week, apparently she was all talk about you, and not a damn thing about your cousin."

"I hurt her?!" I sat up and looked at him incredulously. "All she's ever done is rip my fucking heart out!"

My dad didn't seem surprised by my outburst, just stood there waiting to see if I was finished.

"I hate feeling whatever this is, and caring so much about her. There's no reason some insignificant girl should make me this crazy."

"Insignificant?" he said after I'd lain back down with a huff. "You really think that?"

"No, Dad . . . I don't. I'm just mad right now. Even after what happened this morning, I came here and thought about every part of the house I knew she would love. What I still wanted to add for her, and about how she would make this our home." I sat there clutching my chest, the ache there almost unbearable. "But that won't happen."

He opened his mouth but shut it and continued to stare at the fireplace.

"I can't take this. It's like I told you a week ago before they showed up. I already hurt thinking about not having her in my life somehow. Even as just a friend. But I don't know how to do that. I love her too much to just be her friend, and it kills me seeing them together. More so now. I don't know what to do. I know I need to move out, but I know I won't be able to stay away either. It's like I'm asking for her to keep breaking my heart."

"I don't know what will happen. But I think you should give it some time. You're a part of the triangle, which means you didn't get to see things the way the rest of us did. I admit it's strange the way she clings to Tyler, and if I'd never seen her look at you, I would think they're a couple too. But I did see the way she looked at you, we all did, and there's no doubt—well . . .

"Maybe you should move out. Do that, and you can decide from there how to approach her. Whether that's as a friend or if you keep fighting for her, you'll decide then. You have three more weeks until you go back to Austin. Let's finish out the summer work, then you can find a new place, concentrate on finishing school, and let the rest happen as it's supposed to." He made his way to the door. "I'll explain the situation to the girls, but you should come back to the house soon. I know you've been gone all day; you need to eat something, and there's a storm rollin' in. Should be here for the next few days."

"I'm right behind you," I said from the spot on the floor I hadn't moved from since that morning.

"It'll all work out the way it's supposed to."

I thought about Tyler holding Cass that morning. "That's what I'm worried about."

7

Cassidy

"QUAD ICED VENTI MOCHA for Natalie," I called out, and looked at my watch face on the inside of my wrist; only five minutes left. I could do this. I set out making the last few orders of drinks and walked over to the supervisor taking over for me. "Do you need me to do anything before I head out?"

She glanced at me and gave me a bright smile. "No, Cass, see you Monday."

I was shaking so much it took me three tries to get my code in so I could clock out. It had been almost three weeks since I'd seen Gage and I knew he was coming home either today or tomorrow since classes were starting back up on Monday. I was a wreck, to say the least. Ever since Gage told us to get out and then walked away from me, I hadn't spoken a single word to him, and my heart broke a little more with each passing day. I had no idea what happened or why he was so mad all of a sudden that morning. Tyler had been just as confused as I was. All I knew was Gage and I had gone right back to our normal back-and-forth routine of flirting then avoiding each other, only this time it was worse since I couldn't see him. Tyler and everyone at work was worried about me, but I knew I just had to make it until Gage was back, then we could talk about everything face-to-face and try to fix whatever had gone wrong this time.

I walked home, my heart racing the entire time as I went through different conversations and scenarios for when he showed up. Most of them ended with me in his arms, his mouth on mine, and by the time I got home, I'd convinced myself this was all going to work out. Shutting the door behind me, I saw a grim-faced Tyler standing in the living room, arms crossed over his chest.

"You okay, Ty?"

He took a deep breath in and out before answering. "He's gone, Cassi."

"Who's gone?"

"Gage. He showed up right after I got home from dropping you off this morning, moved all his stuff out."

My heart painfully skipped two beats before I took off for his room. A sob stuck in my throat when I saw his bed still there, but bare, and nothing was in his closet, in his drawers, or haphazardly thrown around the room. He had made sure to do all this while I was at work; he left and didn't even say good-bye. I tried to slip into indifference so Tyler wouldn't see me lose it over this, but I couldn't. My knees were weak in the worst way possible, my lips were quivering even as I tried to force them firmly together, and tears were blurring my vision.

"I'm sorry, sweetheart." Tyler wrapped his arms around me and pulled me into his chest.

"I d— I don't—why?"

"I don't know, Cassi, but I'm so sorry." He turned me so I was facing him and cupped my cheek with one of his hands. "What can I do to make this better?"

"Nothing."

"Cassi—"

"I'm serious, I just . . . I just need to be alone right now." I moved out of his arms and went to our room, curling into a ball on the bed. When Tyler opened the door I spoke before he could. "Please, Ty. Just leave me alone for a while."

After giving me a kiss on my forehead, he turned and left the room.

"SWEETHEART, COME ON. Get dressed, let me take you out to lunch or something."

I sighed deeply and wrapped the pillow closer to my chest. "I'm not hungry, Ty."

"You need to eat, you're losing too much weight."

"I'm fine." No, I wasn't. This couldn't be normal, not that anything between Gage and me had ever been normal. Not the sudden love I felt for him, not how I felt like I couldn't breathe unless he was near me, and especially not how I'd slipped into a "zombified version of myself," as Tyler liked to call it. I stopped doing Saturday shifts, but other than that I still went to work and continued to cook dinner for Tyler and the guys. When I wasn't doing either of those two things, I was curled into a tight ball in bed, trying to ignore the intense pain of Gage ignoring me. It had been another three weeks since he'd moved all his stuff out,

making it a month and a half since I'd seen or heard from him.
Tyler still saw him at school, and I was glad that their relation-
ship hadn't suffered as well, seeing as they were still doing their
Saturday-morning breakfasts at Kerbey Lane.

With a huff, Tyler walked out of the bedroom and shut the
door behind him. Four hours later, I was just starting to think I
should get up and start making dinner for him when he walked
back in. His long strides were determined as he made his way
to the bed; lifting me up into his chest, he slammed his mouth
down onto mine.

I started to protest, but my heart was so shattered, I could
barely find the will to turn my head away. "Ty—" I finally managed, but when I opened my mouth, he forced his tongue to meet
mine as he laid me back down, his body following.

"Damn it, Cassi," he growled against my mouth when he realized I wasn't kissing him back. He pulled away slightly and
searched my eyes, pain filling his. "What do I have to do? I've
loved you since we were kids. What do I have to do to make you
love me too?"

"I *do* love you, Tyler."

He shook his head. "Not like that, Cassi, I want you, all of
you. I want you to be mine, I want to take care of you in every
way possible for the rest of our lives. Can't you see that?"

I just continued to stare into his brown eyes, unblinking.

When I didn't say anything, he let his head drop into the
crook of my neck and sighed. "I can't keep doing this. I can't
keep waiting for you to see me the way I see you. I kept—I kept
hoping one day you would get it. But I see that's not going to
happen. I'm sorry, Cass, but I can't do this anymore."

"Wh-what do you mean?"

"*This,* Cass, all of it. Living here with you, only being your friend. I can't keep doing this. I want all of you, or nothing at all."

"What?!"

"You ne—"

"I thought you were my friend!"

"I am, damn it, Cassi, haven't I always been that? But I'm tired of just being your friend! I can't keep doing this with you."

"Tyler—" My chest was heaving up and down quickly. I felt like I was on the verge of a panic attack. "How can you do this to me? I can't lose you, you're all I have!"

"Then don't fucking lose me!"

"That's not fair, I've never thought of you like that, Ty, and Gage—" Tyler's eyes narrowed and darkened at the mention of his cousin. "You know what he meant to me!"

"Why can't I be that for you? At least I won't make you destroy yourself like he has from the heartbreak he's caused you! So decide, Cass, right now. You're with me, or you leave."

My jaw dropped and I couldn't stop the tears that escaped my eyes. Why was he doing this? *How* could he do this after all these years? "You're breaking my heart right now!"

"And you think you haven't broken mine? How do you think it felt that after years of being there for you, taking care of you and loving you—you took one look at Gage and you're ready to give your heart to him."

Words escaped me for a few seconds and my head quickly shook back and forth as I floundered for the right thing to say. I couldn't lose Tyler. He was my rock, and with Gage gone, he was back to being all I had left.

"Let me love you, Cassi." His voice went soft and low. "Let me be who you need."

"Ty—" I cried, and shook my head once more, and instantly his features hardened as he started to push himself off me and the bed. *Oh God, no.* I realized right then I'd do anything—just as long as he wouldn't leave me too. I grabbed his face and held it just inches from mine. He'd been the only reason I'd stayed in that house all my life, and he'd been the only reason I'd survived it as well. I did love him, more than I could ever explain to anyone. I owed him my life. But he was right, it wasn't in the way he was describing his feelings for me. Could I love him in that way too? No one got me like Tyler did. Our relationship, however weird it may have been, was the result of leaning on and loving each other for most of our lives. He knew exactly what I needed and always made sure I was taken care of before himself, just as I did the same for him. I took a shuddering breath in and let my gaze fall from his eyes over his face and to his wide shoulders. There was no doubting he was attractive, I'd always thought that, but now that I was trying to look at him differently, I realized he wasn't just attractive. He was sexy. His entire body screamed raw masculine beauty and I felt my heart kick up as I studied the parts of him I could see. His piercing eyes were so dark right now that they were almost black. They were hidden behind thick blond lashes that matched his short-ish, unkempt, dirty-blond hair, which I'd always secretly loved. His strong nose led down to his mouth, which was full but not too full. More like it had a constant perfect pout unless he was giving one of his heart-stopping smiles.

My heart and mind instantly wished for green eyes, black hair, and deep dimples, but I pushed it away. Gage didn't want me. I glanced down at his hard jaw and my eyes kept going to his neck and the tops of his shoulders. He'd been a swimmer throughout school and his best stroke was the butterfly; because of that he had shoulders that were broad and covered in muscles, and I started to wish he had his shirt off so I could finally study the rest of his muscles too. Could I do this? Could I be selfish enough to try to make myself fall in love with him in that way just so I wouldn't lose him? It wasn't fair to him, and I would probably be a horrible person for it, but yes, I could. And I would. I couldn't lose Tyler, and if that meant trying to give him my heart when it would always be lost to his cousin, then that's what I would do.

I looked back into his eyes and continued to convince myself that I could do this as I slowly brought his face down to mine, leaning up slightly to meet him halfway. Our eyes were still locked on each other as I pressed my lips softly to his once, then twice. Tyler searched my face for a moment before bringing our mouths back together, soft yet firm, and moved his lips against mine. It felt wrong, so wrong. This wasn't like kissing Gage; I didn't feel like the world fell away when Tyler kissed me, and I started to feel sick knowing I would never have this with Gage again. Squeezing my eyes tight, I took myself back to the hill next to the creek on the ranch, to the best night of my life. I thought about Gage's hot breath on my neck as he made a trail of light bites and kisses from the hollow at the base of my neck, up my throat, and back to my mouth. I thought about the weight of his body on mine as we tried to pull each other closer together. I thought about the overwhelming sense of joy and belonging I felt in his arms. I thought about all these things, and tried to throw them into my kiss with Tyler.

When Tyler's tongue slid across my bottom lip, I parted my lips slightly, this time meeting his exploration of my mouth with one of my own. He moaned and pressed my body deeper into the mattress while his mouth trailed down my neck and across my shoulder as he slid the strap of my tank top down. My breath caught when he went back and nipped my neck before lightly sucking at the sensitive spot behind my ear.

"You can do better than this, Cassi. I need to know that you want me as much as I want you," he whispered against my skin.

I grabbed fistfuls of his hair and forced his head back up to mine. I wanted to yell at him, tell him he wasn't being fair considering I was still completely not over his cousin. Instead, I crushed my mouth to his and sucked on his bottom lip before capturing it in my teeth. Grabbing the bottom of his shirt, I ripped it over his head and ran my fingers over his muscled body, causing him to shiver and his hard-on to become disgustingly apparent. I wanted to throw up. Trying to picture him as Gage wasn't helping at all; if anything it was making it worse. There was no way to fool my mind into thinking this was the man who would always hold my heart. Every touch and every kiss was completely different, and lacking everything that was just . . . *us.*

Tyler's hand was running up my bare stomach toward my chest, and just as I was about to stop him, and hope he wouldn't be hurt by that, his cell rang. I tried to suppress my sigh of relief when he rolled off me and grabbed his phone to answer. When he hung up he walked back to the bed and hovered over me on his hands and knees, placing two soft kisses on my cheek.

"Ty—" I had to clear my throat before continuing. "You're going to need to be patient with me. Other than kissing Gage at the ranch"—Tyler's eyes narrowed again—"I've never done anything. I don't want to do anything yet, I just . . . I just need time if that's okay."

"That's more than okay, Cassi, take as long as you need."

"And I think I should move into the other bedroom."

"What?" He backed up farther, his eyebrows shooting up. "Cassi, why?"

"Because it will be awkward to sleep together now."

"Cass," he said, rolling onto his side and propping his head up on his hand, "you've slept in my bed for years; that shouldn't change now."

I thought about all the times when Ty would wrap his arms tighter around me, making his hard-on more apparent, and we weren't even in any kind of relationship when that happened. If we were, I could only imagine how much more often that would happen and I already felt disgusted just thinking about it. I really didn't want anything related to that with Tyler . . . not after I'd spent a year fantasizing about Gage's naked body against mine. "I'm sorry, Ty, but if we're going to try to be in a relationship, I can't start one in bed with you."

Tyler exhaled slowly. "Okay, if that's what you need, Cass." He leaned down to press featherlight kisses to my jaw. "So we're going to do this? You're gonna be my girl?"

"Yeah, Ty," I said softly, "I will."

He grinned wider than I'd ever seen and kissed me softly. "Thank you. I love you."

"I love you too. It might not be the way you want yet, but I'll get there. I just . . . as long as I've known you, I've only thought of you as a friend. I never considered anything else with you until about five minutes ago, so I'm sorry if this takes longer than you'd like."

"Don't be sorry, I know it'll take time." His nose skimmed across my collarbone, and my eyelids actually fluttered shut. "I've wanted this for so long, I'm just happy you're finally giving us a chance." He hopped off the bed and pulled his shirt back on. "Come on, let's go."

"Go where?"

"Well, if you're leaving my bed, I'm not about to let you sleep on a bare mattress in a bare room. Let's go get whatever you want."

"Really, Ty?" I smiled at him; this was my Tyler. "You're not gonna be mad at me?"

Pulling me off the bed, he wrapped his arms around me and kissed my nose. "I couldn't be mad at you if I tried."

"DO YOU LIKE IT?" Tyler asked hours later.

We'd made a trip to a few stores, and for the first time since I was six, I had a room and bathroom that were completely and utterly *me*. From the curtains and bedding to the lamps, throw rugs, and towels, all of it was warm, designed to be an escape, and would be perfect for curling up in and getting lost in books. "I love it."

"I'm not going to lie, I'm gonna hate not sharing a room with you, but you did good. This screams Cassi."

"I was just thinking that." I sighed into his arms and let my head fall back to his chest. Now that we were dating . . . I guess . . . it was weird going from being so comfortable with Ty to having all our touches mean something. With the exception of actually kissing, every little thing we'd always done made it look like Tyler and I were already together. I hadn't noticed it until tonight, and when I did, I couldn't help but think about Gage and what he must have thought while we lived together. If he *had* ever wanted me, I was now understanding why it took him so long to act on it. I sucked in a quick breath and bit on the inside of my cheeks at the realization that Ty and I could have been a reason that nothing ever happened with Gage.

Tyler slowly rubbed my arms and kissed my neck. "I'm sorry

you're still hurting. I know I'm not him, but I'll try to make it better."

Of course Tyler knew what I was thinking without my telling him. I turned in his arms and let my hands glide through his hair. "You do. You always do, Ty. I don't know how you haven't noticed that you're the one person in my life who it would kill me to lose. You've made my entire life better, you've always taken care of me and put me before yourself." *Now it's my turn.* I brought his face down to mine and kissed him slow and hard.

Gage

I DIDN'T KNOW what was easier, living with them and stomaching her walking out of his room every morning, or not living with them and not seeing them together. But of course, with the latter, I hadn't seen her at all. It was the first of November . . . meaning I hadn't seen her in three months. Three slow, torturous months. I still saw Tyler every Saturday morning, but for some reason he'd stopped mentioning her and stopped throwing their awkward relationship in my face every five seconds about a month and a half ago. It killed me not knowing how she was, and I hated missing her birthday, but I didn't know how I would handle seeing her.

Last Saturday, Ty had asked me to start coming back to dinners, at least when all the guys came over, and I was seriously considering it so I could get my Cassidy fix, but there was something I had to do first. I had to see her without Tyler around, and since I had no idea what his schedule was like this semester, I was now driving up to Starbucks and hoping she would still be there.

I parked and walked around the side to the front doors; opening them, I swear to God my heart stopped right then. She was there, and she was more beautiful than I'd ever seen her. She was busy at the bar, so I ordered my drink without giving my name and, like the creep I was, stayed off to the side so I could watch her for a few minutes. Her long brown hair was pulled back, and her honey eyes were wide and bright as she smiled at something a coworker said. *God, that smile. I would do anything to make her smile again.* When her arm stretched out to pass a drink to a customer, I saw something on the inside of her forearm, but she moved too quickly for me to get a good enough look.

Sooner than I'd wanted, she was calling out my drink order and I had to take a deep breath in before walking over there.

"Thank you!" she said brightly, flashing me a quick glance before turning back to the bar. Sucking in a startled gasp, she looked back up, her eyes wide, mouth slightly open. "Gage," she whispered softly.

"Hey, darlin'."

Her cheeks went red as she continued to stare at me.

"Are you off soon?"

She glanced down to the inside of her wrist. I smiled at her too-large watch that always slid over. "Um . . . te-ten minutes."

My eyes went wide as I got a good look at her forearm. I had no doubt what that was. She had a tattoo. A cluster of stars. Ursa Major. I thought back to that night by the creek, we'd been talking about constellations, and she'd pointed it out first, telling me it had always been her favorite one. I remembered adding that to the list of reasons why she was amazing, since that constellation was the reason I'd named my horse Bear. I'd told her as much and she'd given me a soft smile and reached over to brush her hand against my arm. I'd have been damn stupid to think she'd gotten that because of that night, but I wanted to know if she thought about it at all when she looked at her arm.

I looked over to the cups that were lining up next to her and grabbed my drink. "All right." I wanted to tell her I'd wait for her, but I didn't know if she'd even want to talk to me. She'd broken my heart, but I'd been coldhearted and a straight coward when it came to her. So I just turned around and went to sit on one of the big chairs in the corner.

Cassidy

OH MY GOD, he's here. Gage is here. My heart stopped when I looked up and saw those bright green eyes staring down at me. Dear Lord, he was so handsome. My dreams over the last three months hadn't done him justice at all. I tried to go back to work, but I was so flustered, I could barely concentrate on the drinks I was making.

Why is he here? And is he waiting for me, or is he meeting someone here? He wouldn't have asked if I was off soon if he wasn't waiting, right? Damn it, Cassidy . . . calm down and just breathe. I put out another two drinks and couldn't help looking over at him. Like he could sense that I was watching him, he lifted up his head and met my gaze. I couldn't look away and I wished desperately that he would for the both of us. God, it didn't help that he was wearing my favorite shirt of his; it was an old Ramones shirt, and the color green was almost the exact same color as his eyes. I needed him to stop looking at me; I could get lost in those eyes on any given day, even from across a coffee shop.

I was finally able to tear my eyes away when Stacey, one of my coworkers, asked about a few drinks she was waiting on in the drive-thru. Why did he have to come to this Starbucks? There were tons in the area, and dozens of other coffee shops. I didn't know where he'd moved to, but this couldn't have been the only one close to him, and even if it was, you only had to drive an extra five or so minutes before finding another. I needed these ten minutes to go by faster; I felt like I was going to break down right there in front of everyone. In the last six weeks since Ty and I had gotten together, I'd slowly been able to start having a normal life. It wasn't overnight by any means—I still ached for Gage, still dreamed of him on a nightly basis—but I was finally laughing again. And now here he was. Bringing back every good and bad memory of him. I didn't want to still be in love with Gage, and his being there wasn't going to help a thing.

For the rest of my shift, I kept my eyes on my drinks only; I knew it was rude to the customers who came up to the bar, but if I looked at them, I would look at Gage. And I just couldn't handle that right now.

"Cassidy." Stacey grabbed my arm and I jumped.

"Huh?"

"You're off, clock out and go home . . . Are you okay?"

I took a shaky breath in and mashed my lips in a tight line as I barely shook my head.

"Come on." Her hand, which was still on my arm, led me to the front to clock out, then dragged me to the back. "What's wrong?"

"He's here!" I blurted, and tried to calm my shaking.

"Who is?" Stacey looked up to the monitor showing the store's cameras.

"Gage . . . Gage is here. Oh my God, why is he doing this? He doesn't want me! He never did, and he left without so much as a good-bye."

Her eyes went wide. "Oh shit. Tyler's cousin?"

I nodded and took off my green apron. "I think he's waiting for me. Should I talk to him?"

"Do you want to?"

"I don't know. I do, but I don't know if I can."

"Cassidy," she said with a sigh, "just because you're with Tyler now doesn't mean he can control who you talk to."

"No, no. It's not that. It's just—I still love him, Stace. I don't want to, but I do. I thought I was getting better, but when he showed up just now, I don't know."

She gave me a quick hug. "It's up to you. Before you go back out there, just think about whether you'll regret it if you don't talk to him."

I nodded and waited five more minutes, deciding that if he was still out there and alone when I walked out, then I would go up and talk to him. With one last deep breath, I walked out from the back and around the corner. He was in the same spot, head down and spinning his most likely empty cup around in his hands. Like earlier, he stopped abruptly and his head slowly came up. He looked at me, then to the door that I was next to, and started to stand up, his eyes pleading. When I began walking toward him, he sat back down and seemed to clear his throat a few times. I sat in the chair next to him and pulled my legs up underneath me, so I wouldn't continue to bounce them up and down nervously.

"How are you?" He finally broke the silence after a few minutes.

"I'm fine." I hated that my voice sounded so small. "You?"

"I'm all right. You, uh—you look really good, Cassidy."

Please don't tell me that. I need to get over you, I need you to be mean again or just go back to avoiding me. "You left."

He sighed. "Yeah, I needed to."

I nodded. "Look, I understand you were mad for what-ever reason, but you didn't even say bye. You were just gone, Gage. Was it that bad having to live with a girl, or was it just me?" I shook my head and grumbled to myself, "Of course it was just me."

"I should have said good-bye, I should have told you I was leaving. I just, I didn't know how."

"Why are you here, Gage?"

Pain flashed through his green eyes and his brow furrowed. "Um. I, uh—needed to see you. Tyler's been asking me to come around; I needed to know if that would be a bad idea."

"You're grown, you're free to do whatever you want."

"If you don't want me around, Cassidy, that's all you have to say."

My eyes narrowed. If I didn't want him around? He was the one who left me! "I would never get in the way of you and Ty."

"That's not what I'm asking."

Well, I don't want to answer that. I looked away and tried to slow my racing heart again. Gage brushed my arm and turned it slightly, running his fingers over my birthday present to myself.

"I like this."

"Me too." My voice was shaky and I tried to disguise it with a small laugh. Of course I had gotten it for me, but I'm not going to lie and say that Gage had nothing to do with my decision on that tattoo. I knew he was gone from my life, but even though nothing had ever come of us, he would always be the man I was in love with. I was sure of it. Over the almost year that we lived together, we'd found plenty of things that we had in common, but looking at the stars that night, followed by those amazing kisses and falling asleep in his arms . . . That constellation was by far my favorite thing we shared. "And yes, I want you around.

It's been . . . different without you there." *Miserable. It's been absolutely miserable.*

He nodded and continued lightly running his thumb over the stars. "I'm sorry I missed your birthday, and I'm sorry I up and left. I've missed you so much, Cassidy."

A strangled sigh escaped my throat and I had to look away again to compose myself. "Why did you leave?"

"You know why. I couldn't stay there with y'all anymore."

Right, because I was getting in the way of his relationships. "You couldn't stay with us? Or just me?"

His jaw tightened and he leaned away.

"It's fine. I don't need you to answer that."

"Cass—"

"No, really, Gage, don't." I stood up and walked toward the doors. When I was outside he caught up with me; putting a hand on my shoulder, he turned me around and I stumbled back when I saw how close he was.

"I don't want to keep staying away from you; you have no idea how much you mean to me."

Why is he doing this? Why is he always playing with my heart? I wanted to scream at him for leaving me, for making me fall in love with him, for continuing to keep me wanting him like he was right now. But then I figured that was probably what he wanted. He probably loved having girls basically fall over themselves for him.

He wrapped his arms around me and pulled me close. "Can we at least be friends again? I miss talking to you, I miss driving you to work in the morning, I miss our morning hugs . . . I just miss you."

I tried not to get lost in his scent, or how I finally felt like I was where I belonged for the first time in three months. I didn't know if I could just be friends with Gage, but anything would be better than the hell that I'd been through without him. I pulled back slightly, and he wrapped a big hand around my neck, reminding me of all those times I'd thought he'd been about to kiss me. "I miss you too, Gage. So much. I would love it if you came around. Do you, uh, is there anyone who cooks for you?"

"No, it's just me there." He paused for a minute. "I'm not seeing anyone if that's what you're asking."

Of course that's what I'm asking! "I wasn't, but I know how bad you are at cooking. I'm surprised you've managed to last this long." I tried to laugh, but it sounded wrong. "I'll make dinner for you every night, if you'll be there. I know Tyler really misses having you live with us; I think he'd like it if you were there."

"I have night classes on Mondays and Wednesdays, but if you want me, I'll be there."

God, I wanted him in so many ways. Ways that I shouldn't . . . couldn't. "Then I guess I'll see you every other night."

8

Cassidy

"DINNER WAS GREAT, Cassi, see you on Thursday!" Jake gave me a quick side hug and headed for the door.

"Thanks again, Cass. Can you make your lasagna next time?"

"Sure, Grant." I hugged him back after letting him see my eye-roll. "Any dessert preferences?"

"Your triple-chocolate cake!"

All the guys moaned and then turned to look at me with the poorest excuse for puppy eyes.

"Please, Cass, you haven't made that in weeks." Adam's bottom lip trembled lamely and I had to stop myself from rolling my eyes again.

"You guys are pathetic. Okay, well since it'll be our last night together for a few weeks, lasagna and triple-chocolate cake on Thursday. Now get out or help me with the dishes." I've never seen an apartment clear out that quickly. Jerks.

Gage started walking into the kitchen and froze when the door opened suddenly and Ethan and Adam ran back in, grabbed the rest of the peanut butter chunk brownies, and ran back out the door. Gage chuckled softly and stepped up next to me. "You washing or drying tonight?"

"I dried last night, I'll wash tonight."

He picked up a dish towel and stepped to the side as Tyler walked in and gave me a peck on the cheek. "Good dinner, babe. Do you need any help in here?"

I raised an eyebrow and stopped scrubbing the pan. "Did you want to do the dishes?"

"Err, uh . . . I'm gonna go check the score of the game."

That's what I thought. I went back to the pan and handed it off to Gage when I was done. This was our new routine. Gage would help with the dishes before he went back to his place, and Tyler would come in to make sure there wasn't anything going on he wasn't okay with. After a month and a half of Gage coming around again, you'd think he'd have been over it by now. Apparently not. Ty continued to kiss me too often and make his presence known whenever Gage and I were in the same room. Not like we ever did anything. I got a hug when he walked through the door and before he walked out it. Other than that, it stayed strictly friend-level.

"Y'all gonna come visit? My sisters have been asking about you a lot."

"Uh, I don't think so, Gage." The last time I was there I'd fallen in love with his family almost as fast as I'd fallen in love with him. I still had dreams at night of us living together somewhere on the ranch, or close to it. There was something about that ranch that felt more like home than Mission Viejo ever had. But being there would just bring back that awful morning, and

I still wasn't ready for that. "Besides, we're not even going back to California this winter. I haven't gotten any time off at work; most of the employees are taking long vacations. So they need all the help they can get."

"Well"—he nudged my side with his elbow—"you're welcome anytime. You know that, right?"

"Yeah." After a quick look at Tyler to make sure he was deep in the game, I turned slightly toward his cousin. "I just don't think that's the best idea considering . . ." I trailed off and braved a glance into his green eyes, only to find them fixated on Tyler, jaw clenched so hard I could see the muscles working.

"Probably right. Merry Christmas then, I guess. I'm gonna head back to the ranch in the morning; I'll be back in three weeks."

"Merry Christmas, Gage— Oh! Wait, I have your present."

"Present? Cassidy, you really didn't need to get me anything."

I smiled and grabbed his arm, towing him back toward my room. "I didn't *get* you anything. And if you don't like it, don't worry about it. It won't hurt my feelings or anything." I was surprised that Tyler didn't jump up and follow us in there, but I figured I only had a minute or so before he realized we weren't in the kitchen anymore. "Here you go." I worried my bottom lip as I shakily handed him his gift.

Gage walked over to his old bed and sat at the edge, just staring at the wrapped present for a few seconds. With a slight shake of his head, he unwrapped it slowly and paused when the front was revealed. His next intake of breath was audible and an oddly pained expression crossed his face. "Cass—" Looking up, he broke off quickly as his eyes narrowed on something behind me.

Tyler wrapped his arms around me and rested his chin on top of my head.

Gage stood up quickly and strode out of the room. "I gotta go. I'll see y'all in a few weeks."

"Later, man," Tyler called after him, and waited for the door to shut before speaking again. "Did he not like it?"

My heart sank. "Guess not."

Gage

WHAT THE FUCK? Was she trying to twist the knife that was already in my heart? She just had to throw the best night of my life back in my face even though it already hurt like hell watching them together. And I had no doubt they were together too. I don't know if they'd always been like this and I'd just missed them kissing each other, or if I was just so in love with her I chose not to see it. But I was definitely seeing it now. It's like Tyler couldn't keep his damn hands off her. Not that *that* part was new, but now he kissed her so often even I could see how uncomfortable he was making her. I slammed my hand down on the steering wheel and cursed Tyler. It didn't matter that I was still completely torn up from what happened last summer, or that she was bringing that memory back up; I hated seeing him touch her. She was mine. Granted, the flirting had stopped completely, but she still looked at me the same way she had all last year. Then she went and gave me that picture? I knew she was amazing with her camera, even if she thought her pictures weren't anything special, and I saw her take it out often while we were at the ranch, but I had no idea she'd taken a picture of our spot. I'd barely looked at it for more than a few seconds, but it was perfect. The tree, the creek, and the hill we'd slept on were all there, blown up in black and white. Her tattoo and this? It's like she was trying to make sure I couldn't forget that night, which of course made me unable to forget the morning that followed. My eyes rolled when my phone rang; I figured it was Tyler getting ready to throw a bitch fit at me for leaving the way I did.

"What?" I all but growled.

"Oh, uh . . . sorry? Did I interrupt something?"

Glancing at the screen, then back at the road, I brought the phone back up to my ear and sighed. "Sorry, Cara, thought you were my cousin. What's up?"

She giggled and paused before continuing. "Well, I know it's not Monday or Wednesday, but I'm leaving to go home for break tomorrow and I was thinking we could get together . . ." She trailed off suggestively.

Thoughts of Tyler's arms wrapped around Cassidy's waist as she watched me open that picture flashed through my mind and I tightened my grip on the steering wheel. "I'll be at your place in ten."

"I'll be waiting."

I ran a hand through my hair, pulling at it slightly. Cara was one of the girls I'd been seeing since I started hanging around Cass again. *Seeing* might be the wrong term, since we never did anything outside of a half hour in the bedroom. Once I realized that Tyler wasn't full of shit and they were actually together, I'd stopped waiting for a girl who would never be mine and did the one thing I knew would piss Cassidy off more than anything. I slept with every damn girl who was the exact opposite of her. Including Brynn. Tall, red or blond hair, and any eye color other than the golden honey of Cassidy's eyes, and I was game.

It's not like I rubbed it in her face; in fact I knew she didn't have a clue about it, and I wanted to keep it that way. I secretly hated what I was doing . . . I was disgusted with myself but I couldn't stop. I wanted to forget her, forget the way her small frame felt beneath me and curled up in my arms.

Pulling up outside Cara's apartment, I hopped out of my truck and made my way to her door. She opened it before I could knock and stood there in black lacy underwear and bra, holding up a foil packet between her index and middle finger with a satisfied smirk or her face. After I grabbed the packet from her, she took my hand and walked me back toward her room, shutting and locking the door once we were in. She turned and wrapped her arms around my neck, bringing my face down to hers, but I removed her arms and pushed her back toward the bed. I couldn't stop the roll of my eyes when she pouted but kept from saying anything; she knew how it was, and the fact that she was trying to change it just made me know nothing could happen between us after tonight. No kissing, and no holding each other after. The only two things I'd done with Cassidy, and I couldn't bring myself to do them with anyone else now.

Cara's pout turned into a hungry grin when I shed my clothes and rolled the condom on. Crawling onto the bed with her, I pulled down her underwear and threw it to the floor before sliding into her. My groan was matched by hers and I had to force my eyes back open before I could get lost trying to picture Cassidy beneath me. I'd made that mistake once already with a girl, Hannah, and the impressively forceful slap I'd received across my face from saying Cass's name as I came served as a reminder to always keep my eyes open.

An hour later I was back at my place and taking a scalding hot shower, trying to wash away everything Cara. Cassidy's sweet face when she told me she had a present for me kept flashing through my mind, making me feel even more nauseated over what I'd just done. I was drawing a blank as to why I was still trying to push her out of my mind this way, since it obviously wasn't working. And God, if she ever found out, I knew she'd never look at me the same way again. The thought of her looking at me with the disgust I already felt had my gut churning even more and I had to steady myself against the wall when I felt like I was going to lose my dinner.

"God, what the hell is wrong with me?" I said out loud. "She doesn't even want me."

Shutting off the water, I stepped out of the shower and had just haphazardly tied a towel around my hips when my phone beeped. I cringed at the thought of Cara asking me again to be exclusive when we got back from break. I'd thought it earlier, but knew it for sure now: there was no way in hell I could see her again after tonight. Warily, I picked up my phone and let out a relieved yet strangled breath when I saw Cassidy's name.

> *CASSIDY*
> *I'm really sorry you didn't like the picture. You told me it was your favorite spot on the ranch, and I realized I'd taken a picture of it at some point that week when we got back . . . I just thought . . . Well anyway, like I said you don't need to keep it. I hope you have a good Christmas and New Year, see you when you get back?*

What was I supposed to say to that? I wanted to ask how she could possibly think that was something I'd want to remember. I wanted to tell her I loved it just so she wouldn't feel like I hated something she'd given me. I wanted to say the part I didn't like was that she had gone back to Tyler like she always had, and I wanted to beg her to come with me to the ranch and leave Ty there. Jeez, why did she always turn me into such a fucking girl?

I do like the picture, Cass. I'm sorry I left the way I did, there were just a few things I needed to take care of before I left tomorrow. Enjoy your holidays, see you in three weeks.

Three long weeks of my life without Cassidy. Again.

9

Cassidy

I WAS JUST ABOUT TO SLIP into bed when Tyler came walking into my room with a hungry look on his face. Crap, not again. I'd done all our laundry, gone grocery shopping for us and for Gage since he was supposed to be back tomorrow or the next day, and all I wanted to do was lie down. Before I could say anything to him, he picked me up and laid me on the bed. "Ty, I'm really tired— Oh!"

All coherent thoughts left me when he sucked on that sensitive spot behind my ear and made his way down my throat with soft kisses and barely-there licks. He grabbed the neck of his shirt and pulled it over his head before letting it drop to the floor and pressing me into the bed again. I let my fingers softly trail down his back and up his sides, causing him to shiver and his ever-present hard-on to make itself known. Heat swirled in my lower stomach and my heart raced when his hands glided across my waist under my shirt. My eyes were shut and I let my head fall back onto the pillow as I pictured Gage's body pressed on top of mine. Before I realized what he was doing, my jacket was unzipped, my shirt was pushed up over my chest, and his mouth was sucking on my hardened nipple through the satin of my bra.

We'd never even gone this far, and although it felt incredible and part of me wanted him to take my bra off so there was nothing between me and his mouth, my body started shaking. And not in a good way. My mind may have been conjuring up images of Gage, but there was no way I could keep telling my body it was him when everything was so distinctively Ty. He slid the cup of my bra down, freeing my breast and resuming what he'd just been doing.

"Ty," I breathed, and tried to ignore my body shaking even harder. "Ty." The last one came out as more of a moan.

"I know, baby." His hands left my bra and made quick work of unbuttoning my jeans and trying to shove them down. He growled and pushed up off me to take them the rest of the way off and came back down onto his elbows, so only his mouth and hips were against me. "Cassi," he whispered against my skin when he rocked against me. The pressure and roughness of denim sent tingles through me, and he did it again.

When his hand traced over my underwear and moved it aside, my body froze momentarily and then started shaking in full force. "No, no no no no. Tyler, I can't, I can't do this."

"You'll enjoy it, Cassi, I promise."

I knew I would. It wouldn't be my first orgasm; it would just be the first one done by anyone other than myself. But I wasn't ready for this. Not with Tyler. "Ty, please—" I groaned when his fingers trailed against my most sensitive area and I cursed myself for feeling any type of pleasure while my body and mind were obviously sickened at the idea of allowing this to continue. "Tyler, seriously, stop!"

His fingers stopped just barely inside me, and his head jerked up to look in my eyes. "Are you kidding me?" He didn't remove his hand as he looked at me suspiciously. "You want this, Cassi, don't tell me you don't. Your little moans and sighs, and damn it, Cassi, you're wet as fuck. So why are you telling me to stop?" Tyler searched my face and shook his head slightly. "I swear to God, if you say you don't want this . . ."

"I—I—I do." I took a deep breath and forced my eyes to stay open and not make any noises when his fingers curled inside me. "I do want this, Tyler, but not yet. I'm not ready yet."

"You're—"

"Tyler. Please." My body was shaking harder now and for some stupid reason I was on the verge of tears. "I do want you, and yes, it feels"—I floundered for the right word—"incredible. But we've never done anything more than kiss, and this is moving way too fast right now. Can we please just ease into this?"

"Ease into this? *Ease?* Damn it, Cassi! We've been doing nothing but making out for almost four months."

"I meant—"

"You have got to be shitting me." He got off the bed, grabbed his shirt, and stormed across the apartment to his room.

I shakily pulled my pants back on, and fixed my shirt and hoodie before going to his door. "Tyler, please, talk to me." I tried the knob but the door was locked, and though I stood there begging for him to open it, there was never a response.

MY BACK ARCHED as his mouth sucked in one of my nipples and a soft moan escaped my throat. His hand came up to my other breast and gently massaged while his other hand started dropping lower, teasing my waist and hip before resting at the top of my underwear.

"Gage, please," I begged, and grabbed fistfuls of his black hair.

"Please what?" If I couldn't already feel it against me, the tone of his voice would have made it obvious he was smiling.

"Touch me."

His hand slipped inside my underwear and I groaned embarrassingly loud when it finally touched where I wanted it most.

"Gage—" I moaned, and arched against his hand.

"The fuck did you just call me?"

My eyes shot open to find a pair of dark brown eyes looking down at me instead of green, his mouth in a straight line as his jaw ticked under the pressure.

"Ty—" I tried not to panic over the possibility that I had said his cousin's name while we were kissing. Oh God, if the kissing was real, was the rest? I took a moment and almost sighed in relief when I noted one of Tyler's hands was in my hair while the other was under my back, holding me closer to him. My shirt was on and the comforter was up to my waist and keeping an extra layer between us.

"What. Did. You. Call me?"

"I—I don't know."

His eyes went flat as he pushed himself off me and the bed. Last night came rushing back to me and I prayed the morning wouldn't start off the same. He started to walk quickly out of my room, and I fought with the covers and comforter to run after him but he'd already thrown on his jacket and was walking out the door by the time I made it to my bedroom door.

"Shit." I ran back to my nightstand, grabbed my phone, and called him, but it went straight to voice mail. Hoping it was a fluke, I waited a few minutes and tried again with the same result. I left a message begging him to call me and come back.

Two hours passed without a word from him, and I finally called Jackie, flipping out. "I'll be right over!" she promised.

"Jackie—I need to go find him!"

"Um, no! No, you do not! I'll be right over and we're going to talk about this."

We said our good-byes and I dressed for the freezing weather in case she decided to help me go looking for him. She showed up with two coffees and muffins, told me I better get comfy again because we weren't going after him, and plopped down at the dining room table.

"Okay, spill."

"What? I already told you everything."

"Not really, you told me you called him Gage and he got pissed and took off. How did this even start though? Is Gage back?" Obviously Tyler had known about my feelings for Gage, but Jackie was the only one who knew the extent of them.

I got up and walked to the breakfast bar, grabbed the paper, and gave it to Jackie as I went to sit back down. "He must be. I found this note from Ty saying he was going out to break-fast with him. He must have written it before coming to say good-bye to me . . . and, well, I'd been having a dream about Gage—"

"Dream? What kind of dream?"

I raised my eyebrows and just continued to stare at her.

"That kind, huh?"

"Well, we weren't actually doing anything yet, but I kind of moaned his name and all of a sudden it's Tyler's voice and he was asking me what I'd just called him. I tried not to freak out, but the way Ty was looking at me, I knew I had actually said Gage's name out loud."

"What was Tyler doing? Had he been doing what Gage was in your dream?"

Thank God she got it. "No, but I was worried he had been! I'm guessing he just came to kiss me and I responded because of the dream, and . . . shit, Jackie, I didn't even tell you about last night!" I quickly told her everything about last night and waited for her to respond.

"And nothing happened between you and Ty while you were alone these last three weeks?"

"No, nothing beyond kissing. I mean there were a few times when the kisses started getting to be too much while we were on one of our beds, but I always stopped it before it went farther than that. And his parents came for a week and a half, so thank God that always kept it pretty clean. But last night was definitely the farthest he's ever tried to push it."

"Has he been trying a lot?"

I nodded and rolled my eyes. "And he's always getting mad about it too. Like actually yelling at me because I won't sleep with him; last night wasn't the first time it ended badly."

"Whoa." Jackie put both hands up, palms facing me, before letting them slap down on the table. "What?! He doesn't hurt you, does he, Cassi?"

"*No!* Tyler would never touch me that way." I didn't know how to assure Jackie of that since she knew nothing about my life before Texas, but I knew Tyler would never hit me. "No, he just gets mad is all."

She was still looking at me, a little unsure. "If he ever hurts you, you let me know. I'll kick his ass."

"And how are you going to do that?"

"I have my secrets."

"Uh-huh. I'm sure you do." Actually, I didn't doubt it. She

was one fierce little Asian. Ethan called her his little firecracker, and it fit her perfectly. She was tiny but came with more energy than anyone I knew and threw it into her emotions; whether it was happiness or anger, love or depression, she exuded it. And Jackie angry was pretty terrifying, if I say so myself.

"I'm serious. If he ever touches you, tell me."

"Jackie, I swear to you. He wouldn't. But he yells, saying that he's waited long enough, and wants to know if it's still because of Gage. He didn't ask that last night, but with last night and then this morning, I know I've hurt him, Jackie. Maybe I should just do what he wants."

"Cass, no, this is a big deal. Don't just sleep with Tyler because it's what he wants and he acts like a child when he doesn't get his way. No one should ever push you into something like that, Cassi, and it's not like you're teasing him with it. We've all seen you two together, and I know you're honest with him about not being ready. You're really subdued when it comes to any type of affection with him; he's the one always pressing the issue, even in public. Besides, he *knows* about your feelings for Gage, you didn't ever try to hide that from him. Maybe y'all should take a break."

"I know, I've thought about that too, I just—I'm afraid of losing Tyler in my life. He's my best friend; I don't know how I'd be able to deal without him there."

"With how close y'all were before you moved here, I can't see you losing that kind of friendship if this didn't work out."

I decided against telling her that Tyler had said it was all or nothing between us. I worried my bottom lip and glanced down at my phone, only to confirm what I already knew: he still hadn't called or returned any of my texts.

Jackie left five hours later and I tried to occupy my mind with reality TV to pass the time. I hated having Tyler mad at me, and it was making me sick that I still hadn't heard from him. I could have called Gage to find out if Tyler was still with him, but I didn't know if Tyler would have told him what happened, and if he hadn't, I didn't want to be the one to do it.

After a few shows and a movie, I tried to call Tyler one last time before peeling off my clothes to take a long, hot shower, hoping the water would relax my still-tense body. I had just pulled on a pair of sleep pants and tank top and was running a brush through my wet hair when I heard a key in the lock. I ran out of the bathroom just in time to see Tyler stumble in with a tall redhead attached to his face. He shut the door and pushed her up against it, grabbing behind her thighs and lifting her so she could wrap her legs around his waist.

"Tyler?" I choked out, and he turned their bodies so he could see me.

"Oh, hey!" His eyes were glazed and though his speech wasn't slurred, it was slower, and I knew he'd been drinking. "Cara, this is my sister Cassi. Cassi, this is Cara, she's in a couple classes with me."

Sister? Sister?! I opened my mouth but nothing came out. I just sat there watching as he walked them back to his room. Seconds later he walked back out and grabbed a couple beers from the fridge before turning to me.

"Sorry, did you want to say something?"

"Tyler, wh-what are you doing?" My voice was shaky and barely above a whisper.

"Finding someone who will take care of what you won't," he sneered, and his eyes narrowed on me. "What do you expect? For me to just wait for you forever? I can't believe I wasted all that time on you, waiting for you to be ready. I should have just taken it from you."

"Ty!"

"I have needs that you aren't filling, *Cassidy*. Either give me what I want or get out."

"What? Ty—I—I don't—"

"Save it, Cass." He grabbed my hand and led me toward the front door. "I'm so damn tired of being your crutch; find someone else for that." He shoved me out the door before shutting and locking it.

"Tyler!" I pounded on the door for what must have been five minutes straight and he still never came out.

My teeth were clattering and my body was shaking. It'd been in the low thirties yesterday while I was out grocery shopping, and the sun had been out then. Now the wind was blowing hard and it was pitch-black outside. I couldn't even begin to fathom what the temperature was. But here I was with wet hair, in socks, thin flannel pants, and an even thinner tank top. No phone. No keys. I didn't know any of our neighbors, and after getting no answer when I knocked on their doors, I started walking to Gage's town house. Not even a mile into my already-freezing walk, it started sleeting . . . hard. I could have gone into a store and asked to use the phone, but I didn't know anyone's number by heart, and I wasn't about to ask some stranger for a ride. Hoping to warm myself up, I attempted to jog, but my body was so cold I felt like I was going slower than when I'd been walking.

Gage

I STOPPED ON THE WAY to my room and turned slowly to look around. I don't know what I heard but when I didn't hear it again, I continued on in and shut the door before turning on the

TV. Thank God Cassidy had gotten groceries before I'd come back. Even though I'd finished dinner with the guys only a few hours ago I was already starving and about to finish off an entire bag of chips. Another muffled sound from the front of my place had me muting the TV and grabbing my Sig. I crept down the hall and heard a loud thump against the door. Looking out the peephole showed nothing, but I wasn't stupid enough to leave it at that. Before I could reach the blinds I heard sobs and a soft, melodic voice calling my name.

"Cass?" I asked even before I swung the door open to reveal her little body curled up in a ball at the base of the door. "Shit. Cassidy!" I put my Sig on a table near the door and went back to her.

"G-G-G-Gage?" she stuttered, and looked up at me as I scooped her into my arms.

She was fucking freezing. Her hair had literally frozen and even in the soft light from above my door I could see her face was blue. Why wasn't she wearing a damn jacket or shoes?! Where the fuck was Tyler? I ran back to my bathroom with her in my arms and turned the hot water on as I sat her on the counter. Flipping the light on, I got my first good look at her and a string of expletives left my mouth. Her lips and the surrounding area were blue, as were the tips of her fingers. The rest of her was bright red and shaking uncontrollably. Her eyes fluttered as she tried to keep them open before she gave up, letting them close. Her lashes, eyebrows, and hair were all frozen and her damn socks were stuck to her feet. I tried to lift her shirt off her but it was stuck as well, causing her to cry out and start sobbing again.

I wanted to scream at her, ask her why she would go outside dressed like this when it was sleeting and at most twenty degrees, ask her where her damn boyfriend was and why she hadn't called me. But I was so scared all I could do was whisper that she would be okay as I hugged her and tried to transfer some of my body heat. The shower was warmed up so I took off my sleep pants, leaving on my boxer-briefs, and took us both into the shower. She cried out again and I knew it must have been burning her, but she needed to heat up—like half an hour ago. I kept my arms around her and rubbed them vigorously up and down her body, and as her clothes loosened on her, I took those off and threw them onto the bathroom floor. She brought her hands up to my body and I flinched as the contrast between the hot water and her frozen fingers hit me. We were in a burning-hot shower, and she was making me freaking cold. My stomach dropped when her head fell hard to my chest and her body gave out.

"No, no, no. Wake up, Cassidy! Wake up!" I shouted, and sank down into the tub, glad I'd put the plug down so it would fill up while the shower ran. "Cassidy!" I grabbed her chin and brought her face up, cringing when I saw how blue her mouth and the surrounding area still were. "Wake up, darlin'!" I pressed my mouth to hers as if I were doing mouth-to-mouth and blew hot air onto her frozen face.

"G-G-G-Gage?"

"That's right, Cass, wake up. Keep talking to me." Her eyelids fluttered shut and I shook her body. "No, Cassidy! You can't sleep right now. Stay awake, talk to me. Why were you outside?" I grabbed her fingers and blew more hot air on them before shoving them into the collecting water, turning the shower up even hotter, and grabbing her chin again.

"T-T-Ty."

"Where was Ty, Cass?"

"K-k-kicked-d m-m-me out-t."

My body stilled. "Dressed like this?"

She nodded even though I still gripped her chin.

"Why didn't you call me, Cassidy?!" I shouted at her, and tried to calm myself when she recoiled from the sound.

"H-h-he locked-d m-me out. N-no ce-ce-ce—"

"Locked you out without your phone?"

She nodded again and I squeezed her body tighter to mine. "Jesus, Cassidy. I'll kill him. I'll fucking kill him." I looked down to see her jaw slack and her eyes closed again. "No! Wake up, baby. You gotta stay awake. Come on, Cass." I shook her again. "I need you to stay awake!"

"S-so c-cold."

"I know, Cass. I know. I'm so sorry. I'm sorry I wasn't there for you."

"G-Gage?"

"Yeah, darlin'?"

"I'm t-tired."

"I know." I sighed in relief when I looked down to see only red on her beautiful face instead of blue. "You can't go to sleep yet though."

Cupping water in the hand that wasn't holding her upper body, I let the water fall down her hair a few times before running my hands over it to make sure it was completely thawed out and warm. I kept her talking until her teeth stopped chattering and her body stopped shaking. It wasn't until I had us out of the shower and was wrapping numerous towels around her that I realized I'd been in a shower with a naked Cassidy. But I could barely even think about that now, let alone then. I was terrified for her, and now I was shaking with built-up rage at my cousin.

Her eyes closed again when I took her into my room to grab a shirt and sweats to dress her in.

"Cassidy, I need you to sit up and stay awake. I'm going to start a fire. I know you're tired, but if you can stay up for another half hour, I'll let you go to sleep then, okay?"

She nodded and sat up, wrapping her arms around herself in my baggy clothes.

"I'll be right back. Stay awake."

I grabbed my phone and changed into clean boxers, jeans, and a hoodie before running into the living room and starting a fire.

"Adam. Hey, man, I'm sorry if I woke you, but can you do me a huge favor?"

"Uh, yeah." He whispered to someone that it was me and asked, "What's up?"

"Are you with Dana?"

"We were just watching a movie. What's wrong?"

"I need someone to come watch Cassidy while I go beat the shit out of Tyler. But if you're with Dana, I'll call someone else."

"No!" He sounded alarmed. "No, no, it's fine. What happened to her?"

"I haven't gotten the whole story, but he kicked her out of their place, locked her out in nothing but a tiny shirt and pants, without her phone or anything. I guess she walked all the way over here; she was blue and frozen when I opened my door." The firewood had caught and I waited for it to stay burning before turning off the gas.

"Are you serious?" He spoke away from the phone and whispered for Dana to come with him. "We're on our way. Do you need us to get her anything?"

"No. I just need someone to watch her, make sure she stays

awake for a while. I had her in a hot shower for a while and she's in some dry clothes now. I just got the fire started and I'm gonna make her some coffee."

I heard him relaying the story to Dana. "Damn. Gage, that's a good three- or four-mile walk from their place. My car is saying it's sixteen degrees and it is sleeting really bad."

"I know," I growled, and started the coffee. "She had to have left at the very least an hour and a half ago, and Tyler hasn't called me once to tell me she's gone. I swear to God, if he's just sitting in that apartment when I get there . . ."

"Gage, maybe I should go with you to make sure you don't kill him. Dana can stay with her."

I wanted to say I'd deal with it alone, but I knew he was right. "Yeah, okay. How long until you're here?"

"Less than five minutes."

"'Kay, the door is unlocked. I'm gonna go check on her."

"All right, see ya."

"Darlin', you still awake?" I asked as I walked into the room.

Cassidy had a few tears on her cheeks when she looked up at me, and my heart about broke.

"Come on, the fire is going and the coffee is probably ready by now." I didn't wait for her to try to get up; I wrapped the comforter around her, scooped her back into my arms, and carried her to the couch I'd pulled up in front of the fire, then sat her down. "You okay?"

She nodded and stared into the flames.

"I'm gonna get you coffee. Once you drink it you can lie down, all right?" When she simply nodded again, I walked into the kitchen and poured her a mug before putting some milk and sugar in there. "Here you go, Cass. Drink all of this." The door opened and she jumped. When Dana and Adam walked in she looked back at me and grabbed the mug.

"Hey, sweetie," Dana said softly, and sat next to her. "What happened that you'd do something as crazy as walking in this freezing weather?" she asked with a quiet laugh and nudge.

I was glad she was asking, because that was exactly what I wanted to know. I was afraid Cassidy was going to break down crying again, and I knew how much she hated for anyone to see her cry, but instead her eyes narrowed and she harshly whispered to Dana about Tyler walking out that morning and coming in late that night with some redhead whose name she couldn't remember. Said he introduced Cassi as his sister and took the redhead into his room, and repeated what Tyler said when he came back into the kitchen. That was the last thing I heard before grabbing Adam's arm and stalking out to my truck. I was going to kill the prick.

We were there in six minutes, and I didn't even bother knocking when I saw his Jeep in the parking lot. I used my old key and charged in, my anger building when I heard some chick's loud moans in the kitchen. Rounding the corner, I paused only momentarily when I saw Tyler screwing Cara on the kitchen counter before continuing toward him.

"What the hell, man? Get out!"

I didn't say anything, just grabbed his shoulder and turned him as my fist connected with his nose.

"Gage!" Cara screeched, and tried to cover herself when she realized Adam was with me. "You had your chance with me, you passed it up!"

"This has nothing to do with you and me, Cara. I honestly couldn't care less who you decide to sleep with. But he has a girlfriend and he could have killed her tonight because he was being stupid. Now get dressed and get out!" I grabbed Tyler's arm and dragged him over to the couch, letting him fall onto it and throwing the blanket at him.

"Damn it, Gage! You broke my nose."

"I want to break a lot more than that. But I'm going to give you a few minutes to explain yourself first. Where's Cassidy?"

He looked at me incredulously. "How the hell am I supposed to know? I told her to leave and now she's gone."

"Your Jeep is here."

"So?"

"Did you give her your keys?"

"No." He picked up a pillow and held it to his face.

"How did you tell her to leave?"

"I walked her outside. Why do you care? What's with all the questions?"

"You locked her out of the damn apartment without a way to go anywhere or call anyone! She was in her damn pajamas and, if you didn't notice, it's fucking freezing outside!"

"Wait—if you knew all this, why are you even asking me?"

"Because I was hoping what she told me wasn't true! She walked to my place and by the time she got there she was blue and completely frozen! She could have died, you son of a bitch!"

"Shit, I didn't even think—oh God, is she okay?" He stood up and I punched him again before he could go anywhere. Adam came up behind me and kept a firm hand on my shoulder.

"You are a worthless piece of shit. Do not come near Cassidy again, you hear me? I don't know why she's clung to you her whole life; all you've ever done is let her get hurt. I didn't understand how you could let her get hurt in the past, and I sure as hell don't understand why you would treat her like this just because she wouldn't have sex with you. You don't deserve her, and I'll kill you if you hurt her again."

"Can you just tell me if Cassi's okay?"

"She's fine. And she'll be fine as long as she's with me."

"Whoa, wait!" We all turned to see Cara standing there with a disgusted look on her still-flushed face. "You're dating your sister?!"

"She's not his sister, and he's not dating her anymore. He's all yours." I jerked my head in the direction of my old room and Adam followed me in there. I grabbed Cassidy's bag from her closet and shoved as many of her clothes as possible into it, grabbed her phone and charger, and headed to the bathroom before throwing everything in there in another bag Adam was holding. When we walked back through the living room, Cara was on her knees in front of Tyler with a towel wiping the blood off his face and chest.

"Gage—"

I cut him a hard look and he stopped talking. "I'm serious. Stay. Away. From Cassidy."

When we got back to my place, Dana jumped up and put her finger over her mouth before whispering, "She finished a second cup of coffee and just fell asleep like three minutes ago."

"Did you put sugar in it?" The coffee was decaf; I wasn't trying to make her stay up the entire night, but I wanted her to drink something hot and wanted the sugar in her system.

She nodded. "And milk."

"Thanks, Dana, I appreciate it, and I'm sorry for interrupting your time together."

"Don't even think about it. She's one of my closest friends and takes care of you boys all the time. I owe her for keeping my guy fed."

I grunted in agreement and couldn't help but smile when I walked around to the front of the couch. She looked adorable. There was no other word for it. She was drowning in my sweatshirt; the hood was up over her head and her wavy hair spilled out the sides. Her cheeks were pink from the heat of the fire and she was still fully wrapped up in the comforter.

After a quick good-bye to Adam and Dana, I took both of her bags into the spare room before going back out to the living room and picking up the girl I love. When she was all settled in the guest bed, I pulled the hood of my sweatshirt off her head and brushed the hair from her face. *God, she's beautiful. And she's here.* She'd run to me. For the first time ever, she'd gone to someone other than Tyler. Granted, all this was his fault, but she'd gone somewhere else, and it'd been to me.

"I love you, Cassidy," I whispered, and pressed my lips to her forehead before reluctantly leaving her to go back to my own room.

Cassidy

THE SMELL OF COFFEE woke me the next morning and I was briefly disoriented when I didn't recognize the room I was in. When I started to get out of bed and fell back with a groan, the night before came rushing back to me and I wanted to die when I realized how Gage had taken care of me. And Tyler—what the hell? How could he do that to me? I'd never once kept my feelings for Gage a secret, and he knew I needed time to get used to us as a couple. I thought I'd progressed significantly, but apparently not enough. I couldn't believe he'd just bring someone home like that though. It wasn't like my Tyler at all, and I was surprised by how much it hurt. It wasn't anything like when Gage broke my heart, but it still felt like someone had punched me in the stomach. Or maybe that was just a side effect to whatever was going on with the rest of my body. I tried to sit up again but didn't make it far before my head hit the pillow.

There was a soft knock on the door and Gage poked his head in. "Mornin', how are you feeling?"

"Like a truck ran over me."

"What were you thinking, Cass?" His eyes narrowed as he sat on the end of the bed.

"Wait . . . you're—are you mad at me?"

"Mad? Darlin', I'm furious. You could have died! Does no one understand that? Because apparently Tyler didn't get the memo either."

My breath stuck in my throat. "You spoke to Tyler? When?"

"When I left you with Dana last night, I went to go talk to him." His green eyes flashed and he looked away quickly before settling his narrowed gaze back on me.

"I don't remember a lot of last night. Just coming here, and parts of the shower."

His eyes softened for a second. "Cass—just tell me why you didn't try to get someone to help you. Or ask someone to use their phone."

"I don't know anyone's number; it's all just saved in my phone. And it was really late, I didn't think it'd be safe to hitchhike over here."

"And walking over here in sleet wearing your pajamas *is* safe?"

"Seemed like it at the time," I mumbled lamely as I finally managed to get off the bed and tried to ignore the way my entire body felt like it was two seconds from collapsing and never getting back up. "Sorry I bothered you, Gage. Thanks for taking care of me. I'll see you later."

"What? Where are you going?"

My eyes widened in surprise from the anger in his tone. "I'll go to Jackie's until I can get my own place." I stopped walking and stood there still as stone when Gage's sweatpants fell off me and straight to the floor. Let's just add on one more thing to be humiliated about when it came to Gage. At least his sweatshirt was big enough that it still covered everything important. I flushed when I realized he'd already seen everything last night. "Can I please use your phone so I can call her? Or Ethan," I asked through clenched teeth.

"Cassidy, why are you leaving?"

"Because I shouldn't have come here in the first place! Obviously it was a bad idea."

"I don't want you to leave." His voice softened drastically and he reached out to grab my hand to pull me back to the bed, coughing out a laugh when I tripped out of his sweatpants. "Sorry, that's the warmest clothing I had for you last night."

I just nodded and turned my head so he wouldn't see me blush.

"Hey." He put his fingers under my chin and turned my head so I was looking into his dark green eyes. "I'm sorry. I'm not mad at you; you just scared the crap out of me last night. I was seconds from calling an ambulance. I probably should have but I was too focused on warming you up."

That just made my blush get about ten times worse. *Oh my God, I can't believe I was in a shower with Gage. Not that I was able to enjoy one second of it or even realize at the time what was really happening.* "Gage," I began after a few silent moments, "was she still there when you got there last night?" I almost told him not to answer that, but then his face morphed into one of pity and I no longer needed him to. "I'm kind of tired," I said, quickly changing the subject. "Is it okay if I go back to sleep for a bit before I call Jackie?"

"You can go back to sleep; you need to rest as much as possible after last night. But I want you to stay here, Cass. Adam and I brought most of your stuff over last night. You don't have to, but you're more than welcome to live here. As long as you want."

Live with Gage again? But he hated having me with him last time. "I appreciate what you're doing, Gage, but you don't owe me anything. And I don't want you to give me a place to stay because you feel sorry for me."

"That's not it at all. I want you here—honestly I'd rather have you here than anyone."

I doubted that. But the idea of being this close to Gage again had my stomach fluttering. I realized I still hadn't said anything when he stood up and walked over to me.

"Just think about it." His raspy voice got even deeper. "But go back to sleep now, darlin'. I'm gonna go for my run. I'll check on you when I get back." His hand brushed across my forehead once I was under the comforter and he frowned. "Are you hot?"

"No, actually I'm still kind of cold. Can you throw me your sweats?"

Gage cursed under his breath and headed out the door, tossing me his sweats on his way out. Before I could try to pull them back on he'd returned with the comforter from his bed. "Here you go." He brushed his hand across my forehead again and down my left cheek. "I'll be back soon, okay?"

"Have fun," I mumbled as I curled into a tight ball. I didn't even have the strength to try to put the sweats back on.

Gage

I HADN'T EVEN gotten down the driveway when I ran back inside and grabbed my keys. I couldn't run. Not right now when I was worrying about her so much. As soon as I was in the truck, I called my mom. Yeah . . . I know. I was that desperate.

"Why doesn't it surprise me that you're already awake? It's your last day before school starts back up; you should be sleeping in."

"Hello to you too, Mama."

"How's my boy?"

"All right. Hey, Ma, I need your help on something. Cassidy's burning up, and I don't know what I should do. I'm on my way to get a thermometer, but is there anything I should buy . . . like food, drinks, or medicine?"

"Cassidy?" She couldn't hide her surprise in that one word. "Shouldn't Tyler be helping her if she isn't feeling well?"

"Uh . . . long story short?"

"Sure." She sighed, letting me know I'd have to give her the full version later.

"He brought home another girl and kicked Cassidy out last night."

"He what?! Are you sure?"

"Ma, yes. I'm sure. I even asked him myself. But that's not the worst part. He locked her out without her phone or keys or anything and she ended up walking to my place. It was sleeting really bad and she was in her pajamas; she didn't have a jacket or anything."

"Oh, that poor girl. Is she okay? You said she's burning up?"

"Yeah." I blew out a deep breath and tapped my thumb on the steering wheel furiously until the light turned green again. "She's in sweats and I cranked the heater up really high last night. She said she's cold but she's bright red and really, really hot."

"Just get the thermometer for now, and some NyQuil. Call me back after you've taken her temperature."

"All right, thanks, Mama, love you."

"I love you too. Bye-bye now."

I ran into the drugstore and got the most expensive thermometer I could find and a few bottles of NyQuil before heading back to the house. I'd only been away from Cassidy for maybe twenty-five minutes, but there was no doubt she was worse than when I'd left. I could feel the heat emanating from her skin and she was shaking again.

"Cass, wake up, let's take your temp."

She groaned and pulled both comforters up to her cheeks.

I continued trying to wake her up while I tore open the box. She finally nodded when I showed her the thermometer and I slipped it into her mouth. While I waited, I touched her cheeks and forehead and had to stifle the urge to yell at the damn thing to hurry up. I'm pretty sure the people who made the thing laughed at being able to torture people with the wait. Not able to sit there doing nothing, I called Mama again and told her about the changes. If I'd thought she was hot earlier, she was on fire now. Finally the stupid torture device from hell beeped and I gently but swiftly took it from Cassidy's mouth.

"Shit, that's high," I breathed.

"Gage Michael Carson!"

It took me a second to realize what happened. "Sorry, ma'am, but it says one-oh-five-point-two. What should I do?"

"Take her to the hospital right now. If she stays at that temperature for too long she can start having seizures or go into a coma."

What?! "Okay, I'll talk to you later."

"Call me as soon as the doctor tells you anything, you hear me? I want to know immediately."

"Yes, ma'am." I hung up and scooped Cassidy into my arms; she'd already fallen back asleep and didn't so much as move until after I already had her in the ER. And then it was only to start shaking uncontrollably, and I wished I would have thought to bring one of the comforters with me, or at the very least put the sweatpants back on her. I'd never had to take care of someone, and I felt like I was doing a fucking awesome job . . .

I LOOKED UP when I felt a hand on my back and smiled softly. "I really do appreciate you being here, Ma. I didn't have a clue as to what I was doing." I raked a hand through my hair and sighed when I looked back over at Cassidy, who was asleep in my bed. "Obviously."

"Hush. You did everything you could."

"If I would have just taken her as soon as she got here—"

"She would have had pneumonia either way, Gage. She was out in that weather without the right clothes and had wet hair. You can't blame yourself. Tyler, on the other hand . . ."

"God, I want to punch him again."

"For once," she said with a sigh, "I wouldn't try to stop you."

Cassidy rolled over and I stopped breathing for a moment so I could listen to her soft, rhythmic breaths. She'd been back at my house for two days now after four days of monitoring in the hospital to make sure she was on the mend. Mama had left the cooking and cleaning at the ranch to my middle sister, Nikki, and had rushed to Austin as soon as I told her that the doctor said Cass had pneumonia. She refused to let me miss my classes, and if I couldn't be sitting next to Cassidy, at least I felt better knowing Mama was there with her instead of Tyler. Who, by the way, had shown up at the hospital while I was in class and, after a verbal beating from my mom, left and had only tried to make contact by phone. Thankfully Cassidy hadn't wanted to talk to him, not that I would have let him talk to her anyway.

Mama had been great though. She'd been cooking for us and taking care of Cass in a way only a mother could. I could see Cassidy didn't handle being taken care of in that way very well at first, but with how weak she was, she didn't have much of a choice and I knew she now loved having a mother figure looking after her for the first time in years. Mom was sleeping in the guest room, so naturally I put Cassidy in my room, and honestly I wouldn't have had it any other way. Technically, I'd been sleeping on the bigger couch, but I always ended up sitting in a chair next to the bed so I could make sure her breathing stayed normal. Or at least, that's what I'd been telling myself. Cassidy was the only one who believed that. That knowing smile Mama gave me every time she saw me in there let me know she wasn't fooled; she knew I just wanted to be near her. There I went, being fucking creepy again.

"Come talk to me, Gage," Mom whispered over her shoulder as she made her way out of my room.

I stood up and stretched before bending over the bed and pressing my lips to Cassidy's forehead. She looked and felt so much better, I had no doubt she'd be trying to get out of bed and

back to work on Monday. I choked on a laugh on my way out to
the kitchen, thinking about how cute Cassidy got when she tried
to get her way, but there was no way in hell I was letting her out
of that bed for at least another week. "Yes, ma'am?"

"I just wanted to see how you're doing with all of this."

"I'm fine." My brow furrowed. "Why?"

"I meant, how are you with Cassidy being here? After they
visited this summer, and over winter break, you were just so . . .
I don't know. Heartbroken? And now she's here after there was
trouble between her and Tyler. I just want to make sure you don't
get hurt again, son."

"Yeah, I understand. I don't know what to make of a lot of
this. I was—*am* still messed up over the whole thing, but I can't
stop . . . I'm still in love with her."

"I know you are."

"I've tried getting over her, Mom"—Mama didn't know exactly *how* I'd tried to get over Cassidy, but that was something
that was better left unknown to anyone other than myself and
the girls I had been with—"and I've tried to figure out why she
would do certain things . . . there has to be something I'm missing. Cassidy's not the type of girl to purposefully hurt someone, and if I didn't know her as well as I do, I wouldn't see that
she was hurt too. For some reason, I found myself apologizing
to her after I got back this summer. She was so mad that I left,
and even though she tried to hide it, I knew she was upset. And
then . . . I don't know. Maybe I'm just making myself think all
this is happenin'."

"Well, I'm not so sure about that. You only have to be in the
room with the two of you to know there's something there. She
looks at you like— Well, anyway. Just be careful. Whether she's

doing it on purpose or not, you've been hurt by her too many times already."

Not like I needed that reminder. But she was right. I knew if I kept reading too much into her running to me, something would bring me crashing back down to reality and I'd end up even more pissed off than the last few times that had happened.

She began to say something, then hesitated and opened the fridge and freezer to browse.

"Might as well just say it, Mama."

"Are you sure it's the best idea to have her living here with you? Don't get me wrong, sweetheart, I absolutely adore that girl. But with all that's happened, you really think you should be doing this?"

"Yes." I didn't even hesitate. "I'm sure and I do."

"All right." She raised her hands, palms facing me. "All right, I got you. Just making sure," she added with a wink.

10

Cassidy

I WAS JUST rinsing out my mug in the sink when there was a hard knock on the door. It was only six thirty in the morning, for crying out loud; who was crazy enough to go around waking people up this early? Not that we weren't awake. Gage had come to check on me before he left for his run not long ago and I hadn't been able to go back to sleep. I tiptoed over to the door and looked out the peephole.

"What the hell?"

He knocked again, and even though I was watching him, the loud sound made me jump back.

"What do you want, Ty?" I practically growled as I swung open the door but stood in the doorway so he couldn't come in.

"God, Cassi, I've been going out of my mind. How are you? Are you feeling okay?" He reached his hand out toward my face and I smacked it away.

"I'm fine. Why are you here?"

"Baby, I'm so sorry. You have no idea how sorry I am. Please let me in so we can talk about what happened."

"There's not much to talk about. You brought a girl home to screw because I wouldn't. That about covers it all, don't you think?"

"I—" He ran both hands through his hair and pulled them out hard, leaving his hair sticking up in all directions. If I hadn't been so upset from seeing him again, I might have laughed. "I fucked up! I'm sorry, I was wasted and pissed because of what you called me—not that that's an excuse, I know you had been asleep, I just wasn't thinking. I mean, I was . . . but—"

"Wow . . . this is already starting off so well. You were wasted, you weren't thinking, you *were* thinking. You know, you seemed pretty coherent to me."

"Cassi—"

"No, I need you to go."

"Can we please just talk about this? I'm *sorry*, Cassi."

I put my hand on the door and started to step back. "I would say I'm sorry too, but I can't, Ty. I'll never be sorry for not giving you my virginity, especially when it made me realize what kind of guy you really are."

"I'm not that guy!"

"Are you serious right now? Ty, you *are* that guy. I wasn't ready and you kept pushing me. When I wouldn't budge, you not only found someone else, you made it a point to insult me in front of her and then kick me out of our place." I began shutting the door but he put a hand out to stop me. "I thought you did a pretty good job of saying this, but it seems we aren't on the same page. So let me try. We're over, Tyler."

"Cassi, please! I'll wait as long as you need! Cara was a mistake."

My body was shaking and I was dangerously close to crying. I couldn't believe I was actually doing this. Saying good-bye to my Tyler. I was literally seconds from giving in and rushing into his arms and begging him to make this better, the way he always had. I wanted what we had before, before I made the mistake of agreeing to turn our friendship into something more. But that was gone now. "It's too little, way too late, Ty."

"Babe," he pleaded, and his eyes took on a strange heat as I began closing the door farther. Before I realized what he was doing, one arm was wrapped around my waist, the other hand curled around the back of my neck, and his lips were hard against mine.

I struggled so roughly against him that when Gage suddenly appeared behind him and pulled Tyler from me I landed hard on my butt with a low *"Oomph."*

"You okay?" Gage asked. His bright green eyes were fixed on me and he was still trying to catch his breath from his run. Even in the situation I couldn't help but admire his amazing body. His long-sleeved shirt was soaked and clinging to his chest and abs, and his loose mesh shorts showed his tight calves.

"Yeah." I nodded and pulled myself up. "Fine."

One hand reached out and slid down my arm until it wrapped around my hand, and his eyes roamed over my face for a few seconds before he spoke again. "Go get back in bed, Cass, I'll be in to check on you in a minute."

"This is why you won't talk to me? You and him?! How long has this been going on?"

My eyes went wide when I looked over at Tyler. Was he serious? He knew better than anyone how Gage felt about me, or—didn't feel about me. "Ty—"

Gage pulled me so I was somewhat hidden behind his back.

"Don't even try throwing this onto her for something that isn't even happening. You messed up. Your actions are what brought her here to me. You're the reason y'all are no longer together."

"I told you from day one, man, I *told* you to stay away."

Before I could ask what Tyler meant by that, he was stepping up so he was chest to chest with his cousin, and I knew this was going to escalate quickly. "Tyler, just go," I demanded as I pulled on Gage's arm to move him back toward the entryway; his hands clenched into fists and I swear his body started vibrating. "Gage, come on. Let's go inside." *Please, please, please don't fight.* I honestly couldn't stand to watch anyone throw a punch, and Tyler knew that. I knew he wanted Gage to be the one to start it, because he figured it would freak me out enough to make me want to leave. "This is what he wants, please just shut the door."

"What?" Tyler taunted. "Too good to hit me this time?"

I froze. Gage had hit him?

"For all the shit you've put her through, you deserved it and more."

"What are you waiting for? I'm standing right here."

Gage gently pushed me farther back and straightened up to look down at Tyler. "Darlin', go into your bedroom."

I watched Tyler's smirk grow into a wide smile; he'd hinted at Gage's temper before, but he knew I'd never seen it . . . and I didn't want to. My body was shaking, and though I felt like I was nailed to the floor, I forced my feet to move and stepped right in between them, facing Gage but keeping my head down so I wouldn't see the way he was looking at Tyler; his stance was telling me all I needed to know.

"Darlin'."

"Please." My voice was soft and shaky as I made myself reach out and grab his clenched fist. I ground my jaw as I held it and tried to stop how my body was violently shaking. Seeing this side of Gage would change everything; I couldn't let him do this. "Just don't."

Gage's body tightened before he hunched down, his hand going under my chin to tilt my head up. I had squeezed my eyes shut and they slowly opened when I heard his soft voice. "Cass." His green eyes were wide as they looked all over my face.

"Please," I whispered again, and he nodded. The hand not holding my chin relaxed and squeezed mine as he moved us away from Tyler.

"You need to go. Don't show up here without an invite first, you got me?"

"Cassi—" Tyler began, but Gage shut the door and flipped both locks before wrapping his arms around me.

"I'm sorry."

"Gage, I don't want what's happening between me and Tyler to ruin your relationship. You're family. Maybe I should go—"

"Nope. You're staying here. I don't care if he's family—hell, I've already dropped too many things he's done because we're family. But not this, not the way he treated you."

"But—"

"We'll be fine, Cassidy. He's being a dumbass, I'm allowed to not want to see him."

I just nodded my head.

"Are you okay? I'm so sorry I scared you."

"I'm fine, I just— I'm fine."

His hand trailed soothingly up and down my back. "I'd never hurt you."

"I know that, Gage," I said on a sigh. He wouldn't hurt me, but he didn't understand I couldn't see him hurt anyone else either.

Gage

THINGS WERE NEAR PERFECT over the next few weeks. Cassidy had gone back to work the Monday after Tyler showed up, and he hadn't bothered her since. I still saw him at school, and we were back on for going to breakfast Saturday mornings, but even though things were getting back to normal, they were still strained. I was taking Cassidy to and from work, and failing at helping her in the kitchen at night, but damn if it wasn't one of my favorite times with her.

All the guys came over to my place for her cooking about once a week and I was glad it was less than what they'd been doing at Ty's. I knew I was being selfish, but I loved our time together, and having a bunch of people over just got in the way of that. When it was just us, we'd curl up on the main couch and she'd watch TV while I did homework, and more often than not, I got to carry her to bed at night. If others were over, she always kept at least a foot between us, and even though it was small, I hated any distance from her. We didn't touch a lot, but knowing I couldn't put my arms around her sucked. Like now. We'd gone out to grab dinner with a bunch of our friends, and even though she was in the seat next to me, there might as well have been a damn table between us.

"Yo, Gage."

"Hmm?" I reluctantly tore my gaze from Cassidy to look at Grant and throw back the chip he'd thrown at me.

"Shit, I thought you'd gone deaf for a minute."

"I was distracted. What?"

"I bet you were." Adam and Jake laughed next to him and Grant pointedly looked at Cassidy. My foot shot out and connected with his leg when his look turned hungry. Grant grunted and fixed his eyes back on me. "Guys' night tomorrow. You in?"

"Yeah, sure." Cassidy laughed at something Jackie said and like an addict drawn to heroin, I couldn't help but look over to watch her. My first observation still held true; it sounded like damn angels when she laughed.

Ethan looked past Jackie and Cassidy. "You're going tomorrow?" When I nodded he continued. "All right, as long as I don't have to be the only one to deal with their drunk asses at the end of the night, I'm in too."

Cassidy laughed softly and turned to look at me with a smile that had me fighting not to lean over and kiss her there in front of everyone. Wait, tomorrow? Tomorrow was Saturday. "Ah, never mind, sorry, I forgot what tomorrow was. I can't go."

"What?" Jake and Grant said at the same time, and Grant continued. "No. Guys' night. Which means both of y'all need to be there."

"Sorry." I shrugged; I was anything but sorry. "Tomorrow's Saturday, I already have plans."

"Bro. Two words. *Guys'. Night.*" Grant looked at me like I was missing the hidden meaning and losing my damn mind.

I knew what guys' night entailed, but until a few months ago when I realized that Cassidy and Tyler were really together, I hadn't cared for guys' night much. And was kind of relieved I had a legit excuse not to go now. "I have a date. Sorry."

Adam stopped kissing Dana's neck and looked at me with one brow raised and shot a quick glance to Cass, then back to me, and shook his head. He knew about all the girls I'd been with at the end of last year, why I'd been with them, and how I felt about Cass. I'd spilled everything in my truck on the way back from punching Tyler that night. It was obvious he thought I was going out with some random girl; I'd have to clue him in that my date was with Cassidy. I turned to say Ethan was on his own but stopped when I saw Cassidy's stiff posture. Her face was completely blank. If it weren't for Jackie shooting daggers at me, I would have thought Tyler had shown up. Even still, I looked around me and couldn't figure out why Cassidy's mask would be back. Didn't she want to have our Saturday night together? We'd started watching movies every Saturday night when I lived with her and Tyler, and we'd easily fallen into the same routine since she'd moved in with me. Maybe she'd made plans with Jackie, and that's why Jackie was looking at me like she was about to go psycho firecracker on me.

My confusion only intensified, and by the time Cassidy got back from getting groceries with Jackie the next day, I was completely dumbfounded. She hadn't said a word the entire way back to our place last night, hadn't gotten up for our morning hug before or after my run that morning. And I cut breakfast with Ty short so I could be home when she got back. She still didn't say anything and kept taking the groceries I was trying to help put away out of my hands and doing it herself. After *she* finished putting everything away, she walked into her room and shut the door.

I finished the rest of the homework I had for the weekend and decided to order pizza so she wouldn't have to cook that night. After hanging up the phone, I walked over to her room and knocked on the door.

"Yeah?"

I turned the knob and pushed open the door, worrying when I saw her curled up in bed. "You feeling okay, darlin'?"

She sighed and turned so she was facing me. "What's up, Gage?"

"Uh—I ordered a pizza." It sounded more like a question, but

I was so damn confused I didn't know what to say or do anymore.

"Thanks, but I'm pretty sure I can fend for myself when you're out. I've been known to get in the kitchen every now and then."

Man, with that tone, she'd skipped snarky and gone straight California bitch on me. "Um . . . I'm not going out."

Her eyebrows shot straight up and she mashed her mouth together tightly before forcing a smile that looked pained. "So your date's coming here. Did you want me to leave?"

"Cass, seriously? It's Saturday."

"Yeah, I know."

"So . . . ? It's movie night."

"Wow, um . . ." She shook her head slightly and her whiskey eyes got even wider. "I'm sorry, but I'd rather not be watching movies with you and your date."

Holy shit, she really thought I had a date with someone other than her? I knew this wasn't exactly a date, and she lived with me, but these were *my* nights with her. She had to know I wasn't about to let someone come between us and our night together, much less another girl. I mean honestly, it's not like I was subtle with everything I felt about her. I was pretty damn pathetic when it came to Cassidy; anything involving her and I was there with a smile on my face. Not that I cared; I was in love with the girl, and everyone knew it even if I hadn't told them. Shit, even the guys last night were talking about how I couldn't stop looking at her, and she'd been right there. "Darlin'," I said softly, "you are out of your damn mind if you think I have a date with some chick tonight."

Her face scrunched up and she looked so damn cute I had to force the corners of my mouth not to turn up. She had been upset because she thought I was going on a date. Everything from last night through today finally made sense, and yeah, it felt damn good to know she'd been jealous. "But last night . . . you told everyone—" She stopped and tilted her head to the side. "You don't have a date?"

"Oh no, I do. But apparently my date would rather spend the night alone in bed than on the couch with me, a movie, and a pizza."

"You didn't go out with the guys because of our movie night?" she asked softly.

God, I was in love with this girl. "Uh, yeah. Now are you gonna come out there with me, or do I have to throw you over my shoulder, hold you down on the couch, and force you to watch a movie with me?" Damn if my pants didn't get tighter thinking about pinning her down on the couch.

She failed miserably at hiding her smile and slowly got out of the bed, making her way toward me and the door. When she passed me she paused and turned her head up to look back at me. "Thanks, Gage."

11

Cassidy

GLANCING DOWN AT MY WATCH, I almost sighed in relief when I saw there were only five minutes left of my shift. It was Friday and, for whatever reason, this Friday seemed like a Monday. We had angry customers in the drive-thru who yelled at Lori because it took her almost three minutes to get their six-drink order out to them, then a snotty kid threw his hot chocolate on the ground because it had whipped cream—seriously, what kid doesn't like whipped cream?—and his mom demanded we make him another for free, even though she'd never mentioned anything about the whipped cream *before* I'd made the drink. Lori had gotten emotional after the six-drink order, and we'd traded spots right after, so she had gone out to clean up the mess while I started on another hot chocolate, and in her barely two months of preggo glory . . . she proceeded to get morning sickness, right there in front of everyone. This, incidentally, made said snotty kid throw up right next to her as well. If that hadn't been enough, the mother started yelling that she was going to sue us for causing her child to throw up from, and I quote, "forcing that awful whipped cream into my baby boy." I hadn't meant to, but I was so over the day already I'd snorted out a laugh when she said that, and she decided to take her anger out on me. Said that it wasn't saying much for Starbucks if they'd let a drugged-out child with track marks make their customer's drinks as she pointed to my tattoo of Ursa Major on my arm. Yay me.

I was just slipping off my apron and punching in my code when Stacey walked in with an older woman I'm assuming was her mother. Stacey looked amazing; she was glowing and couldn't stop smiling, exactly the way a girl should look the day before her wedding.

"Hey! Didn't expect to see you today, but I must tell you, you missed one awesome day."

"Really?" she asked, her eyes getting bright.

"No. It was awful, be glad you weren't here."

"Oh." She scrunched up her nose at me and smiled. "Well, we're meeting up with my girls to get our nails done but I'm glad I caught you before you left. I was wondering if you're going to bring a date tomorrow. I know things with Tyler ended a few months ago, so I didn't know if you planned on bringing some-one else . . ." She trailed off.

"Huh. I hadn't even thought about that. I guess I'll just go by myself. If this is about the price for catering, I'll totally eat for two if you want me to."

She and the older woman both laughed. "No, it's not that. Well, I was talking about you with Russ, and he said there were a few guys from his fraternity coming who are single, and that I should set you up with one of them." My eyes got wide but she kept talking. "Obviously, I would have rather talked to you about this first, but Christian, one of his frat brothers who's coming, was sitting right there and one thing led to another, they got on your Facebook page . . . safe to say Christian is dying to meet you now."

"Uh . . ."

"He's really cute, Cass, he's twenty-two, he's a baseball player—"

"I'm taking Gage," I blurted out when I saw his truck pull into a parking spot.

Stacey sucked in a deep gasp and her eyes got wide. "Oh my God. Really?" She squealed. She actually. Freaking. Squealed. "How come you didn't tell me about this? Oh, Cass, when I get back from my honeymoon you are telling me everything!"

Oh crap. "Um, well, it's new."

"Cassidy, this thing with Gage is *not* new. It may have taken forever, but it sure as heck isn't new."

Gage got out of his truck and started making his way in, so I hurried around them so Stacey wouldn't get a chance to say anything to him, especially since Gage knew nothing about Stacey's wedding or our relationship, which was so new, you could practically say it was nonexistent. Since it was. "Yeah, well . . ." I smiled and hugged her hard. "We're being kind of quiet about it right now because of Ty, so—" I broke off when Gage walked in and smiled his heart-stopping smile, dimples and all. "See you tomorrow, Stace!"

Gage's arm had just settled around my shoulders when Stacey called out in a singsong voice, "Good-bye, Gage Carson, I'll see y'all later."

His smile stayed but you could see the confusion in his features at the way Stacey was speaking. "Bye, Stacey." It came out more of a question and he cocked his head to the side as I hurried us out the door. "She seemed like she was in a good mood," he stated as he opened the passenger door for me.

"Uh, yeah . . . something like that," I mumbled, and tried to figure out how I was going to ask him to the wedding and keep him out of the loop about our "relationship."

"GAGE?" I TIMIDLY CALLED from the hallway. I knew he would come with me, but if I was being honest with myself, I was afraid he'd see just how much I wanted him to be my date to this stupid thing.

"Yeah, Cass?" The door to his bedroom swung open to reveal Gage in nothing but mesh shorts, his hair still wet from a shower, a few drops of water running down his broad shoulders and chest.

I failed at stifling a gasp and tried to focus on his eyes. That didn't help either; I could get lost in those dark green-and-gold eyes. "Um . . ." I realized I was biting my lip and looking at his well-defined stomach again. *Get a grip! This is not the first time you've seen him half-naked.* I mentally shook myself and looked at the floor instead. "So Stacey's getting married tomorrow, and before everything happened, I'd already RSVP'd with a plus-one for Tyler. But since that's obviously not an option, I was wondering if you'd maybe be my date? As a friend, I mean! Go with me as a friend." Okay, this was going exactly how I hoped it wouldn't. I'd managed to get lost staring at his body, I'd asked him to be my date, and I knew my entire face was beet red from embarrassment.

He didn't say anything, but I could practically feel his silent laughter making its way through my body. I sighed and turned back toward the living room. "Don't worry about it, I'm sure you're busy tomorrow." No, he wasn't. Tomorrow was Saturday, our movie night.

"What time is it at?"

I stopped walking but didn't turn around. "Starts at five."

"Well then, it's a date." His next laugh wasn't silent.

I grimaced thinking about our "date" misunderstanding last week when it came to our movie night and actually smacked my face as I walked into the living room, groaning into my hand. "Awesome," I mumbled to myself.

Flopping onto one of the couches, I closed my eyes and tried to think of anything but Gage's amazing body. I'd seen him without a shirt on hundreds of times, and of course my pulse had started racing every time, but I'd always been in control of myself. Unfortunately, I was once again letting myself believe a relationship could happen between us and stupidly thought that Gage wanted me too. I silently cursed myself for the thousandth time for thinking that living with Gage could possibly be a good idea.

CRACKING MY EYES OPEN, I glared at the sun coming through my window. I grabbed an extra pillow and put it over my face. Wait . . . extra pillow? I was in my bed, and it was now morning. *Gage.* Didn't matter how many times he put me in my bed, I was thoroughly embarrassed each morning after I woke up. Who knows if I was snoring, drooling, or talking when he did it? I dragged myself out of bed and toward the kitchen, where I could smell fresh coffee.

"Morning."

"Ugh." I slumped into his chest as he pulled me in for my

morning hug. Not gonna lie, it was still my favorite part of each day with him.

He chuckled and kissed the top of my head. We both stiffened for a moment and I had to rein in my smile before I stepped out of his arms. It wasn't the first time Gage had pressed his full lips to me since the ranch, but usually it was a peck to my cheek or forehead when he was putting me in my bed, and even then I was still mostly asleep, so I always figured I was dreaming it.

"Coffee ready?" I asked while scrounging around the fridge for the creamer that was hiding.

"Yep." He leaned over me to pluck the creamer out of the fridge from directly in front of my face. "Looking for this?"

"Whatever, it's too early." I grabbed my mug and went to sit on a bar stool.

We drank our coffee in silence as I continued to mull over the kiss and stress about Stacey saying something to Gage about our "relationship" tonight. After he was done, Gage went to his room to get ready.

"I'll be back in a while, but after that I'm heading out for breakfast with Ty."

"All right, I may not be here when you get back. I have some errands to run. But so you know, we need to leave around four fifteen, 'kay?"

"I'll see you later then." He smiled at me as he picked up his iPhone and headed for the door.

One of these times, that smile was going to make me come completely undone.

I glanced at my phone and cursed the speeding time. We needed to leave in ten minutes and I still hadn't tried on my dress. After Gage left that morning I'd taken a shower, gone with Jackie to get manicures, and done some quick shopping for a new summer dress since it was the middle of March and the weather had been in the mid-seventies all week. I would've had more than enough time to get ready, but I'd spent twice as long on my hair trying to make it look perfect. I couldn't think of one time in my life that I'd ever spent so much time on my appearance. The entire time I told myself I was just trying to look nice since we were going to a wedding, but I knew I was doing this for Gage. And that was a bad thing.

Finally happy with the big spiral curls in my hair, I ran to my closet and slipped on the dress. It was a deep-green halter that had reminded me of Gage's eyes, so naturally I'd fallen in love with it. It was form-fitting on my chest with a V-cut, making me have cleavage for practically the first time ever, and lightly flowed out to a few inches above my knees. It was the perfect mix of cute and sexy. I desperately wanted to pair it with the cowboy boots Gage's sister had bought me last summer but grabbed a pair of black heels instead. Glancing in my full-length mirror, I slowly turned to make sure there were no more tags on it and smiled at my reflection. I wasn't normally one to think this, but dang, I looked good.

Taking a deep breath, I opened my door and tried not to trip over myself as I took in the sight of Gage. He looked beautiful, in the most masculine way possible. He was wearing khaki slacks with a black button-up shirt that had the sleeves rolled up to his elbows. I looked up to his face and tried not to smile at his openmouthed stare.

"Wow, Cassidy. Just . . . wow." His eyes slowly raked over every inch of my body.

I tried to sound like he wasn't making my heart race and my

stomach do flip-flops. "Not so bad yourself, G." *Does he even know what he does to me?* "You ready?"

He simply nodded and led me out to his truck. The ride to the outdoor ceremony and reception was intense, to say the least. Neither of us could say anything; we both just kept looking at each other from the corners of our eyes. You could feel the tension between us and it took everything in me not to slide over toward him. Once we arrived and were around other people, the tension quickly left and we easily slipped back into our familiar banter. I only knew a handful of people there, other coworkers, and though we were all pretty close, I was immensely grateful that Gage had agreed to go with me. It would have been awkward without him, especially when Christian introduced himself; after one look at Gage's arm around my waist, he smiled politely and walked away. Stace was right; that guy was seriously cute, but he was no Gage. The ceremony was quick and moving, and Stacey looked stunning in a strapless mermaid-style dress.

Not long after the reception started, Stacey and my other co-workers pulled Gage and me onto the dance floor with them. I figured he would go to sit back down but he stayed out there having fun with the rest of us, and he never left my side. We joked and danced crazy with each other as everyone made up their own moves to some oldies, as well as newer music that you couldn't exactly dance to, not that anyone cared. I sucked in a quick gasp when Gage put his arms around my waist and pulled my back against his chest after a new song started. The song had a sensuous beat and it caused the tent to get a clublike feel. As our bodies slowly started moving together, I became hyperaware of every part of my body that was pressed against his and couldn't stop my breath from quickening. His hands were on my thighs, clutching the bottom of my dress, and I put my left hand back, sliding it through his hair. I dragged my hand out of his hair and down his cheek before putting both my hands on top of his, wishing he'd grab me harder, but wishing he'd let me go. This could only break my heart when the song ended. Putting a hand low on my stomach, he pushed us closer together as his other hand moved all of my hair to one shoulder. My head dropped back to his chest as his lips touched the base of my neck, a soft groan escaping my lips. My heart pounded in my chest as my insides tightened—was this really happening? Flashes of his coldness the day after our night on the hill at the ranch danced through my mind but I tried to push them away. He wouldn't do that to me again, right? I left my head resting against him until the song ended, allowing him to press his mouth to my neck and shoulder a few more times. I wanted to turn to look into his eyes, to question what was happening, but Lori grabbed my hand and pulled me to where the bride and groom were about to cut the cake before I got the chance.

I didn't see Gage again until after Russ had flung the garter and Stacey had thrown her bouquet into a sea of single women. I was starting to worry when the DJ stated there was only one song left before the happy couple would be taking off, when his warm hands found mine.

"One more?" he mumbled, his face a carefully composed mask.

"Of course." I tried to smile but his look was worrying me.

He put a hand gently on my waist and grabbed one of mine with his other, clutching it to his chest. I laid my head next to our joined hands as we swayed back and forth to our first slow dance of the evening.

Halfway through the song he spoke again. "Cassidy." I looked up into his eyes and he forced his gaze on something behind us, shaking his head slowly back and forth. "Look . . . I—"

I cut him off, not wanting to hear whatever regrets he was having from today. "Don't, Gage."

"No, I need to tell you this."

He held me close as I quickly tried to back away from him. I shut my eyes so he wouldn't see my hurt. "I get it. You don't—"

"I'm in love with you," he blurted out.

There was no way I had heard that correctly. My eyes popped open and I studied his face. "You— What?"

He blew out a long breath before looking at me again. His voice was so deep and full of emotion it caused a warm shiver to go up my spine. "I'm madly in love with you."

My eyes grew even wider as I let that sink in.

"I've tried to keep my feelings to myself, and I know I'm no good at it, but I can't keep doing it anymore. I don't just view you as a friend, Cass. I never have. I thought you should know. I know you don't feel the same but I'm tired of lying and hiding it from you."

"Why didn't you ever tell me?"

"When was I supposed to? You've been dating my cousin since we met."

A lump formed in my throat as I realized all the time I'd wasted thinking Gage could only ever be my friend. "Gage, I'm so in love with you."

"But Tyler . . . ?"

I shook my head and cleared my throat. "Wait, why did you think Tyler and I were together when we first met?"

"Because he told me you were." His brow furrowed.

For obvious reasons, I wasn't a fan of violence, but I instantly wanted to punch Tyler. "Tyler and I only dated for a few months.

You didn't want me and you left, and I was afraid of losing Tyler too, so I agreed to be his girlfriend a little while after you'd moved out."

Gage stopped swaying us, his face full of disbelief. "What? No." He shook his head. "You were the one who didn't want me. You told me you weren't okay with what I felt; you were with Tyler while we were at the ranch—he told me what you did for him the morning y'all left."

"What I did for him? What do you mean? Tyler was my best friend and nothing more. Gage, you were the one who told me to leave at the ranch. I was going to ask if I could stay with you, I was going to tell you that I was in love with you, and you kicked us out; Tyler told me you moved out of the apartment because you couldn't stand living with me. He'd been telling me that since the first day after we moved in with you."

"You were going to tell me you loved me, that last morning at the ranch?" When I nodded, Gage looked up and hissed a curse. Cupping my face in his hands, he pulled me close. "Tyler lied."

He crushed his mouth against mine and my knees buckled under the wave of emotions swarming through me, but Gage's hands left my face and he tightened his arms around me to keep me standing. How had I ever been able to kiss Tyler after having these kisses from Gage? He slid his tongue between my lips and I softly moaned into his mouth. A chill went through his body when I pressed myself closer to him and gripped his messy hair; I smiled at the knowledge that I could do that to him. Gage moved his lips across my jaw toward my ear.

"Let me take you home," he whispered huskily into my ear.

I'd let him take me anywhere.

We started making a beeline toward the cars but that was the same moment the bride and groom were going to take off, so we not-so-patiently stood in lines with everyone else and blew bubbles at them as they ran to their awaiting limo. Once their taillights had faded into the distance, Gage grabbed my hand, intertwined our fingers, and walked me to the passenger door of his truck. Planting one searing kiss on my lips, he gently lifted me up onto the seat, letting his fingers trail down from my waist to my knees. My heart about stopped.

He rounded the front and, after hopping in, pulled me across the seat and kissed me senseless. Not long after, with both of us struggling to catch our breath, he broke away, but I wasn't ready for it to be over just yet. I turned to better face him and eagerly pressed my lips to his neck, alternating between soft kisses and little nips, giving him a taste of the torture he'd put me through earlier. His fingers gripped my hips and a low moan escaped from him as I lightly trailed my lips along his jaw. The sound warmed my body and I could feel my control slowly slipping away. One of his hands made a trail down my thigh and curled around my knee, pulling me over so I was now sitting on him. I gasped and brought his mouth back to mine. I needed him. All of him. I ran my fingers through his hair and arched my back so I could press my body more intimately into his.

"Cass." He spoke around our kisses. "Cass, we should stop."

I bit down on his lower lip and gently tugged in response.

The next noise coming from his throat could only be described as the sexiest growl I've ever heard from a man. He fiercely attacked my mouth again and soon the windows were completely fogged up. Gage slid his hands under my dress and traveled up toward my underwear. Thank God they were cute and lacy tonight. His fingers had just started curling around the sides to pull down when his hands and mouth froze.

"No, Cassidy, we need to stop." His hands were now cupping

my cheeks and holding my face a couple inches from his. "I'm not going to do this here with you."

I shook my head and tried to kiss him again. "I don't care, Gage."

He stopped my advance and looked directly into my eyes. "No."

A huff of air escaped my lungs and I lowered my head dejectedly. I tried to move away, but his hands kept me anchored to him. Pressing his forehead to mine, he held us there while our breathing returned to normal. What felt like an eternity of trying to hide my embarrassment later, he finally slid me back onto the seat and pulled out of the parking area. Neither of us said anything until we were five minutes from the house, then he took my hand and pressed it lightly to his lips.

"Don't be upset, Cass . . . please."

Easy for him to say. I shrugged and looked out the window. "I'm not."

We pulled up to a red light and he took my chin in his hand, forcing me to look up at him. He knew I was lying. "I swear to you, it's not that I don't want to." I suppressed an annoyed laugh; of course he would say that. "But I'm not about to take that from you, especially in my truck. You deserve better than that." Someone honked behind us and he started driving again.

The distraction couldn't have come at a more perfect time, because my eyes were huge and my cheeks were now bright red. I'd forgotten that during my rant to Gage, Adam, and Dana about why Tyler had brought that girl back to our place. I'd also disclosed the fact that I was still carrying my V-card. *Someone please kill me now.*

As soon as the car slowed in the driveway, I left my heels in the truck, jumped out, and ran for the door, key already in hand.

"Cassidy, wait!" Gage yelled as he threw the truck in park.

I know it's childish, but it's what I've always done. Bad situation came up? Run away. Kind of hard to break that lovely habit. Only this time, I didn't have Tyler or Gage to run to. I thought about calling Jackie and packing a bag, but first I needed to get the damn door open. After almost dropping the key, I finally got it in the lock and opened it as Gage called my name again. I slammed the door shut behind me and raced for the closet in my room, grabbed my duffel bag and threw it onto the bed. I'd thrown the contents of one drawer into the bag and was heading for another drawer when Gage reached me.

Grabbing my arms, he spun me around so I was facing him, and though his grip didn't hurt, it effectively held me there. "Damn it, Cassidy, what are you doing?" He was searching my eyes, and I saw his were full of confusion and I watched as they filled with pain and fear when they flicked over to the bag on my bed. It could have been seconds, minutes, or hours. Time seemed to stop as my heart broke looking at this amazing man. Blowing out a breath, he stood up straighter and released my arms so he could push the hair away from my face. "Don't run to him. Not from me."

I let out a strangled sigh but couldn't think of what to say. *Hey, Gage, I appreciate you trying to protect my virtue. But in case you didn't notice, I just put myself out there and you freaking rejected me before bringing up the fact that I'm still an inexperienced virgin.* I wasn't mad at him; I got it. Who would want to be with someone who has absolutely no idea what they're doing?

"Please don't go, Cass. I want you here, with me."

I'd never had anyone ask me not to leave, and he'd just asked me twice. "I won't." It came out soft as a whisper. He raised an eyebrow and let out a humorless laugh. I quickly said, "I promise."

Pressing a soft kiss to my forehead, he released my hair and stepped away. His eyes looked so hurt and it took every ounce of control I had not to throw myself into his arms. He was giving me my space even though he was so sure I was about to leave him. It was practically written all over his face with a bright red Sharpie that he didn't think I would stay. With a final sigh he turned and left my room. When he hit the living room I heard his deep voice trailing behind him.

"I love you, Cassidy Jameson."

Dear Lord, I was so in love with him. I didn't think I could ever get enough of hearing those words coming from his lips. No matter how much my gut screamed at me to grab my stuff and leave before he had the chance to hurt me again, I forced myself to unpack the duffel bag and get ready for bed. Pulling on a pair of sleep shorts and an old concert tee, I went to the bathroom to wash my face and throw my hair into a messy bun. Hoping to assure him I wasn't running from him, I walked out to the living room and went to his door, but it was locked and there wasn't any light coming from under it. I sighed and reluctantly walked back to my room.

Gage

How HAD I FUCKED UP so bad last night? I couldn't believe what I'd heard from Cassidy about Tyler, and God, did it make me want to punch him all over again. Realizing just how much he'd lied to both of us to keep us from each other pissed me off to no end. But having Cassidy tell me she loved me took all that away. Kissing her and having her kiss me back again had felt so right, and I hated how much time we'd wasted, but damn if I was ever going to let anything stand between us again. And then I'd gone and done the job myself.

I'd checked on her that morning before my run, so I knew she'd stayed, but I didn't know if she was planning to, or if she was just waiting for today so she could move out. Thinking about her leaving punched a hole through my chest, but I wouldn't force her to say. I wouldn't force her to do anything; she'd had enough of that with Tyler. I would treat her like I always did and let her make the moves. It terrified me, not being in control of the situation, but I knew Cassidy needed to be the one to do this, so I'd sit back and wait. Praying to God that at the end of the day she was still in my place and wanting to be with me.

The coffee had just finished brewing when she stumbled out of her room and once again I was stunned at how beautiful she was. Her hair was a disaster, she looked half-asleep, and that Sex Pistols shirt about swallowed her whole, but she was still the most beautiful girl I'd ever seen. Her cheeks reddened when she saw me standing there and I held my breath until she staggered into my chest for our morning hug. *Thank you, God.*

"Mornin'."

She mumbled and I laughed.

"How are you?"

Those whiskey-colored eyes looked up at me and for a long while she didn't say a thing, just continued to stare at me. I wanted to kiss those naturally pouty lips so bad but I forced myself to let her do this at her own speed. "I'm fine," she finally said, her voice raspy from sleep. "You?"

"I'm good." *Not anymore,* I thought when she stepped away and made her coffee. She drank two cups without saying a word, and after she put her mug in the dishwasher she turned and faced me for a minute.

"We didn't get groceries yesterday, so we're going today."

She's getting food; does that mean she's staying? "All right, I'll take you."

"Uh, no, I always go with Jackie. She's going to pick me up soon, I'll just go with her."

Definitely leaving. Damn it. "I'll be here, Cassidy." *Whenever you decide to come back.* Before I could make an ass out of myself and drop to my knees and beg her to stay, I forced myself into my room and went to take a shower.

Cassidy

"I JUST DON'T UNDERSTAND. I thought he'd be happy I stayed." I looked up at Jackie to see her face full of disbelief. I'd just told her everything from the night before.

"Um, I'm sure he's thrilled that you stayed, but did you really think he was just going to pick you up in his arms and kiss you to death this morning?"

"Well . . . yeah."

Jackie snorted and picked up a packet of sliced fruit. "Cassidy, you ran from him last night and started packing a bag. Granted"—she cut me off with a hand when I started to speak—"you did stay. But he probably doesn't know how to act around you now. From what you're saying, he thought you *did* something with Tyler after the first time you kissed, and the second time, you run from him. What is he supposed to think?"

"Damn," I whispered.

"If it were me, I'd go right up to that boy and kiss him."

"Really? But what if I'm wrong about all of this? What if he was lying last night?"

"Do you think he was lying to you?" she retorted.

"No."

"Well, then it's settled. When you get back march that tiny ass of yours up to him and kiss him good. He'll wrap you up in his arms, you'll say, 'Take me to bed or lose me forever,' he'll go all Maverick on you and take you to his bed to ravish you for hours."

I rolled my eyes at her. "*Top Gun,* Jackie? Really?" I smiled at her and grabbed a grapefruit. "And your ass is smaller than mine."

JACKIE GAVE A WRY "GOOD LUCK" as I hopped out of her car and made my way to the house. For some reason, I still half expected Gage to slam his mouth down on mine as soon as I saw him, but that didn't happen. Actually, I'm not really sure *what* happened. I opened the door and found Gage sitting at the kitchen table with his head in his hands. As soon as I shut the door he looked up and his eyes got wide, his jaw dropped, and he just stared at me.

"Um, I'm just going to put these away . . . ?"

Gage stood up so fast, he had to catch the chair before it toppled to the floor, and he hurried to the kitchen with me to help me put away the groceries. He didn't say a word as we did it, though more than a few times I caught him looking at me from the corner of his eye. His weird silence confused and unnerved me, so instead of taking Jackie's advice right then and there, I did the cowardly thing and headed for my room.

"I'm just going to take a shower," I mumbled as I headed

away. When I reached my door I chanced a glance back at him to find him walking slowly toward his own room, his head down and a hand rubbing the back of his neck. "Gage?"

He turned quickly, his green eyes shifting through a range of emotions while his face stayed impassive.

Before I could talk myself out of it again, I walked quickly over to him, rose up on the balls of my feet, wrapped my hands around his head, and brought it down to mine. His arms pulled me into a tight embrace and he smiled through our kiss. It was long and slow and oh so perfect.

"You're not leaving?" he whispered against my lips.

"I can't." I shrugged, hoping he'd understand exactly what that meant.

Gage pressed his lips to mine again and lightly brushed my tongue with his. "God, I was afraid I'd never get to experience that again," he confessed when we separated.

"Wait, then why were you so distant this morning and when I got back?"

"I'm not Tyler, darlin', I'll never push you. I'm taking all my cues from you. But can you please tell me what happened when we got home last night?"

So he *was* waiting for me to do something? God, Jackie was brilliant. "Gage, I was humiliated. Still am, actually." He wasn't getting it. "You rejected me, only to remind me soon after that I've never been with anyone. It makes sense that you wouldn't want to be with me because of that, but that doesn't make it hurt any less."

"Whoa, wait . . . what? How did you even come up with that?" I opened my mouth to respond but he continued. "Cassidy, you being a virgin doesn't make me *not* want to be with you. If anything it makes me want you more, so I could claim you as mine. All I want is for your first time to be perfect, and my truck in a parking lot at your friend's wedding is anything but perfect."

"I really screwed last night up, didn't I?"

He laughed and wrapped his arms around me. "I'm just glad you stayed." He peppered my cheeks and lips with soft kisses.

"Gage, did you really just say you wanted to claim me?"

His husky laugh went all the way to my toes. "I've wanted nothing else since you spilled your beer on me."

"Oh God, we're back to that again? Are you ever going to let me live that down?"

"Never." He grinned wickedly as he bent down to kiss me again.

"Gage?" I asked through a breathy moan when he placed an openmouthed kiss on that spot behind my ear. "I'm in control with what we do?"

He brought his head up to look me in the eye. "Completely, Cass, do you want me to stop?"

"No, but if I do want to stop—"

"Then we stop. No questions asked."

I nodded and sucked my bottom lip into my mouth, thinking about finally making my dreams of him a reality . . . well, some of them anyway.

"Come on, let's just watch a movie." He mistook my silence and grabbed my hand, towing me to the couches.

Before we got to the couch, I tugged on his arm and slowly backed up toward his room.

His eyes darkened and he looked quickly between me and his bedroom door. "Cassidy, don't do this for me."

"I'm not," I said softly. "Did you already forget about last night?" I asked with a sly grin.

"You'll let me know—"

"I'll tell you when to stop, Gage," I assured him.

With that, he put his hands on the back of my thighs and picked me up, and walked us to his room, his mouth never leaving mine. He gently laid us down on his bed and kept most of his weight off me while still pressing his body to mine. Bringing his knees up, he put his weight on them and unzipped my thin hoodie before peeling it off me and covering my body with his again. My hands went to the bottom of his shirt and I pulled up until he helped me get it off, depositing it on top of my hoodie on the floor. I traced the contours of his shoulders, chest, and stomach while letting my eyes memorize every square inch of his upper body. He had an amazing body—I already knew that—but to be able to freely touch it, and have the weight of it pressing down on me . . . I couldn't help but smile as I lifted my head off the pillows to kiss him again. He met my kiss greedily and soon I was shivering when he moved lower and his teeth lightly grazed my throat. Arching my back to press my chest into him, I silently willed him to touch me. His kisses alone were making my insides heat, but I wanted more. It took me another minute to realize he wouldn't do anything until I told him. I still couldn't believe he was putting me in control.

"Gage," I said around his mouth, and he just moved it to kiss along my jaw.

"Tell me what you want, darlin'."

"Undress me."

I was expecting him to rip my clothes off, but God, what he did was so. Much. Better. The first to go was my shirt, and as he slid it up inch by inch, his mouth and tongue followed the hem of my shirt. When it was finally off, he captured my mouth with his and kissed me until I was completely breathless. Then he tortured me the exact same way with my jeans, placing hot, open-mouthed kisses all the way down my hips, thighs, calves, and feet. I knew I should have been at the very least a little embarrassed by the way I was writhing beneath him, but I just couldn't bring myself to care right now. He hadn't even touched me yet and already I was shuddering with pleasure. He retraced his way up my body and, without lifting his head from my upper stomach, brought his hands under my back and unhooked my bra, slid the straps off my shoulders, and pulled it from my body.

Placing a hand on either side of me, he lifted himself off me and shamelessly studied every inch of me. One hand came up slowly and touched down on my lower stomach toward my hip. As soon as the tips of his fingers were on my skin I knew where they were, what he was looking at, and my body instantly locked up. I'd never let anyone other than Tyler purposefully see my scars, but I didn't exactly have a choice since he was the one who always took care of me. How could I have forgotten about the hideous lines marking my body? *Especially* at a time like this. I didn't want Gage to see this part of me. *God, I should have waited until it was completely dark in the room!* He'd seen the bruises for a brief moment when I moved here, but I'm sure he hadn't even noticed these the night I walked here from Tyler's. I preferred it that way. There were only two outcomes to this: disgust and pity. Neither of which I could live with coming from him. My hands blurred as one tried to push him away and the other stupidly tried to cover the biggest scar on my torso.

"Stop." Gage's voice came out so softly I almost didn't hear it.

"Please let me put a shirt on," I begged shakily.

"No, babe." He gently but effectively pinned my hands against the bed. "I want to see you."

"Gage—" I sucked in a deep breath as he dipped his head and gently placed his lips on the right side of the large scar and slowly made his way to the left.

Without looking back up at me, he broke the contact with my skin until he came upon another, slightly smaller scar and bent to kiss there as well. Over and over, Gage kissed my stomach, thighs, arms, and shoulders until every scar on my front made by my mom and stepdad had been covered. When he was done, he resumed his earlier study. Gage said something I couldn't make out, and after another minute looked directly into my eyes, his green ones dark and full of want. "You're perfect, Cassidy."

Gage

OH MY GOD, how is she mine? I couldn't have taken my eyes away from her even if I wanted to, which I definitely didn't. Her small body lay there; the only part moving was her chest, which was rapidly rising and falling as she watched me look at her. "So beautiful," I muttered, and she was. Every part of her, scars and all, was absolutely beautiful.

My eyes raked over her perfectly curved hips and flat stomach leading up to a tiny waist and perfect breasts. *Perfect.* There was no other word for this girl lying underneath me. How could I have wasted a second of my time on any other woman than her? And yet, I'd never paid a tenth of the attention to them that I was giving to Cassidy. Every other woman had been a means to the end result, but I could have spent the rest of the night simply looking at Cassidy, and it wouldn't have been long enough. My jeans were uncomfortably tight, but I resisted the urge to let them join the rest of the clothes on the floor and continued my visual exploration of her. I glanced over her small shoulders, dipping into her neck and up her throat before looking at her full lips, swollen from kissing and partially open. And finally, finally, I reached her gold eyes, bright with unshed tears. *Mine. This beautiful girl is mine.*

"You're perfect, Cassidy."

A sound that was a mix between a laugh and a sob left her and she tore her arms from under my hands and threw them around my neck, burying her head in the crook of my neck. She was shaking slightly and I ran my hand through her long, thick hair.

"Are you okay?" I asked when she still didn't let me go.

Her face flashed before mine for only a second before disappearing again down my chest, where she began to place damn near torturous openmouthed kisses. But that second was enough; her eyes were still wet but she had the softest, most beautiful smile I'd ever seen on her. It was more than just my smile, and I wanted to see it again.

With a gentle tug of her hair, I brought her lips back to mine. They moved against each other for a short time and I about thanked God out loud when she arched her back and guided my head to her chest. Her hands moved to the top of my jeans when I brought my mouth to the swell of her breast and I groaned against her skin at the extra space she'd given me by undoing my jeans and pulling them down slightly.

"Touch me," she urged, and I once again forced myself to move slowly.

My fingers had just glided over the soft cotton of her underwear and curled around the top, ready to push them down, when the doorbell rang quickly three times. "Ignore it," I growled against her breast.

"'Kay." Her voice was low and breathy and a shiver went up her body when my fingers trailed over her heat as I pulled down her underwear. The bell sounded again and her body locked up. "The guys are coming for the game and dinner!"

I almost told her that they would get the hint when I remembered I'd given Adam a key after the whole Popsicle Cassidy incident. *Shit.* "Adam has a key," I said in a rush just as I heard the front door open and voices enter the house. With a frustrated growl, I kissed her hard one more time, jumped off her, and had my shirt back on in a few seconds. Adjusting my painfully hard erection and buttoning up my pants again, I looked back to see a flushed and frustrated Cassidy watching me from the bed. "I'll tell them to go."

"No, it's fine. They'll be gone later tonight." There was so much promise in that last sentence; I knew it'd have to be enough to get me through the game.

I nodded and opened the door slightly so I could slip out without anyone seeing in if they were near the hall. Glad I did, because Ethan was just starting to walk down it.

"Hey, man, we thought you guys weren't here."

"Nah, I was just busy. Anyone want a beer?" I called as I walked uncomfortably into the kitchen, hoping to get their focus away from my bedroom door. It was a futile attempt though, because as soon as a fully clothed Cassidy stepped out with her somewhat messed-up hair and red cheeks, the living room went completely silent.

My beautiful girl straightened her shoulders and walked confidently into the kitchen, keeping her eyes on me the entire time. "Any requests for dinner tonight?" she asked when she finally looked at them. I saw her cheeks flush even darker, but she kept her chin up as they all gawked at her.

Ethan glanced at me with a sly grin and mouthed, *Fucking finally,* before looking back at Cass. "Uh, can you make your inside-out burgers?"

"Sure." She glanced at the rest of the guys, who still weren't talking, but Adam was smiling at her. Trying to avoid the stares, she set about getting out a massive amount of snacks for us. When she pulled all the ingredients out of the fridge for the burgers and put them on the counter, I stepped up behind her and put a hand on each side of her.

"You okay, darlin'?" If the guys didn't start talking soon, *I* was going to get uncomfortable.

"I'm great." Her head tilted back and she smiled widely at me; her hand came up around my neck and brought my head down for a slow kiss in front of everyone. Knowing how much she hated showing affection with Ty in front of anyone, that kiss meant the damn world.

I smiled down at her and kissed her softly once more before straightening up and facing the guys and a gleefully happy Dana and Jackie, who must have come in sometime after I'd pinned Cassidy against the counter. They shuffled past me toward the kitchen and I grabbed the remote out of Jake's hand and turned on the TV.

Tossing the remote back at his stomach, I said, loud enough for him and Grant to hear me, "You come over to watch the game or stare at my girl? 'Cause if it's the latter, y'all can leave."

"You and Cassi?" Jake finally asked with raised brows.

"Yeah, me and Cass. If you have a problem with it, you can take that as another invitation to get the hell out."

"I'm good," he said, and I looked up at Grant, who had just pulled his eyes away from Cassidy and given me a satisfied smirk before settling into one of the couches.

I FINISHED SAYING BYE to Grant and Jake after practically throwing them out of the house. Everyone else had left an hour before, and I wasn't dumb enough not to realize they were staying to piss me off. I'd had a hard-on practically the entire night and I couldn't stop touching Cassidy in some way or another. We'd been anxiously waiting for everyone to leave, and those two settled in further and started flipping through the guide on my TV when the game was done. Trying to give them a hint, Cass and I had done the dishes and stood in the kitchen talking after we were done. When I realized they weren't going on their own, I made sure to let them know their time was up.

Turning around after dead-bolting the door, I caught sight of Cassidy dropping her shirt to the floor with a *Come get me* look on her face as she turned to go down the hall toward my room. *Hell. Yeah. My girl is damn sexy.* I didn't wait for the bedroom either; my shirt was forgotten somewhere in the living room and my jeans made it as far as the bedroom door before being left behind as well. Cassidy had just slipped off her bra, and I picked her up and tossed her on the bed; a throaty laugh filled the room as she landed. Before the bed was done settling from my having her thrown on, I was on top of her and claiming her mouth. She moaned and secured me to her body with her arms and legs, but it wasn't close enough . . . I doubted it ever would be. I would always want to be closer to my Cassidy.

Her hands trailed up my back, over my shoulders, and then one continued down to my hand, which was in her thick hair. Grabbing my fingers, she moved my hand and slowly brought it down her body, keeping our fingers intertwined as she led our hands to remove her underwear. I stopped kissing her to watch our hands make their way back up her leg and stop below her left hip. Looking down into her now-dark eyes, I held her gaze as I took my hand from hers and slowly ran it over her before sliding one finger inside. She gasped and let her head fall back as her eyes fluttered shut and her mouth opened slightly. I watched her face as every sensation ran through her body and soon added a second finger, earning a soft whimper from her. Holy hell, she was so tight. Glancing down again, I watched my hand teasing her body and got the strongest urge to do something I'd never done. I know I told her she was in control, and she was, but I couldn't stop myself from asking. Hell, I was about ready to beg her to let me do this for her.

"Darlin', I—"

"Please, Gage," she said soft as a whisper, and her heavy-lidded eyes looked up at me. "I've wanted and dreamed about this for so long. I don't want you to stop." She brought her shaky hands up to my hips and slid the band of my boxer-briefs down enough to take my erection in her hands, and a shiver ran through my body.

She'd barely touched me and already I had to work at not coming yet. I'd never had an issue with this, but then again, it'd never been Cassidy touching me. I focused all my attention on what I was doing for her and couldn't wait another second to take what I wanted. The instant loss of her hands on me was like a physical blow, but this was about her. Sliding my body down the bed, I continued to work her with my fingers and leaned forward to taste her. Cassidy roughly whispered my name and her hands flew to my head, but instead of pulling me away like I was expecting, she held it in place. And thank God, because now that I had a taste of her, I didn't want to stop.

When her body shook and she cried out my name, I pulled my boxer-briefs off the rest of the way and positioned myself between her thighs. She looked up at me after I cupped her cheek with a hand and I kept our gazes locked on each other. "You say stop and we'll stop. Okay?"

Cassidy nodded and wiggled beneath me as she said, "I want this, don't stop."

All the muscles in my body locked and I clenched my jaw as I slowly entered her. God, she was so damn tight. "Fuck," I growled. I saw the uncomfortable pleasure on her face and gave her time as her body stretched around me. I wasn't even halfway in when her body locked and she huffed out harshly. I looked into her wide, trusting eyes. "Are you sure you're ready for this, Cass?" The first girl I'd ever been with had been a virgin, but since her, Cassidy was the only other one. My first time I hadn't realized what I was doing until it was practically over, and even then I didn't care that she was probably hurting. But knowing I was about to deliberately hurt Cassidy had my chest tightening.

Her only answer was to hitch her knees up onto my hips and wrap her hands around my neck.

I pulled back slightly and pushed back in the inch I'd just given up a few times to ready her. The fourth time I pulled back farther before filling her with my entire length in one swift, but as gentle as possible, thrust. Cassidy's mouth and eyes clamped shut as her forehead pressed into my neck and her hold on me tightened. A whimper escaped her, and there was no doubt in my damn mind that it was a bad one. I didn't move until she lay back against the pillow, and when I saw her face I about died. Her eyes were bright and a few tears were on her cheeks and spilling down into her hair. The pain in her face was evident, as was the love she had for me.

"Cassidy—" I whispered as I slowly started to pull out.

When she realized what I was doing, her eyes went wide and she dug her heels into my lower back as she shook her head. "No, Gage, don't."

"I'm hurting you."

"It's okay, I'm fine." Her voice shook slightly and my jaw clenched. "You'll crush me if you stop now. I want this with you so bad, don't stop this. I love you."

Pressing my lips to hers, I slowly inched my way back in and cringed when another muffled cry left her chest. "I love you too, darlin'."

I kept everything slow and easy for a few minutes, listening intently to every sound she made and watching every expression cross her face. Her head dropped back first, then another couple minutes after that her body completely relaxed and her sounds started turning into breathy moans. I picked up the pace slightly and later, when she dug her nails into my back and her thighs tightened around me as she came for the second time, I pulled all the way out and slammed back into her. And God, that erotic moan that sounded in my ear almost pushed me over the edge. She started matching me thrust for thrust and soon her moans turned into pleas to go faster, harder, and I was more than happy to give my girl what she wanted. Right before I gave myself over to her, I felt her tightening around me for the third time. God, she was so freakin' responsive! I ground my teeth and held off until she came undone once again; her name ripped from my throat as I came crashing down with her. My arms gave out and I rolled us so she lay on top of me as our breathing slowed and returned to normal.

Cassidy's eyes started growing heavy, so I kept her in my arms as I rolled off the bed and walked her into my bathroom. I set her on her feet, turned on the shower, and walked toward the trash to discard the condom when I stopped dead. Oh. Shit.

"Gage? Are you okay?" She ran to my side and looked down to where my gaze was and covered her mouth as her cheeks got red. "Oh God, that's really embarrassing."

I looked at her and looked back down, realizing what she was seeing. Her innocence was on me, and I knew it was on her as well, which was why I'd brought us in here. But that's not what stopped me. I hooked one arm around her and brought her face up to look at me. "Cassidy, you were a virgin, that's nothing to be embarrassed about. But, darlin'—I didn't wear a condom."

She still looked mortified but shook her head and dismissed my words with a wave of her hand. "I know, I'm on the pill to regulate my cycle. It's okay."

Hearing that relieved me, but I still couldn't believe it hadn't once crossed my mind. I'd never once forgotten to wear a condom; it was always my first thought as well as my last when it came to other women. But I guess I should have known I wouldn't be able to think of anything but what was happening when I was with Cassidy. Now that I knew she was on the pill, I was actually excited as I realized I didn't want anything to be between us ever. "Cassidy, look at me. You just gave me something incredibly special; I'm going to cherish that, and tonight, forever. Tonight was perfect, don't be embarrassed about it, okay?"

She nodded and smiled when I kissed her quickly.

Cassidy

MY HEART WAS SWELLING as Gage once again took care of me in his shower. This time was vastly different from the first, but it somehow made me fall in love with him even more. His hands were tender as they washed my hair and my body. And as I did the same for him, he continued to pull me into his arms and press light kisses to my lips and whisper in my ear everything from sweet nothings, to his love, to how he wanted to have his dirty way with me again.

Experiencing all of that with Gage was more than I could have ever hoped for or imagined. He was right, tonight was perfect. It had hurt way worse than I was expecting, but he'd been so gentle with me until I was ready for more, and then the more had been earth-shattering and yet still so full of passion that I didn't want it to ever end.

When we were dried off, he led me back into his room and pulled me onto the bed before bringing me into his arms and curling his body around mine. It reminded me of that night on the ranch and I relaxed into his chest, knowing that this time, Tyler wouldn't be around to ruin us the next day.

"Do you ever think about that night?" he asked as he pulled my arm up and ran his thumb over my tattoo. Apparently our curling up in each other's arms hadn't reminded only me of the ranch.

"All the time. Until tonight, that was the best night of my life," I answered softly, and looked at the cluster of stars with him. "I had finally acknowledged that you would never be in my life the way I wanted you to be. But you had turned my life completely upside down, and I knew I'd never be the same, just as I knew I'd never find anyone like you. I didn't want to ever forget you or that night together. Knowing the constellation was special to you too, and having found out on that night together, I decided I wanted that to be my reminder of you."

Gage kissed the top of my head. "I've been wondering since the first time I saw it if that night had anything to do with it. And, Cassidy?"

"Hmm?"

"You won't ever have to worry about forgetting me. I'm not going anywhere."

I thought about his moving out without a word. "Promise?"

"I promise." His arm tightened around my waist and my eyes drifted shut.

GAGE WOKE ME UP early the next morning with soft kisses to my neck and I rolled over to face him, trying to ignore the deep ache that radiated between my legs and low in my stomach. An involuntary groan left my lips and he looked up at me, worried.

"Are you feeling okay?"

"Honestly, I feel amazing." And I really did. Waking up in his arms knowing everything was finally okay made me feel better than amazing. "A little sore, but it's a good sore."

"I'm sorry for hurting you," he said against my neck, and I felt his erection against my stomach.

Funny that when that happened with Tyler, even if we were fully clothed, I hated it. Now, lying here naked with Gage, I couldn't think of a better way to wake up. "I'm not; I wouldn't mind if you did it again either."

His lips froze and he lifted his head so his dark green eyes were searching mine. "Cassidy, I don't—"

From his expression, I knew he thought he'd be hurting me again, but I cut him off and faked hurt. "Oh . . . I understand, I'll just go get ready . . ." I trailed off and laughed when he rolled me back underneath him and pressed his mouth onto mine.

"You are seriously mistaken if you think I don't want you." He ground his hips against mine and separated my legs with his knee. "Sorry, darlin', but you're gonna be late for work today."

I groaned in both pleasure and slight pain when he pushed into me. "I'm sure I'll get over it."

12

Gage

I HONESTLY THOUGHT nothing could bring me down from the mood I was in. Cassidy and I spent every spare moment together, and while our times together in bed . . . and the shower . . . and the couch . . . and the kitchen table . . . hell, all our times *together* were amazing, I loved just spending time with her too. It was better than before; now that neither of us was trying to hide our feelings for the other, we were able to talk freely about everything. Every night I fell asleep with her in my arms and woke the same. It had almost been a week since the wedding, and like I said, I thought nothing could bring me down. But then I saw Tyler at school.

"Son of a bitch . . . this isn't gonna end well."

"Sorry, what?" I glanced over at Ethan, then followed his stare over to see Tyler stalking toward us. "Crap, he knows."

"Were you gonna tell me?" he demanded when he reached us.

I blew out a deep breath to relax myself; I really didn't want to do this on campus of all places. "Tell you what, exactly?"

"Don't play dumb with me, Gage. You're sleeping with Cassi."

I kept my mouth shut, letting my silence answer for me.

"I can't believe this!"

"Ty, come on, man. Let's talk about this somewhere else."

He let out a frustrated laugh and ran a hand roughly through his hair. "My own cousin is fucking my girlfriend!"

My eyes narrowed and I spoke through clenched teeth. "First off, she ain't your anything. Second, we know what you were doing. We know you played both of us."

Tyler's eyes widened momentarily.

"Yeah, we told each other *everything*. Every damn thing you told us. And I gotta say, *cousin*," I sneered, "that's a really fuckin' shitty thing to do. You're gonna pull the family card with me? You knew how I felt about her and you were so threatened by that because she felt the same that you had to tell me she was your girlfriend? That she was blowing you when you knew, you *knew* we'd just spent the night together? You had to tell her that I couldn't stand her and later that I thought of her like a sister? Ty, man, you were like a brother to me. And you repeatedly screwed both me and Cassidy over."

"I told you she was mine and you wouldn't back off!"

"Once again, you hurt Cassidy. Do you know how much I hate you for everything you've put her through over the years?" I stepped closer so our chests were touching and lowered my voice so it was practically a growl. "You let her get beat. You almost let her die by their hands. You broke her heart over and over again because she found someone she wanted to be with. And when you weren't getting any, you broke her heart another way by breaking whatever fucked-up bond the two of y'all had by bringing home another girl . . . forcing her to leave . . . and almost letting her die again." I backed up a step when his body started vibrating. I wasn't finished with him yet, but I wasn't about to get in a fistfight with him out in public. "I never understood why she needed you in her life, and it pissed me off more than I could ever care to explain. But I don't have to worry about it now; she finally sees you, Ty. So, I guess I can thank you for that at least. I'll never have to watch her run to you again. Thank God."

"She's mine. She'll always be mine. You weren't there for everything in her life. You didn't take care of her . . . keep her alive. I did!" He hissed, "I'm what's best for her. I'm what's safe and familiar and comfortable to her. Cassi will always come back to me. I look forward to the day she runs from you to me. And trust me, that day will come. When it does, I'm not letting her go again." Before I could speak, he continued. "So enjoy her while you have her, because in the end, it's me and her."

Screw being in public. My hands curled into fists and I took a step toward him but Ethan stepped up and pushed me back, saying, "Let it go, Gage. Just let it go."

"It'll always be me and Cassidy. You've got a temper; you think with her life she's going to want to be with a hothead just waiting to explode? Or that I would *let* her go into a life where she would get the same treatment she had for twelve years?"

"I would never touch her that way and you know that!" I shrugged Ethan off and stepped back up to my cousin, grabbing the collar of his shirt in my fists.

He glanced down to my shaking hands and scoffed. "Actually, I don't, and she has no idea what she's getting into with you. The minute she catches a glimpse of your anger—because we both know she didn't see anything that morning at your place—she'll be gone and I'll be there to hold her and take her away from it, like I always have."

"And let me guess, you're gonna try to make that happen again, am I right?"

He tapped my clenched fist and Ethan put his hand on my shoulder to pull me back again. "Like I said . . . temper." With a twisted smirk, Tyler pulled my hands off, turned, and headed back the way he'd come.

"Seriously, Gage, no hard feelings or anything, but your cousin is a dick," Ethan said as he slapped me on the back. "C'mon, we gotta get to class."

I watched as Tyler rounded the corner, then checked my watch. "Nah, I'm gonna skip today."

"Need to go unwind? We can grab a beer."

"I'm gonna get Cass. Catch you later, yeah?"

Ethan smirked. "Yeah, I bet Cassi is *much* better at helping you calm down than a beer."

"Smartass."

"Have fun *unwinding,* Gage." He winked as he started backward, then suddenly stopped. "On second thought, Jackie's already home waiting for me . . . unwinding sounds like a damn good idea right about now." He grinned wickedly and grabbed his keys out of his pocket, heading toward his car down the street.

I checked my watch again and took off for my truck, hoping I made it to Starbucks before Cassidy started walking home.

Cassidy

"LORI, YOU OKAY?" How could she walk out of the bathroom smiling? She'd just puked.

"I'm great! Sorry I had to run out in the middle of taking the order though."

"No worries, do you want to go home now, and I'll work your last two hours?" I really was exhausted; Gage and I had hardly slept that week—not that I was complaining—and I was looking forward to getting a nap in before he got home in a few hours.

"No way! You didn't even take your lunch, and don't think I didn't realize you clocked out for it and continued to work. Seriously, Cassi, I'm fine. Go home! I'll see you next week." She popped a piece of gum in her mouth and started rocking out to the song playing throughout the café as she went about washing her hands before fixing the pastry case.

Pregnant women. I swear, they're crazy.

I glanced over at one of our newer guys and grimaced. He made perfect drinks, but I made a mental note to never put him on bar again during a Friday morning since he tended to take his time on each one. This was only my second time working with him, but one of the other shift leaders said he'd done bar really well a few times during the afternoon, then again last weekend; however, I'd had to take over for him four different times when we got slammed.

"Hey, Jesse, want me to get you caught up before I go?"

His almost-black eyes widened slightly with relief, but he kept his face composed. "You can say it, Cassi, I suck at this."

"You don't." I laughed and moved in front of the bar where the two espresso machines sat side by side, steaming milk on each machine and getting espresso shots ready as well. "You've only been on bar a few times and it's been during dead hours. First few Monday and Friday mornings will be a little overwhelming, but you'll get it."

Jesse blew out a deep breath and grabbed two of the cups to

make tea. "And there you go putting me to shame in no time at all."

"Jesse," I said softly, and caught his eye before turning to grab the shots and dump them into cups and start new ones, "if I've been embarrassing you because of this, let me know. I really was just trying to help; I know how stressful it can be."

A deep laugh rumbled out of his chest and he smiled crookedly at me. "You're not embarrassing me. I feel like I'm just makin' an ass outta myself in front of you."

"Uh, you're not. You're learning, like we all had to." I called out three drinks for the café and gave two to the girl at the drive-thru register as Jesse handed her the two teas. His arm brushed mine so I took an unnecessary step away to grab the three milk pitchers and clean them out.

Jesse began making the last two drinks sitting on the bar and I purposefully took my time cleaning and restocking the area so I could watch to see if there was anything I could pick out that he could change to help on his times. Unfortunately, there wasn't. He just needed to speed up, and now that he had all the drinks down, I had no doubt he would. He called out the two drinks, cleaned up, and for the third time since he'd started making those last two drinks his right hand went down to his leg and touched it quickly before he sighed heavily and kept wiping down the bar.

"Your phone vibrating?"

He glanced over his shoulder with that crooked smile that was really too adorable for his own good. "That obvious, huh?"

I shrugged. "Maybe I'm just observant."

"Maybe . . . or maybe you're just checking me out."

My eyes widened and my stupid cheeks instantly filled with heat. "Uh, no. Definitely not."

"Not like I haven't been doing the same to you."

"Jesse . . ." I began to tell him about Gage but his grin and laughing eyes fell as his hand went back to his leg. "You know I don't mind if you check your phone as long as it doesn't interfere with taking or filling orders. If you want to run to the back and take a ten-minute break, I'll cover."

He glanced down at his thick-banded watch. "Cassi, you were supposed to be off five minutes ago."

"Well, whoever it is obviously needs to talk to you if they've called you four times in a row. I'm fine, go take a break."

Jesse shook his head and tried to force a smile but didn't succeed. "I'm sorry, but I know who it is and it's most likely an emergency. I won't take my full break. I'll be right back, I swear."

I finished stocking the bar, checked the whipped creams and syrups to make sure they weren't going to be running out any time soon, and stocked the cups just as Jenn came back in.

"So sorry! There was a line at the bank that took forever. I'm here now, go home. And Lori told me about your lunch, Cassi." She narrowed her eyes at me. "You should actually be *taking* your lunch, not just saying you are."

"They were slammed all morning, it wouldn't have been right to leave." I punched in my numbers to clock out and leaned over to her. "Hey, I sent Jesse on a ten; his phone kept going off in his pocket and he looked nervous about it. I mean, it was on vibrate and all, but every time it went off, his face just dropped and got really pale. Whoever it was called four times in a row that I noticed. They could have been calling for longer. He said he knew who was calling and it was probably an emergency. He's in the back right now and I'll see if he's good before I head out, but I just wanted to warn you. I don't know what the emergency is or if it's something that'll make him have to leave; in case it is I didn't want you to be blindsided."

"Oh, that sucks." She chewed on her bottom lip as she looked over the schedule to see who was coming in next. "Hmm, well if he has to, at least we have two more people coming in within the hour." Jenn looked quickly at the door that led to the back, then leaned closer. "He's seriously hot though, right?"

I untied my apron and moved it over my head. "Jesse? Yeah, I guess." No *I guess* about that guy; he was some serious eye candy. But when compared to Gage? There really was no competition. Jesse was probably a little shorter than Ty and had naturally olive-tan skin with eyes so dark they were almost black, matching his short hair. Like Ty, though, he looked like he'd spent a lot of time at the gym. And while it looked good on him, especially in the white button-down shirt he was wearing with the sleeves rolled up to his forearms, I preferred Gage's longer muscles from working on the ranch all his life rather than the compacted ones the guys got from bulking up in a gym.

"You guess? Oh, Cassi, I know you're taken, but, girl, I know you're not blind. Now go see if he's coming back, then get your ass home."

"Yeah, yeah . . . I'm leaving." I walked to the back and tried not to make it obvious I was walking silently so I could hear Jesse's conversation.

"Do you need me to come home? . . . You sure? . . . Yeah, okay . . . Don't worry about it, I'll get another job . . . No, I don't want you to worry, I'm serious, I'm gonna take care of you, all right? . . . All right, love you too, see you when I get home." As I silently rounded the corner, Jesse dropped to the chair at the desk and let his head fall into his hands. "Son of a bitch."

I cleared my throat and felt guilty for eavesdropping when he spun around quickly. "Everything okay, or do you need to leave?"

He stood and shook his head. "Nah, I'm good. Thanks for giving me that break."

"Of course . . . Uh, Jesse? Are we going to have to look for someone else to work mornings?" When his expression turned to complete confusion, I continued. "I heard you say you were going to get another job?"

"Oh, no, nothing like that. I just need to get an additional job for a while." His face was so tortured I had the oddest urge to hug him.

"Do you want to talk about it?"

"No—" His phone started vibrating again and he dragged his hand roughly over his head before answering it. "Yeah, Ma? . . . No, that's fine, I'll pick some up on my way home . . . Do you need anything else? . . . Okay, if you do just call and leave a message, I'm about to go back to work . . . Love you too." Jesse sighed deeply and glanced up at me from under thick lashes as he tapped his phone in his hand a few times. "My mom is dying. She's got cancer and now it's just spreading real fast. Dad was always a douche, but as soon as she found out she had cancer over a year ago, he bailed and took all the money. She hadn't worked a day since they married and couldn't really start back up then. I'd been in the air force for almost four years when we found out. I kept sending her all my money, but she can't even take care of herself anymore. So when it came time to reenlist just a month and a half later, I decided not to and moved back. I've been going to the police academy at night and have been working a few odds-and-ends jobs, but with her bills my money ran out kinda quick." He looked around, embarrassed, and took another deep breath in. "So here I am. Really I would have taken any job that paid somewhat decent and had benefits, but it's not cutting it." He lifted up the phone as if to say that's what the call had been about. "I'm about to graduate from the academy, but then I still have to apply to departments and who knows how long it'll take to get hired on somewhere. So, as you now know, I gotta find something to go with Starbucks for now."

"Jesse, I'm so sorry. Is there anything I can do?"

"No, that's not why I told you. It's just . . . it's kind of nice to just tell someone, you know?"

"Yeah. What does she need you to get? I can go pick it up for you so you don't have to make a stop on the way home."

"Cassi." His dark eyes lit up and that crooked grin was back. "You're a sweetheart, but no." He glanced at his watch and frowned at me. "Because of me you've been here an extra twenty minutes. Go home, I'll see you next week, right?"

I tried to keep my smile to myself. "Right." I stood there as he walked past me to go back onto the floor and tried not to flinch when he brushed his hand against my arm. I needed to make it a point to tell him about Gage soon. I sighed and walked over to where we kept the employee files, glanced around to make sure no one had come in there, and hurried to jot down Jesse's address on a piece of paper. I was sure I could get in trouble for looking it up, but it was for a good reason. I slid the paper into my back pocket and walked out of the back room, my head bent down as I texted Gage to let him know I was about to walk home. For whatever reason it made him feel better knowing when I left and when I got home—something about knowing I was safe. I'd just hit send when I heard a deep gravelly voice.

"Hey, darlin'."

My heart took off and a huge grin spread across my face as I quickly took the last few steps that separated us. Gage wrapped his arms around my waist and lifted me slightly to kiss me good and hard before setting me back down. "Were your classes canceled?"

"Wasn't feelin' up to it today." His green eyes glanced up above my head before focusing back on me. "How was work?"

"It was all right, kinda busy. Want something before we go? I'm exhausted and have a feeling now that you're skipping your classes I'm not going to get any sleep."

Gage's lips curved up in a slow, incredibly sexy smile that had my stomach heating. "And I have a feeling you're right. Let's grab some coffee."

We ordered, and after Jenn, Krista, and Lori—Lori . . . pregnant, married Lori—all drooled over Gage again, we stood off to the side of the bar talking quietly, me in Gage's big arms.

"You wanna tell me why this guy keeps looking at me like he's gonna jump over the counter and rip you away from me?"

My brows bunched together and I turned around to see Jesse look back down at the drinks. "Jesse?" I chuckled softly. "I don't think he knew I had a boyfriend."

Gage's eyes narrowed again and he looked up at Jesse. I swear his chest rumbled and something that sounded like a growl left his throat.

"Easy there, tiger," I whispered, and wrapped a hand around his neck so he'd look at me again. "Trust me when I say there is *no* reason for you to worry about him. But when we get to your truck, I do want to talk to you about him."

His body tensed. "Did he try something with you?"

"No, Gage, seriously, it's nothing like that. You need to calm down. I'm telling you, you don't have to worry about that, it's about his mom. We'll talk on the way home, all right?"

"Drinks are done, Cassi," Jesse said gruffly from behind the bar.

I grabbed Gage's hand and walked to the counter. "Thanks, Jess. Jesse, this is my boyfriend, Gage. Gage, this is Jesse."

Jesse nodded his head to himself as he cleaned off the bar. "Boyfriend." He muttered something that sounded dangerously close to "Figures." "Great girl you got there, Gage."

"Isn't she?" Gage said, challenging him with a smirk, and unlinked our hands to wrap his arm around my shoulders as he turned us to leave the café.

"Well, you didn't have to be rude," I said when we got into the truck. "Look, after the way you just reacted to him, this might be a bad idea, but I want to cook a few dinners for his mom."

Gage's head whipped to the side to look at me like I was insane, his hand halted in the air on the way to turn on the car.

"Let me explain first." I told him what Jesse had told me before I left and watched as Gage's frustrated glare turned to guilt. "So, I was thinking I could cook a few meals that they could eat now, and some they could put in the freezer for later. I don't even care if Jesse knows it's from us—actually I'd prefer he didn't—but I want to help out somehow. And this is the only way I know how."

"God, I feel like an ass now."

"As you should," I teased, and slid over the seat to lean my head on his shoulder. "We don't have to, it was just an idea."

"No, it's a good idea, we'll do it today. Well, *you'll* do it today; I'll just watch you and help you take it over there." He pressed me closer and kissed the top of my head. "God, you're sweet."

I just shook my head and smiled softly. "Thanks for agreeing to help, Gage."

WE STOPPED BY THE STORE on the way back home to get enough food to make meals to last them at least a week and started preparing dishes right away. It didn't last long though; not even twenty minutes in, Gage and I ended up on the kitchen floor making love to each other. After another round in the bedroom, we made our way back out to the food and spent the next few hours making things that could last for a few days and preparing foods that could sit in the freezer until they popped it into the oven.

Gage was bringing the last load of food up to Jesse's porch when the front door suddenly opened and Jesse stood there staring at us with wide eyes. He'd changed into a fitted gray shirt and low-slung jeans since getting off work, and after a quick assessment, I confirmed that while he was attractive, he had nothing on Gage.

"Cassi, what are you doing here?" He looked down at the piles of boxes, Tupperware, and casserole dishes in between us. "What is this?"

"Please don't be mad!" I said, and took a step out of a few boxes I'd surrounded myself with. "We just wanted to help in some way, and I love to cook. I just, I just . . ." I trailed off as I saw his dark eyes glisten as he continued to stare at everything on the porch.

What felt like an eternity passed before anyone spoke.

"You really do have a great girl, you know that, right?" He blinked back his tears when he looked up at Gage.

Gage's voice was soft and low. "I know I do."

A weak foreign voice came from somewhere inside the doorway and Jesse tilted his head into the house as he answered back in what had to be Italian. "Ma wants to meet y'all. C'mon in." When Gage and I bent down to pick up some of the piles, Jesse shook his head and began helping us. "I can't believe y'all did this. Thank you so much."

"It was all Cass, trust me. If I would've helped, it wouldn't have turned out edible."

Jesse laughed and led us into the kitchen. When everything was put away, he took us back into the living room to where his mom was sitting on the couch. She murmured something in Italian and smiled brightly; even ill, there was no doubt she was beautiful. "Ma, she heard me on the phone with you earlier, she knows you speak English." He rolled his eyes when he turned back to us but the love for his mom was obvious. "She said it's refreshing to see true love in a couple."

"It isn't something you see often." Her voice was still weak, and her English was perfect but held a hint of her accent. "Especially in young couples such as yourselves. I pray I get to see it for my son before I go."

"Ma," Jesse said softly, and went to stand next to her. "Cassi and Gage, this is my mother, Isabella; Ma, this is Cassi and her boyfriend, Gage."

"It's nice to meet you," Gage and I said at the same time.

"It's such a pleasure to meet the two of you. And what was that I heard about you making food for us? Darling girl, that is too sweet of you."

"Really, I wish there was more we could do, but unfortunately all I'm good at is cooking."

Isabella laughed softly. "Oh, my dear, I have a feeling we would get along very well."

"Hey, Jesse, mind if I talk to you for a minute?" Gage asked, and when I tilted my head up to look at him with a worried expression he squeezed me tightly and kissed my forehead. "Talk to Isabella for a bit, darlin', I'll be right back."

"Be nice," I whispered so only he could hear.

Gage flashed his dimples at me. "Promise."

I watched them walk outside but didn't have any time to worry; Isabella patted the couch and told me to "talk food" with her.

Gage

"HEY, MAN, I can't thank you enough. Ma was an amazing cook—her parents owned a restaurant in Italy up until they passed—but she can't do anything anymore, and honestly I have to be the worst cook ever. I can heat up soup and that's about it, so what y'all did is really amazing. Thank you."

"Like I said, it's all Cassidy. I understand what you mean though; me and the guys would starve without her." I laughed and he cocked his head to the side.

"Her name's Cassidy? That fits her; I like it better than just Cassi."

I cleared my throat as my earlier irritation with his obvious affection for my girl came back. "Yeah, I agree. But hey, I wanted to talk to you about something, and I want you to keep an open mind. Cassidy doesn't know about this; I went to the other room to make the call while she was cooking some of the stuff. I figured if you want to tell her, that's your business. Also, I don't want you to take this as me thinking you aren't capable of—"

"Just spit it out, man." Jesse's head was still tilted to the side, but now his brows were drawn down and he looked hesitant.

"All right. My family wants to take care of your mom's medical bills, as long as y'all—"

"No." His body straightened and his face grew tense. "No way."

"Jesse, just hear me out."

He leaned close and spoke through clenched teeth, his voice

soft but harsh. "No fucking way. I don't need your help and I'm not gonna be some charity case for your family."

"Y'all wouldn't be charity. Jesus, Jesse. I get where you're coming from, but don't be so stubborn that your mom has to suffer even more watching you beat yourself up as you struggle to take care of her." That may have been a little harsh. I cleared my throat and tried to calm my voice. "Look, my sister Amanda's best friend died suddenly when we were younger. She was sick, had cancer, and her family didn't tell anyone. Why? I have no idea, but they didn't have the money or the insurance to go through chemo or anything like that, so their doctor suggested natural, alternative treatments. By the time even my mom started to notice something wasn't right, Kasey was gone. Everyone in town flipped out over the issue, and Kasey's parents moved away suddenly. Amanda was . . . she wasn't okay for a long time. She was so sure if they had told us, we could have done something. Well, now we have an opportunity to do something. Dad and I, as well as Cass, think what you've done for your mom already is incredible, and I respect you for it. But you shouldn't have to take on a second job while you're going to the police academy, or even while you're trying to get on at a department. You need to spend your time with her, not worrying about making enough money to keep you guys afloat. We want to take care of all of her current and future medical bills, as long as y'all need it. Also, if this house isn't paid off, we'll cover the mortgage too. It won't be charity, we want to help."

Jesse's eyes were glossy again. "I can't, I can't." His voice gave out on the last word and he turned so his back was facing me.

"If you want, you can think about it for a while, but I really want you to consider this. It could help y'all out a lot, and you wouldn't have to stretch yourself so thin. I know you want to take care of your mom, but it's not bad to ask for help. It doesn't say anything against you." We both stood there silently for a couple minutes and I decided to leave him alone for now. I clapped a hand on his shoulder and turned to walk inside when his arm snuck out and clamped down on my shoulder as well.

"You don't understand what this means to me, and what it'll mean to her. After my dad took off, there was no one left, just me and her. I'm not naïve; I know she doesn't have long. She stopped responding to all meds and treatments months ago, so being able to spend more time with her and not be so stressed would—it would just really mean a lot."

"I'm glad. We're more than happy to do it. If you don't want Cass knowing, I'll give you my number and we can set up a time when I can come by and we can go over the bills and start getting them paid off. So if over the next few days, you'll get them together, I'd appreciate it."

He nodded and his eyes seemed to get even darker when he looked back toward the house. "Cassi's more than welcome here too."

My jaw clenched and I couldn't hold back anymore; my voice dropped low. "I'd appreciate it if you stopped checkin' out my girl too. I waited a long time for her, and I'm never letting her go."

"I got you." Jesse tried to laugh and shook his head. "Earlier it didn't bother me one bit to know she had a boyfriend; I wasn't going to stop." His hands went up in surrender. "You have to know how sexy and sweet she is. But hell, Ma had y'all pegged the second she saw you together; that changes everything. She had a shitty husband, but she would have married anyone after what happened to her when she was younger. Guess she'd had this guy she'd grown up with; they both always knew they were going to be together forever and the night before their wedding he was killed. After that, she knew she'd never find someone to love again and agreed to marry the first guy who came around. But Ma's got this sixth sense when it comes to couples. She takes one look at them and she knows if they're the real deal, so if she says it, I'm not about to mess with it. You're safe when it comes to me."

I wasn't sure if I was more relieved with what he said or pissed at his admitting he was about to go after her even though he knew we were together. Deciding not to dwell on either, I said, "Your mom's had it rough, so let's make this time as stress-free for her as we can, yeah?"

The teasing left his face. "Yeah, thanks again. I don't even know how to begin to thank your family."

"No need, just spend time with her."

"GOOD GOD, are y'all ever just hanging out anymore when we get here?" Adam called from the front.

Cassidy gasped and jumped back and off the bed, grabbing for her clothes. "Did they even knock this time?!"

"I have *got* to get that key back from him." I pulled her back to me after I had my jeans on and kissed her roughly. "You almost ready . . . or not?" I deadpanned when I saw she had a different jersey in each hand. I chuckled and kissed her cheek. "Good luck with that one." Plucking my shirt off the floor, I headed out.

"It's about time!" Grant bitched as he flopped onto one of the couches. "It's rude to keep your guests waiting."

"Kinda rude to just walk in. Adam, swear to God, you do that one more time I'm takin' my key back from you."

"Where's Cassi? I'm hungry," Jake grumbled, and looked hopelessly toward the bedroom door.

"You're grown, get your own damn food! Y'all should be

happy she makes you food anyway, *and* that we let y'all come over every Sunday to watch whatever games are on."

"Well, where else are we supposed to go for the game. You have the biggest TV!"

"Your own place? What if Cass hated sports, or better . . . what if she hated y'all?" I smiled and dodged a pillow Adam threw at me.

"Well, thank God you don't have a stuck-up bitch. At least you have . . ." Jake paused as Cassidy walked out of the bedroom with the most gorgeous blush covering her face. "That."

I looked at my girl. God, I was one lucky son of a bitch. Her hair was loose with its natural wave and was somewhat mussed up from the heated session we'd just been having. Those honey-colored eyes were bright and full of promises for later, and I watched as her cheeks got even darker. Looking down over her body, my travel stopped short and I laughed. "Guess you chose? Wrong choice, darlin'. You're in Texas; don't forget that." She'd been flipping out all day over which jersey to wear; she only owned two, both of which were basketball jerseys. One was a Lakers jersey, Lamar Odom's, and the other was a Spurs, Tim Duncan's. Both teams were playing each other today and, according to Cassidy, that "just wasn't allowed."

"This isn't fair!" She pointed at her gold jersey. "They're my team, I can't just abandon them . . ." Her lips stretched into a wide Cheshire cat grin and she lifted the gold jersey up to her chin to show off her white jersey underneath. "But Tim Duncan is my all-time favorite player and the only man I'd ever leave you for, so I decided to keep him closer to my heart."

My eyes rolled and I held back a laugh as Ethan spoke up. "You can't cheer on both teams, Cass. Pick one or the other.

And remember what Gage said: you ain't in California any-more, baby girl."

"But it's so hard!" She stamped her foot. Actually stamped her damn foot.

"Darlin'"—I couldn't hold back my next laugh—"did you really just stamp your foot?"

Her eyes had begun drifting to the TV as Jake got it on the channel where they were still doing pregame footage and she did a double take, her eyes going wide. "*Shh!*" Her hand flew up and she turned more so she could watch, her hand still up in the air, like that would keep us all from still talking. Oddly, it did.

I let out a groan though when I saw what she'd seen and was now intently watching. As soon as Tim Duncan's interview ended I started talking again. "You happy to be gettin' your fix?"

Cassidy turned and her eyes were bright, her smile bigger than ever. I shook my head at her but pulled her close and kissed her hard. I wasn't complaining; she was so damn cute when she got excited over watching Tim Duncan. I didn't even mind that she always reminded me she would leave me for him; if Tim Duncan was the worst thing I had to worry about, I'd say I had it pretty easy.

"You know what I think isn't fair?" Jake asked. "That Gage gets a girl like Cassi. She actually knows what's going on in every sport we watch, and she enjoys watching the game. Where's my Cassi? That's what I wanna know!"

"I'll find you one, Jake," she promised as everyone laughed, and left my arms. "Nothing fancy tonight, guys, I'm just gonna make sandwiches. Anyone wants a beer, we stocked up the fridge at the bar; help yourself."

"And *that. Right. There.* I want a damn SMB too! Doesn't

matter if she thinks it's 'nothing fancy' or not, there isn't another SMB out there like Cassi. That's it, I'm kidnapping and keeping her." Jake sounded exasperated.

"What the hell is an SMB?" Ethan asked, but we all looked confused.

Jake looked at us like we should know this already. "SMB? Sandwich-Making Bitch."

The room got tense as at least Adam, Ethan, and I got ready to rip into Jake for talking about Cassidy like that. But all of a sudden Cassidy burst into laughter so hard she had to grip my arm to keep herself standing. Jake and Grant laughed with her.

"See, she gets it," Jake said, and picked the remote back up to turn up the volume.

Cassidy was wiping tears from her eyes when her laughs turned into soft giggles. "Jake, just for that I'm making your sandwiches first and *I'll* get your beer for you."

"You're serious right now?" Ethan asked her, still looking pissed off. At least there were some sane people in the room still.

"Well, yeah. That was the funniest thing I've heard in a while." She looked at me and her smile faltered when she realized I wasn't finding anything about that funny. "All right, Jake, did you mean that to be offensive?"

Jake said, "*Hell* no. That's the best compliment I could give a chick. I won't let just anyone make me a sandwich." He grinned ridiculously at her.

"And I didn't take it as offensive." I still hadn't relaxed my tense frame, and from the looks of it, neither had Ethan or Adam, so she kept talking. "It's like that whole women-belong-in-the-kitchen-barefoot-and-pregnant thing; it's funny. If Jake meant any of that literally, I doubt he'd be okay with me watching the game with you guys."

"Exactly!" Jake threw an arm out toward Cassidy, pointing toward her. "She gets it, why don't y'all?"

Cassidy kissed my cheek and moved to the kitchen. "But, Jake, I expect an early birthday present this year of a Cowboys jersey with the initials *SMB* on the back rather than a player's name."

"Gage, you are one lucky motherfucker. That's all I'm gonna say," Grant said, soft enough that I doubted Cass could hear him, and Jake grunted his agreement.

"Seriously, man, it's a compliment, you need to relax," Jake said, and turned up the volume even louder.

But by this point, I was relaxed, completely. Something Cassidy said was replaying through my mind over and over again, and I turned to look at her. She glanced up as she finished getting everything out of the fridge and smiled softly at me. That smile I'd realized was reserved just for me. She turned to get a carving board and bread and I let my eyes roam over her again, her long hair reaching her waist, the tank top Lakers jersey resting loosely on her hips, and those super-short black shorts that were driving me crazy right now. My jeans got tight as I continued over her legs down to her bare feet. The corner of my mouth lifted slightly and I snapped my eyes back up a little just in time for her to turn. I kept my gaze in that spot, letting the image she'd put in my mind play through, and finally looked back up to her beautiful face. Was it twisted that I hardened even more at the thought of Cassidy pregnant? Before the guys could notice I was sporting a hard-on again, I turned and headed back for our room.

How many times had I thought about marrying Cassidy and having a family with her? Thousands, at the very least, but for whatever reason I'd never thought of her actually pregnant. And damn if I ever wanted that image to leave my mind. It'd only been a month and a half since we'd gotten together, but I'd been in love with her for almost two years now. *That's not too crazy, to think of this already, is it? Fuck . . . who am I kidding? Of course it is. I'm only twenty-two, and she's nineteen. I shouldn't be thinking about this for years.* And I doubted I would have actually thought about having kids if she hadn't made that one completely innocent comment. But she did, and now it was all I could think of. Cassidy round with my kid. *That* would be an incredible sight.

"Babe?"

I turned to see her worried expression as she closed the door behind her.

"Are you okay? You aren't really mad at Jake, are you? I thought it was funny."

"No, I'm not."

Cass smiled softly before her brows pinched together again. "Then what's wrong? Why are you in here, and . . . I don't even know how to explain your expression. I can't tell if you're mad or confused or—I just have no idea."

God, I wanted to tell her. I wanted to say I was gonna kick the guys out, that I wanted her to stop taking birth control and I wanted to marry her immediately. But I knew I'd freak her out— hell, I was freaking myself out. Not the marrying-her part; I'd have married her in an instant. But the rest of it. I needed to take all this slow; I needed to find a way to ease Cassidy into the idea of even having a family. I knew because of her childhood, she had this fear of having children. She was terrified she'd turn into her mother. I knew there wasn't a chance in hell that could ever happen. Right now, though, if I were to tell her I was imagining her pregnant, I could only imagine that mask I hated so damn much slipping back on her face. It would ruin things for us, not just today, but for some time to come. She'd shut down, I had no doubt about it. So instead, I pushed the image of her pregnant to the back of my mind and smiled down at her.

"I'm fine, sweetheart. I'd just been checkin' you out and got hard thinking about what we'd been interrupted doing. Decided it was better to walk away before any of the guys noticed."

Her honey eyes widened and heated before she looked down. Instantly my erection made itself known again. *Down, boy.* She took another step closer and pressed her body to mine. "I'll take care of that as soon as they're gone," she whispered huskily, and with a suggestive smile, turned and walked out of the room.

13

Cassidy

I'D SPENT MOST OF THAT NEXT WEEK at Jesse and Isabella's, and thankfully Gage went with me. We were both completely enchanted with her tales of Italy and the man she'd grown up with and loved. She was a sweet woman, and we hated seeing her so ill, which is why we'd spent every free second there since the morning after the whole SMB basketball game.

Isabella had some good days and other not-so-good days, but this whole week had been awful, and I could see how much it was wearing on Jesse. That Monday he hadn't been able to even put a coffee with three sugars together correctly, and I'd finally sent him on a lunch, and then home when he told me Isabella couldn't get out of bed that morning, even with his help. It wasn't until this morning that she'd been able to get around on her own and seem like herself again.

In the month and a half since we'd first brought food to their house, it'd become a weekly ritual for us. Every Sunday morning before the guys came over for the game, we'd go over with food for the week and talk with her and Jesse for hours until it was time to go home. After this week though, Gage and I were exhausted emotionally. I couldn't understand how Jesse could do it; after only a handful of afternoons and nights with her, we were both so emotionally drained from worrying about her, all we wanted to do was sleep the weekend away and pray that she got better. But Jackie had called as we were on our way back from Isabella's and said we absolutely had to be at her party tonight.

Figuring we needed all the help we could get to bring our spirits up, we'd decided to go and I was already seriously regretting it.

"Damn it," Gage mumbled under his breath, and I paused. Tyler was there; this was the first time I was seeing him since the morning he'd shown up at Gage's door, and he was with that redhead he'd brought home the night he kicked me out. "Darlin', if you want to leave, tell me and we're gone."

"It's fine. I'm not going to let him control what we do; that's dumb."

As soon as Ty saw me, he broke away from the redhead and walked quickly over to us, giving Gage a death stare before stepping close to me. "Cassi, how are you?"

My heart clenched and my arms twitched, wanting to wrap them around Tyler's waist, but a squeeze from Gage's hand and one look at the redhead glaring at our group reminded me why that wasn't an option. "Tyler."

"Don't be like that, baby."

"Don't. Call. Her. Baby," Gage said through clenched teeth, and pulled me closer to his side.

Tyler's eyes narrowed and swept over to look Gage up and

down. "She's never complained about it." His brown eyes came back to me and turned pleading. "Cassi, can we please talk?"

"I don't think that's such a good idea, Ty," I said softly, fully aware of Grant, Ethan, and Jackie standing near us.

"Why? Did Gage tell you that you can't speak to me now?"

"No, he didn't. I just don't have anything to say to you."

"Hi, Gage." A soft but sultry voice joined the conversation and I looked past Tyler to see the redhead, realizing this was the first time I'd heard her speak.

"Cara." His hand tightened around mine again and anyone near us could feel the tension rolling off his body.

Gage's body was turned so my shoulder was against his stomach and he was staring down at me, but I was looking straight at Cara. Her eyes took on a strange heat when they looked at Gage and she dragged her bottom lip through her teeth. An uneasy feeling filled my stomach and got worse when her eyes locked on me and she slipped her hand into Tyler's.

"Your name's Carrie, right?" she asked with a sneer. I had no doubt she knew exactly what my name was, but before I could correct her she kept going. "I would say I'm sorry for taking Tyler from you. But, well, I'm not." She shrugged and her lips formed into an awkward shape, making her look like a duck. "You're not his type, but I'm sure if you ask real nice, Gage will give you either my Monday- or Wednesday-night slot."

I felt Gage's body lock up even further; I swear if someone had poked him he'd have shattered. But I had no idea what she meant by "Monday- or Wednesday-night slot." I didn't have to ask; Cara didn't leave me wondering for long.

"I mean, it would probably be more of a charity case than anything, but Lord knows you need to learn how to keep a boyfriend and Gage needs to fill his booty-call slots."

"Cara, shut up," Gage whispered. I didn't have to see his face to know what she was saying was true. The horrified tone in those three words said it all.

"Oh." She sucked air in through her teeth. "Whoops, did you already fill those spots? God, Gage, I knew you had a healthy appetite, but I thought you'd at least mourn my loss for a while. Don't worry, honey," Cara said, focusing her attention back on me with an unconvincing grimace, "he doesn't keep any of his girls around for very long. I'm sure a night will open for you soon."

I looked up at Tyler to see his obvious concern for me as he disentangled himself from her, but Jackie was already pulling me away from him, Cara, and Gage.

"Cassidy!" Gage called as I was swept away.

I lived with Gage, I spent every night with him; I would have known if he was going to a booty call at night. But Gage's reaction to Cara told me that what Cara was saying had truth to it.

"That bitch. Don't listen to anything she said, Cass, she was just trying to rub her relationship with Tyler in your face."

"Then why was she talking about Gage?!"

Jackie looked at me like she wished she had the answer, and then Jackie's little frame started shaking and her face turned murderous. "You better hope like hell that what she was saying wasn't true, Gage Carson."

I whirled around to see a wide-eyed, pale-faced Gage shut Jackie's door behind him.

"Babe—"

"Is it true?" I demanded.

"I can explain."

"Oh my God, it's true? You had days? Like . . . you had a fucking schedule for your fuck buddies, Gage?!"

His eyes got even wider and he took a deep, shaky breath in.

"When. Was. This?" What had Cara said? Something about his having a healthy appetite but thinking he'd mourn her loss first.

"Cassidy," Gage said, "I need to explain."

"When, Gage? Because from what she was saying, it didn't sound like it was a couple of years ago!"

"The last time was the night before I left for the ranch for winter break."

That night was the night I'd given him the picture and he'd left quickly. What girl had he gone to screw that night? And then it hit me, and my voice lost all the force behind it and came out soft. "Oh my God, you lied to me." Jackie tried to leave the room but I gripped her hand harder. "Tyler was right, you left the apartment because you didn't want me there with you. I *was* making it hard for your relationships." I had been in the way, just like Tyler said. If Tyler hadn't been lying about that, what else hadn't he been lying about?

"No, no, babe, that's not it at all. I didn't lie to you, I've never lied to you."

"Bullshit!"

I could tell from his expression my language in the room had been surprising him. He stepped closer, trying to pull me into his arms, but I stepped back with Jackie. "Cassidy, that hadn't begun until I started coming around again after I'd moved out. It only lasted for a month and a half. I was just trying to forget you. I thought you'd led me on; you know everything Tyler told me when we lived together and at the ranch! I was pissed, and I wanted to get back at you and forget you; that was my way."

The room fell silent for a few moments while I tried to swallow the lump in my throat. "That is the most pathetic, disgusting thing I've ever heard."

"Cassidy—"

"How many of those girls did you treat the way you've been treating me? Did you tell all of them you love them? That they're perfect? I swear to God, Gage, I knew you were experienced but I had no idea you had a fucking *schedule*!"

"I have never told another girl that I loved them. Only you, Cassidy, it's only ever been you." His green eyes were pained and his shoulders looked like they were hunched in.

"Gage, do you really expect me to believe you? Was this all a game for you? Innocent, naïve Cassidy got dumped by her boyfriend because she wouldn't have sex with him; let's see how long it'll take me to bang her."

He flinched like I'd slapped him, but before he could say anything I gasped loudly.

"Oh my God. How many of them did you screw without a condom? Did you 'just not think about it' with all of them too?!"

"This is getting awkward," Jackie said when Ethan walked in and gave me a double take as I said those last few sentences.

"Babe!" Gage no longer looked just hurt; he was pissed too. "How could you even think that? Are you serious right now, Cassidy?! I have *never*—"

"How do I know that you haven't given me some disease, Gage?!"

"Cass!"

"Get out." I kept one hand gripping Jackie and let the other point toward her bedroom door. "Get out, Gage."

"Darlin'," he said softly, and took two steps toward me, one arm extended.

"Don't fucking touch me!" I screeched at him. "Get. Out!"

"C'mon, Gage," Ethan said as he slowly dragged him toward the bedroom door, "you need to give her time alone; let's go back out here."

"Cassidy, I swear, it's not like you think. I love you."

"Let's go, man." Ethan grabbed his upper arm and pulled harder.

Gage stared at me with the most devastating expression as he stumbled behind Ethan out of the room.

"How could he?" I asked Jackie as soon as the door was shut behind them.

"Come here, Cass." Jackie pulled me toward the bed and sat me down. "I know you probably don't want to hear this, so let me start by saying that I agree with you, it is gross that he had days for girls. I think he's a pig for that, but, sweetie"—she brushed some of my hair away from my face—"the rest of it? You can't really be mad at him for that. Because weren't you doing something similar? You thought Gage didn't want anything to do with you, so you started dating Tyler. And while you two weren't having sex, you made out all the time and you were trying to get yourself ready to go there with Tyler."

I wanted to be mad at her for taking Gage's side, but as always, I knew Jackie was seeing things in a way I couldn't.

"I've known Gage for almost three years. He's had a couple girlfriends, dated a few more girls, but he's never been in love with any of them. He's never once treated any of them the way he treats you. Like I said, what he did was not all right. But at least talk to him about it. Don't break up with him because of something stupid he did while trying to get over you."

"But *her*, Jackie? Why did she have to sleep with Gage and then Tyler?"

"I know, I was about ready to go off on her, but Gage didn't know Tyler was going to do that to you. Don't hold this against Gage." She was silent for a minute before talking again. "I can tell you're not considering my advice, so hear this: everyone does stupid shit when they're upset. Doesn't matter what, could be indulging in pints of Ben and Jerry's, or it could be what Gage did. I did something along the lines of what Gage did once. I dated this guy Anthony all four years of high school; he left for UT right away, but I went to a community college for a year before I decided to come here too. I thought we'd be together forever, but he ended up finding someone else and told me *after* I'd already started school here. I was so upset that I went and slept with his roommate, who just happened to be his twin brother, and made sure Anthony found out about it."

"You didn't!" I said, my mouth wide open, and then started bursting into laughter.

Jackie giggled next to me. "I did!"

"Did his brother not care that you were using him?"

"Nope, he was so mad at Anthony for what he did to me, he was game as soon as I mentioned it. Actually, he and I remained good friends and he's the one who introduced me to Ethan . . . it's Adam."

"You had sex with Adam?!" I whispered, horrified. How were she and Dana friends? How were Adam and Ethan friends? "Do Ethan and Dana know what happened? And where's this Anthony guy?"

Jackie laughed harder and wiped tears from her eyes. "Yes, everyone knows what happened. Adam had actually already told Ethan about me and everything that had happened; Ethan still wanted to meet me. Dana didn't like me at first last year when she and Adam started dating, but after she hung out with me and Ethan she got over it really quick. And Anthony decided he wanted to go into the army, so he left after his second fall semester."

"Oh my word."

"I know." She took a deep breath in and out to calm her laughing. "All that is to say, people do stupid shit when they're upset. Don't be too hard on Gage. He's not cheating on you, and remember, I get to hear what goes on behind enemy lines since I'm dating one of his best friends. He fell for you the moment he saw you. I didn't have to hear that from you to know it; he told Ethan too. We were all just waiting for you guys to come together."

"Ugh, I feel so stupid for overreacting!" I jumped off the bed, pulling her with me. "Thank you, Jackie, what would I do without you?" I hugged her quickly.

"Well, let's just hope Gage is still here so we don't have to go track him down."

Just then there was a loud crash and a few guys started yelling, one of them distinctly my Gage. "Oh shit."

Gage

ETHAN HAD TO PULL ME out of the room so I wouldn't continue to make an ass out of myself and dig myself into an even deeper hole with Cassidy. Was it too much to ask for us to have a normal night out without something happening?

I shoved him. "Get the fuck off me."

"You need to calm down, man."

"I am calm! I just can't fucking lose Cassidy because of Cara!" God, in December I thought I'd die if Cassidy ever found out because I knew she would look at me differently, and I didn't think I'd be able to handle that, but I didn't know just how painful that death would be. I didn't think I could handle seeing her look at me like that one more time. Like . . . exactly what she said: she was looking at me like I disgusted her, and I couldn't blame her; I disgusted myself. But how could she for one damn second think that I would use her as a fucking game, or that I would ever treat anyone else the way I treated her? I hadn't made it a secret since we'd been together how special she was to me and how different she was for me. But apparently she'd never believed any of that anyway.

"Fuck," I growled, and stormed past Ethan toward the living room, stopping short when I saw Tyler and Cara with smug looks on their faces. "Are you happy now?" I asked both of them.

"Told ya, *cousin,* Cassi will always be mine. Now I just gotta wait. She's done with you, and soon she'll realize I'm all she has left. She'll come running back to me."

Cara's eyes grew wide and she turned to Tyler. "What?!"

"Don't act shocked and hurt," Tyler said with a roll of his eyes. "You knew exactly why I brought you with me tonight. You already played your part."

My eyebrows raised high and I almost expected Cara to slap him, but she just turned with a huff and stormed out of the apartment.

"I'm sure you can still catch her, if you think you need to go back to your *days*." Tyler raised an eyebrow in my direction.

"Cassidy's mine. You really think she's going to come back to you after you cheated on her and treated her the way you did?"

Before Ty could respond, Grant decided to step up and put his two cents in. "Honestly, I'm surprised either of you think you're getting another shot with her. Cassi gets done with one of y'all and moves on to the next; now that she's got both of y'all outta the way, she'll be looking somewhere else," he taunted.

"You best shut up, Grant. Now," I growled.

His smile just got wider and the challenge in his eyes was more than a little apparent. "And damn if I haven't wanted to fuck that piece of ass since the first night Ty showed up with her. I promise not to be too rough with her. Now, if you'll excuse me . . ." He smiled wryly at me and started walking toward Ethan and Jackie's room, where Jackie and Cassidy still were.

"You son of a bitch!" Tyler yelled, and stalked toward Grant, but I had already plowed into him and was knocking him into the table, breaking it with the weight of both of us.

Immediately all the guys started yelling at each other and the girls scattered away from us. Adam and Ethan pulled me off Grant, yelling at me to calm down, and Tyler took my spot, slamming his fist into Grant's face—or arm if Grant was able to block it. Jake had just started pulling Tyler away when Sean came to Grant's defense and punched Ty in the stomach. Jake let Tyler go and went after Sean as Ty doubled over and tried to catch his breath.

"Man, is she that good of a lay?" Grant asked even as he spit blood onto the floor.

"You have a death wish, dumbass? Shut up!" Adam yelled, but I was already out of his and Ethan's grasp and charging back toward Grant.

As soon as I landed a solid punch to Grant's jaw someone put me in a choke hold and I tried to bring my arms back to get him off, but Grant grabbed them and sent his foot into my stomach. The next thing I knew my neck was free and I didn't have time to catch my breath before both Grant's feet went into my stomach again. I rolled back and scrambled to my feet, vaguely registering Adam wrestling with Reid and Ethan trying to hold Tyler back.

Grant was getting back to his feet but I swiped his legs out from under him, grabbed his shirt, and lifted him slightly off the ground to deliver another blow to the right side of his face. My arm cocked back again and someone grabbed it; I turned, but Tyler was already punching some guy I didn't know and my arm was free again. After another hit, Grant's eyes started fluttering and I had to struggle to keep his weight up as I was still having trouble catching my breath and was constantly getting hit from all the other fights going on around me.

Cassidy

JACKIE AND I STOOD THERE in shock watching as the party turned into an all-out brawl. Girls were huddled in a group near the patio door, and while a few guys were standing with them, the rest seemed to all be in the fight or trying to pull guys off each other.

I looked up and saw Tyler slam someone onto the hardwood floor and lean back to start hitting him, only to be flipped onto his back and get hit himself. Ethan grabbed the guy and pulled him far enough for Tyler to stand up, but he stumbled into someone else before going back to the guy Ethan was still holding. I realized Gage was the one Ty had just run into and saw him holding Grant up and punching him in the face.

Why is this happening? My body was shaking watching the guys punching, kicking, and choking each other. Different days and nights with my mom and stepdad kept flashing through my mind and all I wanted to do was scream at them to stop, but I couldn't find my voice. My legs were weak as my worst night-mare played out before my eyes and again I tried to yell at them, but my voice still wasn't working. I let go of Jackie's arm and rushed up to Gage before he could hit Grant again. I couldn't deal with seeing the man I love hitting someone else for no ap-parent reason.

Gage

"YOU SAY *ANYTHING* LIKE THAT about her again, I will end you." I brought my arm up one last time, but Grant's eyes rolled to the back of his head and I felt someone try to grab at my arm. With-out straightening my arm or my body I flung my elbow back into the person. Before I could realize that I'd hit a face instead of a torso, I'd turned around and had my arm cocked back, ready to throw another punch, but what I saw stopped my world.

The fighting around me, the yelling, the girls on the other side of the room shrieking, my heartbeat.

Everything. Stopped.

My eyes focused on my beautiful girl on the ground, Ethan's hands under her arms. One eye was wide with what should have been shock but instead was outright fear, and the other was cov-ered by her hand. Her mouth was slightly open, and as she took a staggering breath in and began to cover it with her other hand, my world unfroze and I dropped to my knees in front of her and tried to reach for her, but she flinched back into Ethan.

Cassidy flinched away from me.

It felt like I'd been shot in the chest with a shotgun.

"What the hell is wrong with you?!" Jackie screamed at me.

"Oh God, Cassidy!" I took a short, painful breath in. "Baby, are you all right? I'm—" Another painful breath. "I'm so sorry."

I got to my feet and followed as Ethan lifted her up and walked quickly back to the bedroom with Jackie; Ty wasn't far behind.

"Are you kidding me? You're always going on about me hurting her and you *hit* her?!"

I felt like I was going to throw up. "I had no idea it was her, I didn't even know she was in the room. God. Cassidy, are you okay? Please say something." Ethan had already sat her on the bed so I got closer and gently touched her arm but she jerked away.

"Don't touch her, you asshole!" Tyler pushed me back and went toe-to-toe with me.

"Stop fighting," Cassidy said in a soft, robotic voice. I turned and my heart broke when I saw the right side of her face was in that familiar, lifeless mask. "Tyler."

"Yeah, sweetheart?" He squatted next to her and grabbed her hand, the smile on his face showing how happy he was that she was going back to him, like always.

"I need you to leave, I need some time—"

"Cassi, I've always—"

"Not anymore, not after what you did to me." Her voice lost some of its mechanical sound and got soft as a whisper when her eyes focused on his. "You closed the window, Ty."

I could see that was the one thing that could hurt Tyler the most. Having Cassidy say those last words, confusing as they were, killed him. He stood there wide eyed for a moment before nodding and walking out of the room. As much as I hated him, I still felt somewhat bad for him. I couldn't imagine how much that hurt, but from the way Cass glanced up at me I thought I was about to find out.

"Ethan, Jackie, can you guys give us a minute, please?"

Fuck.

As soon as the door shut behind them, I looked up to see her looking at me. Her hand had left her face and I saw it was a deep red. I had no doubt she was going to have a massive black eye in the morning. I swallowed back bile and took two steps toward her.

"Do not touch me, Gage Carson."

Oh God. What the hell have I done?

"Cassidy." My voice came out rough and quiet. "I swear I didn't know you were even in the room, darlin'. I would *never* hurt you."

"A part of me knows that, Gage."

A part of her. A part of her. What the hell?!

"But I can't—I don't—you . . . you . . ." Her mask slipped and her head fell into her hands; a sob instantly tore through her body.

Fuck this. I took the last two steps toward her and sank to the bed, pulling her into my arms and onto my lap. Her body jerked like I'd shocked her, but I kept my hold tight and didn't let go. No way was I letting go.

"Cassidy, I love you so much." My voice came out tight and I kissed the top of her head. "God, baby, I'm so sorry."

Cassidy

THIS WAS THE FIRST TIME in many years that I'd cried after getting hit. But then again, this one was completely different from all the rest. This one was intended for someone else and was an act of self-defense; I knew that. Really, I did. But this one? This one was by far the worst hit I'd ever taken.

Walking out of the bedroom into the short hall had been like falling into a hellish nightmare. I hated any type of physical fighting. Hated it with every ounce of my being. And walking out to at least ten guys beating the crap out of each other had brought back flashbacks I'd worked so hard at erasing from my mind. Seeing Gage in the middle of it had taken it from hellish nightmare straight to hell. That was my personal hell, seeing Gage beating the crap out of Grant. I still didn't know what started the fighting, or who started it, but that didn't matter. For me, there is only one reason to fight someone, and it's if they're trying to take your life or the life of someone you love. But seeing as all those guys were close, I seriously doubted that was the case.

I shouldn't have rushed in there, I should have yelled at Gage to stop. I'd been trying to yell, but I couldn't make anything come out, and as for rushing in there . . . it was stupid, but I just wanted the fighting stopped. Instead, I'd taken an elbow to my eye. Considering what I've endured, it wasn't that bad at all. I'd been so shocked by the way my head had snapped back so quickly, it took me a second to realize why I was falling backward, until I landed smack on my butt at the same time Ethan's hands shot out to catch me. The pain in my eye and head finally registered as Gage turned around with a murderous glare in his eyes, his right arm cocked back, ready to strike again. And that was all I could see and feel anymore, even now.

Pain rushing through my head. Gage's face twisted with rage and his fist aimed at me, ready to deliver another blow.

His arms tightened around me as he kissed the top of my head again. I brought my shaky hands up to his chest and pushed but he didn't budge. I couldn't be here in his arms, not when all I could see was that horrible image. I didn't know if I'd ever be able to get that out of my mind. It was evident my words hurt him, but I didn't want to lie to him. A part of me *did* know that Gage would never hurt me. Before tonight all of me had known that, and although I knew he didn't do it on purpose and it was my fault, my past wasn't letting me comprehend that.

"Darlin', I'm so, so—" His voice gave out on the last word and his forehead dropped into the crook of my neck.

I put pressure against his chest again and I felt him shake his head.

"Please don't. Stop trying to push me away, Cassidy." Gage sounded so pained, my breath caught and my hands stopped pushing, and I started clenching his shirt in my fists. "I love you." He brought a hand up to my cheek and leaned his head in, pressing his full lips, soft as a feather, to my injured eye.

I tried to back away, but his arm tight around my waist kept me in place.

"I'm not them," he said after he silently held me for a few more minutes. "I'll never be them, darlin'. I saw it—" Gage's voice hitched and he had to clear his throat. "I saw the fear in your eyes, Cass. I can't imagine what you're thinking right now, but if it were me, all I would be thinking about is them . . . what they did to you, and what I—what I just did. Damn it, I'm so sorry." His arm around my waist tightened momentarily and his head went back to my neck.

With his forehead pressed into my throat, I could feel his hot breath against my chest, and then something light and wet was there. My body stilled and I focused completely on Gage. My arms had subconsciously wound themselves around his broad shoulders at some point and I could feel the tension and slight shudders in the muscles of his back. Before I could force myself to relax and run my hand along his back to soothe the rigid way he was holding himself, I felt that light wetness on my chest again, twice. I unlocked my body and wound my hands through his hair to bring his head away from my neck, glancing down at my chest for barely a moment before looking into Gage's tortured, wet eyes.

Gage was crying.

Oh. My. God.

I'd seen him furious, I'd seen him bursting with joy, I'd seen him crushed, and I'd seen the love flowing freely from him as he looked at me. But I'd never once seen Gage Carson cry.

"Please, let me take you home and take care of you." His voice was even deeper and huskier than usual.

If not for the emotional situation, I'm positive it would have sent a shot of desire straight through me. As it was, my body was now covered in goose bumps, and all I could do was nod my head.

HOURS LATER, I lay awake staring at the ceiling fan going slowly around and around in the living room. Gage and I hadn't spoken a word to each other since he'd asked to take me home. When we'd gotten back to the town house, he'd gone straight to the bathroom to grab some Advil, then joined me in the kitchen. After I took a few and pressed the ice pack Gage made me to my face, he'd taken my hand and led me to the bedroom. And for the first time since we became *us,* I'd gotten ready for bed alone. He'd grabbed the mesh shorts he liked to sleep in during the hot months and walked into the bathroom to take a shower, shutting the door behind him and only opening it when he was coming back out to get in bed.

Before I could let myself get even more upset over this, I'd forced myself into the bathroom, gotten ready for bed, and walked into the bedroom, fully prepared to leave it and go to the other one. But Gage was sitting up in bed staring at me with that odd expression again, and when he noticed my body angled toward the door, he crawled off the bed, grabbed my hand, and pulled me back onto it with him, curling my small frame into his large one. With a few soft kisses to my neck and shoulder, he slowly slipped into sleep, and after a couple hours of not even being able to think of going to sleep, I quietly snuck out of bed and into the living room. I hadn't moved since.

My phone vibrated and I frowned as I glanced down at it. It was almost three in the morning; who on earth was texting me this early? When I saw Tyler's name, I almost didn't read it, but with nothing else to do, and seeing as it was only a text, I opened it anyway.

TYLER
Cassi, are you up?! Has your mom called???

Mom? Why would she be calling me? I haven't talked to her in . . . in . . . hell, I can't even remember. Was it my birthday right after I moved here?

Um . . . no? Why?

TYLER
Can I call?

I skipped a step and called him instead; he answered on the first ring.

"She and Jeff haven't called you?" was his greeting.

"No," I said softly, and walked into the guest room to further prevent waking Gage. "What's going on, Ty? I know we haven't talked in months, but you know I don't talk to them. Like, ever."

"Cassi, sweetheart, my dad just called . . . their house caught fire. So bad it spread to the houses on each side."

"Oh God! Ty, did it get to your parents' house too?" There was only one house between mine and Ty's; I prayed it didn't get that far.

"No, no. The firefighters got it contained before it could. It didn't do too much damage to the houses on either side, but, Cassi, your house is gone."

A gasp escaped my throat, but for the life of me, I couldn't figure out why . . . other than shock that a fire could spread so quickly that a house that size would just be gone. Then again, there was a hell of a lot of liquor in that house.

"Are you okay, sweetheart? Dad said they tried calling your mom but she . . ."

"Ty," I said when he didn't continue, "what aren't you telling me?"

"Her car was still there." I could hear him shutting a door and heard the sound of jingling keys. "I just packed a bag, I'm on my way to come get you. Can you pack for me real quick, Cass?"

"Wait. Pack? Why?"

"Cassi, trust me, I hated your mom and Jeff just as much as you, but your house was just burned to the ground, and as far as anyone knows, they were both in there. For multiple reasons, the main being you're their only family, you need to be there."

"Oh, right." My voice sounded soft but was strangely calm. "I'll start packing right away. Just call when you're outside. I don't want to wake Gage."

"You—what?" He sounded completely baffled, but I didn't have time to get into it right now.

"Just call me, Ty, I gotta pack."

After ending the call, I flew into action, thanking God we'd kept all my clothes in the spare bedroom. I don't know why I never moved them into Gage's room; it was just something that never came up. Once my bag was stuffed, I tiptoed back into Gage's room and into the bathroom, grabbing all the toiletries I would need for a while. Ty called seconds after I'd zipped my bag shut, and within another two minutes, I was in his Jeep.

"Dad got us a flight that's leaving in a few hours," he said quietly as he turned onto another street. "You okay, Cassi?"

"I'm fine, I feel—" I cut myself off, not wanting him to know what I'd been thinking since he told me about the fire, but then his hand curled around mine and I couldn't hold it back. "I feel guilty. Because I should be upset, right? But I'm not, and I don't know why, but, Ty, I'm . . . I'm . . . I feel—like it's justice. I feel like I'm getting some sort of sick revenge, and that house, God, that house is gone, Ty. There are so many bad memories there."

"I know." His hand squeezed mine as he drove us toward the airport. "Don't feel guilty, Cassi, I know she's your mother, but she's not your mom. She hasn't done anything in over a dozen years to deserve your love or your sympathy."

"I just feel like I should be upset by this somehow, but I can't find it in me. Not right now anyway."

Tyler nodded like he understood, and his voice dropped lower. "How's your eye?"

"It's fine. Really, it didn't hurt much at all, it was just the shock of it happening, and seeing Gage like that was ju—" I stopped quickly.

"And why didn't you want him to wake up? You didn't want to tell him you're leaving?" When I didn't respond he nodded again and stayed quiet for a few easy minutes before adding quietly, "I know I've fucked up bad, sweetheart, but I have *never* closed that window. Since we were seven, that window has been open, and it will always be open. No matter what."

My heart clenched. "Not now, but sometime during this trip we need to talk about what went wrong with us. But I'll always love you, Ty."

"And I'll always love you."

14

Gage

I DIDN'T HAVE TO OPEN MY EYES to know Cassidy wasn't in the bed with me when I woke up. Not only was my arm not touching anything but cool sheets, but everything *Cassidy* was just missing. Rolling out of bed, I hit the restroom, then stalked quickly out to the living room. Did she not feel comfortable sleeping next to me after what happened last night? I'd been kicking myself all the way home and after we'd finally gotten here. I couldn't believe she'd agreed to come back with me, but even with that, she still looked at me with so much fear I felt sick, even now.

I paused only momentarily when I found the living room and kitchen empty, and went straight to the spare bedroom. After a quick look to see the bed made and no Cassidy, I shut the door and went back to my room for my phone. It was only then I saw the note underneath it.

Gage—

Please understand, I have to do this. I don't know when I'll be back, but I'll call you when I can. I'm sorry for leaving while you were sleeping, but I knew you'd try to stop me. Forgive me.

I love you. Always.
Cassidy

She left. Cass left me.

I grabbed the lamp that was sitting on the nightstand and launched it across the room, listening to it shatter when it hit the wall. Stop her?! Of course I'd have stopped her! I couldn't live without her, I wouldn't have let her go. Glancing at my phone, I realized she must have turned my alarm off too, because it was already a little past five in the morning. I was supposed to have taken her to work already. *Screw this, I wouldn't have let her go if I was awake, and I'm not letting her go this way either. I know I scared her last night, but it was an accident and even with her past I know we can get through this.*

Pulling on the first clothes I found, I started to head out when I had another thought. I walked into our bathroom and had to pull in a few deep breaths through my nose when I noticed her stuff missing. Turning, I walked to the spare room and had to grip the frame of the closet door when I realized she'd cleared out most of her clothes.

"*Damn it!*" I roared as I raced out of the house and to my truck.

I was at Starbucks in no time and rushed in without even turning my truck off.

"Jesse!"

He turned, his face clearly confused. "Gage, man, what's going on?"

"Is Cassidy here?" I asked breathlessly even as I rounded the corner to go into the back.

"No, that's why I'm asking you what's going on. She called about forty-five minutes ago, said she was leaving for California with some guy named Tyler. Do you know who he is and why the hell she'd just up and go to California?"

That stopped me dead. Cass hadn't just left me. She'd left me for Tyler and she'd gone back to California. To what? His parents'? Why wouldn't she have just stayed with him? None of that mattered right now; I felt like I was going to be sick again at the thought of losing Cassidy for good this time, and once again to my cousin. "You're sure?"

"What?"

"Jesse, are you sure that's what she said?"

"Yeah, now what the hell's going on?"

I couldn't answer at first, I just sat there staring at nothing. "It's just what she told you; Cassidy—Cassi's gone." God, she was really gone. I wanted to fly to California and beg her to come back here with me, but she'd made her choice, and honestly, I'd had Cassidy leave me too many times for me to believe she'd come back to me again. A part of me hoped she wouldn't, because I knew in the end she'd just end up leaving again. Just like Tyler said she would, and I'd be in the same fuckin' heartbroken spot I was always in.

"Well, why did she go?" Jesse no longer looked confused; he was glaring accusingly.

"I don't know," I called over my shoulder as I turned to leave. "She told you more than me."

Before I got all the way out the door my phone started ringing, and I almost threw it across the parking lot when I saw Tyler's name.

"What?! Christ, Ty, I swear if you called me to throw all this in my face, we are done. Forever, you got that?"

"I'm not, and I don't have a lot of time, man, Cassi's gonna come back from the bathroom and getting food and she's gonna be pissed if she knows I called you." He let out a hard, fast breath and started mumbling to himself, "I can't believe I'm about to do this for you. I can't fuckin' believe it . . ." Then with a deep breath in he said quickly and quietly, "Look, Gage, by the way you answered the phone, you've already figured out she's gone. So I don't have to tell you that part, but I don't want you to think she just left you. My dad called me early this morning to tell me Cassi's house burned to the ground, and as far as everyone can tell, her mom and Jeff were in the house still."

"Shit," I hissed under my breath. But if that happened, why didn't she wake me? Yeah, there were still a couple weeks of school left before graduation, but I would've dropped everything to have been there for her.

"Yeah, look, Cassi isn't torn up about it, but she needs to be in California right now. I didn't know until I was on my way that she wasn't going to wake you, and I've tried to talk to her about it, but every time I do she starts to slip away. You know what I'm talking about when I say that, right?"

I did. Her mask. My least favorite thing in the world. "Yeah, I know."

"Bro, as much as I hate it . . . swear to God I hate you two together more than almost anything, but I hate seeing Cassi like this more. It was worse when we got back from the ranch last year, like a hundred times worse, but right now she's so focused on numbing herself because of what happened last night that she's able to hide a lot of what she's feeling right now." He paused for an intense few heartbeats before continuing more slowly. "Even with that, she's miserable. She's wearing one of your shirts, Gage, and every five minutes like clockwork she smells the collar; I don't think she even realizes she's doing it. I'm sure her leaving without saying a word killed you, that's why I called—"

"She left a note," I interrupted, and pulled the small piece of paper out of my back pocket to read it to Tyler.

"God, Cassi, that made it so much worse than it had to be," Tyler mumbled, more to himself than anything. "Listen, I was already thinking this, and after hearing what she wrote, that's classic Cassi. I know what she's doing, Gage. She's scared; this is what she does when she runs away. She's not running from your relationship, and I don't know if she would have even left period if I hadn't called about her mom's house. So just focus on that; she's not running from you, she's running from her past and fears, 'kay?"

"I don't know, that's not what it feels like." I climbed into my truck and rested my head against the hand that was gripping the steering wheel. "You called it, Ty, you said I would do something like this to her."

"Gage, I was just trying to scare you off. I know you wouldn't touch her. I was pissed that you had her and . . . I don't know, I wanted you to think you would lose her."

"And now I have."

"You haven't. Look, last night, I was all for making you feel like shit even though I know you had no idea that was Cassi standing behind you. I know you wouldn't hurt her; you're probably the only guy I would ever trust with her," he admitted reluctantly. "So believe me when I say I'm not trying to make you feel bad about this next part. You know what happened to her; you don't know the extent, but you know. Imagine having her past, then seeing your past come out of the person you want to spend the rest of your life with."

My breath came out in a huff and I clenched the steering wheel harder.

"Cassi knows you'd never intentionally hurt her; I can see her struggling with what she knows and what she saw for that split second. I think she's running away just while she tries to work through that, Gage. I saw the way you were beating yourself up before she asked me to leave the room, which means she saw it too. I know Cassi better than anyone. I have no doubt that what's going through her mind is that her struggle to get through this is hurting you more. She probably thinks running away is what you want her to do."

"How the hell could she think that I'd want her to leave?" My voice was shaking and low, but if I tried to push harder, I'd break. My girl was gone, and while I wanted to believe Tyler, I didn't know if I could after all the times he'd screwed Cassi and me over.

"This *is* Cassi we're talking about," Tyler reasoned. "She'll probably be back soon; I should go before she catches me on the phone."

"I can't lose her, Tyler."

He groaned out a breath. "Yeah, I know. Just give her a little time; when she slips away, she's usually gone for a few days at least, a week at most. You've never seen her like that because when I brought her to Texas, a couple times when she began to slip away, I was able to remind her we were away from her mom and Jeff. The only time she's actually *gone away* since we've been here was when you moved out, so you weren't there for that either. That was the worst I've ever seen it, and this one has to do with you too, so it might take a while. Don't give up on her, and I'll keep you updated, all right?"

"Why are you doing this? You've been trying to come between us this whole time, so why back off now?"

He was silent for a second. "I can't lose her either. And last night, it finally hit me that I was about to. If nothing else, she'll always be my best friend and I will always take care of her. Giving her ice packs at night or helping her not make the biggest mistake of her life by running from you—either way, I'll take care of her."

"Thanks, Tyler, I appreciate it."

"Gotta go, bro."

"Keep her safe for me, yeah?"

Tyler grunted in agreement. "Always. She loves you, Gage. She'll come back to you."

I knew she loved me, but nothing could convince me right then that she would come back to me. My head slowly shook back and forth as I dropped my phone onto the seat next to me.

Cassidy

"THIS IS JUST SO—I don't even know," Tyler said with an exasperated sigh.

"It's weird, right?" *Weird* didn't even begin to describe it. It's like I was looking at some stranger's smoldering lot and melted Lexus, which now resembled a marshmallow that had caught on fire, not my mom's. Other than that sick sense of relief, I felt nothing. No pain, no heartache, no longing.

According to the investigators, the fire started in the bar area, which wasn't a surprise. As I said, that house had just as much liquor as an actual bar, and if Mom and Jeff were in there like the investigators believed, that settled that. Jeff smoked a lot, but being the rich prick he was, he liked smoking expensive loose tobacco out of a pipe like he was freaking Hugh Hefner, so he was always lighting up matches to take a couple puffs. Spill some Everclear, Jeff's spirit of choice, and try to light his pipe next to that . . . and *poof.* There goes the bar and house.

We watched as a couple men and one woman walked cautiously around the ashes, searching through piles of brick and avoiding support beams that were still standing. Tyler wrapped his arms around my waist and drew me close into his chest as one of the men called out to the others. They all slowly made their way to him and peered closely for a few moments, called an officer over to them, and showed him whatever it was they'd found. I held my breath and Tyler's arms tightened as the officer spoke to a detective and that detective walked over to where we were standing with Ty's parents and half the neighborhood.

"Miss Jameson?"

"Yes?"

"I'm Detective Sanders, could we talk somewhere a little more private? Or if you would prefer we can speak in my car or at the station."

"Why don't we take this into the house, Cassidy?" Tyler's dad, Jim, suggested.

Detective Sanders looked at a notepad quickly and clicked on a pen. "And you are?"

"This is James Bradley. The Bradleys are practically family and their house is just right there," I answered, and pointed in the direction of their house.

"I'll follow you." Detective Sanders swept an arm out at the same time he motioned to another man wearing a suit who I had noticed watching me and Ty for some time now. I did a double take when I finally looked at his face. I would have sworn I knew him, I just couldn't think of how. The man followed us and was introduced as Sanders's partner, Detective Green, once we were in the house. "Miss Jameson, would you prefer to do this alone?"

"No, as I said, they're practically family. And please, call me Cassidy."

Sanders nodded and accepted a chair from Ty's mom. "Cassidy, I know you already went over this when you arrived on scene, but to confirm what was reported to me, where were you this morning around midnight?"

"I was at my house in Austin, Texas."

"And what brought you to Mission Viejo?"

"Tyler"—I waved over to Ty, who was sitting practically underneath me—"texted me close to three this morning, err . . . central time, asked if I'd heard from Mom or Jeff. I told him I hadn't and after I called him he told me his dad had just called him saying there was a fire. He explained everything and said that he was coming to pick me up, we got on the first flight here, and here we are."

Sanders nodded and scratched his cheek before flipping his notepad shut. "Cassidy, unfortunately it looks like we have some bad news." He paused for a moment and looked up from his hands into my eyes. "The investigators seem to have found two bodies under some of the debris. They are beyond recognition at this point, so we'll have to run some tests to confirm that they are your mother and stepfather. Unless you knew anyone else who was staying there, it looks like once the records come back, we'll find them to be matches."

I nodded and leaned into Tyler's side when he wrapped his arm around me.

"Bradley family, would you please give us a few minutes?" he suddenly asked when Detective Green leaned forward to mumble something.

"You want me to go?" Tyler asked in my ear.

"Might as well, Ty, I'm fine."

He nodded reluctantly and kissed my forehead.

"Miss Jameson—" Detective Green began.

"Cassidy," I said, cutting him off, and studied him. Why did this guy look so familiar to me? There was something about him, but surely I'd never forget a face like that, especially those eyes. He and his partner were complete opposites. While Sanders was probably in his late forties, with dark red hair and graying sideburns, a stomach protruding over his belt, and height that any professional basketball player would kill for, Green was achingly handsome, probably in his late twenties, a little over half a foot taller than myself, with a lean muscular build and short brown hair that he obviously styled only by running his hand through it, just like Gage. Air filled my lungs in a rush as I thought about Gage.

"Cassidy, I find it quite interesting that you don't seem upset in the least that your home just burned to the ground or that it's most likely your parents' bodies that were just found underneath the debris," Green said with a weird, calm intensity that for a split second made my mind go blank and my heart flutter. *What. On. Earth?*

"I don't know how I'm supposed to feel, Detective Green."

"Well, I would understand if you were in shock, but you don't seem to be that either. Like I said, it's quite interesting."

"Are you implying something, Detective Green?"

He leaned forward, putting his elbows on his knees. "When was the last time you spoke to your mother or stepfather?"

Was he serious? Was I really being interrogated right now? Wait! Weren't we supposed to be in a police station for something like that? Deciding that not cooperating would only make this worse, I thought about it for a few seconds. "I haven't talked to Jeff since the morning I left for Texas; same with my mom. But she did text me on my birthday about a month later. So if you count the text, then I would say it's been over a year and a half since I've had any type of communication with her, though I didn't respond."

"Bad relationship with your parents, Cassidy?" Green asked, looking at me with his steely gaze; Sanders had his notepad out again.

"Something like that."

"Bad enough that you would want them killed?"

I looked directly into Detective Green's pale blue eyes. God, those eyes seemed so familiar to me; my stomach fluttered again and I shook my head slowly. "I'm not a violent person, Detective Green, so much so that I can't stand to even watch movies where there's violence. So, no. I would never wish for anyone's death."

"Even not being close with your parents, Cassidy, it's odd that you have no emotion regarding this entire situation."

Taking a large breath, I was finally able to tear my gaze from his and worked at clearing my thoughts. "That house held memories that haunt my every thought; those people are what made those memories into nightmares. So no, Detective Green, I have no feelings regarding any of them being gone. I'm sorry if you think that means I somehow had something to do with this, but I don't have one fond memory from California since the morning of my sixth birthday."

Sanders stopped writing and shared an odd look with Green before Detective Green asked, "And your biological father? Would he have any reason to start this?"

My spine had straightened at the mention of my dad. "Detectives, do you believe this was arson?"

They shared another look and with a sigh Sanders admitted, "Investigators don't believe it was, but that doesn't mean we shouldn't be looking for someone who had a reason to want them dead."

"Well, seeing as my dad died on the afternoon of my sixth birthday from a heart attack, I would say it wasn't him either."

When understanding hit both of them, Sanders attempted to hide a sheepish look as he scribbled more notes, and Green's eyes softened; there went the stupid flutter in my stomach again.

"Honestly, no, I'm not upset that they're both gone. But if you knew about my life, you wouldn't blame me. And no, I had nothing to do with what happened this morning, and I doubt anyone did. Those people were drunks, and they were awful, but they didn't have enemies, because for the last dozen years they've kept to themselves and their liquor. Which is why I'm not surprised the entire house went down so quickly. With the kind of stuff they kept around, it wouldn't be much different from having bottles of gasoline just waiting to explode." I stood and straightened myself to my full five feet, two inches . . . yeah, I'm sure I was real intimidating. "So if there's anything else you need, detectives, I'll leave my number with you so you can get ahold of me. Because of legal matters and funerals, I'll be in California for a while. If you need me here longer, all you have to do is say the word."

Not understanding, or not caring that I was politely asking them to leave, they didn't move a muscle. "We can finish this here or at the precinct, Miss Jameson; sit down," Sanders said quietly as he looked over some notes and crossed something out.

"What did you mean when you said, 'if you knew about my life'?" Green asked.

My mouth shut as I looked back at Green's light eyes; they still held that same intensity, but his face had completely transformed. He knew. I was so stupid; why had I kept talking?

"Cassi, go sit with my parents at the breakfast bar."

I turned to see Tyler standing there staring at the detectives.

"I wasn't—"

"Unless you're about to arrest her, she's done talking to you," he said, cutting Green off, and my jaw dropped.

"Tyler!" I hissed.

"Cass, go. In. The. Kitchen."

The detectives stood and Sanders shook my hand. Green grabbed my hand but didn't shake it; he just held on and stepped close, saying, "That's my card. You need anything, ever, you call me." He looked at my eye for a long moment, then turned his attention to Tyler and glared at him. I could actually feel the anger coming off him in waves and it took me a moment to realize I had a freaking black eye.

Thinking about the shiner, how I must have looked like death after not sleeping at all last night and the emotional drain from the week with Isabella, I stifled a string of expletives that would have made a sailor proud and curled my hand into his, around the card in his palm. I wanted to explain that it wasn't what it looked like, but then I realized that was probably what everyone said. I know it's what I said to every person who wasn't Tyler growing up.

That weird sense that I somehow knew this man came back

when Green looked at me again. I nodded slightly and a soft grin crossed his face before he released my hand. I hurried past Tyler, who was now openly glaring at Green, and walked into the hall a few feet before tiptoeing back toward the den in time to hear Sanders ask Tyler if there was something he thought the detectives needed to know.

"I get it, you think she should be devastated that her childhood home and her parents are gone. It's suspicious that she's not, but she's Cassi, so she's not going to tell you what happened, and I know her not saying anything will only make her look even more suspicious and possibly get her in trouble later. Also, understand that I'm the only person Cassi has ever willingly told. I've told one other person and that person wasn't either of my parents. So this isn't something that she's okay with being spread around; my parents don't even know and as you can see she grew up a house away and we're best friends."

"Are you going to get to it, or are you going to make it sound even worse for her?" I recognized Sanders's voice and was wondering why they went back to having him talk.

"Cassidy was beat by her mom and Jeff every day from when she was seven until I took her with me to Texas a month before she turned eighteen. And before you go judging me, because, swear to you, the guy I told hasn't let it go for the two years since I told him, I wanted to tell someone, I wanted to get her away from them. But she said she'd run away before they put her in foster care, and I couldn't take care of her if that happened."

I pressed my fist to my mouth to quiet my heavy breathing. *Damn it, Tyler! This isn't something you just share.* It happened to me, and I'd only told him; he'd told three people now!

"So like she said, and yes, I was listening to your conversation, she's not sad to see them go, but swear to God that girl couldn't kill a spider. She wasn't lying about not being violent; she hates violence. I already know you saw her face, and before you go looking at me again like you think I did it, I'll tell you what happened. We were at a party and a fight broke out between a bunch of guys; Cassi wasn't even in the room when it started but must have heard it and was so upset by seeing it she tried to stop it and ended up getting hit instead."

My breath came out ragged as he finished; why hadn't he mentioned that it had been because of Gage? Tyler wanted us apart so much, you'd think he'd have just been dying to make it seem worse than it was and say I was in an abusive relationship.

"And as for her mom and Jeff? She hasn't talked to them, and doesn't talk about them. That girl in there has had a shit life, and that shit life was just thrown back at her after two years of trying to forget about it. I get you're detectives and this is what you do, but taking care of her is what I do. So if you want to interrogate someone, interrogate me. Not her. Please, not her." He had started off with an authoritative voice I'd expected the detectives to put an end to immediately, but when he finished, Tyler's voice was so tortured, it nearly broke my heart.

"Are you done, son?" Sanders asked after another moment.

"Yeah."

"Then sit down and tell me, do you or your parents know of anyone who would want to harm Mr. Jeff Kross and his wife?"

"No, like Cassi, I haven't seen or spoken to them . . ."

His voice trailed away to nothing as I went to the living room to lie down on the couch. I should have joined his parents, but at this point, I was so drained I didn't think I could even attempt to hold another conversation. I knew they were itching to find out what happened to my eye, but it would have to wait.

IN THE LAST WEEK, I'd had two more visits from Detectives Sanders and Green within two days of the first: the first to confirm the fire was indeed an accident caused by a candle near the bar—that visit included an apology for the pseudo-interrogation—the second to let me know they wouldn't be bothering me anymore. After examining dental records, the bodies found in the house were of one Jeff Kross and one Karen Jameson Kross. Both times I tried not to study Green, but each time I saw him I'd swear I knew him. We'd had a graveside funeral on Friday and Tyler had gone back to Texas on Sunday, three days ago, since he had finals that week. I still hadn't spoken to Gage, but I couldn't force myself to do it yet.

I had too much going through my mind still: my life with Mom and Jeff, the fierce look in Gage's eyes when he'd turned around to swing again, and most of all the way he looked like he was dying inside every time he looked at me after he'd hit me. Then I'd left him with a note that could have meant any number of things, and I'm sure that had only made it worse. I knew I couldn't have our first conversation over the phone; it needed to be in person. I just wasn't ready for that yet. If I was honest with myself, I was terrified that what had happened last Friday night would change how we were permanently. I didn't want him to treat me any differently, and I was afraid he'd treat me like I was breakable now.

"Miss Jameson? You can go back now."

Glancing up at the receptionist of my mom's attorney, I gave her a small smile and walked down the hall to the open door.

A lanky older gentleman stood up and grasped my hand from across his large desk. "Miss Jameson, thank you so much for coming in. I'm sorry that we're meeting under these circumstances though."

I simply nodded and offered him the same smile I'd just given his pixie of a receptionist.

"Well, this will be fairly quick, since you're the only living person mentioned in your mother's will."

That surprised me, but I didn't let it show. I figured she'd leave me out of it and give everything to Jeff, or hell, even her liquor. She was a bitch like that; it wouldn't have shocked me.

"Though he is not here, we will begin with the only other person mentioned: 'To Mr. Jeff Kross, I leave my car, home, and everything inside them. To Miss Cassidy Jameson, I leave the money in the following accounts.'" Mr. Buckner produced a few pieces of paper stating the bank accounts, not that they meant anything; they were just routing and account numbers. "And she also left this letter for you. Your mother came in about six months ago, Miss Jameson, to change her will and leave that letter. I was surprised, seeing as she hadn't changed her will even after your father passed, but I don't think she was expecting you to have to be sitting on the other side of my desk so soon. Your mother and father were good people, Miss Jameson; I'm very sorry for the losses you've had over the years."

I took the lumpy envelope from him. "Me too," I whispered, unable to force anything louder. I was still in shock that Mom had waited that long to change her will, and then died so suddenly after.

"If you'll give me just a few minutes, we'll get everything squared away here so you won't have to go in to the bank to change everything over, and then we'll be done. I've already called and they're expecting my call again."

"Thank you, Mr. Buckner."

After another twenty minutes and both of us speaking with a manager at the bank, he handed me a few pieces of paper that were faxed over from the bank, giving me the number of the new savings account I'd had everything put into and pages about how best to handle money. I folded them all up and put them in my purse along with the letter, shook Mr. Buckner's hand, and went to Tyler's mom's car, which she was letting me borrow. I drove until I found my favorite coffee shop and pulled into the parking lot. Without shutting off the car, I reached into my purse, opened the folded-up papers, and finally looked at the amount that had been deposited into the savings account. My mouth dropped open and a loud gasp filled the car. *What. The. Hell?*

I'd been fully expecting my mom to not have me in the will at all. When Mr. Buckner said I was getting her money, I thought it was a joke and she wouldn't actually have any. No way did I expect her to have this much, or to leave it to me! Mouth still wide open, I grabbed the letter and broke the seal, and my breath caught at what I saw. My father's ring, the one I'd clung to when he died and my mom had taken from me. I pulled it out of the envelope like it might break and just stared at it as memories of my dad came rushing back and tears instantly blurred my vision. I took deep breaths, slid the ring onto my thumb, and grabbed the letter. Unfolding it carefully, I took one last deep breath and looked down.

My dear Cassidy Ann—

Where do I even begin? There aren't words to begin to describe how sorry I am for ruining your life. Nor are there words to tell you how much I hate myself for what I've done to you, as well as let Jeff do to you. You are so precious, and I don't know how I ever let myself get so lost that I could forget that. Your father was my world. When he died, I didn't know how to go on, so I didn't. I was so weak, and neglected you . . . you were only a child! What's worse is I can't even remember you during that time, which means I can't remember what you had to do to keep yourself alive during those times. I was being selfish and focusing on my hurt, trying to find any way to make it go away. My friends helped keep me intoxicated since they didn't know I was already in that state at home, so I paid attention to them . . . but you? Where was I when you needed me? I don't even know where you were. What kind of mother doesn't know where her little girl is when she needs her the most? All I do remember is looking at you at the funeral and thinking about all the time your father spent with you; he was such an amazing dad, and I just knew I would never be able to look at you again without seeing him. And he was gone. So I did the only logical thing that came to mind at the time: I stopped seeing you.

When Jeff came into the picture, I was so far gone, I just needed someone there with me; I didn't care who it was. Guess it helped that he was rich, since we both had an expensive habit, but he hated kids. Told me the day I met him, and I should have stopped seeing him at that, but what did I do? I married him two weeks later. And then I just . . . became a monster. I know you already know he'd reward me when I would hit or kick you, and thinking about that now makes me sick to my stomach, but at the time for some alcohol-induced reason, getting rewarded for beating you sounded like the most amazing gift. Of course you already know all that, but I had to write it, had to put it out there. And now that it is, I just want to die for almost killing you hundreds of times and beating you thousands more. Gosh, sweetheart, I hate myself. I'm sick with grief and guilt for what I've done to you!

I've been sober three months now; it may not seem like much, but it is for me. Since your father passed, I hadn't gone longer than ten hours without drinking myself back to sleep. In these three months, I've finally realized everything that's happened over the last thirteen

*years, and that's why I'm writing this letter now. You, my sweet
Cassidy Ann, are so strong. What child, what adult even, stands
back up without a tear coming out of their eyes after being beaten
down, just so the other parent can take their turn? We ruined you,
we tried to break you, and gosh, sweet girl, I hope we didn't. You
deserve the best of everything. You deserve a husband who loves you,
cherishes you, and treats you like the princess your father always
said you were. You deserve kids who love you, and give you laughs,
tears, as well as moments that make you want to pull out your hair.
You deserve it all. I've prayed to God every day for the last three
months that you'll get that, and that you'll know you deserve that,
and I will pray it until my last breath.*

*Like I said, sweet girl, you are so strong, I am not. I can't
handle what I've done to you, and I can't handle what Jeff's begun
doing to me now that I'm sober. It doesn't compare to what you
went through, but I still can't take it. I don't know how to begin
to make anything up to you, actually . . . I know there isn't a
way. But I need to do this, for you and for me. If you're reading
this you've already been given the money; I hope it helps you get
started in life. I left Jeff the house and car for a reason; I'm sure by
now you're understanding that as well. If not, please read this next
part carefully and try to understand. I can't live with this guilt,
sweetheart, and I couldn't die knowing Jeff would move on to do this
to someone else. But know this: I love you, I swear I do. I'm so sorry
for everything, my darling girl!*

*I've been spending a lot of time in your room the last few months,
just staring at your wall. Your father wasn't the only one passionate
about the phoenix. Everything it symbolizes fascinates me. Being
given the chance to be reborn and start its life anew from its own
ashes . . . who can say that they've had that opportunity? Through
these ashes, I pray you're able to find peace, knowing that your*

nightmare is now over. I can't give you a new life, but this is your
chance to start your life however you want it to be, sweet Cassidy,
without Jeff or I tainting it. You're beautiful, and you have a bright
light that just bursts from you. Your smile can light up a room; your
father and I always said that, and it's true. Go shine your light on
the world, sweet Cassidy.

    I'll love you forever and always,
    Mom

I read the letter two more times and finally folded it up, put it back in the envelope, and safely tucked it away in my purse when I could no longer see the words. She'd killed herself. Killed them. For her? For me? She left the house and car to Jeff because she knew all three of those would be destroyed in the fire. How did she do this without Jeff trying to get out? They'd been badly burned, but the coroner was certain their deaths were due to the smoke and fire, nothing else. No way he wouldn't have fought to get out. And she just lay there and let herself be burned alive? My entire body shivered with a sickening chill. I didn't understand how someone could be so miserable that they would want to end their life, and to willingly be burned alive? I couldn't begin to comprehend it.

A sob burst through my chest and I covered my face with both hands. The mom in that letter hadn't existed for me for so long, I had never expected to see or hear from her again. And even though I hated her for what she did, I hated it even more that she'd been sober three months and had to go through it alone. At least I'd had Tyler; my mom had no one.

Another twenty minutes passed before I checked to make sure I didn't look like a wreck and walked into the cozy coffee shop so I could allow myself to get lost in a book. Or at least attempt to look like I was. I really just needed someplace where no one was trying to bother me so that I could think about Gage.

I was one person back in line when a somewhat familiar voice called out, "Cassidy?"

Looking to my right and then to my left, my eyes skimmed across the unfamiliar faces in the shop. As my eyes made their journey back to the front I saw a pair of uncertain pale blue eyes looking at me.

I started. "Oh my God, Detective Green?" I'd just seen him a week and a half ago, but he'd been in a suit and looked all badass and older then. Now he just looked like a normal guy in a coffee shop. Looking at him now, the sense of recognition hit full force and I struggled to remember how I knew him. He had on a blue henley shirt that did amazing things for his eyes and a pair of worn jeans that fit him perfectly. In other words . . . he looked good. Too good. My stomach fluttered, and though it took some effort, I was able to stop chewing on my bottom lip when I realized he was studying me intently.

He smiled crookedly. "Unless you want me to call you Miss Jameson, you can call me Connor."

Connor Green. Even his name was attractive. I watched as he ran a hand through his hair, making it stick up like he'd just rolled out of bed. God, I needed to look anywhere else but at him right now. "Please, just Cassidy . . . or some variation of that."

"All right." He chuckled. "Cassidy it is. Let me buy you a drink," he said as he set his cup on the counter and reached for his wallet in his back pocket.

"Oh no, that's not necessary." I gave the lady at the counter my order and reached into my bag.

"I want to, please." He handed the girl at the register his card and she swiped it through the machine.

The girl gave him an appreciative smile as she handed his card back to him, and my stomach and chest heated. I realized I was glaring at her and mentally shook myself. *What the hell? Why do I care if someone else looks at him? He's just an overly confident detective who I must know from a past life and who's done nothing but manage to piss me off . . . and make my heart flutter—nope! Nope . . . just piss me off.*

"Uh, thanks. You really didn't have to do that though."

Connor took a sip of his coffee and smiled softly. "Well, maybe this way you'll agree to sit and talk with me for a while?" My face must have fallen because he said swiftly, "I swear, no type of interrogation, I would just really enjoy your company."

He'd been kind of an ass the last few times I'd seen him, so I wasn't sure if I'd enjoy *his,* but I'd certainly enjoy the view. I thought about Gage and grimaced; I really shouldn't have been thinking of another guy like this. Especially *this* guy.

"If you're busy, I understand. It's probably awkward to talk to the detective who just questioned you regarding your parents' death anyway," he said quietly, and looked out the window, then back to me. His mouth opened and shut again with a hard sigh and shake of his head.

I twisted my father's ring around on my thumb and managed a shrug. "Well, I was going to sit here for a while anyway. I just got back from the reading of the will and have nothing else going on. You can join me if you want." I tried to act like I didn't care either way, but his crooked grin told me he wasn't buying it.

The guy behind the bar called my drink, and after I grabbed it, Connor led us over to a pair of plush chairs that were facing, and almost touching, each other.

"So they read the will today. How did that go?"

I studied his face to see if he was digging for information that would help with his job, but when he just looked worried, my head tilted to the side and I shrugged again. "It went. I was the only one there, so it was over pretty quickly."

He nodded. "So now that everything is over with, how long do you think you'll stay in California?"

"Not sure, I need to go back to Texas. I really just up and left everything, but I feel like I need to figure some things out first. Tyler went back on Sunday so I finally have time to myself. I'll probably take another week or so, unless you guys need me for something . . . ?"

"Uh, no." He huffed and shook his head slightly. "No, the fire and deaths were confirmed accidents. I know I already said it, but I am sorry for the way the questions went the first day—"

"Don't be," I said, cutting him off. "That's your job, right? Can't really blame you for doing that, and I've got to say, you've got it down to an art."

Connor sat back and laughed out loud. "An art, huh?"

"You do! I remember thinking that during. You look completely calm while you're talking, not giving anything away, but your eyes are so intense that it throws the person you're talking to off and I can see how you could get people to start spilling stuff. I know I did . . ." I trailed off and looked to the side.

"Your eye looks much better; the bruising went away quickly," he said, guessing the direction my thoughts had started going.

"Yeah, I hadn't gotten hit too hard. I'd just been trying to break up the fight, and one of the guys was pulling me away as an elbow connected, so it wasn't able to do much damage. And I know what Tyler told you. I was listening, just as he'd been listening to me. There was a reason I didn't tell you and Detective Sanders about my past; I've only ever told one person, and that was Tyler. He's known since it first started happening, and other than him I've never felt the need to share it. With how you were questioning me, I could only imagine how my past would make me look even more suspicious. I hadn't meant to say anything about your knowing anything about my life. It just slipped." I looked into Connor's now-soft eyes and continued. "Like I said, your calm intensity makes people say too much. But I didn't think that was a need-to-know, and it wasn't Tyler's place to tell you."

"I agree completely. And for what it's worth, since you were listening, I thought of a hundred different ways I wanted to go off on him for letting that happen to you growing up. You threatening to run away or not, you could've been killed, Cassidy."

My eyes had popped open the second he'd agreed with me but narrowed into slits toward the end. "You don't understand, Detective Green—"

"Connor."

I sighed. "Connor. You don't understand. Tyler was all I had. If we had told someone, they would've taken me away from the only person I had left. I couldn't let that happen."

"I probably understand better than you'd think," he said softly, and leaned forward, resting his forearms on his knees. "I didn't need you mentioning your life or Tyler telling me about your past to know what had happened. Within the first minute of questioning you, I knew you'd had nothing to do with the fire. Even if you had a rocky relationship and weren't close with your mother and stepfather, you would still have been upset over their deaths and the loss of your childhood home. When you were neither, I knew."

"How?" I asked quietly.

"Cassidy, only someone who would react that way to their own parent dying would understand your reaction."

My brow furrowed and I looked around like the walls would be able to explain that confusing statement. When my gaze met his, I saw it, the tortured numbness. I inhaled sharply and started to reach for his arm but stopped myself. "You?"

He nodded slowly. "My mother was a junkie. I knew who she was, but she wasn't around much. She'd sell herself to be able to afford her addiction, which is how my sister came along, and then me. Through all this, her husband stayed married to her. He didn't do drugs and he didn't drink; I wish he did so I could blame what he did on either of those. But he just hated us because we weren't his, and because of what we represented. My sister was six years older than me, so for the longest time, she was the one who took all the beatings he dealt. When I was old enough to understand what was happening when she'd lock me in the closet, I started holding my own and taking my half of the beatings. She didn't want to tell anyone, said what you told Tyler, that if we told anyone they would separate us. She said if we could make it until she was eighteen, she'd take me away and we'd start over.

"Then one night when I was seven he just lost it. He hit Amy so hard she wasn't waking up and ended up breaking both my legs and my left arm. I waited until he went to his room, like he always did after, and dragged myself out of the trailer and tried to make it to the neighbor's. I didn't get that far, but someone from the park had been walking their dog and found me, called 911. I'd passed out, and with all the blood they had thought I was dead, so police, EMTs, and homicide detectives all came out. My father was arrested, and Amy and I were rushed to the hospital. All I remember from that night other than trying to make it to the neighbor's trailer was waking up to one of the detectives sitting next to my hospital bed. He didn't say a word to me then, but when I woke up the next day he told me he was going to make sure no one ever touched me or Amy again. He and his wife fought hard and were able to adopt both of us. To me, *they* are Mom and Dad."

"Is he why you wanted to be a detective?"

Connor smiled his acknowledgment and his eyes went over my face. "I would never wish death on anyone, Cassidy, and like you, I wouldn't blink if someone told me that man or my real mother was dead." He stayed quiet for a few moments before speaking again. "I had to continue questioning you, even though I knew exactly what was going through your mind. But I hated every second. Looking at you, knowing what I'd come to realize, and seeing you with a black eye, I wanted to grab you and run you out of that house."

"I don't have a reason to lie to you now that you know the truth. I really was trying to break up a fight."

"I know. Once I realized Tyler wasn't your boyfriend, I sat there wondering who was so I could find him instead. But after Tyler basically spilled all your secrets and told us how you got the shiner, I figured it'd be pointless for him to lie about something like that. It's not like he gave us the whole 'she tripped' excuse."

I sighed and mumbled pathetically, "I've used that one before."

He grimaced. "You really don't talk about it often?"

"No. I mean, I told Tyler everything, but it was so he could figure out how best to take care of my injuries."

"I didn't open up for a long time, until I was almost sixteen I think, but once I finally did everything changed. I still don't tell just anyone; you're actually the first person I've told in a long time. But you need to relive it all and get everything out there, or else you're never going to move past it. You may think you have, but it'll always haunt you, Cassidy."

Thoughts of how easily all my fears had surfaced when I saw Gage at the party that night came to mind. Connor was right, but I'd spent so long not talking, I didn't know how, or if I even wanted to start now. "Did you have bones broken a lot?"

"That last night was the only time. Did you?" I don't think he'd even realized it, but his eyes had slipped into that same intensity he'd had a little over a week ago in the Bradleys' den.

"No, they were too smart to break anything. Had a lot of cracked ribs, but anything that would have required a cast they stayed away from. Stitches though . . . they didn't seem to understand or care that people needed to get stitches."

"Did that happen a lot?"

"Stitches? I needed them probably once a month or so, only ever got them a few times though. Tyler was good with butterfly bandages."

Connor's eyes widened for a moment and I bit my tongue.

"Uh, didn't you ever need stitches?"

He shook his head. "No, I didn't. Not until that last night." He paused and then leaned closer, his face only inches from mine. "Cassidy, how often did you get hit?"

I began to back away but one hand snaked up and locked behind my neck.

"Cassidy, how often did they hit you?" he repeated, and that cool intensity in his stare held me where I was. What was it about that stare and those eyes?

"Every day. Is that—is that not like your situation?" I asked when his next breath was audible.

The hand on my neck squeezed lightly and he hung his head. "No. For us it was every two weeks or so."

I mouthed the words he'd just said. I guess it was naïve, but I'd thought all kids who were abused had it pretty much the same as me. "Did you—" I suddenly broke off on a gasp and pushed back against his hand until he let go when he looked up at me from under his lashes. Oh my God, how could I have not recognized him?! I'd dreamed about that look, dreamed about those eyes!

"What?"

"You're that cop!"

His eyes widened and he straightened slightly. "I didn't think you recognized me."

"You knew who I was and you didn't say anything? You've just been acting like—like you cared?" I gasped again. "Were you even—" I backed away from him and grabbed my purse.

"Say it."

"It doesn't matter," I said coldly, and stood up before he could trap me in the chair again.

"Cassidy," he pleaded, but I was already walking toward the side exit door that emptied out into an alleyway. "Cassidy, wait!" Connor's hand grabbed mine and he brought me to a stop. "It *does* matter. You need to talk about it."

My hand involuntarily tightened around his even as I tried to walk away. "Are you a therapist too or does it just come with being a detective?"

"Neither, but you're never—"

"Stop with the hidden interrogation bullshit, Connor!" I cried "I know what you're doing! You're doing the same damn thing you did a week and a half ago! Only now you're—you're—you look like this!" I waved my free hand in front of him. "Did you follow me here? Did you think dressing like a normal person would help me open up to you? Were you even abused as a child or did you use that to get me to talk too? Did you just want to know my past so you could figure out if you made the right judgment on that call all those years ago? And why does it even matter anymore if they're dead?"

His brows slanted down and he backed me up until I was pressed against the wall. "You think this is all some play to solve a case, Cassidy? A case that's fucking closed? That was barely even opened? You honestly believe I would make up some sob story to get you to talk to me?"

"God, just stop! I know all of this was so you could find out the truth about my life! And I know you people do that, you lie about stuff to trick people into saying what you need them to, you make up stories so they think you'll understand. So I hope you feel better now that you've gotten what you're here for, but I obviously have nothing to hide from you anymore! And if you really want to know what I got out of the will, Detective Green, I got her money. I got a lot of it. Yeah, that probably makes me look even worse than before, but I couldn't care less about the money! I was shocked that I was even in her will. And another thing: the fire was no accident, but you won't be able to find the person who did it, because she killed herself in the fire."

"What?" His eyes bulged and one brow raised.

"She left me a letter, and from what she said in it, she was going to make sure both she and Jeff didn't make it out, but I don't think Jeff had a clue. So I don't know how or what exactly she did. But there you go. She killed herself and him. Burned that godforsaken house to the ground and took them with it. There's everything, Detective Green—"

"Connor," he all but growled.

"I know you don't give a shit about me, so drop the act!" I hissed back. "I just found all that out before I walked into the shop, so now you know everything I know. And now you know that yes, we lied to you when you showed up at the house a few years ago, but I couldn't let you take me away; I needed to stay near Tyler. Now, if you'll excuse me." I turned to leave but his grip on my hand tightened and his other hand came up to my shoulder.

"Cassidy, none of this was a damn act!"

"Look, I respect that you love your job, and you're good at it." The hand that was somewhat free tried to flail out. "Obviously. But I've had a crappy week. I've had bad memories resurface. I've visited the—well—now-burned-down house that I wanted so desperately to escape from my entire life. If that wasn't enough I have this annoyingly attractive detective who will *not* leave me alone, and I just found out that for the last three months my mother was sober for the first time in thirteen years! And because she was sober her husband decided to start beating her. She couldn't handle it, and she couldn't handle what she'd done to me, so she decided to kill herself and him, for me! She thought she was doing it *for me,* Connor! If only she had called me, I would have done something. I could have done something, right? I would have gotten her away from him, but she didn't, because she knew I wouldn't answer, because she knew that I hated her. She killed herself knowing that I hated her, and did it for closure for me. So I could start a new life. I just—I don't— why wasn't I there for her?"

Connor's arms wrapped around me, and it was then I realized I was sobbing. What was happening to me today? And what on earth did this man do to me? "Shh, Cass, it's okay. It's okay. Don't let that guilt get to you, none of this is on you, you hear me? None of it. Your mom had demons, and that was the only way she knew how to deal with them."

"But she sounded so much like how she was before Dad died. I loved her then, and I should have been there for her the last three months."

"Don't go down that road. It's going to eat you alive if you do." He held me until I stopped sobbing and shaking, then asked quietly, "What did she say to you in the note?" When I sighed and tried to pull back he added quickly, "God, that makes it sound worse. Please forget I'm a detective while we're together. This isn't an act, Cassidy, I've been thinking about you nonstop since we first left the Bradley house last Saturday. I had no idea you were even still in California, let alone going to be at this coffeehouse this morning. You don't have to tell me, but I can see how much you need to talk about your past. If you don't talk about it and this letter, it'll just get worse."

Without saying anything, I left my forehead pressed against his chest and reached into my purse to pull out the envelope. I held it up for Connor and was surprised when he shifted me so I was still wrapped in his arms while he opened and read it. My left hand was still curled into a fist against his chest and I slowly uncurled it to lay it flat at the same time I brought my right arm to wrap around his waist. Connor's arms constricted and for some reason it made my body relax even more into him. This was wrong, I knew it was wrong. I shouldn't have felt this comfortable, this good, in another man's arms. It wasn't like when Tyler held me; even after all that happened between us, it still felt like he was just my best friend and my rock all last week. But Connor? It felt easy, natural even. Which was more confusing than anything. I'd dreamed about him for years, but I hardly knew him and was still convinced he was just playing his part very well in order to get the information he wanted. That had to be it, right? He'd played me with the story of his "childhood";

he knew it'd get me and it did. I hadn't realized how much I'd craved someone who understood me.

"Cassidy, I have a few more questions regarding your past, and then I'll stop. Anything you tell me after that will be because you brought it up, all right?"

"Whatever," I mumbled so softly, I doubt he heard.

"She said she almost killed you, and you said you should have gotten stitches often. They didn't just hit you with their fists, did they." It was a statement, not a question. But I still nodded my head. "When I was called out to your house for the possible disturbance, why didn't you say anything?"

"I told you, I couldn't be taken from Tyler; he was all I had left in my life after my dad died."

"I saw it in your eyes, Cass, but without your help I couldn't do anything about it. I thought about you so much over the next couple years; I should have come back to check on you."

"I used to dream about you," I admitted into his chest. "There was something about you and your eyes . . . I don't know how to explain it. Part of me wished you'd come back and take me away, the rest knew I wouldn't let you take me away even if you tried."

His hand slid up and down my back in soothing trails. "The woman who called said she'd heard a woman screaming. Had they hit you that night?"

I nodded slowly, wondering what would have happened that night if I had told him everything. "It got worse after you left."

Connor froze and his arms tightened around me again. "How?"

"Jeff was convinced I'd somehow called the police, even though I'd been in a room with them for an hour before you even showed. My mother took off her shoes and came after me. Hit me repeatedly over the head with the heel of her stiletto. I wasn't able to move for hours until Tyler came to get me."

"Shit, Cassidy, I'm so sorry," he whispered, then stayed silent for a minute before asking, "In the letter she said she was rewarded; rewarded how?"

My body stilled and I instantly had to swallow part of my coffee that decided to make its reappearance. "Uh . . ." I licked my dry lips and swallowed again. "Um, sexually," I whispered into his chest. "Usually, I'd get up and leave, but sometimes I wasn't able to move and they wouldn't feel the need to go to their bedroom. So, if I was able, I'd just have to turn my head and try to block out the noise."

"Jesus Christ," Connor hissed as his body and one of his arms left me so he could drag his hand down his face while he whispered, "Sick. They were seriously sick, disturbed people. You didn't deserve that, any of it." There it was again. That tortured emptiness in his eyes. No way you can learn or fake something like that. It's just not possible.

"I know that, Connor." I'd heard it enough times from Tyler to know and believe that before I met Gage, and Gage had only confirmed what Tyler had led me to believe. "And you didn't either; no one does. Not even my mother."

His face changed into a mix of shock, awe, and relief, and his blue eyes seemed to brighten. "What is it about you?" he asked himself softly, and brushed some hair away from my face. We stood there studying each other for minutes before he broke the silence. "I'm pretty sure I've been looking for you my entire life, Cassidy Jameson."

Before I could question that, my back was against the wall again and his lips were on mine. A muffled high-pitched groan left me. Connor's lips were firm and soft all at once, and as they began to move against mine another moan left me at the realization that this ridiculously handsome man could *kiss*. But he wasn't Gage. Just as I'd started to push against his chest, he pulled slightly back and his pale blue eyes bounced back and forth between mine.

"Connor, I have a boyfriend," I blurted out.

He blinked quickly and pulled farther back. "You have a boyfriend."

"Yeah, in Texas. It's Tyler's cousin."

"Where is he?"

"In Texas," I said slowly, making sure he heard me, since apparently he hadn't the first time.

Connor shook his head like I wasn't getting it. "Cassidy, does he know about your past?" He still hadn't released his hold on me, but thankfully he wasn't so close that I was worried he was about to kiss me again.

"He's known since the day I met him; that's the person Tyler told."

"Right." Connor nodded and stepped closer. "Then tell me why the hell he isn't here with you now. If you were my girl, no way would I let you walk into your personal hell without me right there beside you."

"He doesn't even know why I'm here though. I just left."

That crooked smile was back and he leaned in, kissing me harder this time, letting his lean, muscled body press against me. "You aren't helping your argument," he whispered against my lips.

"I don't understand," I whispered back. "I thought you were just doing this to get answers about the fire and that night the police were called."

"No, Cassidy. I told you I have thought about you every minute since I left you that first day and I have been thinking of ways to see you. But seeing as you didn't give me your number, I thought it would be a little much to just show up unannounced. You're incredibly beautiful, Cassidy—God, you're so beautiful. Even when you'd had no sleep and had a black eye, I had to continuously remind myself to not just sit there and stare at you. And I didn't realize who you were until the last time we came to visit; the way you opened the door and looked up at me was what finally brought that night back to me."

"Connor—"

"Today, I swear to you I thought I was seeing things, because that's how bad I wanted to see you again. And you looked so different," he mumbled as he ran a hand through my hair. "No matter what you do, you look amazing. And then you tell me about your past, one that makes mine look like I spent it at Disneyland, and you say we didn't deserve what happened to us, and neither did your mom. Your mother, who did all of those things to you for all those years. And you cried for the woman she was before, and who she was when she died. Cassidy, I gotta tell you, I thought your beauty was only skin-deep when I saw you the morning of the fire, when I figured out your past. I thought you were wasting it when I thought you were in an abusive relationship. Now, after today, God, I know your beauty goes straight through to your soul. It's rare to find someone like you, and until a few minutes ago I hadn't realized I'd been looking for someone just like you. Someone who understands my past, someone with your heart; and as an added bonus, you don't let people intimidate you, and by 'people' I mean me and Sanders." He smiled crookedly. "And I just know the more I get to know you, the more I'm gonna find that I like."

My heart was pounding in my chest and I couldn't stop looking into his smiling blue eyes. The butterflies in my stomach intensified and I knew I was in trouble. "Connor," I murmured around his mouth, which was on mine again, "I'm in love with Gage. I'm going to marry him."

"Are you engaged?" He leaned back suddenly.

"No, but we both know we're going to get married. We talk about it often." *Or at least I think about it often.*

"Then why wouldn't you tell him where you were going, especially when it's something like this? Have you even talked to him since you've been here?"

I bit the corner of my bottom lip and looked to the side. When he smirked again I couldn't stop myself from saying, "He's the reason I had the black eye."

Connor's body went solid and his face fell.

"But it's not like you think, it's exactly how Tyler and I told you. There was this huge fight, and I saw Gage in the middle of it and I freaked. I hate violence, and I couldn't stand to see him hitting his friend. I wanted to yell at him to stop. Thinking about it now, I doubt it would've done any good anyway. All the guys were yelling at each other, girlfriends were shrieking at their boyfriends to stop, and the music was playing. But I tried to yell, I just couldn't get my voice to work. So I didn't think, I just ran in and tried to pull him off. He wasn't facing me and didn't know it was me. I'd been in the other room and as far as he knew I was just another guy getting ready to fight him. He flung his elbow back and turned around to throw a punch and that's when he saw me. It killed him, knowing he did that to me, but all I could see was the look on his face and my past came rushing back to me. Now that's *all* I can see when I look at or think about him. Tyler called to tell me about the house just a few hours later. So I did what I do best: I left."

Connor's arms dropped and understanding covered his face.

"I *am* in love with Gage. I just need to figure out how to not

see that look on his face every time I look at him from here on
out. Until then, I know he'll just continue to torture himself
knowing he hurt me that way."

"Talk, Cassidy."

"Um . . . I am talking . . ."

He shook his head. "That's exactly what I meant about needing to talk about your past, and now that letter. If you keep it
inside, they'll remain demons for you the exact way your mom
had her own demons. Those demons will take away every
happy thing in your life. You need to talk about it. If you don't,
you'll always see your boyfriend the way you saw him during
the fight." Connor blew out a deep breath and ran a hand over
his face. "Shit," he mumbled, "all right, I get it, you love him."
He handed the envelope back to me and pulled me into his arms.
"You want to marry Gage, Gage should be the one you talk to.
You need someone who understands what you went through,
you have my card. And I'll behave from now on." He grinned
at me and kissed my forehead and left his lips there as he spoke.
"Unless you're single. Then it's fair game and I'm fighting for my
turn next."

I laughed and pushed him back, noting that I hated the loss of
his arms around me. And hating that I hated that.

"That letter, Cass? Don't let it get to you. Like I said, she had
demons and that's how she thought she needed to take care of
them. You're beautiful inside and out, so I know you'll be able to
find the beauty in what your mother thought she was doing for
you. She thought she was giving you a new life, Cassidy. Don't
let them ruin this one too."

My heart swelled and my vision blurred.

"Would it be too much to ask if you wanted to finish your
coffee with me? You have a boyfriend, I already got that, but

that doesn't mean I don't want to spend time with you." Connor wiped a tear from my cheek and took a step toward the side door.

With my history of feelings for this man, and how my stomach fluttered and heart picked up its pace when he looked at me, it was probably not the best idea. But as long as he kept to himself, then having someone like Connor to talk to would be a godsend. "I guess it's good I have a lot of free time then."

He gave me a full-blown blinding smile and my heart stopped; my arms and lips tingled. Yeah—this was a bad idea.

15

Gage

LOOKING AROUND AT MY FAMILY, I couldn't help but notice someone was missing. It'd been two weeks. Two. Weeks. And not one word from Cassidy.

"Anything?" I asked Tyler, even though I already knew the answer.

"No, man, I'm sorry. Called Mom before the ceremony; she was asleep in the guest room."

I nodded and tried to swallow past the lump in my throat. I'd just graduated and we were now out to lunch, but I couldn't even attempt to smile or be happy about it. My entire world was in freakin' California and not talking to me. My family had come out yesterday, so they all knew what happened with her, and it was safe to say no one looked particularly thrilled right now. Amanda, Nikki, and Emily were pissed because they thought it was all my fault, which it was. Emily reasoned in her little princess voice that if I hadn't been a mean boyfriend and hurt Cassi she wouldn't have run away. I'd thought Cassidy had taken my heart with her; I was wrong. Because my baby sister definitely let me know I still had it when she helped break it a little more. Mom and Dad just looked worried, whether for Cassidy or myself, I didn't know. Needless to say, things were strained right now.

"We really are so proud of you, son," my mom said with a pained smile.

"Yeah, congrats, Gage," the three girls mumbled at the same time.

I glanced at Tyler anxiously and he just shook his head and leaned in close. "She's not calling me or answering my calls either. But Mom and Dad are watching her. I don't know what happened but Mom said she looks a lot better all of a sudden and she's been gone from the house a lot. It shouldn't be long, Gage, she'll come back." He clapped my shoulder and leaned back in his chair.

The weird thing about all this was it brought me and Ty together again. Like he said he would, he'd kept me updated. He'd texted me every day he was in California and came to my house the minute he got back to Texas to tell me everything he hadn't been able to say through texts. During this last week, he'd continued to give me every update his mom and dad gave him, and we'd actually spent time just catching up while he helped me pack up the house. I'd made Tyler pack up Cassidy's things; I couldn't stand seeing them untouched. For once, he actually wanted Cass and me to be together, but I was beginning to think it was too late.

"So you graduated college, what are you gonna do now?" Dad asked as he leaned back in his chair.

"What do you mean? I'm going back to the ranch." Not like

this was news. That had been the plan my entire life; that's why he'd helped me build my house on the ranch. The house I'd finished last Christmas, with Cassidy still in mind even though she had been with Tyler.

Dad just nodded and wiped food from his lips and massive mustache. "You can do that, if you want."

"If I want," I deadpanned.

"Think it's safe to say I'm speaking for the whole family: we'd rather you go to California and bring home our girl first."

Four sets of female eyes snapped to my face and brightened.

"Dad, she left. Again." I tried once more to clear that lump out of my throat and barely got the next words out. "It's over." Pain worse than I'd ever felt seared through my chest as I realized the truth of those two words.

"Doesn't look like it from where I'm sitting," he said, and played with his knife. "Now, almost everything from your place is already in the trucks. We'll finish and take it all to the ranch. It'll be there by the time you bring her back to Texas."

Tyler had his phone out and to his ear. "Mom, is she—yeah, he did. I'll tell him." He turned to look at me. "She said congratulations." When I nodded he put the phone back to his ear and said, "He said thanks. Is Cassi still there? All right, thanks. Yeah, love you too. Bye." After setting his phone on the table he looked at me. "She ran out to get some coffee."

"I could hear her."

"Gage, you might as well go to her," Tyler continued. "It's been long enough and she needs you just as much as you need her."

Before I realized what he was doing, my dad threw a credit card down in front of me. "Give me the keys to your place. Like I said, it'll all be at the ranch by the time you get back. Now get gone."

I fumbled with my key ring, my hands shaking so bad I wanted to toss the whole thing at him, but I still needed my truck keys to drive. When I finally got the house key off, I kissed the girls on their cheeks and ran out of the restaurant. This was it. This was the last time I could put myself out there for her. If she turned from me when I got there, it would be over. I would always love her; she would always be the girl I was supposed to spend the rest of my life with. But there are only so many times you can handle heartbreak with someone before you have to start protecting yourself.

I was at the airport in no time, but the only nonstop flight had *just* left, and the earliest they could get me there with the different connecting flights was seven hours. At least it was faster than driving. Handing over the card without a second's hesitation, I paid for the ticket. I got strange looks from the woman at the ticket counter and the TSA agents when they realized I didn't have a bag, but I didn't care. I just needed to get Cassidy.

Cassidy

CONNOR OPENED THE DOOR as soon as I started knocking. "Hey, everything okay? Don't get me wrong, I'm glad you called, but I was surprised you wanted to . . . come . . . over . . . holy shit." He breathed the last words and his pale blue eyes slowly danced over my body before coming up to meet my gaze. "Cassidy, you look amazing."

I looked down at my light purple threadbare racer-back tank and tiny black shorts. "Oh, um, thank you." I knew how he felt. He was wearing a pair of gray slacks and a black button-up shirt with a gray tie. The tie had been loosened quite a bit, the top two buttons of his shirt undone, and his sleeves were rolled up to his forearms. He looked delicious. "Can I come in?"

"Yeah, of course."

Connor and I had ended up talking at the coffeehouse for hours that Wednesday, and though I hadn't seen him since then, we'd talked and texted every day. Sometimes about our pasts, sometimes about my fears with Gage, his fears that he'd never find a woman who understood his past, and other times just to get to know everything about each other. I'd never been able to talk to anyone like I could talk to Connor. I'd thought I could talk to Tyler and Gage about anything, but after meeting Connor I realized there was something about our sharing our past that brought us together on a level I would never have with either of them. There was something about it that was just . . . nice, and wanted.

He opened the door to his apartment wider to let me through, then shut and locked it behind us. "So what's going on?"

"Are you going to work? Or am I interrupting something?"

He huffed a laugh and grinned crookedly. "No, I just got home after being on for thirty-six hours."

"Oh my God, Connor! You need to go to sleep, you shouldn't have let me come over." I started toward the door. "Wait, thirty-six hours? Why were you talking to me? You should have been working. Was I keeping you from your job?"

His smile softened and his pale blue eyes seemed to dance as he took a step toward me and wrapped me in his arms, pressing his forehead to mine. "I only talked to you when I had free time. You didn't interfere. I got the confession I needed, and we told the family this morning that the killer was caught." I inhaled audibly and his hand came up to brush my cheek. "You, Cassidy, could never be a bad distraction. When we had a minute, you were there for me to talk to; when we took breaks to eat or drink coffee, you were there. When I felt like I needed to take a step back from the case to clear my head, then go back in fresh, you were there. Now I'm home, and you're here. Honestly, I can't remember a time in my life when I was as happy as I've been since this last Wednesday."

My heart was pounding and the butterflies in my stomach were full force, which I was starting to think was the norm when it came to Connor. I let my fingers brush under his eyes, having just noticed the dark circles there. "You need to sleep, Connor," I whispered.

"I will." His lips brushed against my wrist and I actually had to force down a whimper. "Is it okay if I change?"

I leaned away from him. "How long have you been home?"

He pulled me back and rested his forehead against mine again. "Long enough to take my jacket off."

"Connor—"

"Cass, seriously." He chuckled and lifted his head, only to press his body closer to mine. "When you called twenty minutes ago, I floored it to get home because I knew you were going to be right behind me." His deep voice dropped even lower when he continued. "I wish I could come back to this every time."

My breaths started coming quicker and my eyes dropped to his lips before I could force them down to the knot in his tie. How was it possible to be so completely in love with someone but have this kind of a connection and chemistry with someone else at the same time? I'd felt this connection the moment I'd first seen him almost four years ago, but I hadn't had Gage at that time. To have it come back instantly while with Gage was incredibly confusing. I don't know when my hands had dropped to his neck, but I slid them to his tie and focused on undoing the knot and slowly sliding it off. Connor didn't move once, he just continued to stare at me. I looked down at the tie in my hands, then over at the dining room table, where his jacket sat on one of the chairs. He released me and walked over to the table with me right behind him. I laid the tie on top of the jacket as he started taking things off his belt and putting them on the table. Handcuffs, badge, phone, gun.

"Do you have a minute?" he asked as he began unbuttoning his black shirt. All I could do was nod as he shrugged it off. "Can I go take a shower first?"

"S-sure," I stuttered when my eyes snapped back to his.

His hand trailed down my arm to squeeze my hand before he grabbed the shirt, coat, and tie with one hand and turned away. Before he was out of my line of sight, his other hand caught the back of his undershirt's collar and he pulled it over his head, revealing his lean, muscled back and arms. And I had no doubt he did that on purpose.

Connor was back five or so minutes later, hair dark and messy from the shower, a gray fitted shirt and another pair of faded jeans on that I would bet were made just for him. "You want coffee?" When I shook my head, he leaned against a side wall smiling at me. "So what's brought you here?"

I twisted my dad's ring nervously and bit my lip to try to hide my grin but failed. "I want to show you something." I'd straightened my hair and thrown it up in a high ponytail so you could see the exposed part of my back easily, and with the loose, thin material of the shirt, it wouldn't be hard to move it out of the way to show the entire thing. With another smile toward Connor, I turned so my back was facing him, then looked over my shoulder at him to see his reaction.

The day after coffee with Connor, I'd gone to get a tattoo of a phoenix starting at the top of my right shoulder, covering part of my shoulder blade, and going toward the center of my back and ending at my waist. It had taken forever, but it was colorful and beautiful. I loved it; it wasn't just to honor my dad, it was a way to always remind me of my mom's sacrifice. She may have been fourteen years too late, and it may have been something I would have tried so hard to stop her from doing, but it's what she needed to do for herself and for me. It was the only gift she thought she could give me, and in some sick, twisted way, I understood.

"A phoenix?" His lips twitched up at the corners and he took the few steps up to me to move the piece of material going down the middle of my back. "Damn, this is *really* good," he said softly, and trailed a finger down my shoulder blade.

Goose bumps and a shiver spread over my body and I watched as his pale blue eyes darkened as they locked with mine. "You're going to have to forgive me, Cassidy."

In a move so fast I could hardly comprehend it, he turned my body so I was facing him, lifted me so my legs were around his waist, and had my back against the entryway wall, his mouth on mine and moving aggressively. The tip of his tongue lightly traced my bottom lip and I shivered again.

My mouth opened for him, and we both moaned when our tongues touched. My body was at war with itself. I was hating myself and craving Gage but enjoying this strange connection with Connor.

"Connor, stop," I said breathlessly. One hand was grabbing

a fistful of his wet hair, the other had his shirt clenched in it. Forcing both of them to relax their hold, I repeated myself even though he had stopped and currently had his forehead against my collarbone. "Stop."

Connor was just as breathless from the quick but aggressive kiss. "If this guy doesn't realize what he has, promise me you'll come back, Cassidy."

"What makes you so sure I'd want you too?"

He looked up and grinned mischievously. "One, you think I'm annoyingly attractive and admitted to dreaming about me. Two, you got goose bumps the second I touched you"—his eyes shifted down for a second to look at my arm, then came back to meet mine—"and still have them. And three, even though you fight it when we kiss because of your boyfriend, those high-pitched noises that come out of your throat when our lips meet and the way your body instantly reacts to mine says it all."

My chest was heaving up and down quickly; I knew he was right and was thoroughly embarrassed and feeling guilty about it. "I think you should put me down."

"You're about to walk out of my life, so when you promise that you'll come back to me if you and Gage don't work out, I will."

"I'm nineteen," I blurted out.

He chuckled. "And I just turned twenty-five. Your point?"

"You're only twenty-five? But you're—you're a detective. I thought you were close to thirty."

"Do I look thirty?"

"Well, no." I felt my cheeks redden and I looked to the side. "I just figured you had to be older to be a detective."

"God, I like that too," he said softly as he looked at my cheeks.

"Connor."

His eyes snapped back to mine. "I've always known I wanted

to be a homicide detective, so right away I started working hard for it. Only been in homicide for six months, and the youngest guy next to me is thirty-four. But regardless, I've seen your driver's license; I know you're almost twenty. Not that it matters either way; you don't act your age. You're mature because of what you had to live through, and if I had to guess, I'd say Gage is a bit older than you too."

"Twenty-two," I responded immediately.

"Have you talked to him at all since you left?"

I didn't respond, because I hadn't.

"Has Gage tried to call you?"

My head and eyes lifted slightly to look into his. "No."

He nodded and leaned in so his lips were at my ear. "Cassidy, you're in love with someone who isn't here. He hasn't called, and he hasn't come looking for you. Not only that, you haven't tried to call him either, and we've been talking nonstop for three days, and first thing this morning you're in my apartment to show me something extremely important to you. Not Gage's . . . mine. We have—whatever this is between us, I know you feel it too. So what has to happen and what can I do to convince you to stay here with me, to be with me?"

"I'm sorry, but I have to go back to him. I see how it looks for you, but you don't understand my past with Gage."

"Then promise me, Cassidy."

I waited until he was looking at me again. "I promise if it doesn't work out with Gage, I'll come back to you, Connor. But I need to tell you, he's *it* for me. So I don't want you waiting for me to come back, all right? I won't lie to you, Connor, you mean something to me. I agree we have *something,* I know that and it's pointless to act like we don't. Other than you, Gage is the only guy I've ever felt anything like this for, and if he had never entered my life, I wouldn't be able to walk out your door right now, but he has and he changed me completely. You'll find someone who changes you too, but it isn't me."

"He's very lucky." Connor's eyes roamed my face for a few seconds before speaking again. "I'm guessing you want me to put you down now."

"I'd appreciate it if you would."

He took a step away from the wall and set me on my feet. "I do like the tattoo, Cass. I like it a lot. I'm guessing you've been thinking a lot since Wednesday?" When I nodded he continued. "And you're ready to start talking, am I right?"

I smiled. "I bought a plane ticket last night; I leave in four hours. I just had to come and see you first. I wanted to show you."

"I'm glad you did. Not glad you're leaving though."

"You're an amazing guy, Connor, thank you for everything." I leaned up on my tiptoes and kissed the corner of his mouth.

"I'd ask if I could take you to the airport, and I will if you want me to, but right now I'm going to be blunt and tell you I'm struggling with what I want and what I know you need. You already know I think you're beautiful, but you come in wearing this, and that tattoo? Christ, Cassidy. I've never seen your smile this bright, and God, it's sexy. So unless you're ready for me to kiss you again, it would be best if I didn't take you."

"Then you probably shouldn't take me," I said with a small smile. "In a weird way, you arguing with me and letting me cry into your chest outside the coffee shop helped me more than Tyler or Gage has ever been able to. And you're not the only one, you know. I'll cherish these days I've had with you, I'll never forget you, and I'll always be grateful."

"Cassidy."

"Yeah?"

"Go, or I'm pushing you back up against the wall and this time I'm not letting you leave." He smiled crookedly at me as his hand came to my waist.

I sidestepped toward the door. "Good-bye, Connor."

"Bye, Cass."

"CASSIDY, WHAT THE HELL?" Jesse whispered as he stepped onto the porch and shut the door behind him. "You've been gone, what . . . two weeks? Gage's a fuckin' mess and now you're here all of a sudden?"

"Jesse, it's a long story. A *really* long story. You've seen Gage? When was the last time?"

"I haven't seen him for a few days now, but every day for a while there he'd come into the shop and ask if I'd heard from you. So spill. What's going on?"

I pressed the lock button on the fob for the SUV I went to buy after I'd taken a cab to Gage's town home to find it completely cleared out. He'd graduated that morning, so I was guessing he was back at the ranch; I just hadn't expected him to be gone so soon. Even with help, that was really fast to clear out a house and leave. I knew I had to get to the ranch to talk to him, but I needed to make this stop first.

"I can't go into it all right now, but I need to talk to you about something else. Jesse, I just came into a lot of money, and I know you don't like help but I want to help with your mom's medical bills."

Jesse looked at the Tahoe with wide eyes, then back at me. "First, I don't want to know what you did to come into this money. Second, I'm stealing that car from you. Third, didn't Gage tell you about the bills?"

"What? No, what happened with the bills?"

"Cass." He sighed and grabbed my hand to lead me to the porch swing. "The day y'all first brought food over for us, when Gage took me outside, he said he and his dad had talked and were going to pay for all Mom's bills. They even paid the mortgage last month."

My heart swelled for the man I loved. I knew he had reservations when it came to Jesse, but he'd been silent about them since I told him about Isabella. Still, I'd never expected him to do something like this. "Oh, Jesse—"

"Yeah, tell me about it. And without the stress on either of us, I can see how much easier it is on Ma. Only having to concentrate on fighting the cancer has helped her a lot. It's been a blessing. But, Cassi, tell me why you left."

I took a deep breath in and out. "Can I come in? I grabbed some groceries so I could make you two an early dinner. I went home to see Gage, but he's already back at the ranch. I was going to go there but it'll be too late and I'll need it light when I drive to find my way, so I'll wait 'til tomorrow. If you want, you and Isabella should come with me, so Gage's family can meet her."

Jesse grinned. "I think we'd both like that. Why don't you sleep here tonight, we'll leave early tomorrow, yeah?"

I could have gone to Tyler's, but I didn't know if he was still in town. I hadn't talked to him since he'd come back either. "All right, help me with these groceries. I'll get the food started, then I'll tell you guys everything. But first, I think I need a hug from your mom. I've missed her."

His crooked grin turned into a full-blown, blinding smile that reached his dark eyes. "She's missed you too. It'll be good to have a Cassidy meal again." He winked and nudged my side before helping me up and following me to my new Tahoe. "Stealing this car," he mumbled as we approached it.

"How about this: you can have this if you give me your '69 Camaro."

He looked appalled. "Oh *hell* no."

"That's what I thought. I'll keep my pretty beast, and you can keep your baby." That car *was* his baby. He'd tried to sell it a hundred times to help with his mom's bills but she would hide the keys so he couldn't drive or sell it. I knew he would've in a heartbeat, but I bet he was glad he still had it.

"Stealing this car," he breathed again, and I laughed as we shut the doors and headed back up to the house.

16

Gage

I WAS JUST PULLING UP to the main house on the ranch as Dad
was getting ready to start the day. He took one look at me and
hung his head, let it shake to the side once, then came over to me
and pulled me into a hug. One I didn't, couldn't, reciprocate.

"What happened?" he asked when he pulled back.

"She's gone." I tried to act like it didn't bother me, but fuck, it
did. My world, my heart, was gone.

"She gonna stay in California?"

"Nope." I let the word pop and looked over toward the stables.
"Got to the house and Aunt Steph was surprised as all get-out to
see me. Said Cass asked her to take her to the airport that morning when she got back from getting coffee. Cassidy's words: 'I
need to leave, would you please give me a ride?' She's gone, Dad.
I came right back and drove through the night."

"Shit, son, well, maybe she's coming back to Texas."

"And still not calling me?" I laughed humorlessly and shook my head. "No, Dad, she's gone." I had to bite my tongue and looked over at my hand, which was gripping the door to my truck. Slamming it shut, I yelled, "Damn it!" My hand fisted and I wanted to punch something, anything, but like Tyler had said, my temper was what had driven her away. I let my back hit the door and slid down 'til my ass was on the ground and let my head fall into my now-relaxed hands.

Dad sat down next to me, and before I knew it, Mom was out there in front of me with her hands on my knees, staying quiet, which was completely out of character for Mama.

"She's it. Cassidy's it for me, I've never doubted that, not since I first met her. Y'all know what Tyler did to us; y'all know why it was so hard for us. And now? Now I can't blame anyone but myself. I pushed her away, and this time she's not coming back."

"If she's it, then she'll come back," Mama said hopefully.

"Not this time, Mama."

After a couple minutes, Mom spoke again. "You'll find someone, Gage." But even she sounded doubtful. She'd been worried when Cassidy and Tyler broke up, but after I'd told them about what Tyler had done to me and Cass . . . hell, Mama was practically planning our wedding.

"Yeah, I will," I said, surprising the shit out of both of them by the looks on their faces. "But she'll never be Cassidy, she'll never have me. Not the way Cassidy does. She'll always be the girl for me, no matter what." I mumbled the last part, then stood and walked into the house, up the stairs, and to my room to take a shower.

After, I lay on my bed for a couple hours before going down to the kitchen to grab breakfast. The girls looked at me like they still hated me, and I hated me too. "Goin' for a ride," I announced when their glares got to be too much. Hell, Emily at barely six was glaring just as good as Amanda was.

When I got out to the stables and got to Bear, I just stood there staring at him, thinking about the night on the hill with Cassidy, the tattoo on her arm, and the way it felt to have her sitting in front of me on my horse. With a reluctant sigh, I greeted him and ran my hands over him before saddling him up and heading out.

Cassidy

I HOPPED OUT OF MY SUV and waited until Jesse pulled in behind me. Taking in a deep breath and loving the smell of the ranch, I stretched my body and went over to help Isabella out of the Camaro.

We'd woken up really early that morning, and after a quick breakfast and making sure Isabella felt up to the journey, we set off. Isabella was more than excited; knowing she was meeting the family had her feeling amazing, even through the sickness. I know I should have called, but I *still* couldn't bring myself to first talk to Gage over the phone. His truck and Ty's Jeep were the first things I'd noticed when we pulled up. I was surprised that Tyler was there, but I'd been out of contact for a bit and they'd always been close, so I was really happy for them.

I'd just gotten Isabella out when Tyler came running out of the house, followed closely by all of Gage's sisters. I took a few steps from Isabella, since it didn't look like Tyler was going to stop, and was glad I did when he grabbed me and swung me around.

"Damn it, Cassi, you have so much you need to talk to him about. He's . . . he's really fucked up, sweetheart."

I nodded my head against his shoulder before he let me down.

"Whose Tahoe?" he asked appreciatively. "And who are they?" he asked, looking at Jesse, who was holding his mom up.

"Uh, my Tahoe, bought it yesterday." I grinned impishly. "And this is Jesse and his mother, Isabella."

"You're Isabella!" Amanda gasped, and she quickly came to my side to hug me, touch my cheek gently with her fingertips, and smile brightly at me. "I'm so happy you're here, Cass," she said softly, then turned to Isabella and Jesse to introduce herself.

I was surrounded by hugs from Nikki and Emily and quickly explained to Tyler who Jesse and Isabella were. I'd told them last night about everything, so they knew about the fight, the fire, California, and Tyler, but Jesse still didn't seem to like Tyler all that much. I did notice he and Amanda couldn't take their eyes off each other though, and Isabella took one look at them, turned to me, and winked.

Emily and Nikki tugged me toward the house, Amanda helped Isabella, and Jesse and Tyler got all the bags and followed us in. When Gage's mom, Tessa, heard us all come in, she walked out of the kitchen and actually dropped her wooden spoon as she ran to engulf me in a hug that lasted for what felt like minutes. When she pulled back, her eyes were bright with tears and she was touching my cheeks just as Amanda had done.

"Oh my sweet girl, thank you."

My eyebrows drew together in confusion, but I didn't have time to ask what she was thanking me for because it was then that she noticed Jesse and Isabella, and the next round of introductions took place. Of course, she grabbed the phone and called Gage's dad right away, telling him that he had to come back immediately. Not ten minutes later, he waltzed in, took one look at me, and a huge grin broke out from under that Sam Elliott mustache. He took large steps across the room and picked me up off the floor to hug me before setting me back down.

"Damn, girl, it is good to see you in this house."

"Thanks, John," I said softly. I just hoped Gage felt the same way. "John, this is Jesse and his mother, Isabella. They're the family you've been helping."

Isabella was crying softly and Jesse actually left her side and walked right up to John to hug him. John's eyes went wide with shock and his hands came up and patted Jesse's back. When Jesse stepped back and tried to thank him, no words would come out and he just hung his head. John patted his shoulder and walked past him to sit next to Isabella on the couch and pull her into a hug as the rest of the family had done.

Tyler wrapped an arm around my waist and touched the exposed part of my back. "That's awesome, Cass, when'd you get it?" he whispered.

"Thursday. Where's Gage?" I'd bought a couple of those racer-back tanks; the one I was wearing today was a dark green, the same color as Gage's eyes, eyes that I'd spent way too long without.

He pulled me back a ways from the living room toward the dining room. "The girls said he went out to ride a couple hours before you got here. He must have gotten back sometime early this morning; I was still asleep when he did and when he left."

"Gotten back?"

"He went to California yesterday to get you, Cass; got to my parents' house, and my mom told him you were gone. From what Aunt Tessa said, he thinks you're *gone* gone. I'm tellin' you, Cass. He's. Fucked. Up."

"He went to California? How did he know I was there? Did you tell him?"

Tyler looked at me like I was dense. "Cass, come on, I told him when we were in the airport before we even left Texas. I thought you just left without a word. He'd already woken up and was looking for you. He told me about the note you left him—not a good choice, by the way." He raised an eyebrow at me.

"Wait! He has known where I was for two weeks and he didn't try to come get me or call me before yesterday?" Connor's words in his apartment yesterday morning started flooding my mind.

"Gage and I decided it was best. You were slipping away, and it was because of what Gage had done. If he had tried to push you by calling or coming right away, which he wanted to, we both agreed it would have just pushed you even farther away. We agreed to let you work it out and wait for you to come back to him, but he's been so messed up, yesterday he just couldn't wait any longer."

"But now he thinks I'm gone," I said softly.

Tyler nodded. "Yeah, sweetheart, he thinks it's over."

His words felt like a physical blow and I bent slightly, reaching out to grab Ty's arm to keep myself standing. "It can't be. I just had to deal with what happened, I had to fix me. And I did. I couldn't come back to him without fixing *me*."

"You guys will figure it out—you're meant for each other." He kissed my head and wrapped his big arms around me. "Just be easy on him, all right? Like I said, he's not doing well."

"Yeah," I whispered, and looked back over at Isabella. I remembered all the stories she'd told me of her true love during the times I'd come to visit her, and how she was so sure Gage and I were soul mates and would be together forever. God, I hoped she was right.

Gage

BEAR AND I were making our way over the last hill before the main house came into view. I'd spent the morning staring at the house I'd built with Dad, unable to make myself go inside. We'd run for a bit to get some pent-up energy out of Bear and for me to try to clear my mind, but nothing helped; it just reaffirmed that Cass was gone. As soon as I saw the house, I saw the other cars, and when we got closer, I noticed a brand-new Tahoe and familiar Camaro . . . Jesse's. *Shit,* I thought, *something happened to Isabella.*

Making quick work of taking everything off Bear, I left him out in one of his fields so he didn't have to go back into the stable and forced myself into the house. I'd come to really like Isabella over the past two months; she was just as sweet as Mama, and she always welcomed me and Cassidy. I dreaded the day Jesse would call with the bad news. And today, I just didn't think I could handle it.

I heard laughter when I opened the door and, when it shut, the noise stopped completely. There was a buzz in the air and it was making my heart race. I felt like I should have known what was happening, but I was so far gone from what was going on with Cassidy, I couldn't focus on it enough. Turning the corner to the living room, I stopped dead and gripped the corner of the wall.

Cassidy, Isabella, and Mama were sitting on the main couch, each with completely different expressions on their faces, but all I could focus on was Cassidy's. She looked like she was about to burst, like she'd just seen the sun for the first time and was terrified that it was about to be taken away from her.

She slowly got off the couch and made her way to me, stopping when she was just inches from me. All I could think about was the fear she'd had in her eyes the night she left and how she'd flinch away when I tried to touch her. The fear on her face now was nothing like her fear of me, so I slowly brought my hand up, dragged the tips of my fingers across her right cheekbone, and cupped her face. Not once did she flinch, not once did she blink, and her body didn't still when I touched her; it relaxed.

That was all I needed to know.

I grabbed around her waist to haul her body to my chest and crushed her mouth to mine. Not caring that my entire family was staring at us. Not caring about anything except for that little noise in the back of her throat, and that her arms immediately went around my neck, her hands taking off my cowboy hat and letting it fall to the ground, grabbing fistfuls of my hair. Without another word I walked us out of the house and toward my truck, cursing when I realized it was blocked in. A second later the Tahoe bleeped and the lights flashed, and Cassidy smiled slyly as she handed me the fob.

"How?"

"I'll explain everything. Can we go to our spot?"

Kissing her soft lips once, I whispered against them, "I'll do one better."

I drove us to the house and watched Cassidy's confused face as it came to view. "What is this place, Gage?"

Swallowing hard, I grabbed her hand and looked at her. "It's our house, darlin'."

At the word *our,* her head whipped around to mine and her eyes went wide. "Our house?" she whispered. "We have a house?"

"If you want it." Her eyes went bright with unshed tears and she turned to look out the windshield, taking in everything about the outside. "C'mon. Let's talk and I'll show you around."

We walked around the house first. The entire time she held my hand tightly, and her other hand was covering her mouth, which was wide open. By the time we got inside, I couldn't go any farther; I pulled her to me and kissed her long and hard. Something about being in our house ignited something in both of us and the kiss quickly escalated.

I was kicking off my boots at the same time as I unbuttoned her shorts and pulled them over her hips, taking her lacy black underwear with them. My fingers trailed over her heat and I damn near died when I found her completely ready for me. She moaned and arched against my hand when I slid two fingers in her and her gasp filled the empty house. Her head had fallen back, and she righted it, trying to focus her eyes on my plaid button-up. When she was tugging it down my arms, I took my fingers away and helped her remove the shirt, laying it flat on the floor before standing up and grabbing that sexy-as-sin green shirt she was wearing and pulling it, and another light shirt I hadn't noticed, off her, revealing Cassidy without a bra.

"Babe," I growled, and bent to take one of her perfect breasts in my mouth, loving the way her fingers slid through my hair as she gently kept my head in place.

Too soon her hands were gone, but then they were at my jeans and in no time she had them off and had taken my length in her hands, and I had to struggle to stay standing as I kicked the jeans and boxer-briefs away from us. Removing her hands from me, I hitched her legs up around my hips and helped lay her on my shirt on the floor.

"Gage, I love you," she breathed as she brought my face to hers, and I smiled against her lips.

"God, darlin', I love you so damn much. Don't ever leave me

again." I kissed her once more before making my way down her body.

I should have taken my time kissing every inch of her now that she was back in my arms, but that would have to wait 'til later. I needed to take care of her, of us, and I needed to do it right now. Not wanting to tease her, I dove right in and her back arched off the ground. The sexiest moan you've ever heard filled the room and her hands wove their way through my hair to keep my head where she wanted it. I groaned against her, having missed the taste of her, the way my sweet Cassidy completely let go when we were together, and thanking God that she had come back to me.

She came so hard and fast, I wanted to stay there and make her come again that way, but I knew I'd have time for that later. Now I needed her. Her hands were already pulling my body back up hers, and though I tried to be considerate to her and not kiss her after that, she slammed our mouths together and swiped her tongue against mine, moaning even louder when she tasted herself. Dear Lord, my girl was hot. She wrapped her legs around me at the same time I sank into her and our kisses cut off as she cried out and I groaned. Feeling her around me took away the last of the tension of those last two weeks and I reveled in the feel of her.

"Oh, Gage, please. Please move."

I smiled and bit at the hollow of her neck before whispering in her ear as I slowly slid out, "Yes, ma'am." And slammed back in.

"Gage!" she cried, and her back bowed off the ground again, her head pressing against it.

I wanted to take this slow, I swear I did, but I just couldn't. And thank God she was right there with me, matching each thrust and urging our bodies to go faster and harder. She had just started to tighten against me when her body started shuddering and I rode out her orgasm a little longer before I found my own release and collapsed onto her. Cassidy took my weight easily and wrapped her arms around my shoulders, letting one hand softly caress my back.

"Welcome home," I mumbled into her shoulder, and she burst into giggles.

"I'd say that was *definitely* a welcome home."

"Don't ever leave again, darlin'," I pleaded, and she squeezed my shoulders before releasing them.

"Never." She brought my head up and kissed me softly before looking into my eyes. God I missed those whiskey eyes. "Do you want to get dressed and we'll talk? It's going to be a long talk, I have a lot to tell you."

"Nope." I rolled off her and pulled her onto her side as well. "I want you to stay like . . ." I trailed off as I caught a flash of color on her exposed shoulder and leaned up to look over it. "You got a new tattoo?"

"I did." Her smile was one I'd never seen before and she rolled away so I could see it. It was one badass-looking phoenix, and before I could ask what had made her get that, she rolled back so she was facing me. "I'll get to that part but not yet. It'll be explained though."

"All right, darlin'."

Cassidy

THREE AND A HALF HOURS LATER, and I was sitting up on the floor, looking down at Gage, who was propped up on both elbows, staring down at the hardwood floor. I'd just finished telling him my story, every part of it. He'd thrown on his jeans and I'd put on my underwear and my racer-back tank when he had to go out to my car to get the letter from my mom, but other than that, we'd stayed half-naked and in the same spot where we'd had our "welcome home."

Of course he'd known some things about the beatings from Tyler, but he'd never heard about them from me. I told him about all the different ones that stuck out in my mind, how and what Jeff would reward my mom with right in front of me after they got done almost killing me, and about the times when I'd be able to walk away after they beat me, how I'd still be able to hear their moans filling the house. I told him about how I had to shut off my emotions, what I felt when it was happening, before and after, and how Tyler was my savior during those times.

He flinched, but I still told him everything I felt and thought when I saw him hitting Grant, when he elbowed me, and the flashbacks when he turned to hit me again. I explained how I'd thought that until I was able to be past that, I couldn't talk to him, because it would just continue to get worse for us. Then I mentioned the fire and what led to Detective Sanders and Detective Green questioning me, which led to the reading of the will, all the money, and the letter from my mom. I'd had to stop for a second and take a few deep breaths before I told him all about Detective Connor Green, and when I say "all," I do mean *all*. I told Gage about my feelings for him after he'd shown up that night years ago, the coffee shop this past week, the alleyway, and the hours afterward. Gage read the letter again after I told him about the alleyway with Connor and that was when I told him how I had come to see the beauty in my mother's actions with the fire and why I'd decided to get the tattoo. I didn't need to explain why I got a phoenix, since it was in the letter, but I

did tell him all about my dad's ring and the painting that had
been on my bedroom wall. Gage was pissed that Connor had
kissed me, but his eyes had gone solid when I told him about the
hours on the phone and texting in the days following, and going
to his house Saturday morning. I didn't leave a thing out from
then either; I told him everything, from the way I felt to taking
his tie off for him and watching him take his shirt off. How I
kept thinking about leaving to see Gage while Connor was in
the shower and, as soon as Connor was back, how the butterflies
were back again. What happened when I showed him the tattoo
and how he had my legs around his hips and me pressed against
the wall in under a second, and how I'd started to kiss him back
before I told him to stop.

As I had with the phone calls, texts, and coffeehouse, I told
Gage everything we talked about when Connor had me pressed
to the wall, including my promise to him. Gage's hands had
curled into fists and his jaw started ticking from the pressure.
I wanted to run my fingers down his jaw so he would relax, but
seeing as I was the reason he was so pissed off, I just scooted
back a few inches and held his flat stare as I continued to tell
him how I told Connor not to wait for me and that Gage was it
for me, kissing him, and then leaving. I ended with flying back
to Texas, going to the town house to find it empty, going to buy
my dream car, and stopping to see Jesse and Isabella in hopes of
helping them with their financial situation before going to find
Gage so I could tell him about how I'd been forced to face my
demons, and that I knew what I had to do to overcome them.

Connor, as I'd told Gage, was really attractive and sweet but
didn't hold a candle to Gage. What he had that Gage didn't
was an understanding of my past, and before Connor sat down
with me at the coffee shop, I hadn't known that I needed that.

But what I had come to realize was that it wasn't Connor, and it wasn't that he'd gone through what I did; it was that I was keeping that part of my life from Gage. I wasn't giving Gage a chance to understand it and help me with my demons. He would never know what it felt like, but by telling him everything and by baring my soul to him, I could allow him to be there for me and it could only help our relationship improve. And as I'd hoped, as soon as I told him everything, I felt a new connection in our already unbreakable bond that came from my opening up to him about myself. But now he wasn't speaking, and he wasn't looking at me. And since the better part of the last hour had been spent talking about Connor, I could only imagine why.

"Phone."

"What?"

"Phone, Cass, give me your phone." He turned to look at me and his eyes were still flat.

I nodded and dug through my purse as I held his stare. "I know why you want it, and I'm not going to stop you. But, Gage, I just told you all of this; do you want to talk about it first?"

"No. When I can stop thinking about you and him, I'm gonna come back, and then we'll talk about it." He took my phone, stood up, and walked out of the house.

Gage

I SLID MY FINGER over the phone, and though I wanted to, I didn't check the messages. Cassidy had been painfully honest with me, so I knew she hadn't hidden one damn thing from me. Checking the messages would only be saying I didn't trust her, and I did. I went to her recent calls, and though I knew she'd been avoiding everyone but this detective, it still felt like a blow to see his name as the top four of her recent calls. Next to each of them was a number. Three, five, two, six. It didn't take more than a second to add them up. Sixteen. They'd called each other sixteen fuckin' times in a matter of two days, which he was working the majority of, and one morning. My stomach churned and I pressed on his name. It only rang twice before he picked up.

"Cassidy." He sighed, sounding relieved. "God, I'm glad you called."

"Not Cassidy," I responded.

It only took a few seconds for him to get it. "Gage," he stated firmly.

"Yep."

"So she's there with you."

"Yep."

"And you're calling, which means she's told you about me."

What pissed me off more was that he'd known about me and still kissed her, begged her to stay with him. "Told me absolutely everything about you, including how she felt about you."

"Everything," he said doubtfully.

"Everything, meaning I just had to listen to my fuckin' world talk to me for an hour about a guy who knew about me and still fuckin' kissed and had her up against a wall with her legs around him. She even told me how she helped you out of your clothes before you got in the shower. So yes, I know it all."

"Jesus."

"I don't appreciate people touching what's mine," I said in a low warning tone.

He didn't care or back down. "I've never met anyone like her. It didn't take me more than a couple minutes to know I wanted her, and not just in my bed. Girls like her don't just come around every day—in fact they don't come around ever. You weren't there for her when you should have been. I don't give a fuck if she didn't tell you where she went. I would have made it my mission to find her and not let her go again. You let her go two weeks without even calling her."

"And you let her go four years without even checking up on her. You don't know the first thing about me and Cass, and you and she didn't know that Tyler and I were talking daily while she was there. I knew I freaked her out the night of the fight, so Ty and I agreed it was best if I waited for her to come around instead of pushing her. Since Tyler's the one who took care of her all those years, I figured he knew best, and looks like we were right."

Connor scoffed. "You can't keep her in a glass box. I pushed her and *that's* what helped her. If not, she'd still be battling her demons and she might not be there with you. Since she told you everything, I'm guessing she told you if *you* weren't in the picture, she wouldn't have walked out my door."

My hand gripped the railing on the wraparound porch and my head dropped. Hearing her say that had hurt more than anything else she'd told me. "She did," I said, confirming it.

"Pushing her brought us together, and yeah, it may have ultimately sent her back to you, but it gave us a connection you'll never understand and you'll never have with her. I'm not blind, I know she's completely in love with you. As soon as she says your name those eyes of hers light up and it felt like a punch to my gut every time. But just remember what she said to me. Remember that I do want your girl, and that when you mess up, I'll be ready to take her from you."

"Not gonna happen," I growled, and straightened. "I've had enough of other guys trying to take her from me. So hear me when I say that Cassidy. Is. Mine. She came back *to me.* She's not going anywhere, and neither am I. I hate what she just told me, I hate that she feels anything for you at all, but I will fight to keep her and make her forget about you for the rest of my life."

Connor stayed silent.

"I'm putting a ring on her finger. I'm marrying her. And I'm gonna have a family with her here on my ranch. I don't want to hear from you ever again, and when I say *I,* note that Cassidy will tell me if you call her, you understand?"

"Yeah, I got you."

"Good-bye, Detective Green." Without waiting for a response I ended the call and stormed back into the house.

Cassidy was on her knees, butt on her feet, and looking at me like she had earlier, like she was seeing the sun for the first time and afraid it was going to be taken away from her. I understood the look now; she hadn't known then and didn't know now how I was going to react to the Connor thing. Without saying a word, I scooped her up in my arms and carried her through the empty house into the kitchen. Her eyes didn't leave mine and her hand shakily came up to brush across my cheeks, down my jaw, and across my lips.

"Gage," she whispered.

"You're mine," I informed her, in case she hadn't figured that shit out yet. I set her butt on the edge of the counter and gripped the sides of her underwear to pull them down, letting my hands trail back up the insides of her thighs.

She nodded. "Forever." Her voice was breathy as her arms went back onto the large granite island in the center of the kitchen and her head fell back.

"I talked to Connor."

"Figured that."

Her head was still dropped back, so I let the hand that had been supporting her back slide up until it cupped her neck and forced her to look at me. "Are you mad about that?"

"No, I had a feeling something like that, or worse, was going to happen. But I'm confu— Oh!" She gasped when I slid two fingers in, and had to work hard to keep her eyes open and on mine. "Confused. Aren't you mad, why are you—oh God—um, why are you doing this?"

I smiled widely and leaned forward to suck on that spot she loved behind her ear before telling her, "Always told you I wanted to claim you, darlin'." Cassidy burst out laughing, but the movement it caused, and where my fingers currently were, made the sound cut off, and she moaned deeply. "Plus, we gotta break in all the rooms of our home."

She was biting her bottom lip and grinning, her honey eyes bright. "Then I have a request, since this is my room."

"Anything," I promised, but she gripped my wrist and pulled my hand away from her. "Anything but that."

Laughing huskily, her hands went to the button on my jeans and she looked up at me from under her lashes before leaning toward my ear. "I want my turn. Lie down, Gage."

I kept my eyes on her as I stepped out of my pants and hopped onto the island with her, lying down and letting my legs hang off the end. Before I could pick her up to place her on me, one hand was grabbing my base and her mouth and tongue were teasing the tip for torturous seconds before she took as much of me in as she could.

"Shit, Cassidy." I groaned and raked my hands down my face before looking down at her, only to find her looking up at me again from under her eyelashes. Where the hell did this girl come from? I couldn't take my eyes off what she was doing and cursed the fact that I was getting worked up way too fast and this would all be over too soon. Her hand, mouth, and tongue were working together perfectly and I felt like a damn middle schooler again.

When I knew I didn't have more than a minute left, I put the slightest pressure on her ponytail and she looked up, quickly releasing me with a satisfied grin as she crawled over and sank down on me. Her mouth opened but nothing more than a breathy sound of pleasure came out as her eyelids fluttered shut and she started riding me. On our kitchen island. In our house. On the ranch. Hell. Yeah.

It didn't last long, but thankfully I was able to hold off until she got off first. We lay there, with her draped on top of me placing kisses over my chest, and I couldn't think of anything better than right now. But then again, I thought that every time Cassidy and I were together.

"We need to thoroughly sanitize this island before I cook in here," she said between kisses, and I laughed as I pulled her up to kiss her.

"Does that mean you like the house?"

"You really built this?" Her eyes were wide with amazement as she looked down at me.

"Dad and I have been building it for quite a few years now. The second I met you, I knew I wanted to finish building it for you. Even when I thought you were with Tyler, you were always who I pictured when I was here working on it, or when I was working on plans in Austin. We expanded the kitchen a bit, put the huge island in here, and I haven't even shown you the master bathroom yet."

Cassidy's mouth formed a perfect O. "Is there a tub?" she whispered, like she was afraid there wouldn't be.

I grinned and tugged on her long hair. "A big one."

"Really?!" She squealed and kissed me hard. "Oh, I can't wait to use it."

I couldn't wait for her to see it. She was already dreaming of soaking in it; she was going to go into shock when she saw that monster.

"I love the wraparound," she said dreamily.

"You know, that was the last thing we built. Only added it because that night on the hill you said you wanted to live on a ranch one day and just sit on the porch during the evenings. It was so hard not to tell you right then about the house, but I was going to take you the next day before everything happened with Tyler. Now I'm kinda glad you didn't see it before it was finished."

She didn't say anything, just looked at me with those whiskey eyes, and I knew without her saying the words that she loved me. It was pouring off her, and God, I loved her too.

"Now all that's left is to go pick out furniture and make it our home."

Cassidy's face fell. "What about all the furniture from the town home?"

I shook my head. "I didn't pay for that furniture. Dad did, 'cause he was trying to help me get out of the apartment. So now that Amanda's getting out of the dorms next year and moving into an apartment, she gets all that stuff." Amanda went to A&M, the traitor, and though I wasn't thrilled she was gonna live with a couple roommates off campus, I'd moved into an apartment my junior year too, so it was only fair.

"Gage, is th—" She stopped suddenly and looked down at my chest.

"What, darlin'?"

"Is this really going to be *our* home? Here on the ranch?"

My heart skipped a beat. I could have sworn she'd want this. "Uh, that was the plan. I built on the ranch for a reason. I'd always planned on living here with my family. And you, Cassidy, you're my future. I want a family with you."

Her eyes welled with tears and she did a face-plant onto my chest.

"Cass? Darlin', what's wrong? Do you not like it here?"

She shook her head, but before I could feel like she'd killed my dream, she spoke up. "You don't understand. Since we set foot on the ranch a year ago, all I've thought about was living here with you. It's all I want, Gage, and I was afraid I'd never get to."

I laughed once. "Cassidy, you scared the shit outta me. I thought you didn't like it here or something."

"No, no. I love it, I swear I do. I just didn't want to get too excited about it if you weren't sure about my living here with you."

"I'm sure, trust me. Cassidy, if this is what you want too, then this is our future. This house, this ranch . . . it's yours."

"I want it! I want it so bad."

"I'm glad, darlin'. Now, are you ready to talk about everything? Afterward, we'll get dressed, I'll show you the rest of the house, and we'll go back to the main house for dinner."

"Can you just tell me something first?" she pleaded, leaning up on one arm to peer down at me. "Are you mad at me about Connor? I can't go through talking to you about everything else if I'm worried about the end. I need to get that out of the way first."

I took a deep breath in and out, looked up at the skylights, and ran my hands over her back. "I'm not *mad* at you, I'm mad at him. I'm *hurt* that you kissed him back, and it hurts knowing you have those feelings for him. But you told me everything and that had to be hard, and after all is said and done, you left him and told him not to wait for you because you were coming back to me. And, darlin', I'm not letting you go. I told Connor not to contact you again, and I don't want you contacting him. Other than that, I'm gonna forget about Detective Connor Green."

She nodded and pressed her lips softly to mine. "I love you, Gage Michael Carson."

"I love you too, Cassidy Ann Jameson." I really needed to change that last name of hers.

17

Cassidy

WE'D BEEN GONE for almost six hours by the time we got back to the main house, and from the looks of everyone, other than little Emily, they knew exactly what we'd been doing. Or, at least, the *good* parts. Gage had ended up grabbing one of the spare shirts he always kept in his truck since the one he'd been wearing had been used as a sheet, and I saw that didn't go unnoticed either.

John looked at me, looked over at Gage, then back to me. "Where'd you take her, Gage?"

"To our house," he said proudly, and squeezed my hand.

John smiled big under that mustache. "What'd you think, Cass?"

I let go of Gage's hand to run and fling my arms around John's neck. "Thank you for my wraparound porch, and my bathtub and my kitchen."

Everyone laughed out loud and John chuckled as he set me

back down. "He sure did have a lot of changes he wanted made after he met you. I'm glad you like it."

"I love it," I breathed, and stepped back to Gage. "I can't believe you're going to let us live on your ranch though. Thank you. I seriously love it here."

He shook his head and looked at Gage quickly before quirking a gray brow at me. "Not sure what you mean, doll; you marry Gage, this land is half yours."

"Dinner's ready!" Tessa called from the other side of the breakfast bar in the kitchen, and everyone began moving with the exception of Isabella.

I was still staring at John. What did he mean half mine?

Gage kissed my forehead and ushered me toward the kitchen before he went to talk to Jesse about what Isabella wanted to do for dinner. After getting her situated with food on the couch, the family brought extra chairs into the living room when the couches got full, and we all ate in there. Watching Jesse and Amanda try to be sneaky about stealing longing glances at each other had me forgetting about John's strange comment, and I wanted desperately to ask Isabella what she thought of the two of them. I knew she'd winked that morning, but I hadn't had a second alone with her since, and that lady didn't need time; she just needed to see them together once and that's all it took. Well, according to her and Jesse.

Tessa served pie and we stayed out in the living room for hours talking. It was safe to say the Carson family loved Jesse and Isabella, and they were just as taken with the Carsons. It was weird to have Tyler so comfortable around Gage and me together, but I was happy we could all be normal. Ty and I had slipped back into our friendship during the week in California, and it didn't seem to bother Gage, just as it didn't bother Ty to watch Gage and I kiss. It finally felt right to me, and I couldn't have been happier.

When Emily fell asleep with her head in my lap, and Isabella couldn't keep her eyes open any longer, the family started breaking up for the night and figuring out sleeping arrangements. And since Isabella was being put into the guest room, and no one felt comfortable leaving Jesse or Amanda alone after seeing the way they were looking at each other, I was back in a room with Amanda, and Gage was fighting with Tyler and Jesse over who was taking the bed, the couch, and the floor in his room.

I ran downstairs to grab a glass of water and found Gage's parents talking in the kitchen. It looked like Tessa was preparing some things for the next day; I swear that woman never stopped cooking.

"Hey, sweetheart, whatcha need?" Tessa asked.

"Oh, I'm just getting some water. Do you need any help?"

"No, but can I say again that I'm so happy you're here? You didn't see him when he thought y'all were over. Damn near broke my heart seeing him that way, and then thinkin' of not having you in our family . . . well, that sealed the deal and my heart did break."

"Tessa," I said softly, and put the empty glass down on the counter.

"No, no. Don't go getting weepy on me. I'm thrilled as a pig in cool mud that you're back, and I'm gonna stay that way. Now, when all our visitors are gone, you and Gage are gonna have a sit-down with me and John, and we're gonna talk about everything that went down. But it looks like y'all worked out whatever happened, and when he showed ya the house, that told us all we need to know. Right, honey?"

"Sure did," John agreed, and snatched a bell pepper slice.

"I'm not going anywhere again," I said, hoping it would reassure them for now until we could have our *sit-down.*

"I know, baby girl." She smiled sweetly at me and went back to slicing.

"Hey, John? What did you mean earlier when you said that if I married Gage, half the ranch would be mine?"

His eyebrows raised and he shared a look with Tessa. "He didn't tell you?"

I sighed deeply and hopped onto the breakfast bar. "Apparently there's a lot he doesn't tell me. I found out about your family helping Isabella from Jesse just last night. Gage never once mentioned it."

John made a clicking noise with his tongue. "That's Gage for ya. He doesn't mind being in the background. He prefers it. As for the ranch, guess we should start back when he was fifteen. Of course Gage has been doing chores on the ranch all his life, but when he turned fifteen he started working for me. Worked harder and longer hours than any of my hired ranch hands, so he got paid same as they did and for the hours he worked. That's how he got that truck; paid for it in cash when he turned sixteen. Other than that, he saved practically every cent. Now, when he went to school he wasn't getting paid much because he was only home about four months out of the year, but from what he had left over, and what he hadn't spent on the apartment he shared with y'all, he decided to put it toward something. It took almost every penny he'd saved, but he bought half the ranch and business from me. Signed his half over to him about a week before y'all showed up last year. I was sure he woulda told you then.

"So he struggled for a bit at first, but once his half of the earnings started coming in he picked his life back up and repaid me for what I'd paid to get him into the town house. As for Isabella, *I* didn't take care of her medical bills; Gage and I did. Don't know if Jesse knows that, don't know if Isabella knows that, but I'd doubt it. He called to tell me what he was going to do, and knowing he was going to graduate soon and would be starting a life with you, I didn't want him blowing all his money again, even if it was for a great reason. I knew y'all would have to furnish y'all's house soon and other things like that, so we split it just like we split the business. As for the house, Cassi, sweetheart, you can thank me all damn day, but that house is on Gage's half of the property. And like I said earlier, y'all get married, half this ranch will be yours until he buys the rest of it from me."

I heard movement and I turned to see Gage leaning up against a wall not far from us. His green eyes were on me and it looked like he was fighting a smile since his dimples were showing. God, I loved those dimples.

He walked toward me and put himself between my legs, planting a hand on either side of me.

"So that's why the town house furniture wasn't yours . . . because you'd just bought half the ranch?" Gage just nodded so I kept talking. "Well, I have money now; I can pay for us to furnish our house."

"Darlin'," he said with a laugh, "I have money to furnish the house, I just didn't a year ago. But now that half is mine, I actually make money from the business, not from working as a ranch hand. Promise you, sweetheart, it's a lot better." He kissed my lips softly and pulled me closer to him. "Tomorrow, we're going to get everything we need for the house, 'cause I'm not spending another night after tonight without you."

Tessa clucked her tongue. "You furnish that house, Gage Carson, because you'll be stayin' in it and Cassidy will be stayin' here 'til y'all get married."

Gage's body froze and he turned his head slowly to look at his mom. Before he could say anything she spoke up again.

"And don't try any hanky-panky either. This may be half your land now, and that may be your house. But I am your mother and I am not lettin' no hanky-panky go on between the two of y'all before you're wed."

"Yes, ma'am," I said softly.

"Mama, we've already been living together."

"Nu-uh, not under my roof. And before you say that's *your* roof, don't think I won't come after you with a wooden spoon, Gage Michael Carson! I don't care if you're grown. You're still my son, you're not married, and you're gonna do right by that sweet girl. So, all funny business stops right now, you hear me?"

"Dad, is she serious?"

John shrugged. "I argue with your mama, I sleep on the couch and she doesn't feed me. So I don't argue with your mama."

I laughed out loud at that, but Gage still stood there with a horrified expression. It's not like we hadn't gone almost two years of being in love without having sex; we could go . . . however long until we got married. I pushed on his chest. "You heard your mama, step back, no funny business." When I finally pushed him far enough, I closed my legs so he couldn't step back between them and gave him a sly smile.

"Knew I loved that girl for a reason," Tessa muttered as she went back to chopping. "Got a problem with it, son, I suggest you marry her."

"Ma, I'm gonna marry her. Y'all just aren't giving me a

second to even propose; I just got her back today. I gotta make up for two weeks of thinkin' she was gone first before I can get my head on straight again."

My heart fluttered at that . . . *Am I ready to marry Gage? I'm only nineteen.* But Connor was right, my life had caused me to grow up fast, and I'd never felt fully comfortable with people my age unless it was Tyler. I wasn't looking for college experiences, clubs on the weekends, and flings with random guys. I'd found everything I would ever want the day I met Gage. So was I ready to marry him? Um, *yes.* Yes, I was. I grabbed his shirt and brought him close to kiss him softly once. "Get to bed, baby, you haven't slept in a long time. I love you, sleep well."

He smiled that heartbreaking smile and his green eyes lit up before he touched his lips to mine again, then my forehead. With a heavy sigh and frustrated look he turned toward the living room. "You gotta be kidding me. Can't even sleep next to my girl?" He drawled, "Mama, you better be able to get a wedding together real quick."

"Just give me the date."

"Like . . . yesterday," he said, clearly still frustrated.

"Will do, honey, sleep good." Tessa turned to wink at me and looked suspiciously at my hand. "*Did* he propose? Did I miss something?"

I shook my head twice.

"He better get on with it then. That's gonna be one frustrated boy until y'all are married."

I nodded my head twice.

Tessa and I looked at each other for a moment and then burst into laughter.

"At least y'all can find it funny," John said as he snagged another bell pepper. "Poor boy's gonna go crazy and he's gonna be hell to work with 'til then."

Well, we couldn't have that, now, could we? They thought Gage couldn't last? Hell, I wouldn't last. Hopping off the counter, I finally got that glass of water, drank it, and cleaned the glass before hugging both of them and calling out good-nights. After getting ready for bed, I talked to Amanda about Jesse for almost an hour before she passed out and I made my way to the sofa bed in her room, so ready to sleep. It had been a long, emotional day and I was so exhausted I didn't think I'd be able to get the covers over me.

It couldn't have been more than a few minutes later that I was woken up by Gage crawling into bed beside me and pulling me into his arms.

"Gage, your mom—"

"Darlin', I need you in my arms tonight. I didn't just miss sleep last night; it's been a long two weeks." He kissed the top of my head softly and curled his arms tighter around me. "Night, Cass, love you," Gage managed to mumble before he fell asleep.

Seconds later, I followed him into the best sleep of my life.

"Wake up, darlin'."

I burrowed my head farther into Gage's chest and groaned. Too. Early.

He laughed and kissed a line along my jaw. "Gotta start my day. I'll see you when I'm done."

"You're leaving already?" I turned to look out the window; it was barely turning gray outside. "Mmkay, Gage. Come back soon."

"It'll be a short day since Isabella and Jesse are here. Just gonna feed everyone, make sure none of the cattle broke any of the fences last night, and we'll be back." He trailed his fingers between my thighs and kissed me thoroughly, catching my moan.

"Not nice," I grumbled when he pulled away chuckling.

"Go back to sleep, Cassidy."

Rolling onto my back so I could look up at him, I pulled his lips down to mine one last time. "I'll see you when you get back."

TWO DAYS LATER I was in the kitchen with Tessa and Amanda, and we'd just finished lunch and were already working on dinner and dessert. Well, Tessa and I were; Amanda was focused on her phone. Ever since Isabella and Jesse had gone home yesterday morning, I hadn't seen her set her phone down once. I'd finally gotten to have that talk with Isabella, and before I even got the full question out she was already answering.

"Oh, darling girl, I just knew I would see him find his other half before I went. I can now die knowing he'll be taken care of."

It seemed kind of morbid, but Isabella was thrilled, so I kept the smile plastered on my face. Later that day I'd accidentally walked in on Jesse and Amanda making out in the laundry room. They were so into each other they didn't even notice me walk in or step back out. But that night sure as hell was awkward, and they noticed that. I'd fallen asleep after spending another hour talking to Amanda about Jesse and was expecting to be woken up by Gage crawling into bed with me again as he had the night before. I'd been woken up by Gage all right, just not by his getting in the bed.

"WHAT THE FUCK? Get off my sister!" Gage's voice boomed through the room.

I sat up quickly in bed, just in time to see Jesse scramble off Amanda's bed and Amanda looking mortified that her big

brother had just caught her. I scanned both of them and saw
their clothes were on and mostly straight, so they couldn't have
been doing much of anything.

"Outside," Gage barked. "Now."

"Gage, no, no! Please don't!" Amanda pleaded, and looked
toward me for help.

Jesse just looked like a man who was about to face his execu-
tioner.

"Gage," I whispered, but he pushed Jesse out of the bedroom
door and shut it behind them.

"No!" Amanda whispered loudly. "Cassidy, please don't let
him do anything to Jesse!" She was struggling with her comforter, trying to get out from underneath it so she could follow
them, but I stopped her.

"Stay here, Amanda, I got it."

"Please, Cassidy, we were just kissing, I swear."

"I know." I smiled and left the room. Not like Gage could
say much anyway. Amanda was a month older than me, and we
were obviously doing much more than kissing. Looking down
the hall and listening for raised voices, I tiptoed down the stairs
and walked outside until I found the boys and sighed.

". . . *my* girl, and then you go for my sister? Are you insane?
I don't like you and I sure as hell don't want you touching her."

"Gage, man, just listen to me, it's not like that with her—"

"No. You'll stay away, get it?"

"I can't," Jesse said with an exasperated sigh.

"You can, and you will. Cassidy and my sisters are off-limits,
Jesse."

"Babe," I said softly, and shook my head.

"Cass, no. He had his hands all over her and was in bed with
her."

I raised an eyebrow at him. "And you happened to see that because you were coming to get in bed with me."

"Whose side are you on, Cass?"

"Yours, Gage, of course," I answered honestly, and took a few steps toward him so I could touch his arm. "But, Gage, I talked to Isabella."

"So?" His eyebrows were drawn down, and I knew he wasn't getting it.

"No, I mean . . . I talked. To. Isabella," I said with a jerk of my head toward Jesse, both eyebrows raised this time.

Gage was shaking his head like I'd lost my mind, and then he stopped and he hissed, "No, no way. Not my sister. Not with him."

I just smiled at him and nodded.

"Seriously?" He made an annoyed grunt and looked at Jesse like he wanted him gone. "Him and my sister?"

Jesse's eyes and smile were huge when he looked at me. "You asked Ma?"

"Like you needed to know what your mom said for you to know your feelings for Amanda."

Jesse's smile widened even further until he looked at Gage.

"Damn it." Gage sighed and glared at Jesse. "You hurt my sister, I'll kill you." And with that he grabbed my hand and led me back into the main house, up the stairs, and into Amanda's room.

She was sitting on the edge of her bed with a worried expression, and when she saw me grin mischievously at her, it vanished.

"He keeps his hands to himself, all right?" Gage clarified while pointing his finger at Amanda.

Amanda nodded and rushed toward the door.

"Whoa, where are you going?"

"Gage, he's leaving in the morning. I'm gonna spend as much time with him as possible. We'll be good, I promise."

Gage started to protest, but I put one hand flat on his chest and squeezed his hand with the other. "They'll be fine, Gage. Come on, let's go to bed."

He grumbled to himself as we crawled under the covers. "I don't trust him at night with her."

"Well, the way I see it, they're doing us a favor."

"How so?" he scoffed, still burning holes through the bedroom door.

I sat up and tore my shirt off. "Because now we have the room to ourselves."

His eyes snapped to mine, then down to my bare chest, and his face lit up. "Be a shame to waste that."

MY CHEEKS BURNED as I remembered that night, and I was really glad Tessa was facing the other way. I felt bad for going against her, and I'd vowed after that night to respect her wishes until Gage and I got married, whenever that would be. It would definitely be easier at night now, seeing as we'd gone into town yesterday and bought absolutely everything that we needed for our new place. What we couldn't haul back had been delivered that morning and, with everyone's help, everything was already set up. Gage had officially moved into our home today and would be sleeping there, while I slept here, a good five-minute drive away. During the day, however, I'd need to keep myself around Tessa so I wouldn't find myself wandering over to break in our new bed, and the shower, bathtub, dining room table, couches, and every other surface. The blush came back full force just as Gage and Tyler came into the kitchen.

Gage took one look at my cheeks and smiled wickedly. "Gonna go to town, darlin', we'll be back."

"Oh! Don't forget I need a new phone charger. Did we forget something else?"

"Gotta get stuff for the TV: surround sound, gaming systems . . . stuff like that," Tyler answered, looking bored, and Gage just stared at me.

All that stuff sounded more like Ty, not Gage, and I was pretty sure Ty wouldn't be bored with it. But what did I know? "All right, have fun."

Gage

"GAMING SYSTEMS, TY? Really? Do you not know me at all?"

"Well, I knew you weren't going to want to lie to her, so I stepped in for you!"

"True." I pushed his shoulder and climbed into the truck, waiting for him to get into the passenger side before I continued. "Guess I can thank you for that."

"Uh, yeah. That's what I thought." Ty smirked. "You get that ring-size thing you did?"

Grinning, I held up the piece of fishing line I'd tied around Cassidy's ring finger last night in her sleep. I'd been so damn nervous that she was going to wake up, but I couldn't think of another way to figure out the size without being obvious. Not like she didn't know I planned on marrying her as soon as freakin' possible, but still. I needed to be able to surprise her even with her expecting it.

"So are we getting the whole thing done today?"

"Only if they don't need to resize the ring; if they do, the rest of the surprise has to wait until it's done too."

"And you called the people about it?"

"Did it this morning. No matter what, we're gonna go pick one out today and pay for it, but they know we'll be taking it either today or whenever the ring's ready."

"Not gonna lie, bro, I'm jealous. I might have to use this one day. It's the ultimate *aww* moment." He snickered.

"Yeah, I hope so. I want her to like it."

"Hey," he said, and waited until I glanced at him. "She loves you, she won't care how you ask her. She just wants to be with you. But this? She's absolutely going to love it, trust me."

I couldn't help but smile. I was pretty sure he was right. I still wanted it perfect though. "Weird, people aren't usually on this road," I said as we passed a dark Charger headed the opposite way from us.

"Guy looks familiar." Tyler said quietly, "He's not from one of the neighboring ranches?"

I shook my head and looked in the side-view mirror to look at the back of the car until it was out of sight. "No, don't think I've ever seen him before."

"Huh. Didn't go to school with us?"

"No." I drew out the word, trying to put the face to a name. But I was positive I didn't know that guy.

"Swear he looked familiar," Ty said, more to himself. "Sweet car."

I grunted in agreement and turned on the radio. We had a good half hour before we got to the jewelry store, and I honestly couldn't have cared less whether Tyler thought he knew the guy. All I could think about was the fact that I was going to buy a ring for Cassidy.

"Stop the truck!" Tyler yelled a little over a song later. "Stop the truck, go back!"

"What the hell?"

"Gage, turn the truck around!" He actually leaned over and tried to grab for the steering wheel as I slammed on the brakes.

My truck fishtailed and dirt rose up around it for a few seconds before settling.

"What the fuck is wrong with you?!"

"Dude! That's Green! That was Detective Green! Go back to the ranch!"

"Are you shitting me, Ty?" I'd just told him that morning as he helped me move the heavy stuff into the house about what Cassidy had said about Connor. This was a new low, even for Tyler.

"Swear to God, Gage, that was him. Go back now."

With a curse I flipped the truck the rest of the way around and peeled out. "If you're messing with me, Ty—"

"I'm not!" he snapped. "I told you I didn't like that jackass from the second I met him. He challenged me in my house. I didn't like him then, definitely didn't like him this morning, hate him right now. Get back to the ranch."

I grabbed my cell out of my pocket and called Cassidy twice before calling the main house line.

"Hello?"

"Manda!"

"What'd you forget?"

"Nothing, where's Cass and why isn't she answering her phone?"

"Well, I don't know why she isn't answering her phone but she and Mama went out to the side of the house to pick something that they needed for dinner."

"I'm on my way back, but I need you to get them inside. Someone's coming by to see Cassidy. I don't want him near her, you understand?"

Amanda gasped. "Oh God, Gage, is she in danger?"

"No, but if he goes near her I'll be in a hell of a lot of trouble, Amanda. Get her inside. Mama too."

"Okay, all right, I'll— Oh, Gage . . . is he in a black Dodge?"

I pulled the phone away from my ear and cursed loudly. "Yes, Amanda, he is. I'm flooring it, but get Cassidy away from him. Where are the little girls? I don't want them around when I come face-to-face with him."

"They're taking naps," she said distractedly.

"Good."

"Oh, shit," Amanda mumbled, then yelled Cassidy's name away from the phone and the line disconnected.

"Shit, I think she's already talking to him." I gripped the steering wheel and pressed the gas down farther. "I don't want her near him, Ty. I didn't want her to think of him again, and I thought if he never called her again it would be too damn soon. I didn't think he'd fuckin' show up here! How did he even know where she was?"

"I don't know, bro, I'm sorry I didn't recognize who he was sooner. Just try to keep calm. I don't think it'd be a good idea to fight someone else in front of Cassi, especially a detective. You don't need to go to jail, Gage."

I didn't respond, I just gritted my teeth and focused on not losing control of my truck on the country road as I raced back to the ranch. As soon as I was in the driveway, I made it a point to pull up next to his car rather than block him in; no need to give him a reason to stay longer than he already had.

Cassidy looked up with wide, scared eyes, Amanda looked sorry, and Mama just looked confused. Detective Green didn't even turn around as I slammed on the brakes, threw the truck in park, and jumped out.

"Guess you didn't understand the first time, but I don't want you talking to her. Which sure as hell means I didn't want you showing up here either." I didn't stop walking until I was in front of Cassidy, facing her with my back to him. "Darlin', go inside. Please," I begged softly.

"I'm here to make sure she's all right—you know, what you should have been doing when she was in California."

I turned to glare at him and was extremely happy I got to look down at him. Cassidy hadn't moved, and her wide eyes still looked terrified as she obsessively spun her dad's ring around on her finger. "Cass, baby, *please* go inside."

"You always telling her what to do too? You're the one who called to tell me to stay away, even after what she told you about us. What about what she wanted? I find it hard to believe that she wanted no contact with me after everything she went through with me. So now, if you'd step aside, I'd rather just talk to her."

"Man, what the hell aren't you getting? I don't want you near my girl! Get the fuck off my property and go back to California!"

"Gage Michael Carson," Mama mumbled under her breath, and I knew I was gonna get hit over the head when all this was over.

"Cassidy, are you sure this is what you want? Don't you see what he's like?" Connor asked, leaning around me to look at her, and my body went rigid.

"What I'm like? What *I'm* like? I'm a guy who's trying to keep his girl from the prick who's trying to take her from him! I have every right to hate you right now, and swear to God if you weren't carrying that damn badge I would beat the ever-living shit out of you."

"Gage Michael Car—" Mama had begun again.

"You do not," I said, and turned my body so I was facing him and staring down at him, "*do not* kiss another man's girl repeatedly, especially if you already know she's taken. You do not beg her to leave her man and stay with you. You do *not* keep her pinned to a wall until she promises to come back to you if it doesn't work out with her guy. And you. Do. Not. Fly halfway across the U.S. to talk to her after her man has already warned you to stay away. And while I'm mentioning that, you wanna share how you knew where to find her? If you're stalking Cassidy, I promise you I'll act like I don't know about the badge." Cassidy's body went solid behind me and I worked at reining in my anger. I'd almost lost her once because of it; I wasn't about to go through that again.

Connor had the balls to smirk at me and look around me to smile at Cassidy. "I knew your name, knew you had a ranch in Texas. Your ranch is on Google, dumbass; I'm not stalking her. After what Cassidy's been through, I don't trust a phone call from a pissed-off boyfriend that I already know has given her a black eye to tell me that she's okay. And warning or not, she means something to me, so I need to know she's all right, and since she's not answering my calls, I took the only other option."

Looking over my shoulder, I asked Cassidy, "He's been calling?"

Her head shook and she shrugged. "My phone died my first day here. I lost my charger."

God, I felt stupid. I'd already known that, seeing how her phone was currently in our house being charged with *my* charger. Which would be why she hadn't answered her phone when I called on my way back.

Connor continued like we hadn't been talking. "And *yeah,* I care about her that much that I'd fly to Texas to make sure she's all right. As for kissing her and asking her not to go? I'll remind you she kissed me back, and that promise? She willingly made it, and since you seem to have forgotten this as well, added her own part to it."

"Nah, man, it's kinda seared into my brain. I know what she told you. And I know at the end she told you not to wait for her because she was coming back to me. That should have been the last thing she needed to say to you. All this other bullshit is completely unnecessary. Now I'll ask you nicely one more time. Get. Off. My. Property."

Mama's voice got a little higher. "Gage Michael Carson."

"When you stop talking for Cassidy and treating her like a damn child, and when she asks me to go, then I'll go."

I opened my mouth but slammed it shut as Cassidy stepped around me and started walking up to him. Connor's hands immediately went up to reach out for her hips but Cassidy stopped and took one large step back, shaking her head slowly back and forth. I should have been happy that she stepped back before his hands could land on her, but the way they'd automatically gone out to her, like he hadn't even thought about reaching for her, it'd just happened, was like another punch straight to my chest. Without looking back at me, she reached one hand back and linked it with mine, then dragged me with her as she walked forward, pushing Connor toward the cars.

"What is wrong with you?" she hissed at him as he continued to walk backward, toward his rental.

His face fell. "Cassidy, I had to know. I had to make sure you were okay."

"Of course I'm okay! I'm with Gage!"

"Cass, he can't just make you stop talking to me."

"You're right, Connor, he can't," she said, shocking the hell out of me. "But he doesn't *want* me talking to you, so I'm not going to. I meant every word I said to you in California, and I told Gage that too. Connor, I am in love with Gage. He is my everything; don't you understand that? If he doesn't want me talking to you because I allowed you to kiss me, because I kissed you back, and because I think of you in ways that I definitely shouldn't . . . then I have to respect that. And so do you." She turned her body into mine and let her free hand flail through the air when she continued. "Or don't, but at least respect me and my decisions. You knew I was coming back to Gage, and you knew when I left your apartment that I wouldn't be coming back to you. I'm sorry if this isn't what you want, Connor, but don't make this into the huge, dramatic scene that it doesn't need to be. Or more of one, anyway. I already told Gage about you, and he was the only one who needed to know; now I need to unnecessarily explain you to his family."

"Cassidy—"

"Go home, Connor, you made this into a bigger mess and now I need to clean it up. Just go home."

He stepped right up to her and cupped her cheek with his hand; my body froze before it started shaking. My free hand was already balled into a fist, but I forced myself to remain silent and still to see what she would do.

"Cass, I *need* you."

"And I need Gage," she said softly, and removed his hand while trying to force herself even closer to me, so I grabbed her and took a step away from him. "It will always be Gage for me. *Please,* Connor . . . go home."

I watched as his completely broken face studied her, then turned to me and hardened up into an impressive glare. He wasn't lying; he really cared for Cassidy. Connor didn't seem like the kind of guy to back down from anyone, but as soon as Cassidy started telling him how it was going to be, he'd all but crumbled. With one last pained glance at Cass, he got into the Charger and drove away.

Cassidy relaxed as soon as he was off the ranch and her forehead hit my chest. "Gage, I had no idea. I'm sorry, I'm so sorry for everything. I'm sorry for California, I'm sorry for kissing him, I'm sorry for leaving you." Her chest was heaving up and down quickly and I ran my hands over her back to calm her.

"Darlin', it's fine. He's gone and from the look on his face I don't think he's coming back. Are you all right? You looked terrified, Cassidy, did he say something to you?"

"No, but all I could think about was how mad you were going to be. I was afraid you'd think I'd wanted him here or that I'd be happy to see him."

"And were you?" I asked tightly.

"No! Seeing him here . . . realizing how bad I messed things up and how he could ruin them, God, Gage, I was terrified I was going to lose you." Her body started shaking and she made a choking sound. "I'm so sorry." She burst into tears and her knees buckled.

I easily lifted her into my arms and held her tight, letting her cry as long as she needed. Ever since the letter from her mom she'd been more emotional, but I didn't mind. I loved that she was now open enough that she would easily share this with me too. "C'mon, sweetheart, let's get you inside."

She quickly shook her head and wiped at her cheeks and under her eyes. "No, you and Ty were going into town, and now I have to tell your mom and Amanda about Connor. I'd rather not have to see how I broke your heart again."

"Darlin', I'm not leaving you when you're upset like this."

"I'm fine, Gage, really. I just hate that I put you through that. Go run your errand. I'll tell them and we'll have dinner ready when you get back."

"Cass—"

Her lips pressed to mine for long seconds, and without removing them she whispered, "Go, babe. I'm not running anywhere, I promise. This is my home—*you* are my home. I'm not leaving. Run your errand, I'll be waiting here for you."

My entire body relaxed at her words. "Be back soon, all right?"

"Be safe."

18

Cassidy

I FELT SOMETHING WARM against my neck and smiled, thinking Gage had come for his morning hug. But then it felt like a
weight on my throat and it was cutting off my air supply; at the
same time I felt hot breath and tiny kisses cover my chin, cheeks,
nose, and mouth. My eyes flashed open to see a sun-filled room
and two tiny crystal-blue eyes directly above mine before a black
nose plunged toward my eye and my face was covered in tons of
little puppy kisses again. I reached up to pick the fluffy puppy
off my neck and looked at the most precious face I'd ever seen.
White muzzle and forehead, double mask of light gray with
black spots and a couple brown splashes.

"Hi, precious," I whispered, and giggled when I was rewarded
with more kisses on my nose and cheeks.

"You like her?" a deep, gravelly voice asked from the side of
the bed.

I turned my head and smiled brightly. "Like her? I love her! Is she ours?"

Gage nodded and reached over to scratch behind her ears; she instantly turned and started licking and nipping at his wrist. "She's an Australian shepherd. If you want another kind of dog, I'll buy you whatever you want."

"No, she's perfect! Oh, Gage, thank you so much!" I brought the little ball of fluff to my face and cuddled against her, enjoying her puppy breath. My fingers hit a collar and I pulled her away so I could look at it. Turning it around, my smile widened when I saw the hot-pink color. I would have paid to see Gage buying girly stuff. "Did you name her?" I asked, but where I expected to see a name tag, there was a large white bow instead, and dangling off one of the loops was the biggest diamond solitaire I'd ever seen.

I inhaled sharply and froze, unable to do anything but stare and hold on to the wiggling puppy. Gage sat on the bed near my hip and took the puppy from my hands. Holding her up and keeping her facing me, he gently untied the bow until he could slide the ring off. I looked up long enough to see his green eyes staring at me and his dimples showing his excitement, before looking back down at his hands. The puppy had started chewing on the untied ribbon, but when Gage grabbed my left hand and slowly slid the solitaire onto my ring finger, she started following his hands, licking all the way.

Gage and I laughed softly once, our hands both going to pet her, but always remaining in contact as we looked back at each other. His free hand came up and brushed some hair from my face and held it there as he leaned in until our foreheads were touching.

"Will you marry me, Cassidy?"

"Yes!" I cried, and pressed my lips firmly to his, which were failing at fighting a smile.

The puppy yelped playfully and wiggled her way in between our chests until she felt like she was the center of attention again.

"Then I just need to know one more thing, darlin'." Gage pulled the pup to the side of our bodies and laid us down. "When can I marry you?"

"Whenever you want," I answered breathlessly when his lips left mine.

"Right now."

"Have to give me at least a few months."

"Few months?" He leaned back slightly and pulled the puppy back to the side when she tried to crawl between us again. "Tell me honestly, Cassidy, are you saying that because you want time before we get married, or you want time to plan?"

"*Need* time to plan."

Gage smiled and kissed me thoroughly. "Then no way am I giving you a few months. Few weeks."

"Weeks? Gage, I can't plan a wedding that fast."

"Darlin', I'm not gonna spend the next few months living in our house without you. I'm not gonna spend the next few months waiting to start our life together." He leaned up so he was resting his elbows on either side of my head. "Cassidy, I've wanted nothing but to marry you since I first saw you hop out of Tyler's Jeep nearly two years ago. We have the rest of our lives to be together, yeah, but we've already spent too much time apart."

I smiled softly and ran my hands through his thick black hair. "Weeks." I nodded and then shook my head. "As soon as possible."

"Yeah?"

"Yeah," I agreed, and brought his face back to mine.

"I told y'all no hanky-panky until you marry that girl, Gage! I just knew you were sneakin' in here. You are just like your daddy . . ." Her voice trailed off when Gage, who still hadn't stopped kissing me, took my left hand away from his head and lifted it so the ring was facing Tessa. "Oh my God!" I heard Tessa's footsteps quickly leave as she called for her husband.

Gage smiled against my lips and took my raised hand and brought it above my head, pinning it down onto the pillow.

"And, Gage!" she said, suddenly back in the room. "Get your butt off her and out of that bed this instant!" Gage groaned but only separated far enough to look into my eyes.

"Ma?"

"Nu-uh! I told you no funny business."

"As soon as possible, Ma."

"What'd you say?" She walked over to us and grabbed the back of his shirt and began pulling, only stopping when our little ball of fluff jumped onto Gage's back and yelped playfully at her. "A puppy? Oh, son, I knew I raised you right."

I laughed and grabbed the puppy so Gage could get off the bed, letting his mom feel like she was able to pull him.

"You're gonna be mine, Cassidy," he said with the widest smile I'd ever seen on his face.

I bit my lip and nodded. "As soon as possible, baby."

"As soon as possible," he agreed, and laughed out loud when his mom smacked his head twice for being in bed with an unmarried girl, at the same time that she screamed downstairs to Amanda that we had a wedding to plan, and then told Gage how happy she was that he hadn't wasted any more time.

When they got to the door, he grabbed the frame and turned to wink at me before he let her pull him out, and I about melted.

The puppy wiggled out of my arms, and, after a few seconds of looking a little uncertainly at the ground, she took a step off the bed and half fell, half jumped to the ground. Her paws slid in place as she tried to take off running toward the door before she got traction. By the time she got to the door, Tyler was there and scooped her up.

"Hey, sweetheart," he called, and nuzzled the pup. "Hey, Li'l Bit."

"Gaming systems, huh, Ty?"

He smiled and kissed my forehead as he sat down next to me. "Had to think of something quick. Let me see it on you."

I held out my hand and rested my head on his shoulder as we both studied it. I couldn't stop smiling and my heart had been pounding since I'd seen my beautiful ring hanging from the ribbon. "I think it's perfect," I whispered.

"That's what he said too." The ring fell to the left from the weight of the rock and we both laughed. "I think it's too big."

"Nope." I let the word pop out of my mouth and took my puppy from Ty's arms. "The whole thing was perfect."

"I'm glad you're happy, Cassi."

"Me too," I breathed, and kissed the pup's wet nose. "Hey, Ty, can I ask you something? It's not really conventional, and you might be offended by it . . ." I trailed off as I realized how awkward it might be for him.

"Offended? Oh hell, you have to ask now!" He turned so I could see the wicked glint in his brown eyes.

"Not like that! This is something serious."

"All right, all right. I'm serious, but I get to hold Li'l Bit."

I rolled my eyes and vowed to name the puppy as soon as I handed her back over. "All right, well, I have actually been thinking about this a lot this week. I like your dad a lot, Ty, you know that, but I don't have a connection with him like I do you and your mom."

His eyebrows drew down in confusion. "Yeah . . . ?"

"I could always walk down the aisle by myself if this makes you uncomfortable, but I was wondering . . . will you give me away?"

Tyler sat there quietly for a moment. "Never thought I'd be on this side of things, Cassi—"

"Okay, then we don't have to do that—it's all right."

"You gonna let me finish, sweetheart? I always thought one day you'd see things the way I always have, but you found that in Gage. I know I've been a real dick, Cass, but I *am* happy for you guys. You know, you think your question is weird, but Gage asked for my permission to marry you."

I raised my head up to look at him. "He did?"

"Yep, and I didn't even have to think about my answer. I've been taking care of you for most of our lives, and there's no one I'd trust with you more than him. I would never let you walk down the aisle alone, and since your dad can't be here, I'm glad you asked me to be the one to give you to him."

"Thanks, Ty, you don't know how much this means to me." I sighed happily and caught the puppy with a grunt when she jumped from Ty's arms onto my stomach. "I know things got weird for us, but everything feels like it's back to how it should be; it feels perfect."

"You know I'll always love you most," he said a little loudly, and before I could question his increase in volume, Gage came back into the room and I understood.

"Well, I don't know about that." He smirked and sauntered over to the side of the bed, leaned over, and kissed me softly before grabbing the puppy. It was still so weird to have Tyler not say anything when Gage kissed me in front of him. "You name her yet?"

"Li'l Bit," Tyler said immediately.

I rolled my eyes. "Sky."

"Sky?" Gage asked with a smile, and I nodded. "All right, Sky it is. I'm gonna take her out, and the girls are waiting downstairs for you, darlin'. I'm warning you. You thought a few weeks wasn't possible; just wait until they start plannin'. They're unstoppable until everything's done."

"As soon as possible," I whispered.

"As soon as possible," he agreed, and pulled me out of the bed with one hand, keeping Sky in his other arm, and led us downstairs.

Gage hadn't been lying: there wasn't any cooked food sitting around, and there wasn't any food being cooked; they were *that* serious. Tessa, Amanda, and Nikki were huddled around the kitchen island with a pad of paper. Each had a pen in hand and was jotting things down as they talked chattily.

Emily looked up from where she was sitting near Amanda's side on the island and squealed, "Puppy!"

The rest of the girls looked up and started demanding to see the ring. Gage pushed me toward them as he took Emily's hand and led her outside with Sky. After fawning over my ring, they shoved the pad of paper in front of me and all started talking at once. All I caught were the words, *how soon, colors,* and *in the barn.*

"Wait, I'm sorry, did you say *in* the barn? Like have the wedding in the barn?" They had a massive barn, and Amanda had told me about the dances and numerous parties they'd had in that barn. Granted, I'd never been inside it, but a wedding in there? Um . . . What?

"No, darlin' girl." Tessa laughed, and I relaxed. "The reception will be in there."

Oh. Just as weird.

I must not have been very good at hiding my thoughts that early in the morning, because Tessa and Amanda laughed even harder. "Trust us, Cassidy, it's not gonna be some hick wedding; you'll be amazed what we can do with that barn. Not too far from the barn is a perfect spot for a wedding though; I've always thought that!" Tessa went on and started sketching the trees that formed an arch and the field between it and the barn, explaining where chairs and such would go for the ceremony. "How many people will be coming?" she asked suddenly, and my mouth opened, then shut.

"I don't know," I answered honestly. From Stacey, I knew all about the issues of having too many people to invite, but I had hardly anyone. I had the Bradleys, who were Gage's family; Jackie and Dana, whom I'd met because they were dating Gage's best friends . . . The only people who were solely mine to invite were Jesse and Isabella—hell, even they were technically linked to his family now—and Lori and Stacey.

"Okay, well how many people in the wedding party?"

I glanced at Amanda, then back at Tessa. "I don't know."

Thankfully Gage came back in then and Tessa asked him the same question. "Uh . . . Ty, Ethan, and Adam."

Tessa looked back at me and leaned forward to ask quietly, "Do you have three girls you'd want in the wedding?" She finally understood my sudden awkwardness.

"Amanda, Jackie, and Dana." I looked back at Amanda. "Will you be my maid of honor?"

"Oh my God, really?!" she screeched, and threw her arms around my neck. "Thanks, Cass! Okay, what about colors?"

"Green," I said at the same time Gage said, "Gold."

I turned to him with a confused look and he pointed to my eyes. My stomach warmed and I kissed his lips quickly. "Green on the guys, gold on the girls."

Gage smiled widely and cupped my cheeks to deepen our next kiss. "Gotta get some work done, darlin', have fun. Ma—"

"I know, I know!" Tessa said somewhat distractedly. "As soon as possible!"

As soon as Gage slipped out the door, the wedding planning took off.

Gage

I WALKED INTO MY OLD ROOM, where Cassidy was now staying until she moved into the house with me, and my heart stopped before kicking into overdrive. Cassidy was curled up on top of the comforter with her phone in one hand, that hand resting on a notebook with a list of names, all of which had checks and numbers next to them. I looked at the floor and picked the pen up; put it, her phone, and the notebook on the nightstand; and turned to look at her again. Her hand was still out like it had been when she was holding her phone, and the other was curled around a sleeping Sky. Deciding to let them be, I kissed Cassidy's forehead and turned to leave.

"Gage?" Her voice was husky from her nap, and damn if the sound didn't shoot straight through me.

"Hey, sorry. Didn't mean to wake you."

"It's okay." She patted the bed beside her and I carefully climbed in so I wouldn't wake Sky. "I didn't mean to fall asleep."

"Y'all get a lot done today?"

"Oh my word, like you wouldn't believe. You weren't lying; your mom has connections any wedding planner would kill for."

"Honestly, I'm surprised y'all have anything left."

"We really don't. Just the dresses, shirts, ties . . . that's about it. I decided it's going to be semiformal. I don't want you in a tux."

Thank God. "Sounds good to me."

"Can you tell me something? Why do you want to marry me so soon?"

My body went rigid. "Cass, I thought we already went ov—"

"No, I remember what you said, but is it because we can't do anything with your mom not letting us live together? Because if that's it, Gage, I'll find a way to be with you. I just don't want you to feel like you have to marry me so we can be together in that way."

"God no. The only person who can keep me from you *is* you. If you aren't ready for this, Cassidy, all you have to do is say the word; but if you are . . . darlin', I'm so ready to marry you. The way I see it, I've already found everything I want in you, and I know that's never going to change. So why wait? I'm ready for it all: marrying you, living in our house, having a family. As long as it's with you, I'm ready."

"'Kay, good." She smiled and pulled my head down to hers to kiss me. "Might have to hold off on the family though. I just got used to the idea of having kids; that's gonna take me a while. Oh, but just so you know, everyone except Isabella and Jesse thinks this is a shotgun wedding."

I threw my head back and laughed. "I don't care what everyone thinks as long as I'm married to you at the end of the day." I turned her body to face mine and cringed when Sky made an adorable little puppy grunt and stretched. When she just rolled onto her back and fell asleep I relaxed and took Cassidy's mouth in mine, letting my tongue lightly trail along hers. "Did y'all figure out when we can have the wedding?" I asked when her hands began unbuttoning my shirt, her lips pressing open-mouthed kisses onto my chest each time one was undone.

"Two months."

Fuck. I groaned. "Two months?"

"Mmm-hmm." She finished the last button and ran her hands over my stomach and chest. My hard-on was pressing against my jeans and for the hundredth time today I wished we were in our house. "Or nine days. It was one of those."

"Nine?" I brought her face up to mine. "Nine days?"

Her cheeks flamed as she bit the corner of her lip and nodded. "Adam, Dana, Ethan, and Jackie will all be here in five days to help with last-minute stuff and just hang out, since I made the last two weeks of school kinda crappy for everyone." I squeezed her hip and she continued. "Per your mom, the guys are all staying in our house, and the girls are all staying here. Then come next Saturday, I'll be yours."

Mine. Nine days and this amazing girl would be mine.

Lord, I couldn't wait.

I ran my hands up her body, under her shirt, and loved the breathy sigh that left her when my hands ran over her breasts. Her hands went back to my stomach before trailing down to undo my belt, then the button on my jeans, and her mouth went back to her torturous kisses on my chest. "Did you lock the door?" She grabbed my length in her hands and I groaned some sort of affirmative. "Where is everyone?"

"Downstairs," I roughly whispered, and pulled her shorts and underwear down.

Cass placed Sky on the floor and straddled me, grinding her hips into mine.

"Darlin', trust me when I say that this is something I love about you, but you are *loud,* and it's not exactly something that anyone would appreciate if they heard us. Just let me touch you."

She sank down on me hard and a loud moan left her. I sat up and crushed our mouths together, swallowing the rest of her moan. "I'm sure you can find ways to keep me quiet," she said against my lips, challenging me.

Challenge accepted.

Cassidy

IF YOU WOULD HAVE TOLD ME ten days ago that I was getting married today, I would have laughed, because there's no way to plan this elaborate of a wedding in nine days, right? Wrong. Gage's mom and sisters were a force to be reckoned with—well, except for little Emily. But she helped by playing with Sky when we were too busy to pay attention to the pup.

Tessa had connections like you wouldn't believe with other families from the neighboring ranches and in town, and through their help, we'd transformed the barn into a reception site I was jealous of. And it was *my* wedding. We'd kept the ceremony pretty bare; it was already so beautiful in that field that we'd set up white wooden chairs facing the natural arch of the trees, and nothing else. It was simple, but to add anything else would have taken away from the beauty of the ranch. A few dozen feet from the last row of chairs, we'd set up a tent that had fans in it so the girls could be in there when the guests started arriving and the guys went to stand up front, and I was so grateful for that, because it was that or come from the barn, which was a good five-minute walk.

The barn looked like it always did on the outside: absurdly massive, with faded red paint and clear globe lights decorating the doors and edge of the roof. The inside, which I hadn't seen until it was already decorated, had white, green, and gold tulle with little twinkle lights sweeping in arcs up into the center of the barn, making it look like a large tent. There was a dance floor on one side, tables on the other. The tablecloths alternated green and gold with bowls of floating flowers and candles on top. We had the cake and groom's cake—Tessa had given me a look like I'd lost my mind when I said I didn't know what a groom's cake was . . . whoops—on a table in a corner a little ways away from where the food would be. And thanks to all the dances and parties they'd held here in the past, they had massive fans that would keep it extremely comfortable in the barn, which had been my biggest worry. After all, it was June, and we were in Texas and going to be dancing in a barn. When the girls had laughed at my concern, I'd decided they knew better than me since they'd done this before and kept my mouth shut.

I turned to look at Jackie, Dana, and Amanda all zipping each other up; they looked incredible. They had on summer dresses that were strapless and tight around the chest and waist, and lightly flared out to above their knees. They were gold with eyelet cutouts showing black underneath, and they paired them with black cowboy boots to make them more casual. I loved the look and I was glad they did too.

"You ready, Cassidy? It's supposed to start in twenty minutes!" Amanda squealed, and clapped.

I about tripped over myself trying to get to where my dress was, and Jackie and Dana started laughing.

"I *think* you might be a little excited." Jackie snickered and let go of my arm when I was steady.

"Just a little," I breathed on a smile, and took a normal step in the direction of my dress.

With the help of the girls, we had the dress on and zipped and my brown cowboy boots on, and Amanda was restyling my hair, making sure it was perfect. The guys were semiformal, like the girls, and I was going to go with a white summer dress, but that's where Tessa had put her foot down. Said I had to have a real wedding dress, no exception. I was so glad I'd listened to her.

My dress was a strapless gossamer gown with a drop waist and chapel train. It was soft white and fit my figure perfectly. It was perfect for the ranch, it was perfect for me, and I was hoping it would be perfect for Gage. I skipped the veil and curled my hair into large, loose curls, which the girls spent time playing with so it wouldn't look "styled." Since we were out in the country, Amanda thought it should have the natural look without being natural, and since I had no idea what that meant, I let them do as they pleased. The side where my hair parted was French braided loosely, close to my ear, and pinned underneath the rest of my hair to keep that side from my face. It didn't look like my wild waves, but Amanda was right, it did look natural, almost windblown, but not messy.

I stared at my reflection and couldn't help but mutter, "Oh wow."

"You look beautiful, Cass!" Jackie cried, and stepped up beside me to brush hair over my shoulder, then stepped back.

My makeup was flawless, thanks to Dana, and I made a mental note to steal the eye shadow she'd used on me. It was a soft gold and made my eyes even brighter. Amanda handed me a barely tinted lip gloss, and after putting it on, I turned and faced my friends and almost-sister.

"I'm ready," I breathed, and couldn't stop the huge smile that was plastered on my face.

Amanda grabbed my watch off the table we'd brought in there and said excitedly, "Eight minutes!"

Just then, Tessa, John, Stephanie, and Jim all walked into the tent. There were gasps from the women and broad smiles from the men. We gave each other loose hugs, and kisses on the cheeks, and after a few words they were gone. Before I could grab my watch to see how much longer *now,* Adam and Ethan walked in, whistling low.

"Look at you ladies," Adam said with a smirk as he kissed Dana thoroughly, then gave me and Jackie kisses on the forehead. Ethan had kissed my cheek on the way in and was holding Jackie close to his body.

I looked around for Amanda and saw her at the other end of the tent with Jesse. She kissed him excitedly, then pushed him back, telling him he needed to go sit down, just to bring him back to her and kiss him again.

"Wow, sweetheart," a low voice said from behind me, and I spun to face Tyler. "You look beautiful."

"Ty, look at you!" I hugged him tight, not caring that the girls were telling me to be careful with my dress and hair.

The guys really did look handsome: all three were in black slacks, dark green button-ups with the sleeves rolled up to their forearms, and green-striped ties.

"You ready to do this?"

"I am! How's Gage?"

I hadn't been allowed to see Gage for two whole days, and it'd been torture. I didn't understand why we were having the rehearsal two days before the wedding, but then the girls and guys announced that we weren't seeing each other again 'til the wedding and a look of horror passed over both our faces. I'd had a lot of fun just being with the girls, but I was ready to see him again. Not like we hadn't gone longer, even recently with the two weeks of my leaving, but he'd been a five-minute drive from the main house, and we'd been forced to stay away from each other. Like I said, torture.

"Ready to see you, that's for damn sure. Do you know how many times he tried to sneak out at night?" Adam asked, and Ethan and Tyler chuckled. "When we finally went to bed, we had to take shifts staying awake the last two nights so we could stop him from trying to go see you."

"Well, maybe you shouldn't have stopped him," I teased.

"This will make it better, Cassidy," Dana said, and handed over my bouquet of stargazer lilies, the white ones filled with pink.

I grumbled at Dana and Tyler checked his wrist. "We're up."

My heart stopped.

Gage

I SMILED AT DAD, Mama, Nikki, and Emily, then looked anxiously back toward the tent. What was taking so long? Ty had gone in there like ten minutes ago.

"You ready, son?" Pastor Rick asked, and nudged my side.

"So ready," I breathed, and kept my eyes trained on the tent. *Now, if my girl will just come out here, I could marry her and everything will finally be right.*

Music started playing, and though I wondered how Mama had figured out how to get the music out here without my noticing anything, I didn't think about it too long. Adam and Dana, then Ethan and Jackie made their way from the tent toward the front where I stood. Amanda came next, and when she was standing next to Jackie, the music changed and I held my breath. I'd been waiting for this for two years, and it was finally here. I saw Ty first, and then they turned and began walking toward me, and everything else faded away as I took her in.

I've never seen anyone as beautiful as Cassidy, and I'd never seen Cassidy as beautiful as she was right then. Everything about her was perfect, and she was mine. Her lips stretched into a wide grin, and I felt my own lips mirror them. They finally reached the front, and Tyler put her hand in mine, then went to stand behind me. My eyes locked with her whiskey-gold ones and all I could think about was how this was finally happening, and how our lives were going to be from here on out. I somehow managed to get through repeating after the pastor in all the correct places and saying, "I do." I placed Cassidy's diamond-covered band on her finger, and she slid the black tungsten ring onto mine. When the time came, I cupped her cheeks and kissed her like it was the last kiss we'd ever share. She threw her arms around my neck and I just thought, *Screw it.* I put one arm behind her back and swept her legs out from under her and held her close to me as I continued to kiss her.

We reluctantly broke away but continued to stare at each other when my family and our friends surrounded us and were calling out their congratulations. When I saw the opportunity, I tightened my hold on her and walked us toward the tent at the back of the chairs. As soon as we were in there, her hands were in my hair and she was bringing my mouth to hers.

"I missed you and I love you," she said in rush before she was kissing me again.

I smiled against her lips. "I love you too, Cassidy Carson."

Her lips froze and she looked up at me with those wide eyes and a bright smile. "I like that."

"Love that," I said, correcting her, and claimed her lips. "And, darlin', that dress? Good God, I'm gonna have fun taking that off you."

Cassidy

"WELCOME HOME, DARLIN'." Gage's gravelly voice sent tingles straight to my lower stomach as he carried me through the door of our home. I hadn't been in there since we moved in all the furniture, and I'd missed it. I knew Tessa had rounded up the guys and had them move all my things in there that afternoon, as well as move all their stuff out to the main house. She also said she'd stocked it so we wouldn't have any reason to leave over the next week unless we wanted to.

I wouldn't want to.

The reception had been a blast, but I'd been eager for it to be over. I wanted to be alone with Gage, alone with my husband. He looked so incredible that I hadn't been able to stop touching him all night. He wore black slacks and a dark green shirt rolled up the same as the rest of the guys', but no tie, the top button undone, and a black suit vest. The black and green did amazing things with his hair and eyes, as I'd hoped they would, and it was safe to say my new hubby looked good enough to eat.

We'd danced for hours with our friends and his family. Gage had vetoed the father-daughter dance, but Tyler and Gage had come to an agreement that Ty would get a couple slow dances with me. Other than those two dances with Ty, and a dance split with John and Jim, Gage didn't let me more than a few inches from him. And that was more than fine with me.

I couldn't believe just three months before, we'd been at Stacey's wedding and everything about our feelings for each other and Tyler's manipulation had finally come out. When I thought about it that way, our relationship had moved fast—crazy fast—but Gage was right . . . we'd already spent too long without each other, and there was no point in waiting; he was all I would ever want. And now he was mine.

Looking back at his green eyes, I smiled softly at him and ran the tips of my fingers over his jaw before kissing his full lips. "Take me to bed, Gage."

Without another word, he walked us through the house and into the master bedroom before setting me on my feet in front of the bed. I started to unbutton his vest, but he put my hands back at my sides, then brushed the hair away from my neck, bending to place hot, openmouthed kisses there. He made a trail down my shoulder, then around to my back, placing two soft kisses on my tattoo before gripping the top of the zipper and slowly sliding it down.

"You looked so beautiful tonight, Cassidy."

My breath caught when the zipper hit the end, and holding up the dress with one hand, his other hand trailed along the small of my back, inside the fabric, and around my body to softly caress my stomach. Letting go of the fabric, he let the dress fall into a pool at my feet and turned my body around, all the while keeping both hands on me. His green eyes were so dark I couldn't see the golden flecks anymore as he pushed me gently onto the bed and moved the dress aside.

Taking a step away from the bed, he undid the buttons on his vest first, then his shirt. When both were done he removed them at the same time and tossed them onto a chair in the corner of the room. My eyes trailed over his tanned body and lingered on the long muscles; my fingers twitched with want but he was standing too far away. He leaned forward, cupped my cheek to kiss me softly, and walked over to all the windows, shutting the blinds and curtains at the same time his other hand went to the button on his pants. With pants undone, but still on, he crawled onto the bed and on top of me, unsnapping and pulling away my strapless bra before lowering me to the bed.

His head bent low and latched on to one breast, teasing the nipple relentlessly before moving to the other and doing the same. When he was satisfied with how worked up he'd gotten me, he kissed me long and hard as he pulled my lacy white boy-cut underwear off and placed a knee between my thighs.

"Beautiful," he mumbled, and brought my arms above my head, pinning them down onto the pillow.

Leaning up, he kissed my Ursa Major tattoo, and I was able to sneak in a kiss to his abdomen before he slid back down and smirked at me, then slid *all* the way down. No matter how many times I'd had every part of this with Gage, every time felt better than the last and like I'd been denied his touch for years. A breathy moan left me when he swiped his tongue against me and a shudder rippled through my body. One hand lay flat on my lower stomach as the other went to help with his mouth and I thought I'd die right there on the bed. My body tightened but I held off as long as I could before the heat in my stomach exploded, making it even more intense and limb numbing, and I gave myself over to what I knew would only be the first of many orgasms tonight.

Without wasting any more time, I brought his face back to

mine and used my free hand, with the help of my toes, to push down his slacks and dark boxer-briefs. He finally kicked them both off and positioned himself between my legs, kissing up my chest and throat to my lips. Grabbing his length, I wrapped my legs around his back and guided him to me, gasping out in raw pleasure when he pushed himself inside me.

"Cassidy," he groaned, and pressed his lips to the dip in my neck as he slowly started moving.

Our bodies, as always, moved together in perfect synchronization, and I was once again so thankful I'd never done this with anyone but Gage. He had been the only one for me from day one; there had never been anyone who had made me feel the way Gage did. My bond with Tyler and my connection with Connor would never hold a flame to what this was. This was raw and passionate, it was pure and unconditional, and it was tender and full of an understanding I never expected to have.

Gage propped himself up on one elbow and cupped my cheek with one hand as his pace quickened; my legs left his back only for my thighs to squeeze his hips and my heels to dig into the bed. My hands urged him to move faster and I felt that familiar heat intensify as my body began tightening around him again. His breaths were coming harder and faster, and I begged him not to stop. The hand on the bed clenched the sheet, his forehead hit mine, and the muscles in his jaw worked as he tried to hold off a little longer. My head fell away from his and my mouth opened, but no sound left as I climaxed for long, incredible seconds before crashing down just moments before he did.

We lay there holding each other, still connected, and waiting for our breathing to even out. His lips were pressed to the top of my head while mine were pressed to his chest; the only words we could seem to form were *I love you*.

19

Gage

WE'D JUST FINISHED HERDING the last of the cattle into a different section of the ranch, and God, this day couldn't have been longer. Cass hadn't been feeling that great when I left her that morning, and I hated leaving her when she was sick, but the move couldn't wait. There was a huge storm coming in that was supposed to be there all week, and it's too hard to move the cattle during a storm—point made when the storm came halfway through the day. It was almost the middle of October, and it was already cooling down, but the cold front that came with this storm was wicked, and swear to God the cattle just decided to plop their happy asses on the ground. Not like we weren't expecting them to prepare for the storm, but this storm was why they needed to move in the first place; there were too many creeks running through the part of the ranch they were in, and where they were going was elevated. So when they'd all lain down in groups, I'd groaned and tried to prepare myself for a long afternoon.

It'd ended up taking an extra three hours to get them all in, and by that point I was snapping at some of the ranch hands whom I'd known practically my entire life. I apologized as much as my pissed-off self would allow when we got all the horses back to the stable, hopped in my truck, and drove back home. I had a sick wife who needed taking care of, and she'd expected me home hours ago. Driving up, I hated not seeing Cassidy standing there with Sky—not like I really expected her to be there tonight, but it showed just how bad she was feelin'.

Since our "honeymoon," which was really just an amazing week in our home of uninterrupted time with a naked Cassidy, she'd started her own routine with our lives, and damn, I loved it. Every morning I got my hug in bed; she'd tell me to come back after I finished feeding all the other animals, and she'd have breakfast waiting for me; more often than not, breakfast led to a whole lot else that resulted in our having to sanitize different surfaces of the kitchen again. Then she and Sky would walk me out and stand on the porch until I was gone. Some days I'd come back for lunch if I wasn't busy, but every night she and Sky were waiting on the porch as I drove up. Seeing her waiting with a big smile on her face in the house I built got me every time. I was a lucky man, and I thanked God for giving her to me every damn day.

Sky jumped up from where she'd been lying near the steps on the wraparound, and I barely scratched her ears as I raced into the house. The scent of food caught me off guard and I slowly made my way back to the kitchen. Cass should have been in bed. Rounding the corner, I was relieved but also worried that Mama was standing there making soup.

"How is she?"

She looked up and smiled. "Sleeping. She'll be fine though. Just the flu."

I nodded. "Thanks for comin' to check on her, Mama."

"Of course, of course. Dinner's in the oven, should be done in just a few minutes. And I just need to put the last of this in the pot for her soup. Why don't you go take a shower? I'll be outta here in ten or so minutes."

"All right, thanks again." I kissed her cheek and crept down the hall. Sky had followed me inside and was now stretched out along Cassidy's side, with her head on Cassidy's stomach. Cass was completely out; her face was ghostly white and a thin sheen of sweat clung to her. Kissing her warm forehead, I turned and headed for the bathroom to take a quick shower.

Cassidy

I WOKE UP WITH A START, and it only took a few seconds before I realized why. My stomach rolled and I raced to the bathroom, barely making it to the toilet in time. I groaned and slid down to the cool floor of our bathroom. It felt so good right there, I was going to stay there forever. I curled up onto my side, pressed my cheek onto the tile floor, and hoped my stomach would stay calm the rest of the night.

Gage had woken me up some time ago and fed me a cup of soup. It'd stayed down for an hour and he'd let me go back to sleep, but apparently I still wasn't ready for food. My stomach rolled thinking about dinner and I took calming breaths through my mouth until the uneasiness passed.

I didn't know how long I'd been lying there, but I was still awake when I felt something on my leg. Figuring it was my imagination and not wanting to take my arms from my sensitive stomach, I wiggled my leg and curled back up into a ball. Not a minute later I felt it again and I sat up to look, wishing I'd turned on the light in my race in here. I had to blink my eyes a few times to focus on whatever the large lump was on my leg, and only when its tail curled up above its body did everything become clear.

"Gage!"

Gage

MY BODY SHOT UPRIGHT and I was out of bed before I realized that Cassidy wasn't in bed and had screamed my name. I was already in the hall heading to the living room when a short, pained cry came from the master bathroom. I turned around and burst through the door as soon as I reached it. She was in the bathtub and it took me a second to notice she was fully clothed and there was no water in there. I took two large steps toward her and her hands shot out.

"No, stop!"

I froze.

"It—it's right there." Her hand was shaking uncontrollably as she pointed down.

I looked down but only saw the floor. Taking a step back, I flipped on the lights and had to blink a few times before I could look at the dark tile, and there, not two feet from the bathtub, was a scorpion. I laughed and looked up at a freaked Cassidy.

"Hang on, darlin', I'll get him." I jogged into the closet, grabbed the first shoe I found, and went back to smash the shit out of that ugly thing. "That isn't the first one you've ever seen, is it?"

She didn't answer and I decided it probably was and felt like an ass for laughing. I'd grown up in the country, where scorpions were a common thing; she'd grown up in a country club neighborhood in a rich city in California. I'm sure she'd never once had to worry about these things.

When I had it cleaned up and thrown away and the shoe wiped off, I looked up and noticed she was still violently shaking; her cheeks were wet, eyes were huge, and lips were chalky white and trembling. She didn't look like she had earlier from being sick; she looked freakin' terrified. God, I was such a dick. I lowered my voice and spoke in a soothing tone. "Cass, it's okay, he's gone. Come on, let me take you to bed."

Her head started shaking quickly back and forth when I got to the edge of the tub, and she was still staring at where the scorpion had been.

"Cassidy, it's okay. You need to calm down or you're gonna force yourself to go into shock. Breathe, babe." When she didn't make any move I exhaled loudly and put my arms under hers; it was when I started to lift and her hands slipped from the side of her calf that I saw the trickle of blood coming from a small red circle. "What the hell? Shit, Cass, were you stung?!"

She nodded slightly and a soft sob followed by a huge breath in snapped her back to the present. "Gage! It was on me! I had no idea—I was just lying there and I felt something. I tried to get it off and it was still there!" Another huge breath in. "I looked down and I didn't realize what it was at first, and then its tail, oh my God, its tail did that thing where it, where it, you know . . ." She tried to show me with her hands.

It was so damn cute, but she was freakin' out and had just

been stung. I knew from experience that it hurt like a bitch, and the one that got her wasn't little either, so I kept my mouth shut as I carried her over to the counter where our sinks were and turned the water on, waiting for it to warm.

"A-a-and I just freaked! I tried to sit up and scramble away and it stung me before I could get it off. I've never even seen one before! Why was it here? They aren't supposed to be in Texas, are they?!" She took another shuddering breath in, and before she could continue her chest started heaving up and down quickly.

"Breathe, Cass, deep breath in and hold it, then blow it out. Darlin', you've got to calm down, now, you're gonna hyperventilate. Come on, Cass, deep breath in." I gripped her shoulders and tried to force her to breathe with me for the next couple minutes until she was breathing normal and her head was slumped onto my chest. "Good girl. All right, let's get this washed off, I'll get you some ice, and we'll go back to bed. Sound good?"

She whimpered some kind of agreement and clutched her stomach.

God, I'd forgotten she was sick too. This was just not her day.

After we washed where she was stung, I laid her down in bed and propped her leg up on a couple pillows before getting some ice wrapped in a towel. I held the towel against her calf and rubbed her back until she was sound asleep, then curled around her tiny body, and before my head hit the pillow I was out.

NO WAY IT'S TIME to get up yet. I would put money down that I just went to sleep. My eyes opened and I realized my alarm wasn't going off, and it wasn't even predawn outside, it was pitch-black. I heard Cassidy getting sick in the bathroom and realized that must've been what woke me up. Turning slightly, I checked the clock and saw we'd only gotten back in bed about an hour ago. I wished there was something, anything, I could do for her. I felt so helpless, and I hated it. I'd just swung my legs off the bed when a loud smack came from the bathroom and for the second time tonight I shot off toward it, this time to find my wife sprawled out on the floor, eyes rolled to the back of her head and barely breathing. As soon as I finished checking her, I was at my nightstand grabbing the phone, dialing and running back to her side, sliding up to her on my knees.

"Nine-one-one, what's your emergency?"

"M-my wife collapsed, she's—I don't know, she's barely breathing and she's not waking up." The hand that wasn't holding the phone was going everywhere: her eyelids, her mouth, her neck, her chest, her wrist. Anywhere to get a response or to feel her breaths or pulse. "Cass, baby, wake up, please wake up!"

After telling the woman on the other line where we were, she asked, "Sir, can you tell me what happened prior to you finding your wife in this condition? Had she been drinking or—"

I didn't even let her finish. "No, no, she's been sick all day with the flu and then an hour ago she was stung by a scorpion. I cleaned it and everything and we went back to bed. I woke up and she was throwing up, then I heard her hit the floor." My whole body was shaking and I kept begging Cassidy to wake up. The fact that her pulse was so faint I had to struggle to feel it was scaring me worse than anything had in my entire life.

"You said she was stung by a scorpion?"

"Yeah, about an hour ago. But everyone in my family, including me, has been stung at least once before. I washed it, put ice on it, and elevated it."

"Has your wife ever been stung before, sir?"

"Cassidy, *please* wake up! What? Um . . . no, no, she's never seen one before tonight."

"What does the area look like where she was stung?"

"What? Look, is someone coming? I need an ambulance, she's still not waking up!"

"Sir, I dispatched them as soon as you gave me the address. Now I need you to tell me what the area where she was stung looks like."

I touched Cassidy's face and throat once more before looking down at the side of her calf. "Oh shit," I breathed. "It—it's big." *What the hell?*

"Is it red?"

"Yeah."

"All right, sir, she might be having an allergic reaction to the sting."

"What can I do?"

"I'm sorry, sir, but there's nothing to do right now other than wait for the ambulance."

"She's barely breathing! This isn't a normal allergic reaction. I'm not just gonna sit around and wait for someone to get here!" I shot up and ran into the bedroom, grabbing the first clothes my hands touched. "Do you know how fuckin' long it takes for an ambulance to get out here?! You tell the EMTs they see a black SUV trying to get their attention, it's me meeting them on the way." I hung up and rushed back into the bathroom. Cassidy usually slept in nothing but my shirt, but thank God she'd been sick, because she had little sleep shorts on with her hoodie. Sick or not, I didn't want anyone else seeing her but I wasn't wasting more time dressing her.

Grabbing her up in my arms, I walked as steadily and quickly as possible out to her Tahoe, put the passenger seat all the way down, and laid her in it. After putting the seat belt over her, I ran around to the driver's side and took off while dialing the main house. Dad was outside and waiting for me when we pulled up; Mom was in a nightgown with her hands covering her mouth. Thankfully Dad said we'd call her and she ran back into the house to get ready in case we needed her. He jumped into the driver's seat and I hopped into the back so I could watch over Cassidy as we drove.

About ten minutes after we'd gotten off the property, she groaned and her eyes fluttered open. My heart started racing as I brushed my hands lightly over her throat; her pulse was still soft, too soft. "Cassidy, baby, can you hear me?"

She nodded and it looked like she was still struggling to breathe.

"Thank God," I whispered, and rested my forehead on hers for a moment before sitting up to look into her honey eyes. They held mine for barely two seconds before rolling back again. "No, Cass, no. Wake back up!" My hands started doing their check, and when they passed over her chest, I realized it felt wrong.

Even compared to her shallow breathing in the bathroom, this felt wrong. I put my hand back on her chest and crouched low in the seat, making myself eye level with my hand. It wasn't fucking moving.

"Cassidy, Cassidy, babe, I need you to wake up. You hear me? Wake up, darlin', please, God, wake up." I let one hand go to her wrist and the other go to her throat. "Damn it, babe, *please.*" My hands were shaking so bad, I had to take deep breaths in just to calm them so I could check for a pulse. "Come on, sweetheart . . . open your eyes again." I kept quiet as I focused and about cried out in relief when I felt the faintest beat in her throat. "Keep breathing, Cassidy, ple—" My words broke off on a sob and I let my forehead fall onto the top of the seat. "God, Cass, don't leave me, wake up."

"Gage," Dad said gruffly, and I looked up through tear-filled eyes to see flashing lights. He hit the brakes, put on the emergency lights, and started flashing his brights at them.

They'd just started to pass us when they slammed on their brakes. Thank God for that dispatcher. I was already out of the car and running to the other side when an EMT came out of the back of the ambulance, and another came from the passenger side. I didn't wait for them to ask, I just started saying everything I could think of that had happened in the last two hours as I opened the passenger side of the Tahoe and unbuckled Cassidy. They put her on a stretcher, and once again I didn't wait for them to ask; I got into the ambulance with them. No way in hell they were taking my girl without me.

I held her hand and silently pleaded with her to breathe. Once in there, the EMTs started an IV, shot her with something else, and when they started spouting off words, all I heard was *anaphylactic shock*. My heart stopped; there was no way. No way, she'd never been stung before; that couldn't happen from just one sting, right? I gripped her hand tighter and begged God not to take her from me after just giving me her. Twenty minutes later, just as we were pulling up to the emergency room driveway, Cassidy's eyes opened halfway as she took the deepest breath she'd taken in who knows how long and locked on mine for a split second before the EMTs moved the stretcher out of the ambulance.

I jumped out with them and kept her hand in mine as they

wheeled her in. We'd just gotten to the double doors inside the waiting room when a large male nurse stepped in front of me, stopping me from going farther.

"No, I have to go with her!"

"You can wait out here; if you're family, a doctor will be out to talk to you."

"She's my wife, I need to be in there with her!" I tried to side-step him, and when he put a hand on my chest, I just threw it to the side and kept marching forward. She'd *just* opened her eyes again. I needed to be there for her.

"Sir, I'm going to have to ask that you calmly sit down, or I'm going to have you removed."

"If *that* was *your* world, would you let some nurse with a complex—"

"Gage." I turned to see my dad behind me. As I opened my mouth to tell him how ridiculous this guy was being, he spoke again. "Son, sit down. They'll talk to us when they can. In the meantime, you're not doing Cassidy any good if you get kicked out of the hospital."

He didn't wait for me to respond; he put a hand on my shoulder and led me over to the chairs.

Other than filling out the paperwork for Cass, I didn't move, and I didn't speak. I just stood there staring at the doors, willing them to open with Cassidy's doctor behind them.

Cassidy

I WOKE UP and blinked quickly at the bright lights. What on earth? I went to shield my eyes from the light and something tugged on the inside of my arm. I looked down and saw an IV coming out and let my head hit the pillow. What was I doing in the hospital?! Looking to the other side, I saw Gage asleep on a chair, one hand lightly holding mine, the other wrapped around his broad chest.

"Gage." My voice came out barely above a whisper, but his eyes shot open. "What's going on?"

"Oh thank God." He stood and bent over the bed to cup my cheeks, and his hands trailed down my throat and chest in an awkward pattern before separating and grabbing my wrists. "How are you?"

"What are you doing, and why am I in a hospital?"

"Cassidy," he breathed, and the name sounded so happy on his lips, it almost came out as a laugh. "Darlin', you've got to stop scaring the shit outta me like this. We've had enough trips to the ER this year, all right?"

I nodded; I'd forgotten about getting pneumonia. "But why am I here?"

"You had a severe allergic reaction to the scorpion sting. Scared the hell out of me. You passed out in the bathroom, your eyes were rolled back, and you were barely breathing. You only came to for a second before we met up with the ambulance, and then again when we got here, but other than that you wouldn't wake up and your heart rate was so slow—" He stopped and had to force down a swallow. "Cass, it was like it wasn't there at all. Your chest wasn't even moving."

I gasped softly as I watched the nightmare play out over his face again.

"When we were in the ambulance, they kept saying 'anaphy-lactic shock,' and a part of me knew that couldn't be it since you hadn't seen a scorpion before then, but with how you'd been over those last twenty or thirty minutes, baby, I thought I was going to lose you if they didn't do something soon."

Fat tears were falling from Gage's eyes, and I let my fingers brush them away from one cheek before curling them around his neck.

"You weren't going into anaphylactic shock, you just had a really bad allergic reaction. Your doctor said with already being weak and having a shot immune system from having the flu, it just made your allergic reaction that much worse for you and your body shut down to protect itself from the reaction."

"I don't remember anything after you put me back in bed after getting stung."

Gage nodded and planted his forehead into the crook of my neck, inhaling deeply. "You haven't woken up long enough to say anything; I figured you wouldn't."

"How long ago did this happen?"

He looked over at the clock for a few seconds before turning his face back toward my neck. "Almost seventeen hours ago."

Oh my God. I tried to swallow but my throat was really dry, and just as I was about to say I needed a drink, I felt Gage's body shudder. "Hey, it's okay, I'm okay."

"You weren't, Cassidy. You weren't. I've—I've never been more scared in my life." He admitted softly, "Your chest wasn't moving; you don't know what that was like. And half the time I thought I was making myself believe I was feeling a heartbeat." As he spoke, one of his hands came back up to my throat, then trailed down to my chest and ended at my wrist. All of it was soft as a feather, and very practiced, and now made sense. "I've thought you left me before . . . but not like this, never like this.

I thought you were—" He choked out a shaky breath and didn't speak.

"I'm never leaving you again, I told you." I tried to laugh, but it sounded wrong. I couldn't imagine what he'd gone through, but I knew it would kill me to see him the same way. "I'm sorry," I whispered.

"Sorry? Cass, I almost lost you! Why the hell are you sorry? You had nothing to do with it, and I—I just laughed about the damn thing. I had no idea; none of us have ever had reactions to a sting. God, Cass, I didn't know. All of this is my fault."

"Gage—" I tried to pull his head back so I could look at him, but he just kept talking softly, almost as if to himself.

"I never take care of you. With the pneumonia, I should have called an ambulance as soon as I opened my door and found you like that. Last night I should have been there when you woke up the first time so you wouldn't have gotten stung, and I shouldn't have fallen back asleep after you did. I should have been watching you."

"Stop, please—"

"I've hated Tyler for almost letting you die, but, Cassidy, I could've killed you by being careless."

"Gage, stop!" I finally moved his head back and stared into his dark green eyes, tears still falling steadily from them. "None of what has ever happened is on you; all you've ever done is take care of me. Even when you hardly knew me, Gage, that's all you've done. When I would sleep on the couch, you'd move me to your bed, and you didn't even know me then. You woke up early to drive me to work every morning so I wouldn't have to walk. I would have gotten pneumonia either way, and that's not on you or Tyler, it's on me. I'm the one who walked to your place, but you? You threw me in a shower and made sure I warmed up, bought a new thermometer just for me, and took me to the hospital the next day."

He started shaking his head, so I kept talking before he could.

"And tonight—last night, is *not* your fault. How you're even able to twist it around so that it *is* is just beyond me. But obviously it was some freak accident, and from what you're saying, I'm alive because of you."

"Cassidy, you don't know what you mean to me. I can't—I can't lose you." He tried to clench his jaw shut, but his lips and jaw were still quivering. "I can't."

"I know," I whispered softly, and kissed his trembling lips. "Losing you would kill me too."

Gage exhaled deeply and laid his head on my chest, his fingertips on my throat, not saying anything else. I scooted over and after a minute he awkwardly climbed onto the hospital bed with me; his fingertips went right back to my throat, but this time his head rested on the mattress next to mine and we just stared at each other. His hand wasn't uncomfortable—in fact I barely felt it—but for some reason having it there was a new lifeline for Gage, and he was clinging to it. Hard.

20

Cassidy

IT'D BEEN ALMOST A MONTH since the scorpion sting, and thank God things were back to normal—well, mostly. I'd had to spend the rest of that weekend in the hospital, and when I'd gone back to the ranch, Gage had two different exterminators that specialize in scorpions come out to give bids. He didn't care about the money; he cared about which one he thought "wasn't full of shit." Apparently scorpions were hard to get rid of, but he and the exterminator were confident they'd done all they could. After I was informed how wrong I'd been about scorpions in Texas, I realized they were going overboard, but I let him do what he needed, same as with his pulse checks.

I don't know if Gage knew he was still doing it, if it was just second nature now, or if he thought I didn't realize what he was doing, but every time he came up to me, his fingers ended up on my throat or wrists somehow. He'd actually gotten really good at it, to the point where if I didn't know what he was doing, I would think he was holding me sweetly. When he would pull me toward him, it was almost always done by my wrist; sometimes when he kissed me he would pin my arms behind my back and hold my hands there, but his index finger would always be on a pulse point. Others, he would go to cup my cheeks, but would cup behind my neck instead, which I loved, and I loved the way he trailed his thumb down my throat even more, but like I said, I knew what he was doing.

And although it'd been a month, and I thought he should be able to see me without having to reassure himself that I was breathing, I wasn't about to say a word to him. After all, I wasn't the one who'd seen his chest not moving. I wasn't the one who'd had to search for his pulse.

We were starting to get ready for Thanksgiving, which was a little over a week away, and I was kind of excited and nervous about it. I'd made parts of Thanksgiving for the guys the last two years, but I would be cooking with Tessa and Amanda this year, and from what I'd been told, this meal was their specialty. I'd asked why we were doing a Thanksgiving lunch instead of a Thanksgiving dinner, and Gage had just shrugged while saying, "It's Texas," like that should be the only explanation I needed. I'd just raised an eyebrow at him and waited until he sighed and gave his version of an explanation.

"Everyone spends *the day* with their family, but it's the UT–A&M game, darlin', that takes up the night for us."

My response when I saw his mom and dad look at me like I should understand this by now? "Ah."

If cooking a Thanksgiving meal with Tessa wasn't enough to be nervous about, it didn't help that I'd been having some issues the last week that had my nerves skyrocketing. I called my doctor, and he'd said especially after the shock of the sting and the allergic reaction, I shouldn't worry about it. But I *was* worried about it; in fact it was all I was thinking about. So I told Gage I had to run in to town to grab some things for his mom and would be back before dinner—all true, just not the whole truth. He was already dealing with enough as it was; I didn't need to worry him with how I'd been feeling off . . . and other random things.

With another look at the doctor's office door, then the clock on the dashboard, I grabbed my purse and hopped out of my SUV. It was time to find out exactly what this scorpion sting had done to me.

AN HOUR LATER I was back in my car and just staring at nothing. I tried figuring out how to tell Gage, but I could barely convince myself that it was happening, so how could I tell him? I didn't even know how I felt about it—no . . . that's not true. I did. I knew exactly how I felt. I was terrified, and all I could see was my mom and Jeff. Memories so burned into me, I swear I could still feel Jeff slamming the large vase over my back until it shattered. Could feel my mom taking one of the larger chunks and digging it into the small of my back and making a large, bloody X. Could hear her moans as Jeff screwed her brains out after they let me up to go to my room.

I shivered and actually shook myself as I reached for my purse and the letter from Mom. After reading it three times, taking another few minutes to just clear my mind and find the beauty from their ashes all over again, I took a deep breath and pulled out my cell.

"How's my favorite SMB?"

"Fine." I laughed and ran a hand through my long, wavy hair.

I wasn't fine yet, but I would be. "How long did it take for my jersey to come in last time, Jake?"

"Ha! You liked it, huh? Want another one?"

"Love my SMB jersey, and I do, but I need it before Thanksgiving morning. Do you think that will be possible?"

"Oh, hell yeah, Cass. It'll be there in a week, tops. Another one that says 'SMB'?"

"Uh, no." My hands were shaking and I had to put the one that wasn't holding the phone tightly around the steering wheel.

"You gonna tell me what you want or should I surprise you?"

I laughed nervously and took a deep breath before speaking. "No, I know what I want, but, Jake, you can't . . . let me repeat. *Can't*. Tell. Anyone." When he agreed, I told him exactly what I wanted and he stayed quiet for a whole minute when I was done.

"You're serious, Cass?" he asked, for once completely serious.

"Yeah, I just found out, so could you do that and I'll send you a check in the mail today?"

"All right, I'll get it done, and I won't tell anyone. But no way am I letting you pay me back for this, no way, baby girl."

I smiled to myself. "Thanks, Jake."

THE LAST WEEK AND A HALF had been absolute torture. I'd almost told Gage about a thousand times, but thankfully I'd stopped myself every time. I'd needed this time before I told him, needed the time to get used to the idea and actually be happy about it. And I was; God, I was thrilled now. I'd hardly slept at all last night, knowing that this morning he'd finally know.

After getting his morning hug, he left to do what he always does in the mornings, and I hopped into the shower. I blew my hair dry and straightened it but held off on my makeup because

I was sure this morning was bound to be an emotional one. I threw on my jeans, a pair of gray Uggs, and my new burnt-orange jersey that had arrived just two mornings ago. I stared at myself for a long time in the mirror, looked at the back of the jersey, and smiled before I headed out to the kitchen.

I started on an omelet to split for when Gage came back. Usually I'd make us one each, but we were going to be eating all day; I figured splitting this wouldn't kill him. Just as I was sliding the omelet onto a plate, I heard the front door open and my face broke out into a wide smile.

"That's my girl."

I turned to look at him and saw him smiling at the jersey, then a confused look passed over his face.

"Wait, is this new?"

Holding my arms out to the sides, I couldn't help the smile that so easily came back. "Yeah, Jake just ordered it for me last week."

Gage's head fell back, and he groaned. "Darlin', I'm all for your Cowboys jersey, and now your Longhorns one . . . but *another* SMB jersey? It's not that funny."

"Well, it *was* that funny, but I only have one of those." I turned so my back was facing him and took my time getting the silverware from the drawer.

"Cassidy, I love that you want to be my wife and makin' this our home is what you wanna do. But I would never stop you if you wanted to do something, like with your photography. So even though I love that this is what you've chosen, I think that SMB shit is degrading."

Okay, well apparently he wasn't going to bite on the name I'd had put on it; I grabbed the plate and two forks and walked over to the kitchen table, rolling my eyes at him when he was watching. "Babe. It's Jake. From anyone else it *would* probably be degrading, but no one takes him seriously anyway."

He grumbled and sat down next to me, digging into the omelet and groaning his appreciation as soon as the first bite hit his tongue.

We ate mostly in silence, eating off the same plate and occasionally feeding each other bites. It was gushy, yes, but we were still newlyweds; we were allowed to be that way. When the omelet was gone, he sat back in his chair and pulled me onto his lap. His hand went to brush away some hair that had fallen forward, and his fingertips did their trusty pause over the pulse point on my throat.

"What do you need me to help you with today?" he asked softly as his eyes watched my chest rise and fall.

"Nothing, already finished all the prep work that I can do before we head over."

Watching my chest must have stirred up another emotion in him, because his lips were now kissing my neck and his hands were undoing the knot I'd made at the bottom of the jersey so I wouldn't have to tuck it in and I wouldn't drown in it. As soon as the knot was loosened his hands were under my shirt and on my bare skin. I quickly got off his lap, collected the plate, and headed into the kitchen.

He frowned but followed me to the sink and took it from me to wash it. It's not that I didn't want him touching me, I was just too wound up with my news to think about that just yet. I leaned my hip against the counter to watch him silently. When he was done he turned and smiled. "Amanda's gonna be pissed when she sees that jersey."

"Safe to say she'll be wearing an Aggie one?"

Gage nodded. "So what did Jake do for you this time anyway?"

Oh my God, *finally*! I bit down on my bottom lip and tried not to smile as I let him turn me around and move my hair aside to see the name *Mama Carson*.

His hand froze before he could sweep my hair all the way to the side, and I'd bet he just saw the *Mama* part. I kept silent as I waited for it to sink in. It'd been a difficult pill for me to swallow, but then again I'd grown up never wanting kids. Since starting a relationship with Gage, I'd slowly grown comfortable with the idea and actually wanted a family with him in the future. I thought we were young, way too young, but I knew someday it was what I wanted.

My period had been late, and that's when I'd called the Carsons' family doctor. He was the one who told me that with stressful events, especially the allergic reaction and what had happened following, it was common to be late or miss a period or two fully. But then I'd started feeling extra tired, I'd had to stop cleaning before I even started because the smell of the cleaning supplies made me want to pass out, and one morning I started crying looking at Sky . . . it was after that round of ridiculousness that I'd called an ob-gyn and made the appointment. When they'd confirmed the pregnancy at the doctor's, all my lifelong fears of turning into my mother had come rushing back to me, and it'd taken a lot of work to remind myself I was nothing like the woman she was when liquor ran her life.

So now I still thought we were too young, but I was happy too. Beyond happy. I hadn't been able to stop smiling since I'd gotten home that day, and now I couldn't wait to see what Gage and his family had to say.

Gage finally draped all of my hair over my right shoulder, and his hand passed over the lettering softly before his left hand shot out and gripped the kitchen counter at the same time as he lowered himself to the floor. Or more like fell, right on his butt.

"Gage?" I spun around and squatted down to look at him. I was afraid he was about to faint, but the color in his face was tan as ever, his green eyes were bright and huge, and his mouth was slightly open. "Babe?" I whispered when he still hadn't said anything or moved.

He didn't say anything, but he started to get back up, so I stood and wobbled slightly when he grasped my hips. Looking down, I saw he was on his knees and just staring up at me. I smiled and felt the tears prick at my eyes just before a few fell. I ran my hand through his naturally just-got-out-of-bed hair and about melted into a puddle on the floor when his head bent forward, he lifted my jersey, and he pressed his lips gently to my lower stomach. After placing two more soft kisses there, his hands left my hips and trailed gently over my abdomen before he stood up and kissed me fiercely as he lifted me into his arms, wrapped my legs around his waist, and walked us into the bedroom.

When we were both spent, I looked into his green eyes and almost didn't want to speak. We'd just had the most emotional experience of my life, all without words, and it felt weird to use them now. But I had to hear him say it. "Does this mean you're happy?"

His dimples took up a good portion of his cheeks. "Yeah, darlin', I'm happy."

"You scared me when you wouldn't say anything for so long, and then I thought you were going to pass out on me."

"Yeah." He huffed a laugh. "I, uh, would've hit the ground a lot harder if I hadn't grabbed the counter first. But, Cassidy, I'm so happy; I can't tell you how happy this makes me."

I curled into his body and placed my lips against his bare chest. "I'm glad."

"When we last talked about it though, you hadn't wanted a family any time soon; I didn't even know you stopped taking your birth control."

"Probably because I only stopped taking it about a week and a half ago when I found out I was pregnant." I smiled against his skin when the stillness of his body gave away his even more confused state. "I guess all the medications they had me on after the sting counteracted the effects of the pill and I got pregnant anyway."

Gage's hand slid up and down my back, his light touch leaving goose bumps all over. "I should have thought of that."

"We both should have, but it's too late now and I'm not mad that we didn't."

He pulled my body up until he could look into my eyes. "You're really okay with this?"

"I am." I shrugged and smiled brightly at him. "I wasn't at first; it really scared me. I started slipping back into my fears, but I reread the letter from my mom, and I thought about all of our conversations since I've been back, and the fears just started melting away. It still took a couple days, but I'm really happy now. Seriously, I can't wait to have your baby."

His smile was wide and absolutely breathtaking; those dimples that I knew would get the best of me someday were all I could currently look at. "God, I can't believe we're gonna have a baby," he breathed, and leaned back. "And I can't believe you told Jake of all people."

I burst out laughing and buried my head in his neck. "He's the only one who knows and he was sworn to secrecy. I knew it would hurt you if I wasn't excited about the pregnancy when I told you, and I had a feeling it was going to take a few days or so for me to get there. I sat there thinking of how I wanted to tell you, and I figured I couldn't just randomly blurt it out after knowing for some time, so I thought of the jersey."

"It was a good idea, darlin', I like it. And it'll be fun with the family too."

"Do you think they'll be happy?" I asked, a little anxious. If I thought we were too young, I could only imagine what John and Tessa would think. It would be the same as if Amanda was pregnant.

"Oh hell yeah. Cass, they don't say much around you because they know how you are about having kids, but when you're not around, dear Lord, it's all they ever talk about. Even little Emily wants to know when you're going to have a baby so she can have someone to play with."

"Oh, I didn't know they were trying not to talk about it in front of me. Now I feel bad."

Gage leaned away, placed two fingers under my chin, and lifted my head up. "Don't. I didn't say that so you would feel bad. They just didn't want to make you uncomfortable, sweetheart. But I promise they'll be excited, especially when they see how happy you are." He kissed my lips softly and without moving away asked, "When are you due?"

"July eleventh; I'm seven weeks today."

He repeated the date and smiled. "Holy shit. We're having a baby in July. This is unreal."

"I know, we have the first ultrasound a week from today." Just then my alarm went off and Gage reached over to my phone to shut it off.

"What's that for?"

"Gotta go help your mom cook."

Gage rolled us over so my back was to the bed and he was

hovering over me; he planted a knee between my legs and I will-ingly opened them again. "She can wait."

WE PULLED UP to the main house and I finished putting my hair in a high, messy bun, Gage's request so nothing would cover the name on the jersey. I looked at all the cars and the butterflies in my stomach tripled; Amanda had been home for two days, but Ty's Jeep and Jesse's Camaro were there as well.

Gage stopped me before we hit the door and kissed me thor-oughly. "I love you, Cassidy."

Forcing my hands to unclench from his burnt-orange shirt, I sighed and whispered my love back to him.

As soon as we were in the house, I was pulled into a massive bear hug from Tyler and I thought Gage would have a stroke. I wanted to tell him I was only seven weeks, he wasn't going to hurt anything, but that would ruin our plan to wait for someone to notice the name on the jersey, so I kept my mouth shut. Jesse and Isabella hugged us, and I cringed when I noticed how much thinner Isabella was, but she looked happier than ever.

"Oh, nuh-uh! Get out!" Amanda demanded, and I looked at her with wide eyes. "Both of you, and, Ty, you can go with them! No burnt orange allowed in this house."

I laughed and looked up at Tessa's back. "But your mom is wearing a Longhorns jersey."

I'd thought Gage was joking when he said everyone in the family wore jerseys or college shirts during Thanksgiving, but he wasn't. The only people in the entire house not wearing maroon or burnt orange were Emily, Isabella, and Jesse. Amanda and Nikki were wearing maroon "Twelfth Man" shirts; John was wearing a "Saw 'Em Off" gray-and-maroon shirt; Tyler was wearing a burnt-orange-and-white "Hook 'Em" shirt, same as Gage's; and Tessa was wearing a Longhorns jersey.

Texans . . . they're their own kind of people.

"Now, now, I'm showin' my love for my divided house," Tessa said, and turned around to show the front was an A&M jersey.

My jaw dropped and I pointed. "Not fair! Why is it okay for her to sew two jerseys together, two *rival* jerseys, might I add, but it's not okay for me to wear Lakers and Spurs jerseys at the same time?"

Gage was the only one who understood what I was talking about, so he just laughed and kissed the top of my head. "Darlin', that's 'cause you were trying to bring Texas and California together. Doesn't work that way."

Tessa looked pointedly at the two of us and smirked. "I'd say it does."

Gage winked and kissed me again quickly as I started walking into the kitchen, and he went over to sit with his dad, Ty, and Isabella.

It took much longer than I thought it would, but an hour later Nikki finally said, "Mama, did you let Cassidy borrow your jersey or something?"

My smile grew and my hands stilled momentarily, then I made quick work of washing and drying them as Tessa responded distractedly from the other side of the counter. "No, baby, why?"

" 'Cause hers says 'Mama Carson.' "

"No, I—" Tessa cut herself off and I heard Amanda's gasp from right behind me, followed quickly by Tessa's. I could hear Tyler and Jesse start razzing Gage, and I turned to face the family with the world's biggest smile.

Tessa and Amanda both had wide eyes, hands over their mouths, and were frozen; Nikki looked like she'd just gotten it; and Emily was sitting on the counter just looking at everyone. Before I could say anything, Gage stumbled into the kitchen with Jesse and Tyler clapping him on the back and still razzing him, and John was walking Isabella in. Gage walked right up behind me and wrapped his arms around me, letting his hands rest on my stomach.

Tessa's eyes followed his hands and tears sprang from her eyes as she let out an excited cry, but she clamped her mouth shut. "I'm not going to assume, I'm not going to assume," she whispered, and leaned into John, who was now at her side with his arm around her shoulders.

"I really hope you're ready to be a grandma," I said through my smile.

The same cry came from her and she left John to pull Gage and me into a big hug. When she let us go she cupped my cheeks and kissed my forehead, before moving to do the same to Gage, and I was pulled into another hug from Amanda.

We went through another round of hugs from everyone, and at the end of the line was Ty. He pulled me into his arms and didn't let go for a long moment. He knew what this meant for me, and as Tyler always had, he knew how to respond to the situation. I was thrilled, and he could see that in my smile and laughs as I told everyone the due date and how far along I was. But he knew deep down what this meant for me and that he needed to be my rock. I wrapped my arms tighter around his waist and face-planted into his chest when the tears started falling down my cheeks. This had nothing to do with Gage's not being able to understand what I needed, because he did; it just had everything to do with why I'd asked Tyler to walk me down the aisle and give me away. He was the closest thing to *my* family I would ever have.

Still holding me tightly, he whispered close to my ear, "You're going to be an amazing mom, Cassidy. I'm so happy for you, sweetheart."

I nodded against his chest and brought one of my hands back to my face to wipe my tears, then down to find and link my fingers with Gage's.

Gage

I STRETCHED MY BODY OUT along Cassidy's and kissed her lips softly. "Wake up, darlin'." Her being tired had nothing to do with the massive lunch all the girls had made; her eyelids had already started shutting before we'd even sat down to eat. So I'd brought her up to my old room as soon as we were done eating, since Mama refused to let us help clean up, and Cassidy had fallen asleep as soon as her head hit the pillow.

She groaned and automatically rolled into me; one hand went to my stomach and her head found its way to that perfect spot in between my neck and shoulder.

Kissing her cheek, I brushed my lips across her jaw and repeated in her ear, "Time to wake up, darlin'."

Her eyes popped open and that slow smile she only ever showed me crossed her face. "What time is it?"

"The game is starting in about thirty minutes. Everyone's grabbing leftovers and pie for dinner."

"Dinner?" She asked warily, "How long was my nap?"

"You call that a nap?" I teased. "Cass, you slept for over five hours. I tried to wake you up earlier after I woke up from my *nap,* but you were out. So I went back home, grabbed Sky and the pies you made, and I've been hanging with Ty since."

"Five? Holy crap!"

"Yeah." I laughed and let my hands trail over her neck, reveling in the deep breaths I was able to take now that I could feel her heartbeat under my fingers. "You feelin' all right?"

"I feel fine. I've been sleeping a lot the last couple weeks, I guess from being pregnant, but five hours! Talk about food coma." She pushed on Sky until she jumped off the bed, then scrambled off as well.

I followed her out, grabbed three beers, and headed back to the kitchen table, where Jesse and Tyler were, and handed them each one. Amanda sat in Jesse's lap, and I tried not to let that bother me, but c'mon, she was my sister, there was no way in hell that wasn't going to bother me. So I made sure my eyes never left Cassidy while she grabbed a plate of food and sliced up two of the pies—not like that was hard. She was so damn beautiful, and watching her had been all I was able to do for a year and a half, so it had become one of my favorite things to do. Especially when she was in the kitchen; she moved around the kitchen like it was a part of her, and she always had some song going on in her head, and every now and then she'd start dancing to it. I loved those times, because when she'd notice me watching her, the blush I loved so much would creep over her face and she'd shoot me one of those blinding smiles. And now? I don't know how I hadn't noticed something was going on this last week and a half; Cass had a new smile I'd never seen before, like she had a secret, and it hadn't once left her face today. I only wished I'd been paying enough attention to notice it before, but I had to admit, I did like the jersey idea.

Just as I looked down at her new jersey, her body started moving to whatever song was in her head and I had to hold back a laugh. God, my wife was cute. Tyler stood up and walked into the kitchen and over to Cassidy; when he reached her, he leaned his hip against the counter and draped an arm over her shoulders. He said something too low for me to hear and she looked up at him to respond. She set down the plate of food, her body automatically sagged against him, and he curled his arm tighter around her. Tyler continued to whisper to her, and I waited for it, the jealousy, but it never came. I hadn't felt it since Tyler came back from their trip to California in May.

I'd seen Cassidy and Tyler when they were friends, and then I'd seen them together. By the time Cassidy and I were together, she and Tyler were only ever near each other in hostile environments, so when Tyler was finally done trying to keep us apart, I'd stopped worrying so much. When I saw them together for the first time after she got back from California, I wondered how it'd taken me that long to see exactly *how* Cass responded to him. Like right now, with her leaning into him and his arms around her, sure, they were close, but there was nothing intimate about the way they were holding each other. Ty was her best friend, nothing more.

She laughed about something and turned her head so she and Tyler were both now looking at me. I raised an eyebrow but didn't move; I knew Ty wanted his time with her. Her hand dropped to her flat stomach; she smiled my smile and mouthed *I love you*. My chest warmed and I again thanked God for giving me her, and now our baby.

Epilogue

Four years later

Gage

I WALKED IN and my heart skipped two beats before kicking into overdrive, as was my normal routine when I was looking at my wife. Six and a half years since I watched her climb out of Ty's Jeep, and she still took my breath away. But right now? Damn . . . Cassidy pregnant had to be my favorite thing. Ever. She had less than a month to go until our third was due, and we were finally gonna have a girl. After our first son, Asher, was born, Cassidy hadn't wanted to wait too long and we'd had our second son, Jax, named after Cassidy's dad, Jackson, eighteen months later. Her pregnancy with Jax had been a rocky one, and the delivery was even worse; after both she and Jax made it out fine the doctor delivered the news that Cassidy wouldn't have any more kids. It'd been a hard blow for both of us, but with having a toddler and a newborn, we didn't have time to think about it too often. Then

Molly McAdams

by some miracle, this past May we'd found out she was expecting again, and I prayed day and night we'd have a girl. I loved my boys more than anything, but I wanted another girl to spoil besides my wife. So the day we found out we were indeed having a girl, I'd gone and called Mama, told her to take Cassidy out and buy anything pink she could find.

We'd already added another hall and two rooms to the house when we found out she was pregnant with Jax; this way when the boys were a little older they could have their own rooms, and there was no question my little girl was having her own room. Princesses, ponies . . . shit, I didn't care. As long as she was happy, she could have her room however she wanted. And now we'd still have a guest room for when Tyler and his wife stayed with us.

He'd stayed with us a lot during the winter and summer breaks while still going to UT, but once he graduated, he moved back to California and met someone almost immediately. She was nice, and more important, Cassidy absolutely adored her. They came to stay with us twice a year for a week or so, and although it was already crazy in our house, we loved it. Right now, Aunt Steph and Uncle Jim were in the main house with the family, and Tyler was wrestling on the ground with Asher and Jax while Cass spoke animatedly with Aria, Tyler's wife. I wouldn't have had it any other way.

I almost laughed out loud remembering the first time Aria and Cassidy had met. Cassidy was big pregnant with Jax, and like she and Tyler always did, they fell into each other's arms and caught up since it'd been a couple months since they'd seen each other. All the blood had drained from Aria's face when she saw them together like that, and she had turned seriously confused when Cassidy shrieked and pulled her into a huge hug. I'd made it a point to have a long talk with Aria soon after that, and though she said she understood, we all saw it still took a couple more days of seeing them together before it finally clicked. At least it'd only taken her days, rather than my two years.

Glancing over at the clock on the oven, I scratched Sky behind her ears and straightened to go take a shower before the rest of our friends got there.

Ethan and Adam had been having trouble finding jobs after graduation, and after Dana and Adam found out they would be expecting too just a month after Asher was due, Cassidy had had the idea of offering jobs to Adam and Ethan. Both had accepted right away; Dana and Adam had married and moved closer to the ranch within a month of our offering the job, with Ethan right behind them. Jackie stayed with her family for all of two months before she realized three and a half hours was still too far from Ethan and then she had moved out here too. Ethan and Adam ended up being better than some of our other hired ranch hands, and Dad and I had both been glad for the change with them here. We'd been able to let go three of the slacking hands and hire on only Ethan and Adam. Saved us money, saved us a hell of a headache, and I got to work with my friends.

Dana and Adam ended up having twins and decided to stop there, saying two of the same age was more than enough, and Jackie and Ethan had just found out they were expecting number two about a month or so ago. Cassidy loved having the girls closer to her, and more often than not, all the girls and kids were at our place at the end of the workday.

Our business had more than tripled in the last few years and I'd been able to buy Dad out two weeks before we found out Cass was pregnant with baby number three. He and Mama were happy to be retired. Well, as retired as you can be living on a ranch. He still wakes up at dawn with me to feed everyone, but as for the rest of it, he leaves it up to me.

Basically, life was good. I'd never been happier.

"Hey, everyone," I called as I reached the living room.

"Dad!"

"Daddy!"

Asher and Jax slammed into my legs and latched on as I kept walking into the room. Tyler was too worn out to get up, so I just slapped his hand as I walked by, kissed Aria on the cheek, then bent to kiss Cassidy long and slow.

Her cheeks were red by the time I pulled back. "Hey, baby," she said softly, and her whiskey eyes went to mine as my fingertips went to her throat.

Four years later, and I still needed this. And not once in the four years had she ever said a word, but now I knew for sure she knew what I was doing. Asher had always been healthy; even when he was an infant he never really got sick and I could count on one hand how many colds he'd had. I could look at Asher and know without a doubt that my oldest son was fine, but Jax was different.

The doctor had to tell us throughout Cassidy's entire pregnancy that we had to be prepared to lose the baby because of what was happening, and then with the delivery—God, that delivery almost stopped my heart for good.

Almost as soon as he'd been delivered, the nurses announced Jax's time of death while the doctor and two other nurses tried to make sure Cassidy pulled through the delivery alive. She'd fainted when something had ruptured and she was losing too much blood way too fast. Those moments had been a hundred times worse than the night she'd been stung. Then all at once, Cassidy's eyes shot wide open and she gasped loudly, and Jax started screaming from the table where they'd originally been trying to get him to breathe. The room froze for a whole second before everyone flew into action. Both of them ended up being just fine and were released from the hospital and in our home three days later.

Just a few months ago, I snuck out of bed and went into the boys' room to let my fingertips lightly brush Jax's throat, then his wrists, as I did every night. Satisfied that my youngest son was fine, I turned to go back to bed, only this time Cassidy was standing in the doorway, with my soft smile on her lips. She nodded and reached for my hand, put it to her throat, and just watched me as I took a deep breath in, then kissed me, and we went back to bed. I thought I was crazy for still needing to feel their heartbeats, but thankfully she accepted it.

"Gonna hop in the shower before everyone gets here. Do you need help?"

"Nope, go clean up. I missed you today."

I smiled down at her and kissed her softly. "Missed you too, darlin'."

When I got out of the shower, she was sitting on the bed with a large smile on her face. "So what do you think about Emma?"

"Emma?" Shoot, was I supposed to know who Emma was? Did Emily decide she wanted to go by that now? When Cass pointed to her swollen belly, I smiled wide. Emma was definitely a little princess name. "I think it's perfect."

"Yeah?"

"Yeah, Cass." I finished pulling on my jeans, then sat down with my back against the headboard and dragged her in between my legs, placing my hands on her stomach. "And how's our Emma doing today?"

"She's good. Kickin' a lot. She loves Christmas music."

"Just like her mama."

"Mmm-hmm." Her head fell back to my shoulder when my hands glided up to her breasts. "Oh, Gage."

God, I loved how sensitive she was when she was pregnant too. I nipped at the place she loved behind her ear and she moaned.

"Everyone will be here in twenty minutes."

"I can be fast," I whispered against her ear, and she shivered.

"Gage, I'm huge pregnant. You can't want a quickie with me, and we have people in the living room."

My hands and lips stopped. Was she serious? "Darlin', you pregnant isn't just incredibly beautiful; it's the sexiest thing I've ever seen. You are outside your damn mind if you think seeing you like this isn't a constant turn-on."

"Mama!" Asher called, and Jax was right behind him shouting, "Mommy! Mommy!"

"And that turns it right back off," I whispered, and she giggled.

"What, baby?" she asked sweetly when Jax jumped onto her legs. Asher had climbed onto the side of the bed and was hanging off my arm as he answered for both of them.

"Aunt Dana and Uncle Adam are here. Can we go outside and play with Abbi and Brandon?"

"It's cold outside," I whispered in the ear that was farthest from Asher.

"Ash, honey, it's too cold outside. Why don't y'all go into the game room, and when Aunt Jackie and Uncle Ethan get here with Caden, I'll send him in there too, okay?"

"Go outside, *please!*" Jax begged with a cheesy grin, and I had to shove my face into Cassidy's shoulder so he wouldn't see me laugh.

"Not tonight, baby."

"Mommy!" He sighed. "Said *please*!" Jax said, like that should have ensured they got their way.

I almost snorted.

"Jax." Her voice was still sweet, as only Cassidy's could be, but it'd taken on that mom tone and the boys knew there was no point in arguing further.

"All right, Mama," Asher said, and he kissed her cheek, hugged my neck tightly, and climbed off the bed. "C'mon, Jax, let's go to the game room!"

Jax didn't move but he waved at us. "Bye, Mommy! Daddy, go a room now!"

I knew what he meant to say, but God, that kid was a riot without trying or realizing it. I couldn't hold back my next laugh.

Cassidy lifted him up over her belly and kissed his chubby cheek before hugging him. How she did all that with her belly so big was beyond me. He looked up at me and grinned as he waved at me from behind her head. I kissed his forehead and held the hand that had been waving, let my index finger run over his wrist, then watched him run up to Asher and the two of them leave our room. I couldn't help but smile watching them leave. We had great kids, and I couldn't wait to see how Emma would shake things up. Now that I'd gotten my wish for a girl, I had only one more thing to ask for. Both boys had my black hair and green eyes; I couldn't care less what color hair Emma had, but Lord, I wanted her to have wide honey-gold eyes.

Cass started to get up, but I gently brought her body back to mine. "Babe, they're all starting to get here now; I gotta go make sure the food's all good."

"Sweetheart, you'll have my mom, Amanda, Nikki, Emily, Aria, Jackie, and Dana here. I'm sure one of them is bound to check on the food if you're not in there. I just need a few more minutes with you," I whispered, and reached into my night-stand and dug around in the back 'til my hand hit the velvet box. Bringing it up around her, I set it on her belly and kissed her neck. "Merry Christmas, darlin'."

"Oh, honey," she whispered, and covered her mouth when she opened it. It was a set of three white-gold bands soldered together, each with a large birthstone on it, the birthstones going in a diagonal. The top had a ruby between *Asher* and *July 15, 2013;* the middle had an amethyst between *Jax* and *Feb. 1, 2015;* the bottom had a garnet and was blank on each side.

"As soon as Emma's born, I'll get the bottom engraved." I wasn't worried about Emma going into February; if she didn't come early, Cassidy and her doctor had already decided she would be induced January twentieth. If she came sometime in the next week, which I doubted, then I'd just get the gem changed. "I know this is more of a Mother's Day gift, but I bought it for this last Mother's Day, and we found out about Emma right before I could give it to you. So I took it back and had them add on another ring when we found out the due date, and I'm not about to wait another seven months to give it to you."

"Thank you so much, Gage." She turned her head and cupped her hand around the back of mine to kiss me thoroughly.

When she turned back and took the ring from the box to put on her finger, I fingered the necklace under my pillow and draped it onto her chest, connected the clasp, put my hands back on her stomach, and waited.

Her hand flew up to the long necklace and she brought the pendant up to study it. It was a white-gold phoenix, with a diamond on each wing and yellow gold coming from the bottom of its tail. I'd seen it in passing one day and bought it immediately.

Cassidy had learned from her mom and Connor that you had to find the beauty from the ashes. It didn't take long for us to realize it didn't just apply to actual ashes. Because there were a lot of times in our lives that we'd had to find the light in the dark.

I'd thought I was going to lose her from the scorpion sting, but it'd given us Asher. She'd gone through a rough pregnancy, and God had taken Jax from us momentarily and almost taken Cassidy, just to bring them back, and now Jax was a happy, healthy, and amazing kid. And it was hard knowing she wouldn't have more kids, but it made the surprise of Emma that much sweeter. The phoenix was everywhere in our lives now. From Asher's name and Cassidy's second horse, which she'd named Phoenix, to the only tattoo I've gotten or would ever get: the same one she had on her back. It was our symbol, and her mother's words were now our motto. During hard times, we whispered them to each other to remind ourselves that we would get through whatever was happening and would come out stronger, and when God blessed us with gifts, it was said as a prayer.

Her hand closed tightly around the pendant and she looked up at me; her wide honey eyes were filled with tears. "From ashes?" she asked with my soft smile.

"From ashes," I confirmed.

Acknowledgments

A BIG THANK-YOU to my husband for always supporting me and helping me around the house more than I could begin to explain. I love you, Cory!

More thanks to my Beta readers: Amanda, Nikki, Robin, and Teresa! Y'all are amazing and helped give me so much confidence in my writing. I am so lucky to have women like you supporting me and giving me honest feedback about my work!

Thank you to Tessa, my editor; I love working with you and honestly have no idea how I ever did a book without you! And to Kevan, my agent, you have been more than amazing, and I love that both of you are just as excited about this book as I am!

BOOKS BY MOLLY McADAMS

FROM ASHES
A Novel

Available in Paperback and eBook

Cassidy has only ever trusted two men: her father, and her best friend Tyler—until she meets Gage... And there's something about Cassidy that makes Gage want to protect her—and make her his own.

For a year and a half, Gage and Cassidy dance around their feelings for each other as Tyler tries to keep them apart; until one day Tyler unknowingly pushes Cassidy right into Gage's arms...

TAKING CHANCES
A Novel

Available in Paperback and eBook

Eighteen-year-old Harper is ready to live life her own way, escaping from under her career-Marine father's thumb and heading to college in San Diego. But soon, she finds herself torn between two men...and after one weekend of giving into her desires, everything changes...

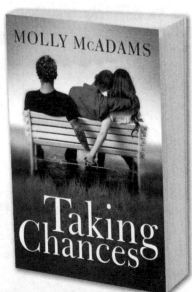

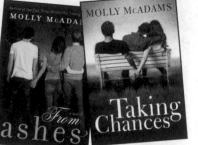

3 1901 05409 4265